crime scene

Jack Furlong

ISBN: 1495940721
ISBN 13: 9781495940729
Library of Congress Control Number: 2014903318
CreateSpace Independent Publishing Platform
North Charleston, South Carolina

"Attorney Bill Carmody has been retained by the parents of Aaron Bellow, a young man who traveled from Wisconsin before being arrested for gun possession in Trenton, New Jersey. It seems like a simple case, but there are some discrepancies....Bill's ramblings, as he discusses prior cases and criticizes the justice system for favoring prosecutors, show him to be a sublimely methodical protagonist who details every aspect of his life. The most resonant scenes take a bare-bones approach; at one point, for example, Bill gives his shrink court transcripts, which showcase Bill's razor-sharp discourse....An atypical thriller, but its winsome protagonist will convince many readers to dive right in."

-*Kirkus Reviews*

"If I had known Trenton was this interesting, I would have attacked two weeks earlier."

-*Gen. Geo. Washington, U.S. Army (Ret.)*

"Crime Scene is not about one crime scene.... It is many scenes in the life of William Carmody. Crime Scene is fiction, but Carmody is more than fiction. His story is reality, the reality of a criminal lawyer's life, his successes, his failures, his frustrations."

-*Albert M. Stark, Founding Partner, Stark and Stark*

"Look, this Carmody chap is not exactly Sherlock Holmes, is he, but they do share a certain kind of noxious narcissism one finds almost charming."

-*Dr. John Watson*

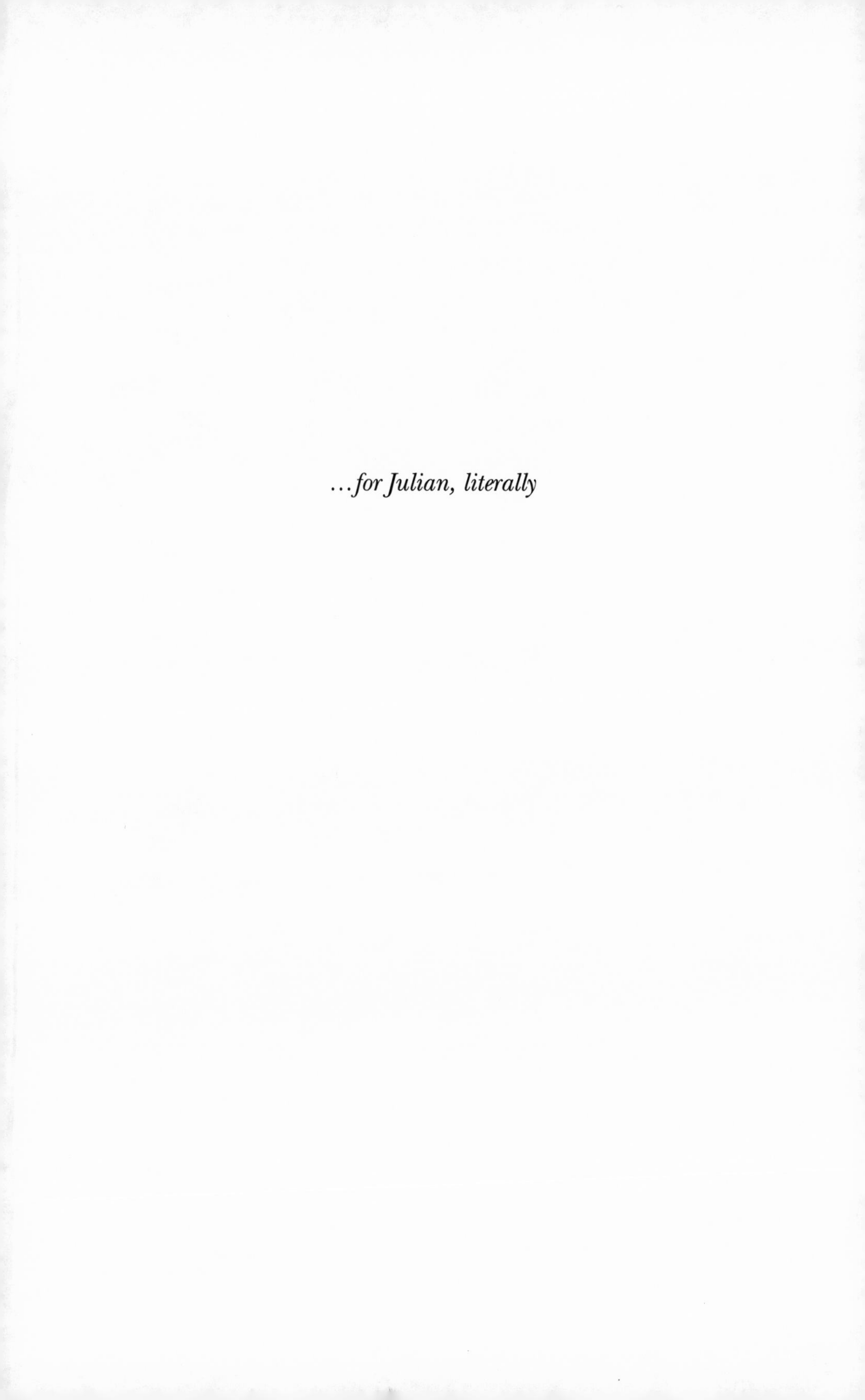

...for Julian, literally

CHAPTER ONE

South of Wisconsin Dells, maybe a mile off I-90/94.

“Welcome to Dapper Dan’s. Cover is $20; need to see your ID.”

“Do I get like drink tickets for the $20?” Aaron Bellow always pushed back. Always.

“Dude, this ain’t the Dells.”

“Just asking.” And needed to get the last word.

“Put these wrist bands on. They won’t serve you unless you’re wearing one.”

“”Got it.” They pulled on Armstrong-style red rubber, coded “Dan’s,” and headed into the main bar.

“Aaron, don’t aggravate the man. We just got here.” Jeremiah Smith, true to his stoic Wisconsin stock, would allow himself to be pushed. In the interest of tranquility. Or survival.

“Relax, Jer. No harm done. These guys aren’t going to bite us.”

“That’s a relief. When we wind up in the emergency room after being beaten with a baseball bat, at least I know they won’t be treating me for bite wounds. I feel better already.” The two young men ignored the anorexic pole dancer sporting a tat of Elton John on her shoulder. They walked to the end of the bar, where a scraggly-bearded bartender pulled a local draft.

"Um, excuse me?" Aaron cupped his hand, not shouting, but making sure to be heard.

Bartender not looking up: "Yeah."

"I'm looking for somebody named Tim, supposedly works here?"

Still watching his glass: "What if he does."

"Well, I'd kinda like to speak to him." Bartender moved away.

"Um, sir?" There stood a fine line between fearless and reckless disregard, often unseen by the young or the restless, too frequently afflicted with hubris and fecklessness. Aaron was both, lacked neither. Point of no return.

Still no eye contact. "Now what."

"Is he working?"

Eye contact: "You want something to drink?"

"I was told to meet him here."

"Who told you?"

"He did."

"Who are you?"

"Aaron."

"Hang on…."

"Where's he going?" Jeremiah sunk his head into his parka as he spoke.

"Probably to talk to Tim."

Bartender returned, scowled, said, "OK, far side of the bar, take the stairs to the VIP room one flight down. His office is next to it."

The magenta Berber carpeting lined the wide steps to the lower level. Everything else was blonde wood. Towards the back of the building stood double doors framed by sconces. To one side, a small room marked "Utility;" to the other, "Office."

A leather-vested biker-type leaned next to "Office." "You Aaron?"

"Tim?"

"Nope. Who's this?"

"My friend. Say hello, Jer."

"Hello."

"You both paid the cover charge?"

"What gave us away? The bracelets?"

"Hang on, smart ass." He rapped twice on "Office." "I was going to offer you the VIP buffet."

"Let's put it this way: I didn't come here for the food."

"You don't like our food?"

"Well, I'm a vegetarian."

"Figures. Go on in, dickhead."

Inside the office sat an unreconstructed, Bobby Ewing lookalike contest winner, circa 1984. His desk featured an ashtray. Of course, there was a couch.

"Aaron?"

"Tim?"

"Who's your friend?"

"Jer? Helping me with the driving."

"Friend? You want to step outside for a second?" No argument. Delicate door click. Then, "What the fuck is wrong with you? Who told you to add a driver?"

"I just figured…"

"You figured shit. What did you tell him?"

"Nothing. I have to make a delivery to New Jersey. That's it."

"Fine. It's your ass. Now, take this. And if I find out you opened it…."

CHAPTER TWO

Session 1. Carmody, William.

...Don't misunderstand me: I am not a nice guy. Whatever I have, I don't deserve. I've gotten some breaks along the way, but those were lucky. Most of the lawyers I know don't know what they're doing. Odds are I'm no different than most of the lawyers I know. In my business, your reputation comes from your biggest cases, especially if you win. But you can lose and still come out smelling like a rose. And some lawyers I know get mixed verdicts, act like they won, and the rest of the world has no idea how much time those defendants actually got because the blowhard didn't do what was best for her client.

So, last November I picked up this kid who was from somewhere around Madison, Wisconsin. Middleton, I think. Apparently, Madison must be the largest urban spa on the continent. I only know this because I had to go out there to meet his parents a little while ago. Always seems to be sunny, around fifty-five degrees, with a nice breeze blowing in from Lake Mendota. Or Monona; depends on the time of day.

When I was there I saw a lot of building going on. New construction blends. It's all that sandstone they use in the Midwest. What is it, prairie style? Everything's fluid, new, old, had an overall impression of Frank Lloyd Wright's nirvana on Earth (he's the guy who designs those buildings that look cool but fall over after a few years.) Saw lots of people walking, riding bikes, driving cars that stopped for pedestrians, probably because the drivers knew they were outnumbered. Or they were being nice. Strange.

Obese people stuck out. As in, I didn't see any. I expected to see cheese heads, but I got a bunch of skinny people in REI workout clothes. I don't think it's that way once you get outside Madison, but when you're there, it's like fit is the new fat. These people expected to exercise, and not on a treadmill at a gym. You think people run harder on paved trails free of charge? Do I sound like someone who's avoiding the issue?

Okay look, this story of how I messed up took place nowhere near Madison; more like its evil twin. Ever been to Trenton? Tell you what Trenton, New Jersey has in common with Madison, Wisconsin: they are both state capitals. And they both end in the letters "o-n." Trenton has a train station. Madison has an airport. Trenton has an airport, but it's in Ewing. Trenton features fried food on every corner, and it shows. I'm not certain how you'd describe Trenton's architectural motif, but consistent would not be part of the list.

Madison can get raw in winter, but it is navigable.

Trenton, it's like this: On a cold November morning, when you least expect it, work crews will shut down the middle lanes of Broad and Market Streets to begin digging up the pavement in order to plant trees down the center.

Seriously. A grassy median project, cooked up in the heart of some public works director's darkness, kicks off after the fall planting season, so we can look forward to earth moving and cement pouring in forms for the next four months. Did I mention there was no parking within three blocks either side of this central intersection? Yeah, they knocked down the decrepit garage and county lockup, built to last in 1975, whacked by the wrecking ball in 2010, when a stiff breeze might have done the same job, more cheaply.

If your building can't survive thirty-five years, you don't get a corner stone or a chance to name it for someone. Not even your uncle who loaned you the down payment on your first house.

Anyway, Trenton actually serves two political imperatives. In addition to the capital of New Jersey, it's also the county seat of Mercer County, one of twenty-one statewide. Come to think of it, Madison has a similar dual purpose, hosting the state capital building and the Dane County offices.

So we're clear, there are no "state" courthouses most places. There are county courthouses, or district courthouses, but not state courthouses. State courts inhabit local buildings. There's a Mercer County Courthouse (where state judges at the trial level hold forth), and there's a Dane County Courthouse (I think it's called the Justice Complex, which is common nomenclature in a lot of counties in New Jersey and Wisconsin. Not sure how this is supposed to make us all feel better.)

The original Mercer County Courthouse has stood tall and dirty at the intersection of Broad and Market Streets since 1839, overlooking the aforesaid beautification project, even as its courtrooms have been abandoned over the last decade. The civil courts now sit in a newer building one block to the north; the criminal courts in a very new building half a block to the west.

The old building sits atop Mill Hill, overlooking Assumpink Creek. If you're not familiar with Trenton (like, I don't know, you're from Princeton, say, or Hopewell Township), it was the site of a fairly important battle or two in the War for Independence.

Most folks are familiar with the surprise attack on the Hessians in their barracks on the morning after Christmas, 1776. Fewer know that the British marched south from Princeton to reinforce the Trenton garrison and tried to displace the rebels from their position behind Mill Hill. While the Hessians suffered casualties in a pitched street battle on December 26th, it was the redcoats who bled and died in numbers on the Assumpink Bridge, a couple of hundred yards from the front steps of the courthouse.

Don't take my word for it. The barracks are a tourist center near the statehouse, but the bridge (or a more modern incarnation of it close to the same spot) stands today. Worth a look.

But this is not about the bridge, but the court where I'm headed on a brisk Monday morning before the regulars show up. The old courthouse still has the video hookup for bail hearings. If you want to get a bail review under the current regime, you have to be in the video-equipped courtroom by 8:30 in order to be there when the duty judge starts wandering down the list of guys (and the rare woman) who haven't made bail since their arrest within the previous week.

Let me translate that, because I am so, so sick of the misinformation campaigns on TV. Bail is a constitutional right. It's found in the Eighth Amendment, Bill of Rights.

Oh, we hear lots of hard words about the First Amendment. Especially around Christmas, which apparently there's a war on. We hear gun crazies rattle their bandoliers about the Second Amendment. Fourth and Fifth Amendments are the daily diet of cops and lawyers. Eighth Amendment? Not so much.

Here's what it says, ready? "Excessive bail shall not be required, nor excessive fines imposed, nor cruel and unusual punishments inflicted." As long as you promise to show up in court, you're supposed to get out. Presumed innocent means not having to do jail time waiting for the grand jury to fart.

My guy gets arrested on a Wednesday night, found in possession of two guns on his back seat (they were in his trunk when he left home, but by the time cops got done searching his car, they were in plain view on the back seat; it's a pattern you get used to.) Cops sign criminal warrant-complaints against him, even though a summons-complaint is acceptable.

A summons is an invitation, including a self-executing RSVP, where "Non, merci" is not an option. Instead of 'regrets only,' it reads, "I'd be happy to attend, on penalty of arrest if I don't." But cops love to haul you off to jail if only to show you who's boss. The warrant lets them do that. It's a permission slip from the court.

The warrant-complaint goes to a court clerk on duty to review paperwork. Although there's a schedule of bails to be imposed based on the seriousness of the crime, the clerks work in the same building as the cops. If Patrolman Muldoon wants $250,000 bail, he's going to get it.

Bail bondsmen take 10%. Most folks understand this. It's a premium on an insurance contract. Give us $25,000 and we will post a bond to get you out. If you don't show when you're supposed to, we agree to pay off the policy ($250,000) to the court. That's why Dog the Bounty Hunter works so hard and gets paid so well. Bail bondsmen don't want to pay $250,000.

But very few defendants have $25,000 lying around to give to a bondsman. If they did, they probably wouldn't be holding a couple of guns they bought in Wisconsin to sell for an $800 profit after driving fifteen hours. (Come on, you knew we'd get back to Madison at some point, right? I'm going to get to why we're here, but give me some space.)

So, they sit in the county jail. And because there are only so many beds in most county jails, people gotta get let out.

This is where the bail review comes in. You're asking a real judge to take a real look at the facts of the case and the measure of the man (occasionally woman) to see if something less than $250,000 is the answer to the question, 'How much incentive do we need to give you to make sure you show up for court?'

The 8:30AM video bail review is quicker than a formal motion for reduction of bail, because there's almost no paperwork involved, and because they don't have to frog march ten guys in a chain from the jail to the courtroom. They can just shuttle them in and out of a waiting area to the other video-equipped room within the walls of the jail.

I'm there at 8:15 for at least two reasons, a chance to look at my client's file and a parking space at one of the few metered spots across the street from the building. I've got Dunkin' Donuts coffee in one hand, a small brief case in the other, and I'm trying to read my messages on my iPhone with the third.

On the street in front of the old courthouse is an historical marker describing the significance of this decrepit shell of a building that for the 30 years I've been showing up is nothing more than an asbestos laden cancer cluster waiting to claim another victim from the ranks of the trolls who work in the basement.

The marker reads: "Mercer County Courthouse, built on Mill Hill, 1839, named for General Hugh Mercer who fought at Trenton and died in the battle of Princeton, 1777. Goodyear vs. Day patent case tried here in 1852. Daniel Webster won for Goodyear. The result was a great impetus to local rubber industry."

Webster actually satisfied a U.S. Circuit Court that Charles Goodyear earned his patent for vulcanized rubber, but if the best you have to offer is the passing attention of a constitutional lawyer (and senator and secretary of state) of some repute a hundred-sixty years ago, you are not the center of the legal universe. Not saying there was any connection, but Webster was dead six months after he came to Trenton.

Tell you something else. After 9/11, the local sheriff banned parking in front of the building. He put the now too common concrete Jersey barriers along the sidewalk and covered the parking meters with burlap and signs reading "temporary police emergency." That lasted three years.

Not so lucky for me, I ran into Dennis Savini, resident civil libertarian...okay, anarchist, ranting at anyone who stopped to listen, which at half past eight on a weekday in the cold was not a large contingent. Convo went something like this.

"Hey, Dennis."

"Mr. Carmody! Why are you here? To answer my recurring question? What is the meaning of these broken cement offerings to the gods of security?"

Took me a minute to realize he was talking about the barriers next to us. "I'm sure you are going to enlighten me."

"Yes, yes, I will! Are you part of the problem, or part of the solution? Who said that? Do you know? Eldridge Cleaver. Black Panther. Ex-pat. Libyan by now, maybe dead for all I know. But we have to exterminate the Muslims, isn't that what they are telling us? Here's the thing for all you security mavens trying to destroy our architecture, common space, sense of independence and trust in one another: Osama bin Laden sent twenty guys to make a statement to all Americans who think we can blow up middle eastern countrysides, killing whoever happens to be there, and not have to deal with the possibility of retaliation.

"No matter how hard it is to hear this, hear this: Muslims didn't pick this fight; we did. But when you're trying to make a statement to all of Western civilization, your target list reads World Trade Center, White House, U.S. Capitol, Pentagon, maybe the Washington Monument. I can guarantee you that the Mercer County criminal courthouse was not sixth on their list. And the same goes for you folks at the New Jersey Justice Complex, or you suits at 477 Sixth Avenue, New York, New York, or even the Mall of America in Minneapolis.

"Now, why can't we rid ourselves of these public eyesores a decade after 9/11 and return to some semblance of normalcy, or as I see it, the endless stream of charges and dispositions...? But I digress, Billy. How are you?"

I'm just trying to get out of there. "Can't complain. No one would listen if I did."

"I would listen to you, defender of the downtrodden, keeper of liberty's flame, last bastion of freedom, or at least bathos."

"But would you be sympathetic?"

"Of course! Is there any other way to listen?"

Okay, stock line banter wasn't getting me out of earshot, so I took a little more direct approach: "Maybe not. Listen, I have an appointment back on the planet Earth, so I'll have to catch up to you when we have more time. Should we grab lunch? We still have to talk about our lawsuit against the warden."

"Perfect. Have your amanuensis call my amanuensis."

"I will do that, as soon as I figure out what an amanuensis is." I turned away from the street as Dennis remained, dragging on his probably tenth cigarette of the morning, his scraggly ponytail wafting in the stiff breeze.

The steps were cracking under my feet walking to the front door of the not yet abandoned courthouse. I think they're marble, but then so is the Parthenon. I've never been to Greece, but I'm willing to bet the steps to the Parthenon are in better shape.

Placards adorn the glass double doors: "Everyone entering this building must show identification. No exceptions." "All persons entering this building are subject to search. John Kemler, Sheriff." "No cameras permitted, by order of the sheriff." I walk through the door, ignore the bag belt, set off the metal detector, and toggle my phone with a camera app on its face. No exceptions my ass.

One sheriff's deputy mans the machine, but we're pals. "Mr. Carmody, top of the morning."

"Hey, J.P. How's your mom?"

"She's better, thanks. Bringing her home tomorrow." J.P. is dark-skinned, six-two when he doesn't slouch, wearing glasses and a navy turtleneck under his navy open-collared uniform, still creased at this hour. His receding hairline reminds me how long I've been passing through that same arch.

"Good to hear." I keep walking up the mezzanine steps to the second floor. Two more turns and I'm in the courtroom.

One more layer of security as another deputy sheriff guards the entrance to the video courtroom. He's sitting on a stool at a podium, eating an egg sandwich, with a list of the morning's bail reviews. If a member of the public tries to get into the courtroom, he asks who the person is there to see. If the person refuses to answer or doesn't know, she's denied entry. To a public courtroom we're talking about. Do I sound angry?

Mike Barnes is an older black guy, wiry, newer to the job, and he says, "Hey, where you going?" I had caught him in mid-chew. I'm pretty sure that's what he said.

I'm mildly aggravated, but containing my contempt. Or not. "What's it to ya', Mike?"

He said, "Did you see J.P.?"

I said, "Yeah; his mom's coming home tomorrow."

He said, "She died four years ago."

I said, "I know. He's probably talking about the urn."

He said, "Where the hell was the urn?"

"I think his sister had it. It's like the Stanley Cup. It moves around." Dropped my coat and bag, kept my coffee and phone, retreated to the Criminal Case Management satellite office across the hall. Needed to talk to John Rooney, one of the helpful case managers. There aren't that many.

"Hey, John."

"Hey, Billy."

"Got time for one lookup?"

"Stand by one. Get out of this program...ok, go ahead."

"Aaron Bellow, d/o/b 6/26/88, don't have a social. Date of arrest was Halloween."

"Gun possession? What's WI?"

"That's him. Wisconsin."

"$250,000, looks like a wrap around on a two-count complaint. Trenton Municipal. Your file number is..."

"Hang on...go."

"12-1194."

"Got it. Thanks."

He said, "Anyone else while I'm in here?"

I said, "I got a list, but let me read this guy's jacket first." I wheeled around, retreating to the courtroom just as Amy Delaney was strolling in with what looked like an intern holding the dozen or so bail review files from the prosecutor's office.

Then I said, "Amy." I think we had lunch once when I was still single. No, I never touched her. Might have thought about it.

"Mis-ter Carmody. Who do you have?" Something about her eyes.

"Bellow. Gun case. You got anything?"

"Doubt it. Let me see." Definitely thought about it, just don't remember what I thought.

I said, "You've got other stuff to do. I'll read the file. Please tell me you have work product."

She said, "Kidding, right?"

I said, "Sorry. Bad joke before my second cup of coffee." Amy was a good prosecutor. No need to give her a hard time.

Work product is what prosecutors in New Jersey are allowed to withhold before letting you see the contents of their otherwise "open" files. Her file had maybe three sheets of paper in it, and I was prepared to bet the ranch none of them was a lawyer's musings on the merits of the case, otherwise known as "work product."

So I sat at the adjoining table, further from the jury box. This is the defense table, typically public defender's private property on a bail review day, because private counsel appear once or twice a week compared to the ten to fifteen per day the PD's shovel through their system. But it was 8:20. I knew I had at least twenty minutes before anyone else showed up.

Aaron Bellow, no prior record, including NCIC check for all fifty states. FBI number assigned with AFIS, but that could mean anything. If you've ever applied for any job, permit, passport, even a safe children's program, you've had your prints taken. Voluntarily, sort of. The print is sent to the FBI for numerical classification, recorded in the Automated Fingerprint Identification System, so learning you have a number assigned can mean more than the prospect of finding a prior arrest where you were mugged and printed.

Savini strolled in behind me, peered over my shoulder, reloaded and ready to launch. "Ah, the NCIC check. Big Brother and Big Sister plotting our every move. Have you no shame? You swore to uphold a Constitution that you now claim gives you the right to collect every mote of my miserable life! Unhand me, I say: unhand me!"

I thought he was done, but then he said, "Which reminds me, all you small government tea baggers telling me how government is invading your space: every last one of you voted for the AEDPA and USA Patriot acts, which are just two of the many Congressional authorizations to set up these protocols for burning us all into a national database. Stop lecturing me about socialism and the Democratic Party."

Of course, I had no idea who Dennis was ranting at, but I'm pretty sure it was time to make space. I slipped backwards out of the courtroom with my coffee. I could almost hear J.P. shouting from downstairs: "Hey Savini! You're part of the problem, not part of the solution."

Checked the file: What else is in here? Warrant-complaint signed by Detective Muldoon, counter-signed by Lourdes Olmeda, DCA. Deputy Court Administrator. That means for getting his probable cause affidavit approved and a $250,000 bond amount fixed, Muldoon had to appeal to a thirty-four-year-old Latina who has worked in the same building as him for sixteen years and may even know what the inside of his city apartment looks like. Of course, he doesn't live in the city, but you have to have a residential address to work for the City of Trenton, so everyone keeps a one-room crib, and wives have no choice but to approve, because the last thing they want to do is raise a family in a war zone.

Affidavit of probable cause, after the pre-printed baloney: "While on a routine traffic stop" –can we stop right there? You're a detective in an elite special investigations unit. You make no "routine traffic stops"– "I observed on the rear passenger seat what appeared to be two boxes containing handguns. Defendant advised these were weapons he had purchased in Wisconsin earlier in the day. He was unaware he needed permits to possess them in New Jersey. Wherefore, deponent asks, etc., etc."

No police reports yet filed, even though it is now more than three days later and the reports are supposed to be transmitted electronically. Routine traffic stop should have been written up before end of shift on the evening of the arrest. And who in his right mind drives across country with handguns in boxes on the back seat of a car. If you say, "How about stupid farm boys from Wisconsin," I know who you are rooting for.

Five minutes later Sasha Taylor plunked into the courtroom with her four-inch stilettos and a body that might be putting some strain on the shoes' superstructure. This is a big woman who dresses in small person's clothes. The day she snaps an ankle will come as absolutely no surprise to me. She didn't look at me as she went from microphone to microphone, tapping on the end.

"Defense table." Tap tap.

Prosecution table." Tap tap.

"Bench." Tap tap.

"Clerk." Once she made sure the video hookup was working at both counsel tables and the bench, she slid into the clerk's chair to the left of the court. Typically she would say hello, but now that I'm representing her son on a schoolyard beef that went hostile until some guy shot some guy, she thinks looking away will absolve her of any potential conflict working in the court system.

Little after 8:30 the Honorable Robert Bannister, J.S.C., strolled into the courtroom without fanfare or an "All rise!" or a "Remain seated." Nothing more than a door opening and a man in a black gown walking to the bench. I never saw this level of informality when I first entered this building thirty years ago.

But there you go. At least he doesn't take himself too seriously, which was a huge problem for some of the old timers, who mistook

"Judge of the Superior Court" for "Justice of the Supreme Court" or worse, "emperor of the universe."

Here's a partial transcript:

THE COURT: Morning everyone. Sasha, is this on?

CLERK: Yes judge.

THE COURT: Who do we have at the Workhouse today?

UNIDENTIFIED VOICE: Your Honor, this is Sergeant Riley.

THE COURT: Thank you sergeant. Do you have our list? And is everyone on it available?

SERGEANT RILEY: Uh, hang on...Eugenio Martinez bailed out last night. Aannnd, Jamar Harrell is in the medical unit, but he should be here in a couple of minutes.

THE COURT: Okay, Mr. Carmody, I see you sitting at counsel table. Who do you have?

MR. CARMODY: Aaron Bellow, Your Honor.

THE COURT: Sergeant, can we have Aaron Bellow brought in?

SERGEANT RILEY: Yes, Your Honor.

Aaron Bellow looks lost. He hasn't slept or had a shower in at least three days. He's got a pale boy's scruff, greasy hair, and eyes sunken into his cheeks. When that happens, the forehead pops out, making your average detainee look a tad Neanderthal, which doesn't help the effort to get his bail cut. We've never met, but he's not too much different than what I expect. At that point I'm banking on his mother having spoken to him on a collect call the day before to explain I would be there. Otherwise, you can get some uncomfortable responses.

> THE COURT: Are you Aaron Bellow?
>
> THE DEFENDANT: Uh-huh.
>
> MR. CARMODY: Excuse me, Your Honor. May I address my client for a moment?
>
> THE COURT: Certainly.

Because the defendants are brought to a videotaping room, they have no chance to speak privately to their lawyers. This entire concept of streamlining bail reviews has raised serious constitutional concerns with traditional jurists and lawyers alike, but efficiency is the new normal, so there you are. But a judge is hard pressed to deny you a chance to tell your client to keep his mouth shut during the proceedings, because likely the kid does not know we can hear everything he says, including muttering under his breath.

> MR. CARMODY: Aaron, please do me a favor. I'll be addressing the court on the issue of your bail, and I know you've never been through this before, so I would appreciate it if you simply did not speak during the proceeding, and I will be up to talk to you later today. Okay by you?

THE DEFENDANT: Uh-huh.

See, I did two things there. First, I told the judge my client has no prior record before the prosecutor started polluting his mind with a bunch of bad facts. Second, I let the judge know the defendant is too dazed and confused to know what's going on. If he says "uh-huh" to the judge the way he said it to me, he intended no disrespect to the court. More likely he's in a kind of delayed shock.

I'm also alerting the judge to my situation. I haven't met this guy before, and the judge will quickly figure I was retained by a mother or father in distress. He'll look for a family member in the court, or assume that someone reached out for me over the weekend. If he looks at the face sheet and sees 'Wisconsin,' he'll be aware that family might not be able to get here that quickly, but the kid's ties are strong enough to have a parent step up to hire a lawyer on short notice.

All of this is to get the judge thinking my guy's way before the prosecutor speaks. Next time you walk into a courtroom, look around. It is set up to favor the prosecution. The prosecutor's table is closer to the jury. The prosecutor gets to speak first, and frequently last as well.

The court relies on the prosecutor being in command of the operative facts to help him form an opinion. By the time defense counsel gets to put in a word, the court's mind has been fixed, and you're trying to alter the course of the brain's existing waves.

The reason the prosecutor gets to write first on the blank slate is because the burden of proof is on the state, and it never shifts–well, almost never, but hopefully we won't get that deep into an affirmative defense as I'm telling you what happened to this guy later on–even after all evidence is in play.

The trial burden is "proof beyond a reasonable doubt," which means something approaching moral certainty. At least it used to.

These days, beyond a reasonable doubt appears to mean "he's probably guilty or he wouldn't be here, unless he takes the stand to convince me he's been set up." Trust me on this one: Casey Anthony and O.J. Simpson are outliers. Worse, when an obviously guilty person gets off on national television, it makes our lives miserable for years afterwards, as jurors swear they will not be goaded into acquittals like those idiots in Florida and California.

> THE COURT: Ms. Delaney?
>
> MS. DELANEY: Your Honor, this is Jim Swaggert, a law student interning in our office under Rule 1:16-1. He'll be appearing for the State.
>
> THE COURT: Good morning, Mr. Swaggert.
>
> MR. SWAGGERT: Uh, Judge, Mr. Bellow was arrested Thursday night on a suspected registration violation. His, um, Wisconsin plates were expired, which led to a routine police inspection of the vehicle searching for ownership or registration information. Police observed two boxes on the rear seat in plain view, which both had the name of Ruger Arms on the outside. They recognized the manufacturer and upon further inspection, both boxes contained a Ruger Arms .22-.45 Lite handgun. Defendant said he didn't know it was illegal to carry handguns in New Jersey since he just bought them, but he was stopped on North Clinton.

THE COURT: Meaning what?

MR. SWAGGERT: Uh, it was off the beaten track?

THE COURT: Prior record?

MR. SWAGGERT: Uh, I don't think so.

THE COURT: Ms. Delaney, can you help us out?

MS. DELANEY: No record we can find judge, but he's out of state. The NCIC comes back negative, but we don't have a Wisconsin printout at this point. Two counts of unlawful possession, second degree, bail fixed in municipal court at $250,000, cash or bond.

THE COURT: Were the guns loaded? Did he have ammunition? Mr. Swaggert?

MR. SWAGGERT: Uh, I'm pretty sure they were.

THE COURT: Well, prohibited ammunition or no?

MR. SWAGGERT: I'm not sure.

THE COURT: Okay. Mr. Carmody?

MR. CARMODY: Thank you, Your Honor. Defendant is 24 years old, no prior record, works in a family business in Middleton, Wisconsin, has friends in this area who he had planned to visit prior to his arrest Thursday night....

THE COURT: Do his friends live near North Clinton Avenue?

MR. CARMODY: Not sure what you mean by that, judge. If you are implying that this young white man shouldn't have friends in a predominantly African-American neighborhood, I understand.

THE COURT: I didn't mean...

MR. CARMODY: I'm not suggesting you did. Not to cut Your Honor off, it seems he had just picked someone up at the Trenton Train Station and headed north on Clinton trying to figure out how to get back on Route 1 towards Princeton. He missed the intersection in front of the cemetery and kept going past the police station and was trying to take a left onto Mulberry, which is where your GPS will tell you is the next place you can get on a ramp directly to Route 1. We can leave to another day the likelihood that two boxes with handguns were sitting on my guy's back seat in plain view, but the operative fact is "in boxes." They were found with purchase receipts, no ammunition, and the clips were still in the box. This may sound obvious, but he's from Wisconsin.

So far I've let the court know that I know he crossed a thin line when he swallowed the North Clinton angle. The last thing judges want is a public perception they are racially insensitive. So, you bring it to their attention, then reassure them you do not intend to make a big deal out of it.

Unless they jack up your guy's bail, in which case, your next stop will be the local press desk to make a statement about how associating with black people is apparently a crime in some parts of the prosecutor's office.

When you take a shot at the prosecutor, or in this case, law student, you're inviting the reporter to review the tape and hear the judge ask the same question. Sounds harsh on a law student? Not nearly as harsh as having my guy's parents fork over $25,000 to a bondsman because you think he's hanging with the wrong crowd, by which you mean black folks. The kid never should have brought it up.

> MR. CARMODY: For the court's edification, I was retained by his parents over the weekend. They own a restaurant in Middleton, more like a diner. They make their own pies, judge. They are prepared to act as community custodians. If Your Honor releases him on his own recognizance, he will sign a waiver of extradition and a personal guarantee co-signed by the parents for the full bond amount should he fail to appear.
>
> THE COURT: Isn't this a guidelines bail?
>
> MR. CARMODY: It is judge, but please recall the last paragraph of N.J.S. 2A: 162-12, which says that nothing in the bail statutes, and surely the guidelines written under those statutes, shall preclude a court from releasing a defendant on his own recognizance if the court finds he is deserving.
>
> (Decision by the court):
>
> THE COURT: Okay, I've heard from the State and defense counsel, and I make the following findings. Defendant is 25 years old, employed, no prior record, strong family ties, and even though this is a second

degree crime, I would normally consider ROR for a defendant with this profile. However, he is out of state, which means I have to find there is some risk of flight, and I think ROR is supposed to be reserved for in-state residents. I'm going to reduce defendant's bail to $25,000 on each count, aggregate $50,000. Wait. Make that a single bond of $25,000 covering both counts on a single complaint. Cash or bond. Defendant must sign a waiver of extradition prior to his release from custody. Mr. Carmody, in addition to preparing that waiver form, please prepare certifications from the defendant's parents that he will be living with them while the case moves forward. Get copies of the waiver and certifications to counsel so she can object to form, but I'm not holding you to the five-day rule. If you get those documents signed today, he can be released today.

MR. CARMODY: Thank you, Your Honor.

(Whereupon the proceedings were concluded.)

Before I left the courtroom I sent an email to my associate to get the documents done immediately. Then I called my ace bondsman, whose name is actually Ace. I think his real name is Lou, but that's only a rumor.

"Yo."

"Ace."

"Yo."

"It's Bill."

"Yo."

"Gotta kid from Wisconsin, good family, two guns, no record, $25,000 bond on both guns. Interested?"

"Yo."

"He's already in the Workhouse. Parents can sign by pdf and give you a credit card. Call McCloud to make sure he's not looking for a source hearing. And don't text me unless there's a problem."

"Yo."

"Can you have him posted and out today?"

"Yo."

"Perfect."

Look, all of this is relevant to why we are here. If you don't understand the context, you'll think I'm nuts.

So, where was I?

I headed back to Case Management with my list of other names to get looked up, made some notes and more small talk with John Rooney, then back to my car for the twenty-minute ride up Route 29 to the jail in Hopewell. This would be the county jail where we send drunk drivers and shoplifters and petty thieves (ok, more shoplifters) to serve three, six, or nine months, or however much time they need to do at $20 per day to pay off fines they can never meet from non-existent employment.

When the detention center behind the courthouse lost its federal certification (built in 1975, it had become a health hazard in about twenty years), they moved all the guys in default of bail into the Correction Center. Now Mercer County has one health hazard instead of the traditional two. Had to get to the Workhouse (what they called the correction center for its first hundred years; name is self-explanatory) before they closed the visitation gate for count.

I stopped at Dunkin' Donuts on my way up to check on Andrew's understanding of the waiver of extradition (easy part, there's a form) and the two certifications from the parents (a little harder).

"Carmody and Scott, good morning."

"Hey. Hola. ¿Cómo estás?"

"Bien gracias, ¿y tú?"

"Cansado. Is Andrew in?"

"One second."

"Hey."

"Hey. Just wanted to make sure you understood the 'I am defendant's father and I live at 1138 Hubbard Avenue, Middleton, Wisconsin, and I am the owner and operator of Hubbard Avenue Pie House' part."

"Yeah, I figured. I'm finishing it now and will pdf it to you in a couple of minutes, unless you want a draft."

"Gimme five minutes to grab coffee."

"Sounds good." I was looking at his certification before I paid for my second cup.

The drive north on Route 29 can be jarring to the senses. Coming out of Trenton, a once elegant post-war city that white people forgot after the riots, you head past Cadwalader Park, designed by Fredrick Law Olmstead (yeah, the guy who designed Central Park and Washington D.C.'s grid), over a small hill, noticing the four flowered crosses still standing where four suburban kids lost their lives when their car went airborne around 110 mph and into a tree on the shoulder. Their parents grieve to this day, wishing the State had installed a guardrail to buttress the trunk and deflect flying, 100-mile-per-hour, two-ton projectiles, perhaps saving the occupants from their fate.

You know, if 'guns don't kill people; people kill people,' it stands to reason that cars don't kill people, but people kill people. Somehow we are fine with all manner of regulation on cars, roads, and drivers, because we recognize the absolute lethality of speeding tons of metal in the hands of drunks, kids, deranged people, angry folk, and just plain bad drivers. Guns? Not so much. And last few years we actually drove car accident deaths down even as miles driven went up.

This is the shit I think about heading up Route 29. Sorry. Is profanity frowned upon in here?

After you round the bend past Sullivan Way (named after the general who lugged cannon down to the river to shell the Hessians from the northwest as the other columns marched in from the north and north east), the houses get larger, the foliage denser, and views of the Delaware open up. Lately, I've been bearing off the highway for a couple of miles through a difficult section in Ewing Township, but that's another story.

Once you hit Hopewell Township, you are on a country two-lane road, winding gently between the Delaware and Raritan Canal and local estates with sweeping water views. One slight problem is the road has become so congested at rush hour that the homes need soundproofing to conduct human conversation inside. But that's trivial, right?

The road turns more rural beyond Washington's Crossing Park, tree lined, bucolic, undulating. Finally, you spy a sign for the county's animal shelter approaching on your right, manned by inmates, who walk down from the Workhouse.

Turn in, away from the river, drive up the hill past the building where inmate work crews still gather for morning muster, and approach the electric sliding gate, the only barrier to your parking in the secure lot close to your entry.

The deal at the Workhouse is this: in order to make sure no one has escaped since last night, they have to lock everyone in their cells to physically count the bodies at the beginning of each shift. This is typically done around 6:30 in the morning, 2:30 in the afternoon, and 10:30 at night.

But corrections staff are pretty tightly wound, so they add other layers of inventory control throughout the day. If lunch starts at 11:30, they want everyone in cell by 11. That means no new attorney visits after about 10:15. If the six interview cubicles are occupado when you get there, you wait your turn in the lobby. PD's ain't going there after 4:30, when interview space is much, much easier to come by.

I needed to get this done early. Bail clerks stop accepting bonds around 3PM, and after that you're begging a duty lieutenant at the classification office to sign your release document.

Front gate security: "Can I help you?"

“Attorney visit?” You have to hand over identification at that point, but for a while they were demanding we show driver’s licenses to prove we had them when driving onto their grounds.

“Ah, ok, we are getting close to a count. You gonna be long?”

“Nope, just getting a signature, and he ain’t on a restricted tier. I’ll be in and out of IDR in fifteen minutes.” (IDR: Inmate Dining Room. Lasted about two months before they converted it to attorney visiting space. Don’t ask. One less movement if they take meals on the tier.)

“I’ve heard that before. You did say you’re a lawyer, right?”

“I get it. If I’m not done, I’m sitting through count, and I’ll get to know my new client much better.” It is not pretty watching grown men beg, which is really what I was doing there. Mostly, this is all about wasting time to do stuff you ought to be able to do online or over the phone but can’t, because corrections officers are the worst combination of paranoid and petty manipulators somewhere this side of Pol Pot.

CHAPTER THREE

Madison, Wisconsin, north of the Beltline, Exit 263.

Best approach to downtown Madison, straddling the isthmus separating Lakes Monona and Mendota, would be cruising mildly up John Nolen Drive. The capitol dome stares blankly back at drivers below, imposing between the newer high rises crowding the avenues spidering outward from the seat of government. Water on both sides, fishermen, bikers, birds, boats, you breathe. Follow the road under Monona Terrace, past Frank Lloyd Wright's moderately modernist eyes on the subtle waves lapping the rocks. Turn back to survey the University, dominating the landscape throughout. Or, stay on Nolen, hit Williamson, take a right, and motor on to a one story squat, yellow cinderblock tub of a building with a sign on an awning: GramPa's Gun Shop.

"Hey Jer, how much cash you got?"

"C'mon, man."

"Seriously. I need about three hundred."

"I have never had three hundred bucks in my pocket in my life."

"Yeah? Even after you cashed that insurance check for your car? You were rolling in it. Listen, if we pick up couple of Glocks or some shit, we can sell them when we get there and make, like, a thousand dollars. I'll split it with you."

"Wow, we take the same risk, go the same distance, and we use my money, and you'll split the proceeds. How can I turn that down?"

"Nah, we're going to need like five hundred a piece. I got six-something in my pocket, but we need gas and tolls and shit. I gotta talk Gramps down off some ledge. C'mon."

Arnold Bruce "GramPa" Clayman ran a simple, honest operation. He knew every gun in his store, which, since they might all be within arms length, was not nearly as impressive as it sounds. But the glass counters and knotty pine walls oozed gun oil and insider's knowledge. Walk into Dick's out at West Towne Mall in Middleton, and you'll see boxes and boxes of shotguns piled in hallways, along with camping gear and hockey bags. GramPa was real.

"Hello, boys. Be with you in a second."

"No problem."

"Aaron."

"What?"

"Are you going to show ID?"

"Yeah, but my name ain't on it, and they don't keep records for more than twenty-four hours. It's cool. Background check will come up negative, because my brother is clean as a whistle. We won't get to where we're going for a couple of days, and by then, the stuff is stale. They toss the backgrounders. We're paying cash. There's no database or inventory. I'm telling ya,' it's clean."

Fifteen minutes and $800 later, Aaron Bellow walked out of GramPa's Gun Shop with two Ruger .22-.45 Lites, no hard questions, no firearms purchaser registration forms, all perfectly compliant with state and federal law.

CHAPTER FOUR

Session 2, Carmody, William.

...and there's another location in the city where too much time goes to waste: the Trenton Police Division TAC squad room. Oh. Sorry, TAC: Tactical Anti-Crime Unit. They have black polo shirts branded with their logo, but I know what you're thinking: Aren't all cops tactical anti-crime units? Isn't that what they do? If you want to get into the heads of the modern soldier in the war on drugs, guns, gangs, and, well, let's cut to the chase, young black guys with more style and swagger than you'll ever have, you have to start with the acronyms of police departments.

You have read of SWAT teams (special weapons and tactics). I have come across legions of SRT's (shooting response teams). TV loves SVU (special victims units, but again, what victim is not special?); CSI (crime scene investigators); and all manner of NARCS (okay, just testing, as Narc is simply short form for narcotics agents. However, one of the best-attended classes for these agents is called NARCO-'narcotics association regional coordinating officers'-swear to god.)

Kids in the streets, they have names for these guys (very, very occasionally gals), regardless of the brand of polo they sport: jump out squads. They drive onto your block quickly, screech to a halt, and two to four cops jump out to grab the nearest pedestrians they can find, push them against a parked car, and go through their pockets.

Do they find drugs? Sure. Guns? Sometimes. Lawfully? Not bloody likely.

Anyhow, the ringleader of the TAC squad is a bullet headed guy named Manny Squitieri. They call him Squid, but eel would also suit. Shaved hair, inked biceps, and a padded middle beneath a heaving chest and popeyed arms. He shows the remnants of obvious steroid use.

Couple of guys in TAC got busted a few years ago for importing Deca from Florida through an on line "physician" named, I don't know, Dr. Vinnie Boom-Bots. Somehow they beat the rap and remained in TAC, but now they're like baseball players who went from fifty dingers to twelve in one season, because when you're no longer juiced, you're left with warning track power.

I'm guessing Squid has a publicist. I saw him and two other TAC guys on the cover of the Trentonian a few weeks back, muscle T's (black); BDU pants (black); shield on a lanyard (gold); Raybans (black); shit-eating grins (white). They were all toting semi-automatics with banana clips, but if you read the story closely, they didn't exactly claim they were displaying guns seized from suspects. They seized a lot of guns, some semi-automatic, but not these guns.

I always thought that if they were getting so many automatics we ought to see more ammo belts, clips, boxes of shells, something. I had a guy charged with shooting up another guy sharing a ride with him. Victim had a six-shot .38 in his coat pocket when he got to the ER, but there were only three bullets in the cylinder, the other three were empty. The gun hadn't been fired.

The TAC unit prides itself on thwarting guns and gangs in Trenton. Every city with a gang problem has a squad equivalent of TAC. And every city has a gang problem. You beat these kids down long enough, and they'll band together to fight back. Like insurgents.

You're roughing them up in their neighborhoods, in front of their friends and family, and then you wonder why they despise you and are willing to give up some part or even all of their miserable existence to have one moment to spit in your face.

The good news is they ain't wearing suicide bomber vests. At least not yet. Push them hard enough, and they might go to school to figure it all out. Go read up on all the sting stories the FBI has played in Miami, Chicago, and New York in recent years. Google "Al Qaeda sleeper cell busted," or some shit. The profiles almost always match up. Local disaffected youth, uneducated, unemployed, unappreciated, not doing well in the gang initiation rites ("You gotta bang if you want in"), still looking for another group to belong to, to empower them.

In walks a sting operator for the FBI to offer them clothes, guns, swag, you name it, all in the name of a religion they likely can't pronounce, let alone understand. They're down with the informant's too often ridiculous plan, because it sounds exotic and dangerous. Along the way, though, you'll see these guys never did anything more serious than put on some fatigues and go to a paint ball range. But we are whacking these moles with dispatch. Has to make us feel better, right?

All I'm saying is, take a look around you. You might start to realize why some sectors in our badly fractured society aren't taking intergenerational poverty and dead ends lightly. They want out, and they are increasingly willing to take risks to get out. On one level, I'm not complaining. For me, it's a growth industry.

But it's also a rush for these guys in TAC. They watched TV growing up and thought, "Give me a gun and a badge and I can do that." If you think these guys get serious psychological testing before they pass muster for local police work, please think some more. They pass a written test, they have sufficient physical skills to handle close combat and they learn to point and shoot. Add to that mix a hulk culture of workouts and steroids, and you've got yourself a budding goon squad.

Mostly they work at night on what was once called "proactive" patrol. They meet in their windowless concrete office in the police division, talk about what sector they will flood that shift, review reports of gang activity, recent homicide investigations, anything they can cherry pick from street patrol roll call, then stick a pin in the city map. Bunch of kids hanging in Prospect Village? Let's roll. Bloods talking trash in the Gut? They ain't that tough. Too many punks loitering at St. Joes and North Olden? Show 'em steel.

My best guess was that Aaron Bellow had been driving north on Clinton towards Olden, headed to Route 1. St. Joe's is a convenient off-ramp stop for white boys from the 'burbs to score some fast weed or worse by driving down the boulevard maybe a hundred yards, turning left onto St. Joe's, pulling to a curb to hand over a couple of twenties and make the turn back to the highway, all in less than two minutes.

You could put a couple of wagons on either side of the intersection and kill the action for a couple of hours, but it would return. It's too easy, and you don't have the manpower to staff it daily.

What I don't like is the way the white kids walk, while the black kids are dealing near a school or park and have to serve a three-year minimum or a ten-year minimum for a couple of ounces of crack or even more for meeting the demands of kids with cash. Why does the buyer get a pass and the seller lose everything?

Tell you what else. When the white kids get busted, their parents charge into my office screaming about denial of their kids' rights. It is, to put it charitably, revolting. Here's my short Letterman list of shit I hear in the office:

"They didn't give my son the right to a phone call!" Sir, they did not have telephones in 1787, so I'm fairly certain there is no constitutional right to use one.

"They arrested my son without probable cause." Would you like to tell me what the standard for probable cause to arrest is? Because I think when your boy dropped those ten bags of heroin onto the floor of the bar, he lost that argument for the time being.

"They never showed me the search warrant they claimed to have." Well, first, they have no duty to exhibit the warrant, just make sure they get it. Second, they usually show it to the person who is to be searched, or the owner of the property. I'm not aware parents of the target have a right to see anything.

One kid told me in his mother's presence, "I will not stand by and let them deny me my constitutional right to smoke pot!" Uh, I re-read my copy of the Constitution, and I couldn't find the pot right anywhere. Actually, that's an expression I've seen in table stakes poker, but never in the pantheon of personal liberty.

So, on a Thursday night the week before Bellow made bail, if I had to guess, TAC decided to take up surveillance at the New York Avenue off ramp, watching for cars from Route 1 turning two lefts to North Olden, then right or left onto either side of St. Joe's. If Bellow was headed north on Olden, away from the train station, he would have driven right by the intersection where the street vendors hawk 24/7. He's white, with out-of-state plates, and absolutely no logical reason for being in that neighborhood, unless you examine the universe of logical reasons, which TAC officers are not well suited to do.

Squid likes to pair with Klingon. Kyle Bradley supposedly got that tag from the locals because of the way he talks, absolutely no one can understand a word coming out of his mouth, or the way his hair sticks up, but someone told me it was actually because he looked like a Klingon (the ones from Star Trek with little spikes growing out of their scalps and down their backs; all very reptilian.)

Both of those guys were sergeants before the mayor took all of their funding away and RIF'd all these supervisors back to detective rank and pay. Once the mayor got indicted, they must have figured they would get their titles back. They still wore their stripes, literally on their sleeves in the form of little brass pins clipped to their pique shirts.

Squid and Klingon and a couple of their boys were likely on patrol, saw this kid driving too slowly for their taste, and pulled him over. At that point, he had no chance whatsoever, because the Fourth Amendment is not something these fellas recognize on their turf. They just don't. If shit gets suppressed in a court hearing after they get caught lying through their teeth, nothing bad happens to them.

Anyway, they've already won: they got the guns or the drugs off the street; they got credit for an arrest; the bad guy had to hire a lawyer, maybe lost his car, and spent countless hours and money defending himself. The Constitution might or might not get vindicated, but that's not really their concern.

And that ain't me talking. I remember talking to an academy instructor many years ago about what they teach on probable cause for warrantless stops. Harry Leahy told me, "Look, we teach them to take the stuff. If it gets thrown out later on a motion, so be it. We got the contraband and the guy is out time, effort, and mooch. It's that simple. We won."

If I were a betting man (and I am), I'd bet they pulled him over on the Wisconsin plates. I wasn't sure that's what happened. It's what had happened in my experience a hundred other times, but you never know. There are something like eight million stories in a naked city, and this would be only one. I had to go see what this kid had to say for himself, then figure out how to get a look at reports before the CAD tapes got erased.

Sorry, forgot again. Computer Assisted Dispatch. Virtually every major police department now has some form of integrated dispatch system so they can monitor multiple channels and 911 calls and seamlessly assign units closest to the emergency call, or the officer needs assistance call or whatever.

All the tapes get saved, and the software records the time each radio call is punched in, the unit making the call, and to some extent the location of the car sending. When you line up those records and listen to all that traffic, you get a markedly different picture of what's going on out there than the calm chronological recitation in the narrative investigation report. Oh, I have examples.

Here's one:

Few years back I had a kid charged with possession of marijuana with intent to distribute over off of New Willow Street, I think on Chapel or Sweets or one of those. Wait, Humboldt. It was Humboldt. Anyway, TAC snatched him in a school zone and he had a prior, so he was extended term eligible (before you get to the three strikes laws, you have to deal with the two strikes versions, which typically double your exposure.) They claimed they rolled up on him as he was in the process of selling a baggie to two guys standing next to him near the curb. Squad jumped out, he got charged, the other two got let go.

When I met the kid, he was scared, he was working, and his mother was behind him. Told me his story, including his walking route before the bust; his having spoken to the same cops a block and a half away five minutes before his arrest; having heard a shot fired which sent the squads back into the area; having met up with two of his buddies on the street as he approached his mother's house half a block away, where his son was visiting with his baby mama, and he was coming to drop off $400 in child support and play with his boy for a few hours.

There was pot on the street, but it was in the hands of the older of the two guys he stopped to talk to. They stood in front of a row house that happened to be the home address of the guy with the pot. A small scale was seized from the windowsill of that house.

For the life of me, I couldn't figure the TAC angle. What did my guy have or do that would make them go after him and not the guy who lived there and whose pot it clearly was? Informant? Didn't like my guy? Knew he had a record?

When I spoke to him, he had a detailed recollection of the events leading up to his arrest. He had been walking up an alley en route to his mother's house when the undercover car rolled up. Black Crown Vic, like he didn't know it was a cop car. The driver asked him if he had heard shots fired moments earlier, and he told what turned out to be Klingon himself that he had heard some noises off to the north, but had neither seen or heard anything close by.

The cops moved on, but returned a few minutes later as my client talked to his buddies on the block. It's a nice street, kind of unusual for many sections of Trenton. Nicely maintained lawns, nice new construction on some of the houses, nice fire and burglar alarms. Nice.

The two cops jumped out of the car, put the three guys against the house, frisked them, and took my guy into custody. Said the pot was his, and the scale, and the $400, which was confiscated as proceeds of a drug transaction. (By the way, try to recall the last time you paid $400 for some pot. Or $300. Kid had ten twenties and four fifties. Did I mention the bank receipt? What are the odds?)

I suppose I should point out to the uninitiated that the $400 turned up on a police report as "confiscated," but discovery did not include a document confirming the cash had been submitted to the evidence vault. And there was no forfeiture action (the civil suit the State has to file to keep the money as actual drug crime proceeds) filed by the prosecutor. I checked.

Prosecutors did offer my client a four-over-two for his second school zone conviction. Four years state prison, minimum two without parole. He had a prior about eight years earlier, which means he was eligible for an extended term: ten-year maximum if convicted, three-plus year mandatory minimum. Did I mention this was pot? About fourteen grams' worth.

His public defender urged him to take the deal, because once convicted, a judge would have no choice but to impose the three-year mandatory, and an extended term could actually turn into a longer sentence. He said no thanks, talked to his mother, and the two of them came to see me.

She was a regal woman, but plain spoken. She believed in her son, could corroborate the story about the child support and the visitation, and appealed to my better nature. That's code for I agreed to take his case with $2,500 up front, balance to be paid as we moved towards trial. I figured three-day trial, $7,500, not my best pay day, but I'd be doing a good thing.

Cops lied. Told the story you just read about the rolling up and finding these three guys with my guy holding glassine bags in his hand extended to the other two, how they were caught by surprise, etc., etc. I hear it all the time.

But we got the CAD reports, which they weren't used to seeing from the Public Defender in those days (now everyone gets them; word does travel.) The radio logs and tapes showed no less than six units in the area, trolling for shots fired in response to a 911 call, and included a brief exchange confirming my guy had just spoken to them. They were blowing up the radio with chatter, including one comment on a TAC line about getting the kid with the cash, let the others go.

Then I found the other two guys on the street. The younger one swore under oath that the guy who lived in the house where they got popped was the guy with the pot. One of the cops admitted that guy had three baggies on him, maybe one gram per baggie. He also was standing closest to the scale. When the State called its expert to testify my guy's stash was "consistent with an intent to distribute," I got to ask him on cross about the guy with the three baggies and the scale. It went something like this:

> THE COURT: Mr. Carmody, you may cross-examine.
>
> MR. CARMODY: Good afternoon, lieutenant.
>
> THE WITNESS: Good afternoon.
>
> Q. Can we settle a couple of issues up front before we get too deep into the intricacies of selling a nickel bag?
>
> A. Sure.
>
> Q. You work for the Mercer County Prosecutor's Office, right?
>
> A. That's correct.

Q. And as you told Mr. McCloud, you have not been paid for your testimony today, as a private expert might be, fair enough?

A. That's true.

Q. But when you get a paycheck at the end of every other week, the Mercer County Prosecutor's name is on it, right?

A. Well, I don't actually get a check.

Q. Direct deposit?

A. Correct.

Q. I'm guessing you're married. Okay, strike that. You get my drift, don't you?

A. Sir?

Q. Well, while you haven't been paid a separate sum of money to render an opinion, you do draw your salary from the very agency prosecuting this case, can we agree on that?

A. Sure.

Q. And while I have no doubt you exercise independent judgment when presented with these cases, the fact is the prosecutor needs your testimony to sustain his burden of proof here, agreed?

A. Agreed.

Q. Because there was no distribution observed, the best you can say is someone looked like he would sell to someone if you had watched him long enough, right?

A. Correct.

Q. I mean, that's what intent to distribute means? Sooner or later, he's going to sell his wares.

A. Correct.

Q. So, in looking at the indicia of intent, you look to quantity of CDS, right?

A. True.

Q. You look for money?

A. Among other things.

Q. You look for drug paraphernalia, like rolling papers, sandwich baggies, scales, etc.?

A. Sure.

Q. So, we can agree that my client had no baggies, right?

A. Yes.

Q. And the money he had on him was a round number in 20-dollar and fifty-dollar bills?

A. I'd have to check.

Q. Why don't you do that, because I'm wondering why a guy selling 10-dollar bags apparently can't make change for anything but a 30-dollar bill.

A. Well, there was the scale.

Q. Right, which was on a ledge of the building where these three men were standing, correct?

A. That's what the report says.

Q. And can we agree that my client was neither the owner nor a resident of that building?

A. I wouldn't put too much weight on that fact.

Q. How about this? Would you put weight on the fact that the son of the building's owner was the one closest to the ledge where the scale was recovered?

A. I'm not following.

Q. You do know that kid was found in possession of three baggies, roughly equal in weight, right?

A. I believe that was in the property report, yes.

Q. And there was a scale nearby, right?

A. Yes.

Q. And he had something like $36 on him in ones and fives, right?

A. I'd have to check.

Q. OK, while you're doing that, here's a question: Did this young man with a dirty wad of singles, three equally weighted baggies, proof of residency in the very home where the scale was recovered, did he possess marijuana with intent to distribute, in your opinion?

A. Um...

Q. I think this is a yes or no.

A. Well...

MR. McCloud: Would it refresh your recollection to see your report, Lieutenant?

MR. CARMODY: Your Honor, did you invite counsel into my cross-examination? If so, I must have missed that. I'm sorry, Lieutenant, you were saying...? Try it this way: Wasn't that proof of "intent to distribute?" Why wasn't he charged?

It went on that way for a few more questions, but the damage was done.

They recalled Klingon to rebut the radio traffic, and he choked on all the critical questions, like, 'I thought you said you were on random patrol and you and your partner just happened on this scene? How come you left out the literally eight other cops who responded to this address at the same time, at least one of whom identified my guy as the one you spoke to earlier?' It got worse for them, better for me. Jury acquitted my kid in a couple of hours.

Point is, you have to get down in the weeds to try to come close to what actually happened. Your client is not a great informant, scared shitless, or high, or ill educated. No matter what, he's unlikely to have known everything going on.

Cops trim their reports to withstand a motion to suppress. So the reports read like an affidavit of probable cause ("I was detailed to the area of St. Joe's and North Clinton in response to numerous quality of life violations, as well as multiple incidents involving open distribution of CDS.... Upon approaching the intersection, I observed several young men, one of whom was holding a plastic baggie with a tie in his hand extended upwards as another male handed him what appeared to be an undisclosed amount of currency.... They appeared startled when we exited our vehicle.") You get the picture.

So, if your client has limited fact recall skills, the cops are playing it not so much close to the vest as actually hiding their cards. If eye witnesses aren't exactly jumping up and down to help out, you're gonna have to look for other sources. In a homicide or a TV show, this is expected. It's like your only file.

In a routine drug case, not so much. Order the CAD's, walk the block in daylight, when the old folks are out and can tell you what they saw from their windows, and interview your guy more than once to see if he remembers something he left out the first time. It might not amount to much, although occasionally clients recall some doozies.

I know what you're going to say: I still haven't explained what we're doing here. I'm going to, but I wanted you to understand where I'm coming from. I know you have a job to do, and I want to play my part, but until you've walked a couple of miles in my shoes, none of this will make any sense. Plus, I like to tell stories. You've noticed?

CHAPTER FIVE

Interstate 80, Eastbound, north of State College, Pennsylvania.

The drive from Madison to New Jersey takes anywhere from fourteen-eighteen hours, depending on condition of car, stamina of drivers, road conditions, and attitude about the trip. General Motors once had plants in Janesville, Wisconsin and Ewing, New Jersey, trucking parts between the two. There was a GM gypsy named Carl who's made that run in thirteen, but he doesn't recommend it. He has family in both towns. He'll tell you to head down through Chicago (avoiding The Loop at all costs, except maybe at 5AM on a Sunday morning, and even then he says you'll hit construction), across the dreary flats of Indiana and Ohio (unless you yearn to see the R/V Hall of Fame, east of South Bend, in which case, this is your destiny and destination) until you get to Youngstown. That's where every driver has a decision to make: I-80 traversing the northern tier of Pennsylvania, or the PA Turnpike, heavy on tolls, tons of traffic, but far less chance of slamming into a blinding snowstorm, unannounced until the squall smacks you in the face.

"Jer, wake up."

"Wha…?"

"Wake up."

"C'mon, man."

“I can’t see a thing. I need help.”

“What the…where are we?”

“No idea. Saw a sign for Williamsport a while back.”

“The world series?”

“What?”

“World series. You know, Little League.”

CHAPTER SIX

Session 3. Carmody, William.

Before you think I'm tootin' my own horn on that bail reduction motion with Judge Bannister, I should tell you I had the place wired. Not in any illegal way, but the way of local counsel since roughly the dawn of man. (I could see some guy in a toga in the Roman courts, where *Lex Romana* jurists invented concepts like presumption of innocence and some kind of burden of proof, walking up to the clerk of the court, handing him a marble bust of Julius Caesar and saying, "You know I can get you tickets to the next big show at the Coliseum. Any chance of your getting my case heard first?")

I've seen lawyers parachute in on bail reduction, having promised a good result, only to have the judge raise instead of lower it. I can tell you family members dump those guys faster than an NFL coach who goes oh-and-six out of the gate.

That wasn't happening here. I had known Bob Bannister for thirty years. We had been admitted to the bar together; we worked on a couple of cases together; he tried to get me to join his firm about twenty years ago (I screwed that up when I had a couple of drinks at the introductory lunch with his partner and started running my mouth); he sat as a municipal court judge in tiny Hopewell Borough where I was a municipal prosecutor for a couple of years in the early 90's; we coached our kids in Little League together; he and I played basketball with his boys when they were in high school; you get the idea.

When he took the bench, I was one of those guys he could count on not to embarrass him if he didn't know something. He had been a civil litigator his entire career, so naturally the higher ups in Smartsville assigned him to the criminal part.

As his friends and protectors, we older guys would walk him through an issue by placing all the relevant arguments in front of him so he could choose from an easy menu, because it's the right thing to do. Young lawyers today are too busy swaggering around the courtroom acting like they know shit, at least until they open their mouths and you realize you're dealing with yet another member of this generation that got trophies for just showing up, even ten minutes late.

Anyway, I got to the Workhouse in time to see my guy before they closed up for count. What you do is drive up the hill to the security gate. Did I tell you this already? Stop me if I did. Officer comes out and over to driver's door and asks for your D/L. Not just your attorney ID, but your driver's license. It has my home address, and he wants to write that down. And you know they keep that information tightly guarded, right? That clipboard will be in the inmate rec room by sundown, with any luck. Here's why they want to see your license: if you're driving while revoked, or if your license is expired, or your car needs inspection, they will call it in. They can't wait to fuck with a lawyer or investigator. Sorry, sorry. I didn't mean to use profanity. It's the Pol Pot mentality I mentioned earlier.

One time I pulled up on a weekend afternoon, and the civilian visitors were lined up in the parking area in front of the gate. The gate was open. I pulled up to it, but no officer. I drove into the visitors' parking area, got my ID and file, and walked back to the guardhouse looking for the security officer. He came lumbering up and essentially accused me of criminal trespass for not waiting for him. Suggesting I didn't see him when I drove up was of no interest to his way of thinking. Really, they are absolute darlings.

Once approved, you pull into a controlled lot inside the security perimeter. Lock your car. Seriously: lock your car. Walk up a ramp past the smoking perch for all the civilians and officers unwilling to mosey to the benches placed on the grass for them. Step over the butts and through the smoke cloud. Remind yourself to get your clothes cleaned. Walk through the glass door and up to a metal detector. No one is actually manning the detector, but you walk through anyway.

Next stop is still another guy who doesn't match up for his job. These are Corrections Officers. Front desk is more visitor's bureau. There are rules. I hate rules. Tell you why later. Another security check. They have a new screening service, the kind of machine a political person agreed to buy from his third cousin's brother-in-law or some shit. It takes your picture and prints a sticky label with your likeness to glue on to your lapel, which will be ruined upon removal. In six months, I have yet to see the machine work. The CO is trying to print out a visitor's pass for the guy in front of me, without much success.

Look, you want to see some ID from the people entering a jail, to make sure they belong and won't smuggle cell phones or drugs to inmates. That's about it. This isn't family visiting. Who goes into a jail unless he absolutely has to? Lawyers, investigators, bail bondsmen, chaplains, doctors, nurses, shrinks, occasionally cops wanting to talk to guys already inside. That's about it.

We all carry some pretty solid forms of ID, and there is an approved visitor list for the professionals who work there under contract. Outside experts make appointments, because they typically need special access to inmates for extended periods of time. It's a crappy county lockup, but you'd think we were entering some amalgam of Ft. Knox, CIA headquarters, and Guantanamo Bay.

I hung up my coat on a hook (you can't bring it in), handed over my car keys and my bar card. I left my cell phone and my briefcase in the car, because they won't let you bring either with you, and you don't want them responsible for keeping those items safe. Not even your wallet. Just trade your personal ID for a visitor's badge. Keep your file folder close with a yellow pad inside; keep a plastic ballpoint clipped to your pad; keep the metal to a minimum. You don't have to, but it certainly speeds the process. Don't believe me? Try it at an airport sometime. Put everything from your pockets into a carrying case, wear a belt with no metal buckle (or no belt). Shoes, bag, laptop, walk through. It ain't rocket science; it's metallurgy.

They'll still wand you down.

"Mr. Carmody, long time no see. How you been, brother?"

"Sammy, what is it?"

"I'm doin.' Who you seein' today?"

"Only got time for one before count. Aaron Bellow. Can you call his name down before I hit the door?"

"Sure. Turn around. OK. Front desk to master control."

"Go master control."

"I got attorney for IDR. Need Aaron Bellow to IDR and an escort."

"Copy."

There is the clang of moving metal doors on a track. Step through. Wait for outer door to close. Step closer. Second door. Step again. Wait for your escort. He calls for the next door. "Twenty seven." Walk down a linoleum laced hall to the Inmate Dining Room, turn left, check in with the desk.

"Who you here to see?"

"Aaron Bellow."

"Sign here. Number Six is open." He pushed the buttons on his circa 1983 Western Electric phone. "This is IDR, I need Bellow, Aaron for attorney visit," turned his head back down to his newspaper and said to his desk, "He'll be down in a few minutes." Cubicle Six is dimly lit with two plastic chairs, a Formica table, walls that rise maybe five feet, all the privacy of a stall in an airport men's room. Less really, because there's no door.

Your mind drifts listening to the muffled (and some not so muffled) voices of lawyers soothing clients nearby. Explaining mandatory minimums, extended terms, progressive plea offers, the modern mantra of pugnacious prosecutors and regrettably too many pusillanimous public defenders. Not sure I can blame them. You don't tell your client he's facing twenty years, ten-year MPI, on an extended term eligible, second degree park zone piece of shit $20 coke sale, he turns down the six-over-three, then comes in second in a jury trial? You got some 'splainin' to do. Sixth Amendment stuff. Ineffective assistance of counsel problem. *Missouri v. Frye* problem. Notify your carrier problem.

What? Oh, sorry: twenty years is the maximum sentence, and the court can impose ten years before you see the parole board, "Minimum Parole Ineligibility." They know that when they offer six over three, which means a six-year sentence, but you have to serve at least three years before they'll think about letting you out. It's a lot of time for bullshit.

Anyway, a kid not more than five-six, 140 pounds soaking wet, hunched over in his orange jump suit, slinks past the opening to my cube, looking around, hair matted, unshaved. Looks vaguely like the guy in the video bail picture.

"Aaron Bellow?" He turns, looks, gaunt. Steps forward. I extend my hand. He takes it.

"Mr. Carmody?" Sniff the air. I'll go with still unshowered as well as unshaved.

"Yeah, have a seat. How they treating you?"

"I've been better."

"Triple bunked?"

"Huh?"

"Do you have two roommates in your one-person cell?"

"I had the floor at first, but now I've got a bunk. Third guy bailed last night."

"Anyone threatening you, hitting on you, stealing your shit? Anything like that?"

"Nah, it's all about control of the TV over there. I'm fine, 'cause I don't care what they watch."

"You okay otherwise?"

"This ain't my favorite place to be, 'but if you've got a warrant, I guess you're gonna come in.'"

"All right, Jerry Garcia, if that is your real name."

"Who's Jerry Garcia?"

"Grateful Dead? No? Let me just tell you: your dad hired me over the phone based on a recommendation of an old pal of mine who practices in Madison, Chris Van Wagner. Do you know who that is?"

"Unh-unh."

"Well, he's been around the criminal courts out there for a good twenty years or so, you can look him up when you get out. Point is this, you don't have to accept the lawyer your dad hires. He can pay, but you have to choose. So, we have to have a conversation, after which you can tell me if you want me to keep going or just bill him for the bail hearing. So far, so good?"

"Yup."

"Let me ask you a couple of basic questions before we get to the main event." And I walked him through his address, date of birth, social security number, prior record, and like that. We always check the DOB and social against what the cops type in the complaint. If they type the wrong number, transpose a single digit, you go in the NCIC (remember? National Crime Information Computer?) with an inaccurate profile. They list you under "alternate SSN's used" as though you were pushing an alias. It does happen; I've seen guys with fifteen different dates of birth, almost as many socials. I finished the intro drill. Then we got to brass tacks.

"So what happened? You're driving from Madison to New York and took a wrong turn in Youngstown?"

"No, we took I-80 like we planned. Got caught in a snow squall though. Pretty scary when you're driving 75 miles an hour and suddenly you can't see the end of your hood."

"Right. So what did you do?"

"Pulled over like everyone else. Found a truck stop around Williamsport. Waited it out. Got back on the road couple of hours later, turned south around Stroudsburg, or wherever, headed down here."

"So you were supposed to be in Trenton?"

"Yeah. I just dropped my friend off at the Trenton Train Station when I got picked up." 'Course as he's telling me this I'm feeling all full of myself for intuiting the train station angle. "Headed up some street because you can't get on Route 1 south from that side of the station or something. Must have turned wrong, got into some section where I knew I was near the freeway, but, like, I was also very far away, you know?"

"Oh, I know. But where were you headed?"

"Back down Route 1."

"Yeah, but where were you going? You just drove all the way out here from Wisconsin, dropped your buddy off at the train, and now what? Round trip vacation?"

"No, I was just..."

"Just what? Cruisin'? That's what Asbury Park is for."

"What's that?"

"Never mind. Let me try again. What were you doing in New Jersey in the first place? Selling those two guns?"

"No, I had a delivery to make."

"A what?"

"Delivery. I had a package in the trunk I was supposed to get to some guy at some mall on Route 1."

"What mall?"

"I don't know, I had it written down, Quaker something."

"Quakerbridge Mall? What were you going to do there?"

"I was supposed to meet a guy in the parking lot next to Sears, the auto center side. Open my trunk, give him the bag, that's it. $2,500 for the job."

"What was inside the bag?"

"Fuck if I know."

"Nothing if not helpful. Where's the bag?"

"Same answer, but I think the cops took it."

"Why do you say that?"

"Cause as soon as they pulled me over, they got me out of the car, took the keys, went through the trunk, and put the guns on the back seat for a few minutes. Then they took the guns, still in the boxes, told me I was under arrest, and next thing I know, I'm in a smelly cell in Trenton Police station."

"So what happened to your guy in the mall?"

"Dunno. They took my cell phone, haven't seen it since."

"And you have no idea what was in the bag in your trunk."

"Nope."

"Did you have a name for the guy you were supposed to meet?"

"Nope, just a, like a code name or some shit, and he'd be in a black Dodge Charger, tinted windows, and he would know my name and have my cell number."

"Ok, well, let's see. What was the code name?"

"Squid."

CHAPTER SEVEN

Interstate 80, Eastbound, south of Mt. Pocono.

I-80 runs the length of the lower 48, from New York City to San Francisco. It found its way into a starring role in John McPhee's *Basin and Range* about thirty years ago (a remarkable history of America's geography), because it was carved brutally out of old rock, as straight as a major highway can be for about 3000 miles. West of Ohio and Indiana, it's mostly free. It's one of two high-speed options across Pennsylvania, the other being the often narrow, always challenging controlled chaos and tolls known as the Pennsylvania Turnpike. The northern route is wide, straight, and heavily trucked. Truckers prefer roads without tolls. More importantly, without tolls, there's no semi-permanent record of a car being on the road for hundreds of miles. No EZPass, no toll receipt, no limited access rest stops for cash register activity to check. In this modern dystopia of electronic footprints wherever we go, I-80 is a ghost road.

"Jer, you awake?"

"What?"

"Wake up, man."

"What time is it?"

"Like 3:30 or so."

"Jeez."

"I need you to look at the map."

"Hang on....Okay."

"Are we taking the Northeast Extension or headed to Route 33 in Stroudsburg?"

"Uhh, let's see, I guess we could stay on into New Jersey and go south at Route 31."

"No, Jeremy, that's a major road. I'm looking for two country lanes, no lights."

"Well, you can't take the Northeast Extension, because that has tolls just like the regular highway. And we passed it a few miles back."

"We did? Huh. Good point; Route 33 then."

"Take that south to Route 22, east to New Jersey, then get off in Phillipsburg. We'll cruise along the river. Trust me on this."

"How long?"

"Another hour and a half, two hours."

"Want me to drop you at the train first?"

"So you can keep all the money? Not sure I'm feeling that."

"Well, we go to the station and check out the schedules, then we'll deal."

"That's fair. But why don't you drop me at the mall an hour ahead of time to keep an eye on these guys.'

"You're not stupid, are you?"

"I'm tellin' you. But you don't listen."

CHAPTER EIGHT

Session 4. Carmody, William.

...couldn't be a mistake, or a coincidence. If he was playing me, he did a bang up job. The kid wasn't sharp enough to make that shit up. What the hell would Squid want with a kid from Wisconsin, whatever he was carrying? Did you ever see those stories about Trenton cops juicing like major league ballplayers? Whole thing was hard to figure, but there was that. I didn't think those guys did steroids any more, and even if they did, it's way too easy to get that stuff online or on a fast trip to Canada. No elaborate drive train necessary. I had to think this one through.

And I had a job. With clients, and bills, and judges screaming for more paperwork to move their cases along. So I thought, let me just ponder what I heard while I deal with this other crap. I had too much on my mind in any case. I hadn't taken my wife on vacation in a year before the, uh, thing, and since then, uh, like I wasn't into... guess you could say I'm back to my old habit of not taking vacations. But I'll get to her, I swear. Please hear me out.

I owed Rooney a call to figure out the bails on another two clients we picked up over the weekend. The one, Joe Wright, was already a client, but they only caught up to him when we surrendered him on Saturday. He was a local kid with a reputation for not taking shit from the cops. So of course he got beat up a lot. Too often I would see him with dried blood in his dreads. They'd get all matted; he didn't care. Had this vacant look in his eyes when he was concussed, but underneath he knew exactly what he was doing.

The other was strange. Fifty-something Irish guy from St. Paul charged with sexually assaulting his nephew. Ex-priest with no prior record, no evidence he was diddling the kid for years, just a one-off event when the nephew came out of the shower naked while they were staying in adjoining rooms. By itself, not the end of the world. What made the case puzzling was that it took over a year for the boy's parents to report it.

Now my guy was locked up in a detention center somewhere in the Twin Cities in default of bond pending extradition, and I had half his extended family calling me for details. Not sure what it is with these big Irish families that they move clan-style through life, no one making a move without half a dozen affirmative votes from siblings, but there it was. The phone call I took at the request of another lawyer I knew went on for almost an hour, finishing something like this:

"And can you tell us what he's facing?"

"Sure; it's a first degree crime to have oral sex with a child under thirteen, so max twenty years, seventeen without parole. But for sex offenders, it only gets worse. Once you do get out, if you get out (escaping civil commitment), you are on lifetime supervision, unable to leave New Jersey, use a computer without permission, live in or near other kids, use alcohol, or basically do anything we might consider normal. They give him polygraph tests annually to make sure he's staying between the lines. He'd have to register annually or more frequently, report to a parole officer as directed, and have no contact with children in any fashion."

"Yeah, but he lives in Minnesota."

"Well, he wouldn't live there any more if convicted, even if he got straight probation."

"Seriously?"

"Sure. There's a statute under the Interstate Compact that permits an application to transfer supervision to another state, but the applications are impossible to process. No one wants to assume the cost of close supervision of a sex offender, even if the risk of him acting out is low."

"Okay, it sounds like you know what you are talking about, so let me put the final question to you: Why should we hire you, as opposed to any other lawyer out there?" Here's what I hate about conference calls. This last question came from the senior brother, the one directing the call. From what I could tell he was some kind of hedge fund guy from Connecticut. I had trouble containing myself.

"I don't think you understand, sir. I've been speaking to you, for nearly an hour now, at no fee, which is contrary to my office practice, at the suggestion and request of Bob Whitehurst, who is a gentlemen and a dear friend of mine. He asked me to answer your questions, and I hope I've done that. But I don't need any more clients. I'm at that stage of my career where I choose the clients, not the other way around. And I have to tell you, respectfully, if I'm expected to answer to a committee every step of the way, I'm not likely to accept representation of your brother or anyone else in that situation."

"Oh, I didn't mean…"

"You know, I think you did. You've taken my time with no offer of compensation, and I'm about to wind this call up. If your brother wants me to be his lawyer, I'm happy to talk to him, but please don't patronize me. I'm too old for that."

"Can we call you back?"

"Why don't you appoint a spokesman and have that person reach out to me if you have any follow up inquiries; how's that?" Did I sound angry there? I really have to work on losing that edge. I'm getting increasingly impatient with people who blithely ignore how they're sucking my blood until I pass out from the poverty of the experience. Okay, maybe that's a tad harsh, but still. How many doctors do you think you can call on the phone, ask a hundred questions, several of them three or four times, keep him or her on the line for an hour, and then ask him if he's the doctor for them? Anyone?

But I have to tell you, the guy's deal was thought-provoking. Sure, garden variety closeted middle-aged man coming out on the back of a twelve-year-old nephew. But for reasons yet undisclosed, no criminal complaint was filed until fourteen months after the event. Most moms would call the cops in seconds. How did he get out the door, on a plane, back to Minnesota, and no movement for over a year?

If I was going to take the case, I knew I would have to track down local counsel in St. Paul to try to get a bail approved for an extradition target. This would be tricky, because here's how extradition works: the Constitution of the United States was designed to protect among other things the southern states' right to reclaim fleeing slaves, but they went a step further, maybe to make it all look legit.

Article IV, section 2 says, "A Person charged in any State with Treason, Felony, or other Crime, who shall flee from Justice, and be found in another State, shall on Demand of the executive Authority of the State from which he fled, be delivered up, to be removed to the State having Jurisdiction of the Crime." What that means is if the governor of New Jersey sends a demand to the governor of Minnesota, there ain't a lot the governor of Minnesota can do except say, "Here you go."

In modern terms the whole shebang is covered by the IAD, uh, Interstate Agreement on Detainers. Bottom line is the "foreign" state is supposed to hold the guy pending receipt of the governor's warrant from the "demanding" state. In other words, no bail. Sit there in your cell until they call your name.

But no one does that any more, because the initial complaint that leads to the guy's arrest is from a local police department or prosecutor's office. Once the guy is arrested, they have to send all the paperwork to the governor's office, where it gets reviewed by governor's counsel for regularity, and all that. None of these folks is in a hurry to help some sex offender (or robber, or drug dealer) get a faster extradition hearing. So the paperwork shuffles, sometimes for weeks.

Is that fair to the defendant? Of course not. He's presumed innocent, but not in this situation. He literally sits as a fleeing felon, forget about this notion that he went home to work for a year before his sister in law got the ass and called the cops on him. He might have been a pedophile, but fugitive from justice? Not bloody likely.

So what's the catch? It costs money to keep a man in jail, especially pretrial detention. It's considered maximum security because the population is diverse, and at risk. You can't mingle drunks with O.G.'s (Original Gangstas). The cost of holding one of these guys runs anywhere from $100-165 a day. And if the governor of New Jersey doesn't get to your detainee's paperwork for a couple of months, do that math: minimum $3,000 a month to hold a defendant for the benefit of some other state dragging its collective feet. If you're holding ten guys pending extradition, make it $30,000 per month. How about a hundred guys?

The response is easy: courts will give your man a bail if he's not signing a waiver right away. If he waives extradition, he's saying he admits he is the guy they want back in New Jersey, and it's a matter of a couple of days before someone comes to pick him up. I had to get someone to get this guy bailed.

Meanwhile, I'm scrolling through my messages, and I see Germaine Green had called, three times no less. This was Wright's half brother and sometime corrections officer. Joe Wright was a good kid, and his word was bond. Green, not so much. I need $1,500 up front before I'm even entering an appearance to do a bail hearing, and he's the kind of guy who will promise you whatever you ask, then show up with $600, figuring you're not turning it down if it's cash. He always seems surprised when we give him a receipt and tell him we post the payments. Then Wright gets on me for postponing his motion, and I have to tell him he's about $900 short of having me at his hearing.

At one point couple of years ago Wright called me in a panic, because his brother had been detained in Los Angeles airport by the feds. They didn't arrest him, but they relieved him of his suitcase, including the $65,000 inside it. "They wiped me out, man."

I tried to explain it to him: the DEA operates on a different platform when it comes to contraband than most states, certainly New Jersey. They take your shit, then give you a piece of paper explaining how you can try to get it back. You have to file an administrative complaint with a certain person by a certain date, under oath, explaining why the shit is yours and why it's not contraband.

Are you following? No? Imagine how the eighth-grade-educated street kid following that on a piece of paper in eight-point font is doing about now. Money's gone. You have to recognize it will be a whole new crime to swear the $65,000 was your life savings right after you cashed in your insurance policy and sold your macked out Civic.

Look, stop me if I'm boring you, but I'm trying to give you some idea of what's going through my mind every time I handle one of these calls. This shit ain't beanbag, and if you don't watch every step to the foul line, you wind up throwing bricks at the backboard.

In New Jersey, civil forfeiture works like this. Say you're arrested for possession with intent to distribute drugs after cops pull you over and find a pound of weed in your glove compartment. That's the crime: possession with intent. Marijuana? Third degree, five years in prison exposure.

Oh, were you pulled over right after you drove past the St. Alban's school gym? Make that five with a three-year mandatory minimum term in prison for possessing with intent, in or near school property. Only the prosecutor can waive that minimum, and he won't do it unless you agree to rat out, say, five of your closest friends. I call it the "I'm in trouble, so you have to go to jail for me" approach. Hell, they actually made a movie out of this syndrome. Look it up: movie's called *Snitch.* Totally appropriate.

But that's just your criminal exposure. There is civil liability too. That's where civil forfeiture comes into play. The public policy deal is, you should not be allowed to keep money you earned on illegal transactions, so if they find $2,500 in the glove compartment next to your pot, they're taking that too. It is "proceeds" of the criminal enterprise. Fair enough.

But what the cops do is search everything and everyone in sight, and anyone with so much as a fifty dollar bill on him gets the money taken and put on a property report as "proceeds." Guys will come into my office with their girlfriends who swear they just took that fourteen-hundred bucks out of their bank account to pay the rent when they got busted, and many times it's absolutely true. Other times, well, that's that.

When the cops take the cash, they retain it as evidence to show you were running a drug distribution enterprise, so the money goes into the evidence vault, perhaps to be produced later at a trial, along with your scale, your baggies, twist-ties, and a black notebook with the names and amounts of everyone you sold to the previous month. If only. The cases are never that clean. Except on TV.

Then there's a separate law requiring prosecutors to move on the cash if they intend to keep it permanently. This is the "civil forfeiture" statute based on the policy position I've staked out here. In New Jersey, prosecutors have ninety days to file a lawsuit claiming the proceeds must be forfeited to the state unless the rightful owner comes forward and swears it is legitimate money from a legitimate source. Cautious defense attorneys will tell their clients not to file any such declaration, for fear it will be introduced in the prosecutor's criminal case as evidence of a defendant's willingness to lie his way out of obvious trouble.

Forfeit "to the state" has its own complications. Time was, the phrase meant to the prosecutor's office, or to the county treasurer. A few years ago, the state legislature got wind of a couple of forfeiture abuse cases: the Salem County Prosecutor taking private flying lessons with his forfeiture account; gym memberships for assistant prosecutors in another county. Next thing you know, forfeiture proceeds are now split fifty-fifty between the Attorney General and the local prosecutor. It's a beautiful scam.

See, the money comes from every kid on the block who gets stopped, for whatever reason. The subtext is invariably, 'What uneducated black man under the age of twenty-five could possibly have twenty-five hundred bucks to his name? Even if he did, he probably owes it to the county welfare board as back child support to his baby mama.' And don't think that isn't exactly what the prosecutors are thinking. I've heard them say it out loud once too often.

But there's more than proceeds; there's "instrumentality." If you use your car to drive the drugs to the sales point, they will take your car as the "instrument" of the crime. No car, no transport, no sale. In Florida, they take boats and planes all the time, and if you want to buy your boat back, raise some illicit cash and launder it through a willing bank for a cashier's check to bring to the auction. Your back in business, and DEA has its' discretionary travel budget for the month. I've seen cars and computers seized as both proceeds and instruments, and child porn cases will always result in a tech haul. If cops don't think you have a job and you've got a flat screen in your apartment, you better hope it's bolted to the wall.

The good news is that many local prosecutors can't keep up with the volume of forfeiture cases, so they are willing to make a deal with defense attorneys, rolling us into the entire scam. Wright got arrested twice before this weekend with cash (don't know how much yet, but if I were a betting man, and I told you I am, it'll be at least four figures), and I know I can call Sean McCloud, forfeiture prosecutor, and suggest a fifty-fifty split, almost by rote. If the guy had thirty-five hundred on him at the time, McCloud will free up seventeen-fifty in a county check payable to Wright "and his attorneys, Carmody and Scott" to resolve the case without filing a complaint. If Germaine Green shorts me, I have a Plan B.

Yes it stinks, because it makes me a tool in the scam. Prosecutors have to know I'm willing to throw my client's property rights under the constitutional bus in order to ensure I get a portion of my fees covered. On the other hand, I can assess quickly the odds against my guy getting back so much as ten cents if he has to swear to the legitimacy of his cash (he can't.) I'll call Germaine back and tell Andrew to fax a letter saying we will be at Wright's rescheduled bail hearing, called "entering an appearance."

Understand, these aren't the only two other cases I'm trying to manage. They just happen to be the ones that figured in how this whole Wisconsin Bellow gun mess turned out and landed me here. I know they want me to talk about the other times I acted out in court, but this is what was weighing me down at the time. I'm telling you this story because at first I thought this guy filed a, um, not a PCR, but an, uh, ethics complaint against me. Then I realized that could not possibly be true. For the life of me, I couldn't figure out why he targeted me, the one guy in a position to get him out of the jam of his life, for extinction. Kind of ironic when you think about it.

Then I realized the judges must have turned me in. Matter of time, really. I've been losing it for a while now. Not sure what they told you. I don't know if you can help me sort through this mess, but I had to talk to someone, even at two hundred per hour.

Okay, maybe I'm required to talk to someone, but I'd rather pick my own listener, thank you. Stop me if this stuff is too hard to follow and I'll try to clean up some of the terms I'm using. So, PCR, that's a 'petition for post-conviction relief,' known in the federal courts and the old world as a petition for *habeas corpus.* What it really is, is open season on your own lawyer, and maybe another bite at the apple you ate last year.

The point was I was shuffling along, picking them up and putting them down as I always did, and I must have taken my eye off the ball. There was a high hard one slotted for my forehead, and I never saw it coming. I think it was because I wasn't looking, but that's what I'm hoping you'll explain to me. Let me finish the story first. Are we out of time yet?

CHAPTER NINE

Route 29, southbound, Market Street, east, Clinton Avenue, north.

Heading into Trenton from the north, drivers can hug the Delaware River and avoid major roads, winding through Alpha and Milford. South from Philipsburg, undulating two-lane blacktop navigates some beautiful stretches until Frenchtown, and from there, Route 29 pours through the old river mill towns, like Stockton and Lambertville, then straight to the Market Street exit opposite the New Jersey Statehouse.

It's a short hop up Market Street to the old courthouse where Market intersects Broad, and in another quarter mile, runs smack into the Trenton Amtrak station linking New York and Philadelphia. The train tracks parallel U.S. Route 1, America's first highway, once a well traveled turnpike of grass, then mud, then gravel, finally asphalt, once unfettered, gradually intersected, then sparsely signaled, finally crushed by lights and jughandles and deceleration lanes and curb cuts for franchises unconjured in the fertile imaginations of colonial engineers.

America's first parking lot groans from the northern tip of Maine to the tail end of the Florida Keys. Never too much information about highways: our roads, our haphazardly wired brains, one organism: in America, we are where we drive.

"Jer…hey Jer, did you fall asleep again?"

"What time is it?"

"About ninety minutes since the last time you asked. Getting dark."

"What's the plan?"

"Let's find the train station, you jump out and pick up a schedule, and then we'll figure out the mall thing."

"Roger. Can we eat?"

"If we have time. Gotta be someplace at the mall."

"I gotta use the can."

"Dude, you're walking into a train station. You should be fine in two minutes."

Jeremy bolted from the car across from the taxi line, south entrance. He found the men's room, the wall monitors, the kiosks filled with folded paper, "NJTransit," "NJ&You," "Visiting The Old Barracks." He reached and opened the "Amtrak" pamphlet, reading and walking, head down, vaguely aware of people moving with purpose.

Outside, Jeremy hunched his shoulders, unaccustomed to the damp more than the chill. Opening a car door, he found himself slapped with warm, fetid air. "Okay, got it."

Aaron: "Well?"

Jeremy: "Nothing going west for a while. Let's go to the mall. How we gettin' there?"

“Look for One North.”

“I think you just missed it.”

“Can’t we follow this street to Mulberry or New York or something? Did I read that right?”

“I would not recommend a U-turn.”

“Jer, what street is this?”

“North Clinton Avenue.”

“Is that a sign for U.S. One?”

“”Next left.”

“Shit…shit. Shit, shit, shit.”

“What the hell is that, Aaron? Tell me those are cops.”

“Those are cops.”

“What do we do now?”

“Just don’t say a thing. I’ll do all the talking.”

“That’s real comforting.”

CHAPTER TEN

Session 3. Carmody, William.

I have to tell you the Joe Wright story, otherwise none of this makes sense. I think this is the part where they started saying I was crazy, because I don't drink the Kool-Aid every time a cop says there was a gun or a furtive movement or whatever happy horseshit they're spewing to prosecutors in their daily diet.

So, the kid's brother calls me a couple of months, maybe a year ago. Germaine Green, remember? He's a corrections officer, so chances are he's dirty at some level, because most corrections officers hang out with hardened criminals and no supervision way too often not to get a taste for how easy it is to be better off than state pay will get you.

If they're not smuggling phones to inmates, they're scamming the overtime rules (calling out sick within an hour of a shift, knowing they have a group of guys waiting to work that shift on overtime—don't take my word for it; check the overtime budgets of every DOC office in America), or flashing tin to get out of speeding tickets. They own guns, fer chrissake.

Germaine Green: when the guy comes to my office, I don't trust him, especially after he pulled that stunt with the six hundred bucks.

Older case: seems Joe Wright was minding his own business on the street outside a club on New Warren Street when a fight broke out as the club was closing. Cops showed up and told everyone to move along. Joe doesn't relate to that kind of talk, so he doesn't move fast enough. He might even start some shit, telling the cops they have no superior right to the sidewalk, and he'll go when he is good and ready.

Now, officer, you can be excused for writing a hand summons to a wise guy, telling him that riot control is part of your job, and disobeying a lawful order is a disorderly persons offense. And if you give the guy the ticket and make him come to court, maybe even pay a fine, you're doing your job. Perhaps a tad overzealously, but it's a matter of opinion. Hard asses are everywhere, but especially in police departments. I get that.

But head breaking is now standard fare with most of these city cops. They jack Joe up against a wall, tell him to spread his legs, then start in on his hamstrings with nightsticks. When he goes down, they kick him in the ribs. People see it; cops don't care. "What are you lookin' at?" Or, "What are you gonna do?" And the answer as often as not is: nothing.

I did that bail hearing. Joe was charged with possession of four-hundredths of a gram of cocaine with intent to distribute. Yeah, I'm thinking the same thing. Really? Four-hundredths of a gram? A little more than a single line of coke you claim you found in his pocket after you kicked the shit out of him, and you want me to believe it's possessed with intent to distribute?

You did this just to teach him a lesson, one which he seems incapable of learning, as this is not his first go round with you guys. Did you know he has a videographer following him around most days taping these encounters? Not every day, but most days. You might want to give that some thought before your next opportunity to knock his head sideways.

...No, I wasn't talking to you. Talking to those cops I can't get out of my head.

Anyway, I get him bailed on the drug charge and he comes to my office to discuss fees. I explain his brother Germaine ain't the most reliable, and that's that. No complications, except getting paid takes twice as long as I had hoped. Gotta start getting more money up front, but the economy is terrible, and I'm asking for families to give me their life savings over one kid who couldn't give up the fast life.

So while I'm waiting for Wright to get me the rest of his retainer, he manages to get arrested again, this time on a gun charge. I'm getting leery of keeping him on as a client: light retainers, dealing with his brother, plus he's a total pain in their ass, so I know cops will grind him down with more charges.

But here's the case. Sheriff's officers claim they rolled up on him in broad daylight in front of his house, he ran inside to avoid them, ran out the back, dropped his piece inside a barbecue grill in the rear yard, ran through a gate in a fence and is still going as we speak. Or so their story went.

They indicted him on this new gun charge right away in order to get a "warrant of indictment," which makes the U.S. Marshals feel better when they kick a door down in search of a "fugitive from justice." Joe remained at large for a month, managing to get his girlfriend arrested for possession of pot when the fugitive task force went to her house on East State looking for him. Searched her bedroom, found an ounce in her shoebox. I got him to turn himself in a week after that. They charged him with hindering his own apprehension. When he turned himself in.

Joe caught up to me after his release. I said, "What happened? You ran through a house and dropped a gun in your grill? Was it hot?"

"Is that, like, Old White Dude humor? Not funny, man. Not at all what happened." He had a decidedly different version on the rear door escape. "I saw those cops in that black Charger, tinted windows and shit. I was standing on the porch in front of my cousin's house in broad daylight, man."

I said, "What were you doing?"

"Nothing. Nuh-thing. I thought I might have a Trenton warrant for fines, so I just walked off. I went around the side of the building and up that driveway to West Paul and kept going. That's it."

Look, I'm not naïve. I was born at night, but not last night. Joe Wright could be lying to me. Wouldn't be the first time. But at least half the young black men in Trenton do owe money on unpaid traffic tickets and ordinance violations to Trenton Municipal Court, so cops can pick them up almost at will and run them in to face the judge on a special brand of payment plan. Pay up, or work time off at $20 a day. Which is why they still call it the Workhouse.

And he wanted no parts of them. He walked over to another street to get away. He did not go through his cousin's house, and he did not drop a gun in a barbecue. He had witnesses. It was worth checking out.

I drove by the row homes in a downscale section of Trenton. (No, not all of Trenton is downscale; there are some elegant sections, including Hiltonia, above Cadwalader Park to the north; Cadwalader Heights, overlooking the park from the south; Mill Hill, near the bloody bridge of Revolutionary War fame, and Glen Afton by the Delaware. You should check them out.) But this is Kirkbride, off of

New Willow, do you know it? Just kidding. Princeton folk don't get to Trenton much, and I doubt you are the black swan in this crowd.

Anyway, I see the layout of the townhouses, including the side driveway of the one house where the junior cop says he ran to watch Wright drop the gun in the Weber grill. There's a chain link fence with barbed wire on top, exactly as he described. The fence is about six feet high, with another foot of barbed wire. He could not see over the top, by his own description. I think I know the guy, and six foot, he ain't. So I wander over there and take a look from his perspective to see how hard it would be to pick up the grill through the back yards of two intervening houses.

One problem: the guy with the barbed wire also has a privacy insert on the west side of his yard. It's this green plastic sheeting you can work through your chain link and give yourself a measure of, well, privacy. I can't see a thing. I walk further back until maybe I could see from a different angle, but the outside fence prevents me from moving around to where I could get a good look. What I needed to do was put the guy on the stand and ask him to show me on a diagram exactly where he was standing when he made his observations.

Then I walked back to the front of the cousin's house to inspect the door. Four panels, lower right has a plywood patch. Must have kicked it in and reached up to unlatch the lock. Was taking a picture with my phone when the next door neighbor opens his door.

"You the cops?"

"Do I look like the cops?"

"Kind of." Might have been that moment when it occurred to me that I looked like your generic middle-aged white guy, gray hair, suit, button down shirt. I really could be the cops.

I said, "I'm Joe Wright's lawyer. Know anything about how this door got broken?"

"They busted it down."

"They what?"

"Busted it down. I was inside. I heard this banging. Opened this door and saw these two dudes with like a metal pipe. Like a battering ram. They told me to shut the door."

"What did you do?"

"What the fuck do you think I did? I shut the door."

"Willing to come to court to say that?"

"Will I get in trouble?"

"You sure there were two guys on the porch with that pipe?"

"Positive."

"No trouble." We exchanged information. I got back in my car before anyone tried to buy it from me for like fifty bucks.

Called Andrew and told him to prepare a motion to suppress, warrantless search, and file it immediately, asking for a hearing in two weeks. Puts pressure on these prosecutors who don't want to do anything for the first six months they have a file. The case managers love us because they think we are trying to move the ball forward quickly. They also hate us, because we don't plead guys with the speed and neglect of some more overworked attorneys.

So what am I looking at? Joe Wright is a twice-convicted drug dealer, albeit a small time player by anyone's estimation. He doesn't roll with any of the colors in Dodge City (no Bloods, Crips, Latin Kings, name your gang), but he's gotten the negative attention of both city and county cops.

On this one, he's charged with unlawful possession of a weapon, second degree (five-ten year sentencing range), possession of a defaced firearm (third degree, three-five), possession of hollow point ammunition (fourth degree, zero-eighteen months) and possession by a certain person not to possess a gun, owing to his prior felony convictions(s). The last is also a second degree crime, but "certain persons" have problems. The range is five-ten, but at least five of those must be spent as actual years in prison.

I've seen nothing on his jacket to suggest he carries a gun, but on the other hand, who doesn't carry a gun in a war zone? An idiot? I have to email Sean McCloud, the guy handling the bail source forms and civil forfeiture.

Oh, I know what you're thinking: with thirty-five lawyers in their office, the Mercer County Prosecutor delegates two very active tasks to the same guy? McCloud also carries a trial load and alternate Drug Court assignments. Makes you wonder what everyone else is doing.

McCloud will try to kill about four birds with a single rock. He'll offer a global resolution of Joe's open criminal files; consent order for all the money taken off of him at the time of his various arrests; look for some kind of stipulation that prevents Wright from later filing a civil suit for police brutality (the so-called 1983 action), and save the county valuable grand jury time by doing all of this before either of Wright's recent cases are presented for indictment.

My cell phone rings and of course it's McCloud, who calls me all the time, and I'm pretty sure he's not gay.

"Hello?"

"Bill, Sean McCloud here." (That's the way he talks, no lie.)

"Hey, Sean, what's shakin'?" (That's the way I talk, but I have an excuse.)

"Joe Wright is shaking in his boots about now, don't you think? We got his knit hat near the back yard where he dropped that .9 millimeter, and I've already sent it out for DNA testing."

"Look at you, Mr. CSI."

"And you know he's got two other files right?"

"I know about the piece of shit resisting arrest charge, if that's what you mean. Was he on probation at the time?"

"No, but he does have a couple of priors making him a candidate for mandatory extended term and certain persons treatment."

"Yeah, and..."

"And he has a conspiracy to distribute marijuana on West State Street from about nine months ago. Co-defendant is Ray Jackson. Know him?"

"Doesn't mean a thing to me."

"Well, we have a decent case for an eye in the sky observation of the last two sales Jackson makes, then they close in on your guy sitting in his car and find close to a pound of weed in his center console. But it's marijuana, so I'm feeling generous."

"Sean, you're nothing if not generous, to a fault."

"It's just the way God made me, what can I say?"

"Don't say anything. What's your pitch?"

"I'll dump the resisting case, as well as the hindering complaint from the other day. I'll let him plead to the certain persons charge, with a concurrent on a single third degree PWI, non-school zone, for an aggregate seven over three."

"That's funny, because Mona Bahadurian already told me you had authority to go to six over two. You're just starting high. Probably all that weed on your desk."

"I have no idea who you're talking about."

"The trial team leader who sits across the desk from you and you're staring at right now? Good luck with that."

"Even at six over two this is an offer he can't refuse."

"You know you get no special credit for dumping the barking dogs on your desk. Hindering? When he turns himself in? Really? And that resisting case. He got like thirteen stitches and you're just ducking a 1983."

"Six over two: going once..."

"Let me talk to him. Can you get me some pre-indictment discovery on the new case? That's driving this bus, so I have to go over it with him."

"I can do that."

"Just reports and affidavits. I don't expect you to have labs on the gun this quickly. And how long to get DNA on the hat?"

"Couple of weeks to a month."

"Let me talk to him."

"Get back to me?"

"Yeah. One other thing. What's the forfeiture case look like."

"Oh, almost forgot. I'll split the entire enchilada, thirty-three twenty from the two earlier arrests. I'll keep two grand, you can have the rest."

"I was thinking the same thing."

"We gotta deal on forfeiture?"

"No, I was thinking 'I'll keep two grand and you can have the rest.'"

"Down the middle?"

"I'll ask; it's all I can do."

"OK, well, you have a wonderful Mercer County day."

"Sean."

"What?"

"No one talks like that."

"I know."

Please tell me you're following me here. This is the kind of stuff that's critical to your understanding how I got into this mess. The U.S. Supreme Court handed down a couple of decisions last spring that make it abundantly clear what we have to do as lawyers in a plea bargain-driven criminal justice system.

There were these two cases where the lawyers did not tell their clients about decent plea offers. In one case, the lawyer didn't pass the offer along. That's the *Missouri v. Frye* problem I mentioned the other day. In the second case, the lawyer apparently went insane, because he told the client about the offer, then told him not to take it, as there was no way client could be convicted of attempted murder when he shot at another guy's legs. I admit I was not aware of the shoot-to-kill-by-aiming-above-the-waist rule, but there you have it.

The failed-to-convey-an-offer case had some language in the opinion along the lines of 'look, when a plea offer goes by the boards, there is no formal rejection hearing. You just don't take the deal. Plea-bargaining is catch as catch can, and nobody in the court system is the wiser. In fact, discussions between client and defense counsel are privileged.'

So, we have to give another bite at the apple if a defendant comes out and says, "I had no idea I turned down a get out of jail free card because my lawyer thought he was Clarence Fucking Darrow and wanted a bigger fee out of me. I would have taken the no-jail deal in a heart beat."

Bottom line was I had to tell Wright about the six over two, but I knew he'd be more pissed about the shakedown on the forfeiture of the money. They hadn't caught him with drugs when they took most of it (and they even took money from his girlfriend's shoe box where they found the marijuana), and he worked hard for his cash. Took some chances and survived on his wits. At the end of the day, he had a hard time accepting the cost of doing business as his operative fact of life.

And these are the operative facts of my life. I can't wait 'til next week. Do you have any more time this week? I gotta get this over with.

CHAPTER ELEVEN

Mulberry Street, north of St. Joe's Avenue.

Most young black men can tell when police are behind them. Ask one. He'll tell you it's more than the flashing red lights, or the white spotlight shining into the back of his car from twenty feet away, or even the sound of a police radio crackling in the background if his window is down. He knows it's the cops because the hair on his neck and arms stands straight up, his heart starts racing before he sees a badge, and his stomach produces enough acid in thirty seconds to burn through the chrome handcuffs he imagines himself in before dark. White kids lack this radar.

If white kids would talk to black, they'd get this advice. The trick is always the same. Less is more. Don't say stuff; it only leads to more questions, more answers not on their clipboard of things they expect to hear. Don't say "sir," it being one of the tells they've been taught to focus on at the police academy. Wanna avoid getting shot? Keep your hands on the steering wheel until invited to remove them to retrieve documents. If you can master it, present calm.

"Aaron?"

"What?"

"These guys aren't wearing uniforms." Jeremy swiveled his head to watch the men approach.

"Just be cool. Stop looking back." Aaron's eyes bored into the rear view mirror, bright, reflecting light banding across his eyes.

"You sure they're cops?"

"Is the Titanic overdue? Of course they're cops. Be cool. Don't say anything."

"What would I say?"

"Let me do the talking." Aaron lowered his window.

"That I can do."

Hulking man in black BDU pants, black sweater, black Kevlar vest, driver's side: "Sir, please keep your hands on the steering wheel." Lowering his mouth below the roof line of the window: "You, sir, place your hands on the dashboard, palms down."

Perhaps too quickly, Aaron said, "Okay." This was his idea of how to get along with police.

"I didn't ask you to talk. I need your license, registration, and insurance card. Where are those things?"

Aaron began climbing the learning curve. "License in my wallet; rest is in my glove compartment."

"I'm going to ask you both to get out of the car, passenger first. Red, open his door."

Second man in black: "Got it, Sarge. What's your name? I said what's your name? Are you deaf?"

"Jeremy."

"Jeremy what?"

"Jeremy Benjamin Smith."

"Okay, Jeremy Benjamin Smith; step out of the car keeping your hands where I can see them." Jeremy moved deliberately, sensing the importance of appearing earnest.

The sergeant stood over Aaron, slightly behind his left shoulder. "Sir, what's your name?"

"Aaron."

"Aaron what?"

"Bellow?"

"You sure?"

"Yup." Aaron tried to turn to look at this questioner.

"Keep looking straight ahead, Aaron. Do not take your hands from the steering wheel."

"I thought you wanted us both out." He slid back on the curve.

"You'll get out on my command."

"What are we doing with this one, Sarge ?"

"Smith? Put him in the cage car; take him to the Island."

CHAPTER TWELVE

Session 4. Carmody, William.

Can I talk sports for a minute? I'm guessing you're not a sports person, I mean not because you're from Princeton, or because you have a PhD (you do, don't you?), but let's face it, you're thoughtful, intuitive, insightful, I mean, I guess you are, since I seem to be doing all the talking. Sports fans don't really do insight, unless you're talking about why a ball fake freezes a linebacker. But if you'll let me, sometimes I use sports metaphors to explain how stuff works in my business. I swear it will make this go quicker.

So, in football and baseball, hockey and soccer (real football), they have halves or periods with pretty long intermissions, which gives coaches time to make adjustments. In baseball, everyone keeps a book on everyone else, and the adjustments get made over a longer time frame, because there are more games.

But the idea is, in football, say, an offensive coordinator figures out during the first half that the other team's defensive backs are playing tight, close to the line of scrimmage, and conceding long passes. But his game plan is short passing, because he's using a second string quarterback while his star nurses an injury.

So, he goes into the locker room at half time and tells his guys, 'Look, they are crowding you at the line. Let's stop and turn for a short hook, then try to burn them up the middle. All we need is an extra two seconds of protection and air the ball out. We'll get that time by rolling you out to throw.' That might not make much sense, but the idea is to change your plan to react to how the defense is playing you.

It happens in our line of work too. I mentioned how these days we routinely get CAD reports, right? Well, now cops switch to an alternate unrecorded radio channel before they close in on a bust.

Another thing some defense lawyers started doing was to go to the police records department, like any citizen can do to get an accident report, and pay twenty-five cents a page to buy police reports on file within a matter of days of an incident. When U.S. Attorneys found out the defense bar was getting early access to raw reports, they went ballistic, because they are used to never turning stuff over until the eve of trial. Local prosecutors have to give us everything in their file once an indictment is returned. But if you can buy it early on the street for a couple of bucks, you can figure out the other side's game plan pretty quickly.

TAC has a new spin on how to deal with that. Those guys don't bother to officially "file" their reports until the case has a grand jury date. They start the reports on their laptops on the night of the arrest, but they keep the report number open so they can edit as they go along, and that way they avoid having me get at their reports before I should. These are the same kinds of adjustments basketball and football coaches make at half time. Other side tries a new tactic, you figure it out, then plan to defeat it.

Reason I tell you is this: here I had this kid in the Workhouse telling me a scary story within seventy-two hours of his arrest. This was not going to resolve easily, even if there was no back story involving TAC officers. Gun cases are next to impossible to plead any more, because the legislature has made every routine gun possession a mandatory prison term, even for possession without a permit. If my gun cases involved white guys, the NRA would be sending me reinforcements, including brigade-strength lawyers and a brief bank to fill my CPU.

So, here's what I had. Parents call to help out their kid arrested for having two new guns in boxes in plain view on his back seat when he got pulled over for being in the wrong section of Trenton. He's facing ten years, but I might beat the case on a motion to suppress. That's the scenario where you argue the cops searched his car without a warrant.

You gotta ignore all those OJ experts who went on TV to say all cops need is probable cause. That ain't it. You need probable cause AND exigent circumstances. You got probable cause to search a house, a car, a kid? Go tell a judge what you think you have and ask him or her to sign a search warrant. You can do it over the phone. If it's a spy case, the FBI can tell the judge after they did the snooping. It's not that difficult. But cops don't want to spend the time filling out the paperwork or depending on some judge they don't trust to sign off quickly.

When they're on the street, most cops will just pull the kid out of the car, go through his pants pockets, search the car, including the glove box and the trunk, and search anything they find inside the car, like a suitcase. Then they'll make some shit up about how your car was weaving within the lane (swear to god this is common), or you had a tail light out. But if you catch them early, it'll turn out they didn't coordinate the excuse-of-the-day for the search. That's why I was taking a shot at the reports.

I left the Workhouse and drove straight to the Trenton Police Division headquarters on North Clinton. This is only a few blocks from where the kid got arrested, so I jumped off Route 1 at New York Avenue and made the left onto North Olden, headed to North Clinton. It goes right by St. Joes, which is where I was telling you suburban white kids love to score pot on a Friday night. You can go stronger, all the way up to crack, but you gotta come late and be patient.

Anyway, as I'm passing St. Joe's, don't I see Artess Nance standing on the corner with that vacant look on his face. I had represented Artess a couple of times, and I knew he had suffered traumatic brain injuries as a child from eating lead paint and falling out of a window. Lawyer got him like half a million bucks in structured settlement money for the two cases, but the kid kept selling his payments to those companies that will buy them up for pennies so you can get cash now. His mother would pay me to keep him out of jail every time he got caught selling pot, which was all the time because he wasn't smart enough to run when the cops pulled up. But that will happen with a 78 IQ and no pattern recognition. She needed him out, because she lived off of his disability payments, which are discontinued when you are incarcerated. Go figure.

"Hey, RT, what's shakin'?"

"You want some pot old man?"

"Artess, it's me, your lawyer."

"Oh, hiya, Mr. uh, Cromartie."

"Carmody."

"Mr. Cromartie."

"You been out here the last couple of nights?"

"Nah, nah, I ain't been here. Cops been here."

"Really? Every night?"

"Every night. Shit's crazy, man."

"Your mom okay?"

"She good, she good."

"That's good. Well, you take care, all right?"

"Mr. Cro...Carmottie?"

"Yeah, RT, what is it?"

"You see my mom?"

"Not lately."

"Tell her I'm arright."

"I will do that."

I turned right onto North Clinton, pulled into the visitor's lot and walked to the main entrance of the police station. On the second floor, the Records Lieutenant was in a light mood, which I ruined.

"Hey Marty, how's it going?"

"Hey Bill, what are you up to?"

"Trying to get a vehicle report on my guy's car taken in Thursday night. Parents' car all the way from Wisconsin and I can't wait for McCloud to figure out if he's involved. Couple of guns found on the seat in unopened boxes, so I don't think he'll be interested, especially if there's a lien." See, if he seizes the car, the third party lender, like Ford Motor Credit, is an innocent bystander and the prosecutor would have to pay off his note to take title. He ain't doing that.

"Hang on. What's the kid's name?"

"Bellow, first name Aaron."

"Let's see, Thursday, still in the filing tray. Wait a second, wait a second, ah, nope. No vehicle report…Wait, wait. Okay, I got an arrest report and underneath that…property report, and vehicle report. Let me make a copies."

"Did they file invest reports?"

"Kidding right? I'm gonna retire before these guys get their reports in. Don't know what it is about TAC, they seem to make up their own rules on this stuff, and nobody cares. When I was on patrol, we would have been suspended for pulling this crap. I mean see this pile over here? These are files we can't forward for grand jury because they still haven't filed anything. It's crazy."

"When are you going to retire?"

"I got three months ten days, not that I'm counting."

"Where you headed?"

"My wife's father is giving us his shore house in Wildwood, because he's moving to Florida."

"Nice."

"Here you go."

"What do I owe you?"

"C'mon, Billy."

"OK, sorry. Hey, if I don't get invited to the party, good luck in Wildwood."

"Thanks, man, but don't you think it's time you tried one of those parties on for size?"

"Not yet. I can't stop now. I'm getting close."

So I'm walking back to my car reading the vehicle report, nothing special. Property report, interesting. Two guns (what the hell was a Ruger .22-45 Lite?), boxes, no ammo, serial numbers intact, nothing else. No cash, no pot, no pipe, no rolling papers, no identification documents associated with the car that might shed light on whose guns they were, nothing. Wisconsin slacker with no pot? Not bloody likely.

As I opened my back door to throw the reports in a bag, I glanced at the arrest report, something caught my eye. I stopped and studied a box on the first page and realized it had been altered. On the submitted page, after someone hit print. Underneath the scratch mark, you could see the number of arrestees was originally "2," straightened to a "1."

CHAPTER THIRTEEN

On Duck Island, South Trenton, below Route 29/129, out of sight from the power plant.

First cop: "Okay, out of the car."

Jeremy Smith muttered to himself, audibly. "Where are we?"

Second cop: "Did we ask you to talk?"

First cop: "Muldoon?"

Second cop: "Yeah."

First cop: "Did Sarge give us an order here?"

Second cop: "I thought he did. You wanna call him on a side channel?"

First cop: "Not sure about this."

Second cop: "You want me to take care of it?"

First cop: "I'm gonna take a walk and see if I can get him on his cell."

Second cop: "Your funeral."

First cop: "That's what I'm looking to avoid."

CHAPTER FOURTEEN

Session 5. Carmody, William.

Duck Island is a spit of land probably too dirty to warrant the name "Island." Frankly, it's not even an island anymore. Lost at the southern end of the city, it's the area north and west of Duck Creek, some ways up from the Hamilton Marshes, and connected to Trenton by Lamberton Road. It's always been a make-out site. You could park there in the dark, and no one could find you for hours or days.

In the 1930's, a serial killer started knocking off lovers who hid out there. Some guy with a shotgun began shooting up couples in their cars. Didn't stop until early 1940's. A poor black guy got pinned with the charge, even though he'd never been in trouble a day in his life and no physical evidence connected him to the crimes. They kept him on ice for like a hundred hours until he confessed and got himself life in prison. But the judge or the jurors must have felt a twinge of guilt, because he denied the crimes on the stand and told about being beaten by the cops. He did 20 and got paroled, and the ACLU took up his cause. Today, the Innocence Project might have gotten him a different result.

Nowadays, the Island has a little more activity. The power plant is still there. And a marine terminal. Not sure who uses the marine terminal. It's more or less next to a nice office building that used to house the Mercer County Improvement Authority, until they moved into even nicer quarters as a result of financing an office complex adjacent to the Trenton Thunder baseball stadium, unobstructed view of the Delaware, and more upscale feel to it. The MCIA office building on Duck Island sat vacant for years, because of course a government agency abandoned class-A offices before they had a subtenant to take over the carrying costs. Something private industry routinely does, but government should never do.

Later, the Mercer County Prosecutor took his special units (homicide, child sex assault, welfare fraud, economic crime, etc.) to the building and solved his space issue, cramped in the old courthouse and spilling into random buildings on South Broad Street. Why this was not done four years earlier will remain one of life's unsolved mysteries.

Trenton Police have long driven suspects (and more frequently, aggrieved prostitutes) to out of the way areas of the out-of-the-way Island, owing to its remoteness and lack of either vehicular or foot traffic. It's hard to get to, harder to find, and easily missed.

There's a graveyard at the north end of Duck Island. Little known fact: General George McClellan, Commander in Chief of the Army of the Potomac during the Civil War, is buried in a nondescript grave there. Shouldn't say 'little known.' There's a sign pointing to the gravesite. What's little known was his rank and historical role. There are signers of the Declaration of Independence buried in Hopewell and Princeton, but McClellan was a big deal in our nation's history. General Grant has a tomb in New York. General McClellan has weeds in South Trenton. The civic comparison speaks volumes.

But not all our capital city's history festers. Trenton spent almost two months as the nation's capital in the early 1780's. George Washington had lunch at a local tavern. The Marquis de Lafayette gave his farewell speech to our nation's congressional delegation here in something like November, 1784. The town has had its moments in the sun.

After the Second World War, when working class black men left the South, the northern Diaspora ran from Chicago to Detroit to Trenton, where the Roebling Steel and Bridge works were still churning out wire cable (they built the Brooklyn Bridge for crying out loud; when they say they have a bridge in Brooklyn to sell you, the Roebling guys say 'no, we actually did sell it to you.') Home Rubber, General Motors, American Standard (the toilet makers?), Delaval (Turbines), a slew of pottery companies, you name it, this was a manufacturing center in America last century.

There's a reason the sign on the bridge leading into the city from Pennsylvania reads "Trenton Makes, The World Takes," but it's just not true anymore. Population in 1950 was close to 130,000, and by 2010 less than 90,000. Two thirds of residents are either African American or Latino, and the 20,000 state employees who drive in every morning drive out every afternoon. Funny how men will brag on where they stand in the fight-or-flight debate ("These colors don't run!"), and white guys in legislatures keep passing stand-your-ground laws. But when folks with darker skin moved in, thousands of Italians and Jews and Irish, once oppressed, fled the scene faster than flies to a sweaty fat man.

From fifty years ago to now, Trenton has fallen on hard times, despite being a state capital where legislators authorize one new building after another to keep construction jobs in the city. State government shuts down at 4:30PM, Monday through Friday. By 5:15, you can roll a bowling ball down West State Street in front of the Statehouse and not hit a thing until you get to Calhoun Street. And who is left to run the city by night? It's not the zombies, at least not yet. And if you told me vampires, I'd give it some thought.

But after dark, the local sets take control at some level. You see guys in Boston Red Sox hats and red sweatshirts gathering in clubs and on street corners. Those are Bloods. Don't be fooled by the East LA origin, where "Blood" was an acronym for Blacks and Latinos Opposed to Oppression and Destruction. When the sets moved east, it was all about banging. Busting heads, robbing people, selling drugs, shooting up your rivals, owning turf, designating outliers as "food" (ready to be killed on sight).

You've got your Sex Money Murder set, "Murder" for short. You've got your "G-Shine," nee, Gangsta Killa Bloods. You've got a few Crips (I had an eighteen-year-old kid looked twelve, drove two older guys away from a liquor store shooting and robbery, caught on video tape; tried to introduce myself to him in the jail, and he starts with, "I roll with the Crips." Calm down big fella.) I had another kid who was protected by the local Latin Kings (they shot a guy in the back who was chasing my client down a street), but they didn't seem to number more than four.

There are plenty of independent or unaffiliated drug dealers all over town, guys with their "flag down" in Blood speak. It's hard to keep score without a program, which is what TAC does. They maintain all kinds of databases, half of which are made up.

By far, the worst one I saw was a pre-sentence report claiming this one defendant was gang-affiliated because he had a tattoo on his right bicep that held the initials "M.O.B." "Member of Bloods," right? Of course, above the letters was a dollar sign, and below was a naked lady. The casual observer of urban culture could tell you the acronym means "Money Over Bitches," (leaving for another day the misogyny infecting African American male circles.) It might be hard on women, but it ain't "The Mob."

But then there was another guy who had a MOB tat and I argued it was Money Over Bitches, until the probation officer grabbed my guy's wrist and I saw on the underside "Bloods Forever." For that guy, MOB was Member of Bloods.

In the midst of this flotsam and jetsam sat Thomas O'Leary, Minnesota ex-pat, late resident of the Trenton Downtown Marriott, a loss leader in hotel circles if ever there were one. Fortunately, the city and state governments kicked in millions of dollars in annual subsidies so the hotel could survive an economy that might fill a dozen rooms a night. Good looking property, great daytime lunch or meeting venue. Located in the heart of Zombietown at midnight.

Thomas had to stay in the city until we could get him to court on his extradition warrant. We had gotten him bailed in St. Paul, put him on a plane to Philadelphia, and promised the local prosecutor we would keep him under wraps in Trenton until we could surrender him to a judge the following day.

So, he learned the ins and outs of Trenton's finest (read: only) hotel. The family had ponied up my retainer, a lawyer in the Twin Cities convinced a judge to bail the client if only to spare the cost of local detention coupled with an expensive plane ride (typically two cops to accompany the prisoner, no advanced purchase rules, one way fare–do the math.)

He had no car, and my fervent hope was he did not elect to take his pasty Irish mug out into the streets of Trenton in search of the vibrant gay nightclubs that flourish in distressed neighborhoods. Once some guys come out, they come way out, and risky behavior is not beyond the pale.

I couldn't meet with him at the hotel. First rule of criminal defense: never meet a client in a social setting. Meet in jail, courthouse conference room, or meet in the discipline of your own office. That's it. I called his cell to verify his instructions.

"Uh, hello?"

"Thomas? You ok?"

Oh, uh, hi, Bill? Yes, yes. Fine."

"Are you in the hotel?"

"Yes, sure, yes....Uh-huh."

"What's your room number?"

"Uh, hold on."

"Do you know where you are?"

"Yes, yeah. Uh-huh."

"Do you have a watch?"

"Yes, sure."

"What time is it?"

"424."

"It's 6 o'clock."

"That's my room number."

"Oh. What time do you have?"

"It says 5:05, but it's dark out. I must have fallen asleep."

"Set your watch to Eastern Standard Time. You have to meet me in court at 8:45 tomorrow morning. It's walking distance from your hotel. Do you need directions?"

"No, no, I'll be fine. Thanks. Thanks. See you then. I'll be fine."

"You sure?"

"Yes, yes. Fine. See you then."

"Ok, talk to you later."

Hard for me to believe this guy was worth a couple of million bucks, which he apparently earned in the day trading market. Probably a savant investor or something, but for those of us not blessed with a special skill, especially in logarithms, it gnaws away, what our society values and how it compensates those skills.

At 8:30 the following morning I toted my Dunkin' Donuts coffee and a mostly empty briefcase (let's see, New York Times crossword, yellow pad, pen, attorney ID, manila folder with a couple of pages of notes from talking to this guy and his family, that's it), this time to the second floor of the new court house girding for yet another bail hearing.

See, bail hearings have become the new trials. Crime might not be up, but defining crime and measuring crime are both up. More things are crimes today than ever before. But no one wants to actually pay for this shit, so we have the same number of prosecutors, fewer public defenders, on again-off again number of judges, static number of courtrooms and grand jury rooms and grand jurors. Petit jurors who approach jury service with the same warm feeling as pending root canal, except they figure out better excuses to avoid it.

You cannot move these cases through the system any faster unless you devote resources to match the increase in cases filed. Weighing down the Public Defender only exacerbates the problem, because the PDs will push back on being overwhelmed; their clients will protest loudly and often that they haven't so much as met their lawyers; post-conviction petitions jump (essentially, 'my lawyer didn't do jack') as those complaints resonate through the system; and judges have to figure out how to cope with all of this even as their authority is being undermined by a new cadre of bean counters called the "Administrative Office of the Courts."

It's the AOC in New Jersey. It's the AO in federal court. By any other name in any other state, it's bureaucrats telling judges how to manage their calendars. When judges had trial experience before they hit the bench, they knew instinctively what the job required and how to manage a trial list. Now we get judges from safe political blocs who have never tried a case.

Quick story: I walk into my office one Friday morning to see half a dozen phone messages from the evening before. 5:45; 5:52; 5:58; 6:04; and 6:15 from Millie Dimond. 6:30pm from George Anastasio. I knew immediately what it was about. Millie was a candidate for a judgeship, and George sat on the P&J committee (Prosecutors and Judges). Because New Jersey runs an appointment system for prosecutors and judges, the governor, unless he doesn't like the outcome, typically asks the state bar association to vet the nominees for a qualification rating.

I knew Millie to be a sharp lawyer with little to no trial experience, but she had been something of an academic in criminal law circles (well, she had married a criminal law professor after interning for him, but you know what I mean). She also had a wonderful temperament and healthy skepticism of prosecutorial baloney, even though she spent her professional life as a deputy attorney general.

During her interview, they must have asked Millie to name one lawyer who had appeared opposite her in a courtroom. Instead of coming up blank, she had thrown out my name. When I had squared off against the Attorney General in the Supreme Court five years earlier, she had sat next to AG to assist in rebuttal. We call that "second chair." "Please use that in a sentence." "Um, when I argued against the AG in Smith versus Jones, Millie second-chaired the AG."

Anyway, I figured the five messages from Millie were to tip me off, but I had her back. She was a good kid. I called George, who had represented my father years earlier. I was surprised he was still practicing.

"Good morning, George. Let me see if I can guess why you called me last night. Millie Dimond?"

"She called you already?"

"Only five times, but I answered you first."

"I'm honored."

"No, you're older. Plus, I didn't need to hear her beg."

"So, what do you think?"

I said, "I think judgeships are a three-legged stool. Temperament, intellect, and trial experience. These days, if we get the first two, I figure we're ahead of the game. It's like Meat Loaf: two out of three ain't bad."

He said, "Meatloaf?" I forgot he had to be eighty. And no one under forty would know what I was talking about either.

I said, "I just mean I don't think she's ever actually tried a case."

He said, "Never tried a case? How about, never taken a deposition. How can that be a good thing?"

I said, "I hear you, but we are all part of a lost generation. We're the dinosaurs now, George. The rear guard action is to make sure they are at least smart and calm."

Point is, if judges don't understand what's involved in a trial, they can never manage a trial list. Non-lawyer bureaucrats handle stuff they cannot possibly appreciate from a constitutional perspective. So, my bail hearing is critical, because in the absence of bail, my guy will sit in detention for months, if not years, waiting for a real day in court. Not a status conference; not a settlement conference; not a pre-arraignment conference or a pre-trial conference. A real, honest to goodness trial date with real jurors and real witnesses. Those days are almost gone, seen in the rarest of cases, the kind that wind up on Nancy Grace's radar.

As it turned out, the prosecutor folded before we stood up. Mike Gallegos was in some ways a stand up guy (he could be a prick, but he was mellowing with age and young children), and he recognized the $150,000 we posted in St. Paul, coupled with the additional $150,000 we were prepared to post here, would be enough. I offered a waiver of extradition (a piece of paper saying if my guy got picked up anywhere in the country, there would be no extradition hearing or governor's warrant, just a plane ride back to New Jersey), and a surrender of his passport. Seems my guy O'Leary confessed on videotape to the detectives in St. Paul, and Mike wanted me to know the game was up before I rolled my first turn on the board. We'll see, Mike. We'll see.

CHAPTER FIFTEEN

**Trenton Police Division, 225 North Clinton Avenue.
Evidence vault, basement level.**

"Evening, LT. Can I borrow your pen?"

"Hello, Bobby. What do we have here?"

"Ah, usual for a night's work. Same ol,' same ol.' Let's see."

"Okay, I got two Ruger .22-.45 Lites. Original packaging. Nice. What do you think these would go for?"

"Gotta be thousand a pop. Ever shoot one?"

"Nope. You?"

"Nah, but I hear they have no kick at all. Nothing. Bip, bip. Done."

"I know you. You're thinking we should head over."

"Don't even suggest it. You taught me better."

"That's right. Okay, I got wallet with identification, Aaron Bellow. No credit cards, no cash. No cash on him at all?"

"That's next."

"Roger. Okay, I got $427 U.S. currency."

"This is the last thing we grabbed."

"Okay, I got one gym bag marked 'Dapper Dan's' with contents, one scale and assorted plastic baggies."

"That's it, lieutenant."

"Sign here. Thank you, and we are good to go. What the hell is Dapper Dan's?"

"Beats the shit out of me."

CHAPTER SIXTEEN

Session 6. Carmody, William.

It was, I don't know, 11:38AM. I said, "Did we have an 11 o'clock appointment?"

Joe Wright said, "Couldn't get a ride, man."

And I'm like, "That's what you said last time."

And he says, "C'mon, man."

And then I said something I shouldn't have, "Awwright, enough. Let's get to it. Now I'm late. I still got a guy with real money coming in before lunch."

He ignored it and said, "Look, it's the search of the house on Kirkbride. I finally got something. I'm tellin' ya.'"

I said, "Hey, I have no doubt the search was bogus. I went out there. No way the guy could see through the fence from the side. There was some kind of plastic screen."

Then he said something that stuck. "I know, I know, but there's something else. It's the money, man. They took my girl's money."

“What are you talking about? They grabbed some gun from somewhere and claimed you stopped to leave it in a barbecue grill. Stupid shit, but there it is.”

“Listen to me. They went into the house, right? Guy says he went straight through, came out the back, following me. Other dude says he saw me put the gun in the grill and keep going. How come the first guy wasn’t right behind me into the back yard?”

“He says he’s battering down the front door while his partner is running around the side, just in time to see you dump the piece and jump the fence for West Paul. He’s trapped on the other side of that fence running the length of the yard, so you get away. Simple as that.”

“I’m telling you, first guy must have gone through the house.”

“How do you know?”

“My cousin. She keeps money in her bureau in her bedroom, second floor. She had like three thousand in her top drawer in an old pickle jar she keeps there. It’s gone, man. Ain’t no one been in the house except her family the whole time.”

“How do you know one of her kids didn’t take his momma’s money?”

“C’mon, man. My nephew is six. Aleesha is two. He can’t reach that high if he knew what money is. Aleesha might have taken it if she got to it, but she would have eaten it.”

“Ok, I got it. I’ll definitely ask him, but you know the drill. It’ll be all deny deny deny, and your word, or her word against his.”

“She already filed a complaint with Internal Affairs.”

"Ok, that wasn't smart. Now they'll know it's coming when I ask in the suppression hearing, and IA will have written this off before we get out of the gate."

"Hey, I told her, but she was pissed."

"Wait a second; which IA?"

"What d'ya' mean?"

"I thought these were sheriff's officers. Which IA did she go to?"

""Oh, don't believe that shit, man. That was one of Klingon's boys. He might wear a sheriff uniform, but he's TAC. You gotta trust me, man."

"How do you know this shit?"

"I know what I'm talkin' about, man. I do."

"Okay. No worries. We'll deal. What else you got?"

"I got eight hundred for you."

"Eight hundred? You owe me seven thousand."

"I'm working on it."

"You always say that. Now go on, get out of here. And for crying out loud, stay out of trouble, and I mean it."

I had to move him out before O'Leary got to the office. This was going to be one of those come to Jesus interviews and I needed a break before the melodrama of a middle aged man confessing to a lifetime of repressed urges and misguided molestation of a family member.

Walking out of my office, I had an Alan Scott sighting. My partner is one of those guys who has a ton of work, fifty civic and bar association commitments, dedication to his daughters' lives, and maybe not enough revenue coming in to support being stretched so thin. It bothers him more than it bothers me, so he keeps running farther and faster to generate more cash, but he doesn't see he's chasing his tail. I've got his back, but he's troubled by that. Seven years my junior, he doesn't like being the younger brother.

"Hey."

"Hey."

I said, "What's shakin'?"

He goes, "You got anything for the criminal practice committee?"

I said, "What the hell is that?"

And he goes, "Judge Cooper has this new committee to get input on stuff he's trying to do in the criminal division, so he brings Black, Bannister and Winters from the bench, Delores and Alex from the prosecutor's office, Nathan or his rep from the PD's, and me and Rob Flacks. He wants an agenda and I'm looking for stuff. Make something up."

So I say, "How about McCloud and those bail source forms. He's holding people in jail because he doesn't like the judges who won't impose all cash on guys with priors or three outstanding files. So, he's faxing letters to classification claiming the bail source forms are inadequate on account of the failure to explain away the presumption of all cash. It's ridiculous. It's contempt. It's a civil rights violation."

And he goes, "That's pretty good. Probably too controversial. Got anything tamer? No water in the water pitchers in the courtrooms? Something like that?"

So I made some shit up. "Last week I was doing a motion to suppress and there was no chart pack in the courtroom. All we had was an eraser board. I drew a beautiful map, had a witness mark it up, left it in the courtroom at the end of the day. Must have looked like it needed disinfecting, so my exhibit disappeared when maintenance came in over night and cleaned it off."

And he goes, "See, that's more like it."

The door of our office opened and a tall, pasty, balding guy of, oh, fifty-five walked in, slouched a bit, looked from me to Alan, to Alan's assistant, and addressed her. "Hi. Uh, I have a 12 o'clock appointment with Mr. Carmody?"

"Your name?" I could have spared both him and her the entire exchange. If this wasn't Thomas O'Leary, my name wasn't Barack O'Bama. Well, that can't be right, because it isn't. But this was O'Leary, right down to his navy blue blazer, open necked blue chambray cotton dress shirt, and pencil thin lipped smile that said, 'I have no idea what to expect, but I am smart enough to be embarrassed I'm here.'

Look, I'm not bragging about this, but you know I represent more than my share of sex offenders, right? They come in all shapes and sizes. Young guys going after even younger girls and boys, old guys going after their grand kids, guys who love to make shit up in the chat rooms, guys addicted to kiddie porn. I even represented a woman who gave her sixteen-year-old stepson a blow job just to get him to stop following her around like a puppy dog, and she got in trouble. Got her a no jail plea, but three years later she found herself having to register under Megan's Law. It's quite a country we live in.

Now, there's one type of guy who stands out in a crowded waiting room of prospective clients. That's the guy who's having sex with his own daughter. He has a special look, and it isn't pleasant. It's a chilling curl to his lip or something, a glint in his eye that says, "I fuck the shit out of my daughter and I'm not embarrassed." It's as close as someone in my line of work comes to vomiting on a client.

Point is, O'Leary didn't have that look. He was on the other end of the shame wheel. I knew O'Leary before he uttered a solitary word, because he was of a type. One, he's a deer in headlights. Knows nothing about crime and punishment and about to get the rudest awakening since the day of his arrest. Two, he didn't do anything wrong; it was all a misunderstanding; the boy's dick just happened to get into his mouth for a split second, could've happened to anyone, right? That's another side of his denial. He'll come around on that, though, because he knew it was wrong when he did it. Sometimes opportunity knocks and you lose your head. No one is judgment foolproof. Three, he's looking at Alan and me, still unsure if he's ready to admit he's gay. It's almost 2013, and he's ashamed of his sexuality. Irish flipping Catholics. Denial is not just a river in Egypt, isn't that what you guys say?

These momentary, silent confrontations were standard fare in my office, but Alan looked at him anyway, with a sideways glance that oozed something between skepticism and pity. Like the minor characters in disaster movies, where you're thinking, "He ain't gonna make it." Dinosaur shows up, eats 'em, and you're yelling at the screen, "I knew it!"

Then Alan turned towards me, his eyebrows saying, "A fee is a fee." I showed O'Leary into my office and shut the door, very quietly. "Do not disturb" rang out from that subtle click of the latch into the hole in the jamb.

O'Leary stood roughly six foot, one-eighty, some skin mottling to raise the question: booze or nerves? I was guessing nerves. His hair was too fine light brown, almost like he colored it, but not quite that repulsive a hue. He had pale eyes and an earnestness about him that made him likeable in spite of what was coming. We exchanged the mildest pleasantries as I sat him in a chair opposite my desk. I took his full name and address, verified his correct date of birth and social security number (like I said before, you never know when a transposed DOB will wind up being the source of an accusation of risk of flight). At some point we started in, but not without the bumpy ride of indignation.

"And how did they treat you in St. Paul?"

"Well, the detectives were very nice."

"You talked to detectives?" Note on pad: 'demand notes of interview or reports of statement taken in Minnesota.' Another gullible suburban white guy who thinks cops are his friends.

"Oh yes, they were gentlemen. It was the prosecutor who seemed a tad heavy handed. He kept insisting I should not get bail, but the lawyer you arranged apparently knew the judge well enough to remind him how long I might have to sit awaiting an extradition hearing. So they gave me a bail, but it was so expensive."

"How much?"

"$150,000. I had to give a bondsman $15,000 just to post a bond. And now I can't get that money back."

"Or, you could have saved all of that money and simply signed the waiver and waited to be moved to New Jersey on ConAir, or more likely ConAir Ground."

He said, "That didn't sound very pleasant."

I said, "No, and it would have been at least two weeks before you got here, all the while staying in local jails as the transport service stopped to make pick ups along the drive from St. Paul to probably New York. It's run by a private company that drives inmates from state to state, but they pick up and drop off along the way."

He said, "Well, it was an expensive lesson, I can tell you that."

I'm thinking, 'Dude, welcome to my world.' But I'm saying, "Can I ask you about your family?"

He said, "Of course, of course."

"How many brothers and sisters, and where do you stand in the birth order?"

"I'm the second oldest of six boys and two girls. Pat's my younger brother, and his wife Joan doesn't care for me. They're the ones in Princeton. They have three children, including two girls and Anakin, their son."

"Please tell me his name is not Anakin."

"You don't like it?"

I'm thinking, 'And white people make fun of black kids' names.' I said, "How many other nieces and nephews do you have?"

"Let's see…well, there's Liam and Seamus…" and he went on for a few moments before tallying the count: "I think thirteen including the three in Princeton."

“Have you ever been accused of, or in fact involved in, touching any of your nephews or nieces, in any improper way?”

“What do you mean by improper?”

“If you have to ask, the answer might well be ‘yes.’”

“No, no, I was just looking for a clarification. “

“I understand. But you are charged with a crime for improperly touching your nephew. You know if I’m asking, I’m asking about sexual contact. I think you know exactly what I meant.”

“You’re right.”

“Look, I’m not trying to be hard on you. I’m trying to get a sense of how well you might hold up under examination by a judge, a prosecutor, even a psychologist hired to evaluate your current psychological functioning. Why don’t you tell me more about how we got here.”

“You mean like getting bailed out?”

“No, I mean how you managed to get yourself arrested in the first place.”

“Well, apparently I wasn’t doing well enough in therapy.”

“Why do you say that?”

“Because we had an agreement that as long as I went to a therapist after this happened, and as long as I stayed with that until the doctor said I was ready to, I don’t know, graduate? If I did that, Joan would not call police for what I did.”

"Why don't you tell me what it is that you did?"

"Well, Anakin and I were in adjoining rooms, which is how it's set up when I visit. There's a guest room adjacent to his room. Anyway, he took a shower and must not have realized I was in my bedroom when he came out, because he came out with no towel on and walked into my room. I think he was surprised I was there, because he blushed. I told him not to worry about it. We were both men, and he had nothing to be ashamed of.

"Then I don't know how it happened, but I told him to sit down and I'd get him a towel, but he sat next to me on the bed, and I'm not sure what happened next, but I touched his penis and I think he wanted me to, so I briefly put it in my mouth. But then I knew that wasn't right, so I stopped immediately and went to get him a towel. I think he got a little nervous while I was gone, because when I came back he grabbed the towel and ran into his room and shut the connecting door."

"Why did you think he wanted you to touch his penis?"

"Because he came over and sat right next to me, and he had no clothes on."

"How old was he?"

"Twelve."

"He came out of the shower with no towel or anything else."

"That's right."

"Okay, I understand that's how it seems to you right now in your mind. But listen to me: nobody does that. Are you sure that's how it happened?"

"Yes, yes. That's exactly what happened."

"Fine; that's bad enough. You've just described a first degree, aggravated sexual assault, and you're facing twenty years, seventeen without parole. We might get you a reduced sentence, but if you are convicted of the top count, the absolute best you could expect to do would be maybe, and it's a huge maybe, a second degree sentence and about six to eight years of actual prison time. Now, tell me what happened after he left your bedroom."

"Nothing right away. The next morning, Joan asked me to step into the kitchen to talk to her, and I could see she was angry about something."

"And you had no idea this might be the reason she was angry?"

"None."

"Okay, go ahead."

"And she tells me I have to get my things together, because I have to leave town, immediately. Then my brother walks in, she basically tells him what happened, and he gets flustered, and it kind of went downhill from there. But finally, cooler heads prevailed and it was agreed she would not have me arrested as long as I got myself into therapy, and let them know I was dealing with the problem."

"And that's it? You pack up and leave?"

"Uh, yeah. I don't really talk to anyone, Pat gives me a ride to the Dinky, and I train to Princeton Junction, then Philadelphia to get a flight back to Minnesota. I knew there were a couple of Delta flights every day and I had a flex ticket to get on without much trouble."

"And what happened when you got back to the Twin Cities?"

"Nothing. I found a therapist and started telling him my story. He was a good guy and didn't put a lot of stock in this momentary lapse. We started talking more about my having repressed my sexuality for so many years and what I needed to work on. Anyway, Joan called him a few months later and asked how I was doing. Apparently, he told her I was doing well, and somehow got into my having moved on, beyond my indiscretion with Anakin, and that we were more involved in my own issues, and somehow this really pissed her off, and next thing I know I'm under arrest. Well, not right away."

"Not right away? When did the original thing happen?"

"Labor Day weekend last year."

"And when did she call your therapist?"

"I think in March or something this year."

"Well, what happened between March and October?"

"I don't know."

"Did she try to talk to you about why you had moved on in therapy?"

"She didn't talk to me at all."

"Huh. What do you make of that?"

"I don't make anything of it."

"Okay. I think I have enough for today. When's your flight out?"

"I'm leaving for the airport as soon as I leave here."

"Good. Let me know when you make it back, no drama, no contact with your brother or his family. No calling one of your other brothers to talk to him either. Are we clear on that?"

"What if…?"

"Seriously, are we clear on the no contact order? No contact means no contact, direct or indirect. Otherwise you'll get arrested and I won't be able to get you bailed out. Are we clear on this?"

"Okay, okay."

"Any questions? Anything at all? Any part of this you don't understand?"

" I do have one question?"

"Go ahead."

"If I can't contact my brother, when can I ask for my money back?"

"What money?"

"The money he borrowed. He promised to repay me with interest, but so far, nothing."

"Who?"

"Pat. He said he needed money to close on a real estate deal and just needed a few bucks to get to closing, but I haven't seen a penny in over a year. Long time to wait on a bridge loan."

"How much are we talking about?"

"It's been, like, $25,000 a month for the past year or so, like $350,000 so far."

"You're kidding."

CHAPTER SEVENTEEN

Mercer County Courthouse, Criminal Case Management.

To: *William.Carmody@Carmodyscott.com*
smccloud@mercercounty.org
From: Ethel.Yeats@judiciary.state.nj.us
cc: Theodore.Winters@judiciary.state.nj.us

RE: State v. Joe Wright, PF# 12-1321; Ind. 12-10-987

Counsel:

The court is in receipt of Mr. Carmody's motion to suppress returnable November 16th. We are proposing to schedule the matter on Tuesday, November 27th, 2012, at 9:00AM. The court will consent to briefing the motion after testimony is received. Please advise how many witnesses you anticipate calling at the hearing.

Ethel Yeats, Team Leader
Hon. Theodore Winters, J.S.C.

•••

"I lost Jer." Aaron sat on a bench outside the Case Management offices, waiting for his case screening interview, wearing stale clothes, using a borrowed phone, talking to a temperamental Tim.

"You what?"

"I lost Jeremy."

"What do you mean you lost him?"

"He's gone. Cops took him, haven't seen him since. Wasn't with me in the city lockup or the county jail."

"Well, he can't just have disappeared. Did you call him?"

"His cell phone doesn't answer. Doesn't even ring. Makes a funny noise then you get a recording. Not in service."

"Well, what do you want me to do?"

"Can you call his parents and ask if they've seen him?"

"Okay, I'm not doing that. Any other ideas?"

"Call his girlfriend. She's in Madison. She's kinda out there. She won't know enough to get scared or ask questions. Just want to know if he's contacted anyone."

"Did you make the drop?"

"I told you already. We got arrested. At least I did. They stopped us in Trenton and took us both out of the car. That's the last I saw of him."

"And you're sure he's not in another part of the jail separate from where you were."

"Pretty sure, but you could call and ask if you don't believe me."

"Does your lawyer know?"

"I don't think so. Told him I put Jer on the train. He sounded skeptical, but he's old and a little crazy himself, so I'm not sure he's going to care."

"How old and how crazy?"

"Ancient; like over fifty, and he's talking to himself or to someone half the time. But he got the job done, so I ain't complaining."

"I gotta make a couple of calls and I'll let you know."

"Who can you call?"

"Who do you think? I think you've fucked up enough for one week. Now go home and don't talk to anyone."

"I'm gonna try to get my car out of impound, then I'm out of here."

"Don't wait for your car. You might not get out of there alive."

"Kidding, right?"

CHAPTER EIGHTEEN

Session 7. Carmody, William.

...Look, I know you want to get into this other stuff, and I will. But I have to tell you how lucky I was to get Wright's motion to suppress scheduled so quickly. I had three independent witnesses, all old guys from the block, all ready to testify that the cops just busted in the door of this row house and later claimed to have found the piece in the grill. Anyway...okay, I probably am ducking the questions, which I would never tolerate in my line of work. You've been very patient.

Let's see. Can I start with this? I get the importance of placement. When I stand up to give an opening statement, the prosecutor has already talked to the jury. And before he's talked to the jury, the judge has already read the indictment to the jury panel. And before that, they've seen a video in the jury room about the trial process that emphasizes what good guys prosecutors and cops are. And before that, they've probably read some newspaper stories about how someone got away with murder on a technicality. I still call it the OJ effect, much more powerful than the CSI effect.

Tell you a quick story. Back in the day I did death penalty work, when we had a death penalty. Anyway, I taught a class at TCNJ one night to help Bob Bailey out. Local lawyer who likes to teach classes to flog his book and CLE classes. Continuing Legal Education. What he does is, he asks all the trial lawyers to take his class for him for one night. By the end of a semester, he's taught maybe three of the twenty classes or something. I say fine, but can I poll the class on my current death case so I can use the data in jury selection, and he says okay.

So I ask the folks about things like, would it make you less likely to vote for the death penalty if you knew the guy was going to spend the rest of his life behind bars? And they were like, yeah, except he's going to get out on parole in what? Twelve? Fifteen? What if he gets a weekend furlough? Didn't that one guy go crazy on a weekend out? Why should we take that chance for this client of yours who raped a woman, shoved a stick into her vagina, down her throat, then strangled her.

See, I figured out that the old Willie Horton issue still lives. He was the guy featured in the Bush-Dukakis campaign that they painted Dukakis with. Guy got out on a weekend furlough and raped and killed someone. I think Dukakis lost. What I did was, I made a point of calling a bunch of people from DOC to testify to this jury that my client would be thirty years behind the wall before he would see the parole board, and even then his chances for release were not good. This was before mandatory life, no parole. Jury gave my guy life, and I never forgot the importance of getting accurate information into the hands of people whose primary source might be television or worse, television news. DOC? Oh, Department of Corrections.

My point is about pre-existing bias. Everything I just described, all of this happens before I say word one. It's the way the mind processes information. So if I start by telling you my mother is in a psych ward, that will be your first impression of my background. If I tell you this with my arms akimbo, you'll think I'm a frightened kid hiding his insecurity. If I start with a story about my childhood, that will color your view. And I guess if I stall like this, that's got its own ramifications. What I'm asking is, please don't put too much emphasis on my order of presentation.

Let me try chronological.

Give me a second...let's see: I was a middle child of two parents and two sisters. We grew up in Ewing, when it was safe to grow up in Ewing. My sisters went to Ewing High, but my mother thought I should go to private school, so I did. Went to college and law school in Newark, and joined the prosecutor's office in 1983. Did that for five years, then into private practice, where I've been ever since. Was on my own for a year, then with a couple of small firms until I got recruited by a larger firm here in Princeton. That didn't work out. My first week they rejected a cash fee from a drug dealer with the "We don't take those kinds of clients" routine. When I tried to explain, "but those are my kinds of clients," I ran into a brick wall. Then I ran out the front door.

I set up shop on my own for a couple of years, but I learned the importance of having a partner, or at least someone who could answer the phone if you were in the can or out to lunch. So, I tracked down Alan Scott, who I knew to be a solid trial lawyer getting underpaid by his partner, an older guy whose ego wouldn't recognize talent around him not related to him. And by 'recognize,' that's short for 'pay.'

Anyway, I watched Alan one day in a trial with a bunch of guys in a prison beating case, and I saw a guy who could handle a witness, wasn't afraid of the courtroom, and had some presence of mind and direction in his cross examination. I'll say it: I saw a younger version of myself with bad teeth. I took him out to lunch and offered him a job. I could tell he was scared to leave the safety of his older firm, but I had skills, and I hoped he saw that. He did, and that was that. Fifteen years later, here we are.

Now, I know you're going to say something about how this isn't too touchy feely in terms of what you're looking for, but I think you've got to understand the practice if you're going to tell these bean counters whether I'm good to go. I've got a segue. And it's this: Alan is the first real relationship I've had with a guy. My dad left my mom when we were young, so I was raised by wolves, or, as they are known in certain circles, women.

I didn't get along well with guys growing up, because I didn't understand what I was supposed to do. Guys hung out and talked sports. My mother and sisters talked about guys and how stupid they were, always talking about sports. It was confusing for me, I'm telling you.

I played baseball. I was tall and left handed, didn't hit much, so of course I pitched. I thought I could play basketball, until one day a coach told me I couldn't. He was right. Most of what I learned about other guys, I learned in those locker rooms and in that private high school, which means I did not understand too much.

With women, I had this fear of getting my head handed to me, so I kind of steered clear of anyone who might piss my mother or sisters off. Which was pretty much every woman I ever tried to date. It was amazing my wife married me when she did. I think if my sisters hadn't been on some kind of magical mystery tour of the Americas, my wife never would have stuck around long enough to get to know me. They would have scared her off in a New York minute.

Luckiest day of my life, when she said okay, I'll marry you. I didn't deserve her. I'm not being self-effacing. I really didn't. She was tall and beautiful and I was tall and not. At least I wasn't fat. That is not a good look.

We've had a wonderful life, but I get stuck in work sometimes, you know? We've been to some wonderful places, and we've always worked as a team, but lately, it's been really, really hard. Do we have to do this part? Can't I tell you about the rest of what happened that got me landed with you? Can we come back to this later?

I know about this stuff. I've represented more than my share of dysfunctional clients with issues that light up the DSM-IV. I've had pedophiles and ehebophiles, exhibitionists and voyeurs, sadists and masochists, and even those inclined to frottage. What? You're not familiar with frotteurism? The guys who bump into you on the subway on purpose? And this is just the chapter on paraphilia. I've had paranoids and bi-polars and active psychotics. Schizoids off their meds because they don't like to feel fat and sluggish. I know what you need to know. I don't know if I can contribute.

...Because it's not in my nature to talk about myself. I talk about clients all the time, try to help them, get them a better deal, or just stand in front of the steamroller for a few minutes to slow the death march. You know who I liked? I liked that Chinese guy who kept jumping in front of the tank in Tiananmen Square in 1989. The tank kept trying to go around him, but he kept moving to stop the tank. The tank driver could have crushed him, but he didn't know what to do and he didn't want to kill his countryman.

You want me to tell you about myself, but I don't know how to do that. I've spent my life talking about other people. How about J.D. Salinger? Did you ever read *The Catcher in The Rye*? That's what I wanted to be: the adult who saves the kids from falling off the ledge into the abyss or the hole, or whatever it was on the other side of the tip of today. If I had to guess, I'd say no one ever looked out for me. Not my father or my mother. He was gone and she was struggling to survive. Not my sisters. Most times I was saving them from one thing or another, even if they won't admit it.

The only one who ever tried to save me was my wife, and I screwed that all up. I really can't explain it, I just did. I got too comfortable with the idea of someone taking care of me for a change, and I let my guard down. Promise it won't happen again.

So if you'll let me tell you what happened with these three guys, I can explain how I got so pissed off in front of these judges, which is kind of why I'm here, no?

I gotta tell you about Wright, because that's where I first figured out that something was rotten in Denmark. We had the police reports talking about this gun in a grill, and our own field investigation pointing to the usual conclusion that cops made something up to get what they thought was a bad guy.

Then they doubled down with their counterfeit crap in the hearing, and by that point, I'm figuring they might actually have gotten the wrong bad guy. And maybe he is a bad guy, I don't know. Does he sell drugs? He might. Based on where he lives and the opportunities out there, it's entirely possible. He pays in cash, which is usually a sign on this question.

He doesn't pay nearly enough, but I called McCloud to get some of the money seized, and I figured I could work a split to get the rest of my retainer if I caught him in a good mood. But when I called to work it out, Sean started yelling at me. As soon as he said hello, I said, "Hey Sean."

He was like, "I thought I told you not to call until I got the reports. If you'd get me the goddam reports once in a while we could do something here, but all you guys keep telling me is that the shit's in evidence. I never see a property report and you guys don't file anything on time. Judge Cooper is putting most of these cases on the hit list to be dismissed for failure to indict, and we don't even have labs back on half this shit. Don't mind me, but I have to ask what the hell you guys are doing down there?" I realized he hadn't recognized my voice, or I had called at the same time he was expecting another guy's call, or something, because he obviously wasn't talking to me. I just said I was sorry and hung up the phone.

Then I went back and checked the pre-indictment discovery I had on Wright in his other cases. No property reports on the seizure of cash. They mention it in the body of the investigation report, amounts, denominations, turned it over as evidence, the whole bit.

But no property reports. So how were we supposed to know where the stuff actually was? The evidence travels with the report. If there was no report, where was the evidence? I took a chance and directed a letter to the prosecutor a couple of days before the suppression hearing, asking that he be prepared to produce all contraband at the time of hearing. If there was a problem, we'd hear about it when I asked for S-1 in evidence. S-1 would be the gun, but all property seized should be on the one report.

I started prepping for the hearing by going to the neighborhood to talk to the guys who saw what happened. Then I went to the house the cops broke into and met with the mother who made the complaint to IA. If you can bear with me, I want to tell you how that hearing went down. I have a transcript.

CHAPTER NINETEEN

New Jersey's Capital City.

Trenton measures roughly eight square miles. It is smaller than most suburban townships in New Jersey. The gritty working class neighborhoods have swallowed up the once regal sections, like Greenwood Avenue, even Cadwalader Heights. The Italians have mostly ceded control of Chambersburg to the Latinos. The Polish community remains unmoved in North Trenton. Mill Hill has tried to make a comeback, but largely failed.

The last bastion of affluence remains in Hiltonia. This mix of stately stone, Tudor, and late fifties hodgepodge homes maintains its distance from the abyss using Cadwalader Park as a grassy moat. On its northern border are the grounds of the now depleted Trenton Psychiatric Hospital, the Ann Klein Forensic Center, and the Department of Corrections' Central Reception and Assignment Facility. Across the street from that complex sits the Trenton Country Club.

The rest of Trenton features streets whose names ring familiar to anyone who reads the police blotter. Cops patrol these zones, looking for idle young black men. In a town of thirty percent unemployment among black males, idle young black men stand on curbs, the dominant demographic.

One of those patrol zones is the area between Princeton and Calhoun Streets, another enclave of hard working people that cops would call a "high crime" neighborhood with many "quality of life violations." Police will tell you open drinking of alcohol, loud music, even a broken window, all qualify for this description. But the TAC cops conduct themselves as though the actual violations are young men like Joe Wright.

If TAC arrests an out-of-state white guy, it's typically a heroin addict from Morrisville, Pennsylvania, jumping across the river for a couple of decks of wet dope. Skinny white boys from Wisconsin might not register at first.

At 6' 5," but a meth-thin 195, Tim Thomas, naturally nicknamed "Tiny" behind his back, was not amused. "What did you do with the kid?"

"What kid?"

It was the kind of answer that brought Tim to his feet while barking into his phone. "What the hell do you mean, what kid? You know damn well what kid. Where is he?"

"Your kid? He bailed out."

"Not that kid. The other kid. The one you dragged off without a charge."

"Oh, that kid."

"That kid. Stop it, man. I haven't got time for this shit."

"Listen, don't get antsy. We had issues."

"Really? You arrest my kid and you have issues? What kind of fucking issues are we talking about? I can't wait to hear this."

"All right listen: we picked these kids up early when they came to town. They weren't hard to spot with their Wisconsin plates, and we appreciate you giving us the make and model. We put a car on them when they crossed the city limit. They tried to put counter surveillance on us. We do not like that. From anyone. Least of all from your guys."

"What the hell are you talking about? These kids can't buy socks, for crissake. Counter surveillance?"

"Yeah, they go to the train station. They drop one kid off while the other kid circles the block. First kid walks inside and out the other door. Gets back in the car on the other side. They drive to the meeting place at the mall, drop the same kid off on the far side from the meeting point. Kid walks through the mall, upper level, and out the other side to where he can look down and watch our meet. They're an hour early. Then they go back to the train station for a second time, and we start getting a little paranoid. Who are these kids and who do they work for? So, we stopped them after they left the station for that last time before they could get set up again. We didn't know what they were into, so we decided not to take a chance."

"Okay, I get that, but you didn't answer my question. What happened to the other kid?"

"We put him on ice."

"Put him on ice? Who are you, Frank Nitti? What the hell does that mean, and where is he?"

"He's in a safe and secure place."

"I'm sure. But is he alive?"

CHAPTER TWENTY

Session 8. Carmody, William.

Brenda Norris kept a neat home. This would be the key fact in Joe Wright's suppression hearing, and I need you to understand it's also key to how I got into this jam. But let me tell you about the hearing. Did they give you these transcripts too? Really? Have you read them? Read this one:

> THE COURT: This is the matter of State versus Joe Wright, Indictment number 12-wait a second, no indictment. Oh, wait, yes, 12-10-987. This is a motion to suppress on prosecutor's file number 12-1321. Appearances of counsel.
>
> MR. MCCLOUD: Sean McCloud for the State of New Jersey.
>
> MR. CARMODY: William Carmody, Carmody and Scott, on behalf of defendant who is seated to my right, Your Honor.
>
> THE COURT: This is a warrantless search, Mr. McCloud; you have the burden. Is the State prepared to proceed?
>
> MR. MCCLOUD: We are, Your Honor.

THE COURT: Call your first witness.

MR. MCCLOUD: Your Honor, the State calls Detective Edward Nestor.

(EDWARD NESTOR, sworn)

THE COURT: Pull that microphone towards you, will you Detective? Thanks. You may proceed, counsel.

(Direct Examination by Mr. McCloud)

Q. Good morning, Detective.

A. Good morning.

Q. By whom are you employed?

A. Mercer County Sheriff's Department.

Q. How long have you been with the Sheriff's office?

A. Just short of five years.

Q. Is this your first job in law enforcement?

A. I was with the Trenton Police Division for six years before that.

Q. Can you tell the court what duties you had when you were with the Trenton Police Division?

A. Sure. I started in patrol, stayed there for four years, then got moved to what at the time was called the Pro-Active Unit, now known as the Tactical Anti-Crime Unit.

Q. Did you attend a police academy?

A. I did; Trenton Police Academy. You were one of my instructors.

MR. CARMODY: That explains everything, Your Honor. (Laughter)

MR. MCCLOUD: I didn't ask him if I taught him everything he knows, although I probably did.

THE COURT: Let's try to stay focused, gentlemen.

Q. What are your duties with the Sheriff's Department?

A. Well, I'm assigned to the detective bureau, so mostly detective work.

Q. Have you had any specialized training for any of your assignments?

A. I've been to the NARCO school for narcotics training. I've had in-service training for fugitive recovery. I've had the standard training courses, including domestic violence prevention and firearms qualification. Those are the main ones.

Q. Are you generally familiar with the various sections of Trenton, including which ones are considered high crime areas?

A. I am.

Q. And directing your attention to October 19, 2012, can you tell me if you were on duty that day?

A. I was working days, eight to four in the fugitive squad.

Q. Were you working alone or with a partner?

A. I was paired with Detective Sam Amico.

Q. And what were you doing during that shift?

A. Well, we took the outstanding warrant list and were looking for known fugitives in certain sectors.

Q. Were you ever in the area of Kirkbride and Princeton Avenue?

A. We were.

Q. Were you looking for anyone in particular?

A. We were looking for a known fugitive from Passaic County. African American, mid-twenties, dreds, baseball cap.

Q. While in the area of Kirkbride and Princeton, did you see anyone fitting that description?

A. We did.

Q. What happened?

A. Well, like I said, we were on fugitive patrol, which means we were riding around the streets with pictures of known suspects or fugitives in our possession. We would look at those pictures to familiarize ourselves with the people we were looking for. Then if we saw someone in the street who looked like one of our guys, we would try to detain that person until we got positive ID one way or another.

Q. What if anything unusual happened?

A. We turned the corner from New Willow onto Kirkbride and we immediately saw a man fitting the description of this fugitive from Passaic. African-American, dreds, 20's. So, we approached him to investigate.

Q. To be clear, this was not in fact the fugitive you were seeking, correct?

A. As it turned out, no. But he fit the description.

Q. Please continue.

A. Well, as we drove towards him, he was obviously startled by our presence, and he had this look in his eye like he wasn't expecting us to be there. So, he moved his hand towards his waist and pulled an object that resembled a handgun and shifted it to the back of his pants.

Q. And what happened next?

A. I asked my partner if he saw what I saw, and then we drove directly towards the suspect.

Q. What did he do?

A. Well, he didn't hang around, I can tell you that. As we approached his position, he looked right at us, turned, and headed straight to the door of the house he was in front off. We called for him to stop, but he went inside, ignoring our verbal command. So, we got out of our vehicle, my partner heading to the side of the house, and me going to the front door where he entered.

Q. Did you enter the house?

A. Not immediately. I went to the door and realized he had locked it. It was a wood frame door, and it appeared to have a dead bolt. Then I heard him moving around or something, and my partner radioed that he was going out the back. That's when I forced open the door and entered the home.

Q. Was he inside the house?

A. No, the back door was open, and I could see him running.

Q. Where was your partner during this time?

A. He had run to the right side of the house, and he radioed that the suspect was exiting the back door. Apparently there was some kind of fence obstructing his ability to give chase. When I went out the back door, I saw a gate open at the back of the fenced yard, and off to my right, I could see chain link that ran all the way to a garage. My partner couldn't get to the back yard.

Q. Where was the suspect?

A. He took off for West Paul Avenue. I radioed for assistance from units in the area, and we set up a perimeter, but we were unsuccessful in finding him.

Q. Did you find anything of evidential value during the course of your pursuit?

A. We found a baseball hat he must have dropped when he was running. I had seen the hat on him when we first approached, and this was the same hat we found over on West Paul, near the curb where I lost sight of him.

Q. Okay, now once you lost sight of him, where exactly did you go?

A. First, we walked the length of West Paul while waiting for other units to respond. We were trying to figure out if he might be hiding in one of the houses or garages in the immediate area. Then we went directly back to the backyard he had run through, because my partner had seen him discard evidence there.

Q. What did your partner tell you?

A. Just that he had seen him drop something in the barbecue grill next to the back door as he left out of the house.

Q. Was that your purpose in returning to the back yard?

A. Sure. We wanted to secure the area, because we thought he had a gun, and we thought it likely he had dumped the weapon while making his run for it.

Q. Did your partner accompany you to the rear yard?

A. Yeah, we met at the gate and he walked me to where he saw the defendant stop and put an object in the grill. We opened the grill and lying on top was a .9 millimeter Glock.

Q. Which is what?

A. Excuse me?

Q. What is a ".9 millimeter Glock?"

A. Oh, sorry. Semi-automatic handgun.

MR. MCCLOUD: Your Honor, I would like an exhibit marked for identification.

THE COURT: S-1 for identification. Did you show it to your adversary? Very well.

Q. Mr. Nestor, I'm showing you what has been marked S-1 for identification. Do you recognize this object?

A. Yes. This is the weapon we retrieved from the barbecue grill that afternoon.

Q. How do you know it's the same gun?

A. Well, first of all, it has a green handle, which I'd never seen before. Second, it bears a serial number, which I recorded in my report, and right here is the number I recorded.

Q. And is this weapon in substantially the same condition as when you retrieved it from the grill?

A. It is.

MR. MCCLOUD: Your Honor, for purposes of this hearing, I move S-1 into evidence.

THE COURT: Any objection?

MR. CARMODY: None, Your Honor.

THE COURT: S-1 for identification is now S-1 in evidence.

Q. Now, Mr. Nestor, do you see the man who ran through the house in court today?

A. I can't say for certain, but the defendant resembles the man I saw.

Q. In what respects?

A. Well, he has the same dreadlocks, same build, same skin tone, same kind of slouch to his shoulders. I can't swear it's him, but he strongly resembles the man we chased.

MR. MCCLOUD: Your Honor, I have no further questions.

THE COURT: Okay, let's take a five minute break. Off the record.

(Whereupon proceedings were in recess.)

Okay, look. If you started reading these transcripts, you read them in this order. And this is what I meant when I was talking about spin control. He who controls the order of presentation controls the order of reception of information.

And because it's a Rule 104 hearing–sorry, fact finding by a judge without a jury, preliminary kind of thing, evidence rules like hearsay typically don't apply–anyway, he gets to shovel all that hearsay in, where one cop tells the court that what the other cop is going to say next is what he told his partner as well. Now the judge is asking himself if it's possible one cop is lying, what are the odds two cops are lying?

You probably think all cops are sworn to uphold the law, and therefore they naturally tell the truth. Trust me on this: they don't. They are actually trained to lie. Not in a corrupt way. Well, I guess corruption is in the eye of the beholder. In what they think is a noble way.

Cops are told from the academy that there are nothing but scumbags and their lawyers on the streets and their job is to interdict the drugs and guns and rampant crime. They give classes on constitutional law, what the courts say is okay from a Fourth Amendment perspective; you know, search and seizure.

So, they actually tutor these guys on what will or will not pass muster. If you tell them they need consent to search, they will ride around with consent forms and ask guys to sign on the dotted line. They tell him he can sign the consent form, or they will go get a warrant, and if they have to get a warrant, things will be a whole lot worse. If the guy refuses, they detain him and tell the judge the facts supporting the request for a warrant include defendant's refusal to consent.

They are already calling him a defendant when he hasn't done anything. They pull him over on the Turnpike for being black in a white Lexus. They do stuff to black guys like drive up close behind them to freak them out. Guy speeds up to move into right lane. They pull him over for speeding up, or unsafe lane change, or driving too slow, or obstructing traffic. We see these bogus tickets all the time.

And that's just road troopers. Local guys will say they recognized the driver driving by as unlicensed. Really? You memorize the list of unlicensed black men in Trenton? Or do you figure your odds are at least fifty-fifty that will be the case? Or he has a taillight out. Or he didn't come to a full stop at a stop sign. And it's your word against the criminal. Remember, we don't see the guys they searched and let go without finding anything.

Whatever the deal is, it winds up being a full blown search of the black guy and his car. If this shit happened routinely in Princeton, there would be civil war. Black guys just accept it as a part of their daily lives. Don't take my word for it. Check out the stats for stop-and-frisks in New York City. They pull literally millions of kids off the streets every year who just happen to be black and Latino. For doing absolutely nothing. The difference is that the Supreme Court has said you can't pull a car over for doing nothing, so when it comes to car stops, you have to make some shit up. And they do.

I'm not trying to browbeat you here. I just want you to get some perspective on my line of work. It'll make it easier for you to understand why I did what I did. In legal terms, they might call it the doctrine of necessity, but that actually applies to something else. Anyway, I'm asking you to think about all of this when you read the cross examination.

THE COURT: Okay, back on the record. Mr. Carmody, you may cross examine.

(Cross examination by Mr. Carmody)

MR. CARMODY: Thank you, Your Honor. Good morning, detective.

THE WITNESS: Good morning.

Q. Let me start by asking you a few additional questions about your training in the conduct of search and seizure, okay?

A. Sure.

Q. When you first approached the person you believe was the defendant, did you think it was the person you had a warrant to arrest?

A. I didn't really know. You know, he was about the same height and build, and he had dreadlocks, but other than that, I couldn't say. He was worth talking to, I can tell you that.

Q. Did you have probable cause to search him as you understand that phrase?

A. I don't think so.

Q. You understand the concept of stop and frisk?

A. Yes.

Q. Did you have reason to believe he was armed and dangerous, such that you could have done so, as of when you first saw him?

A. Not until I saw him move the handgun from his waistband to his back.

Q. You're sure it was a handgun?

A. Not a hundred percent, but it certainly looked like one.

Q. While we're on that subject, were you riding in a marked police car?

A. Unmarked.

Q. Black Dodge Charger with blacked out windows?

A. The windows are tinted, but I wouldn't say "blacked out."

Q. Standard undercover cop car?

MR. MCCLOUD: Objection, Your Honor.

MR. CARMODY: I'll withdraw the question.

Q. So, a plain black Dodge Charger with tinted windows starts driving right at a guy on a street in broad daylight, and the guy's first instinct is to pull a gun out of his waistband, display it momentarily, and put it back in his waist band, simply moving it from his front to his back?

A. You'd have to ask him.

Q. Well, I'm asking you, but let me try a different question: would it be fair to say that momentary display gave you a basis for stopping and frisking the man had he stayed in place?

A. Sure.

Q. And that's because you've been instructed that the display of an object that resembles a firearm can provide an "articulable basis" for detaining and frisking a man on the street, right?

A. If I see something that looks like a gun, yes.

Q. Does that same training tell you that you have the right to pursue that person if he refuses to obey your command to halt?

A. I believe it does.

Q. And you gave such a command here?

A. I did.

Q. I'm curious, what exactly did you say?

A. Something like, "You in the baseball cap, stay right where you are." Words to that effect.

Q. Were you using the car's bullhorn, yelling out the window? What?

A. I did not engage the bullhorn. I'm not sure that car has one.

Q. Well, it was late October. Were your windows up or down as you approached?

A. They were up, I believe.

Q. And you were driving?

A. Yes.

Q. And as you approached from New Willow towards MLK, the suspect would have been to your left, correct? He was standing in front of 18 Kirkbride, or the north side of the street, right?

A. Correct. Yes.

Q. So, your partner couldn't have been shouting at him from the passenger window, right? He would have been looking out on the odd numbered homes.

A. Yes.

Q. So, I'm guessing you pulled your car straight at him on kind of an angle, like it's a fire drill?

MR. MCCLOUD: Objection.

MR. CARMODY: Sorry, Your Honor.

Q. Did you pull straight towards him, such that had you not hit the brakes you would literally have struck him.

A. If the car jumped the curb, I suppose so.

Q. And you're trained to approach in that fashion, isn't that so?

A. True.

Q. And he would have been startled to see a car coming straight towards him at speed in the middle of a block, can we agree?

A. Well, I don't know what was going through his mind.

Q. Have you ever had a car driven straight at you, where you weren't sure if the driver saw you?

A. Actually, I have.

Q. Gets the adrenalin pumping, right?

A. It can.

Q. So, if I understand you correctly, you aim your car at him, put the window down, yell to stop and jump out of your car. Did all of that happen?

A. I wouldn't say "aim."

Q. Did you drive at him?

A. Yes.

Q. What word would you use?

A. I drove at him.

Q. Okay, did you put your window down even as you were maneuvering the car to a stop?

A. I believe I put the window down, yes.

Q. And you and your partner got quickly out of your car, correct?

A. Yes.

Q. Okay, at what point in this little sequence did the suspect pull a gun from his waist to transfer it to his back?

A. As we approached him.

Q. That's your story and you're stickin' to it?

MR. MCCLOUD: Objection.

MR. CARMODY: My bad, Judge.

Q. So, you jump out of the car, and the suspect is how far away from you at that moment?

A. A few feet.

Q. Like, he's right in front of you, turning towards the door of the house?

A. Correct.

Q. So this must have happened pretty quickly, can we agree on that?

A. I would say a matter of seconds.

Q. And if I understand you correctly, he turned, ran to the front door, opened it, went inside, shut and locked the door and ran out the back. Is that about it?

A. Well, if you put it that way.

Q. I don't want to put it any way. How would you put it?

A. The suspect fled and failed to obey our command. He escaped through the house.

Q. Yeah, but he got into the house before you could get out of your car and grab him, right?

A. That's true.

Q. And it wasn't like he knew you were coming, because he was "visibly startled," did I quote your report accurately?

A. Yes.

Q. So, he has a split second to react, turns to the door, gets to the door, opens it. Did he need a key to enter?

A. I don't believe so.

Q. May I assume the door was closed, even if not locked, as he came up to it?

A. The door was closed.

Q. So, at a minimum he had to turn a knob and open the door. Did it open inward or outward?

A. I don't recall.

Q. Well, you went through it yourself a few seconds after he did, didn't you?

A. Yes.

Q. When you went through the door, did you have to pull it towards you or simply push it inside?

A. I don't recall.

Q. Was there a screen door or storm door in front of the main door?

A. I don't recall a storm door.

Q. Tell me how you got through the door.

A. I forced it open.

Q. Was it a metal door?

A. I think it was wood.

Q. What kind of wood? Oak?

A. I don't know what kind of wood.

Q. Well, was it a heavy door?

A. I don't recall.

Q. Did it have panels or was it flat?

A. I don't recall.

Q. Did it have a dead bolt?

A. I don't recall.

Q. What color was it?

A. Dark. Brown, maybe.

Q. Did you force it with your shoulder?

A. I pushed it in.

Q. Right; how?

A. How?

Q. Yeah, how did you push it in? A minute ago you couldn't remember if it opened in or out, now you're telling me you pushed it in. How exactly did you do that?

A. With as much force as necessary.

Q. How much force was necessary?

A. Enough to get it open.

Q. Well, if it was a heavy wooden door with a dead bolt, it would have taken more than a hefty push, right? Did you kick it in?

A. I used enough force to get it open.

Q. Did you use any kind of ramming tool?

A. Ramming tool?

Q. Yeah, like a heavy piece of pipe that you keep in your car for such occasions?

A. I don't recall that. [See, if you read this and wondered why I'm flogging this pipe point, it's because I spoke to the next-door neighbor, who told me he watched from his living room. When Nestor couldn't open the door, he went back to his car and got out some kind of heavy pipe and busted the door open with it.]

Q. Okay, let's move on. Once you got inside the house, what did you see?

A. A living room.

Q. Well, was anyone inside the house?

A. No.

Q. How do you know?

A. I did a quick protective sweep for my own safety.

Q. And when you say "protective sweep," you mean you checked out all the rooms and closets to see if anyone was hiding or lying in wait?

A. Right, exactly.

Q. So you went upstairs?

A. Briefly, yes.

Q. How many bedrooms?

A. I believe there were three.

Q. And you went into each one, checked closets and under beds, that sort of thing?

A. Anywhere I thought someone might be hiding.

Q. Just out of curiosity, did you start by heading for the back door of the house to see if your suspect had run out the back?

A. Not right away, no.

Q. Did your partner radio you that the suspect was fleeing out the back yard, even as you were inside the house?

A. I know I heard from him at some point, but I couldn't tell you exactly where I was when he was telling me the guy got away.

Q. Okay, you checked out the upstairs. Was there a bathroom up there?

A. I believe there was.

Q. Did you enter the bathroom?

A. I went into every room on the second floor.

Q. Did you notice the conditions of the bedrooms, or for that matter of the rooms downstairs.

A. The conditions?

Q. Right, conditions. Were the rooms tidy, messy, clean, dirty, any word you might use?

A. I would say the rooms were neat.

Q. Well maintained?

A. Well maintained.

Q. How long did all that take, walking into each room, checking out closets, looking under beds, et cetera?

A. Matter of a few seconds.

Q. And did you find anyone up there?

A. No.

Q. Could you tell from your time up there how many people were living in the house?

A. Well…no, not really.

Q. Can we start with this: it was in fact a residential home and not a crash pit for a bunch of guys selling drugs?

A. Oh, no. It was a home.

Q. Was there a basement?

A. I don't recall.

Q. Well, did you walk down into a basement as part of your protective sweep?

A. No.

Q. If you were intent on finding if anyone was hiding in the house, wouldn't it have been prudent to check out the basement?

A. I don't know if there was a basement.

Q. Wouldn't it have been prudent to check to see if there was a basement, or a crawl space, or someplace for a person to hide below the main level of the house?

A. Perhaps.

Q. Okay, and at some point you get to the kitchen or the back room or whatever, and you realize there is a back door, correct?

A. There was a back door, yes.

Q. When you approached the back door, was it open or closed?

A. I believe it was open.

Q. Wide open, air coming in?

A. I don't recall, to be honest.

Q. I hope you're being honest with every answer. Do you recall if there was a storm door or screen door inside the kitchen door? I'm saying kitchen door, but do you recall the back room being a kitchen?

A. It was the kitchen, yes, and no, I don't think there was a storm door.

Q. Do you recall if this door opened in or out?

A. I think it opened out.

Q. And was it wide open, like someone had just run outside as you first observed it?

A. I believe so, yes.

Q. And you're telling me you did not see the door open when you first entered the living room directly in front of the kitchen all of 15 feet away from this door?

A. That was not the focus of my attention.

Q. What was the focus of your attention?

A. There was a stairway immediately inside the front door, and I was concerned someone may have run up stairs to avoid detection.

Q. So you went upstairs first as part of your protective sweep.

A. Correct.

Q. How much time do you think you spent inside the house in total that day?

A. Until we finished the job?

Q. Right; front to back.

A. Oh, I'd guess half an hour.

MR. CARMODY: Your Honor, this might be a good time to take a break.

THE COURT: Why don't we do that? 20 minutes everyone.

(Whereupon the proceedings were in recess.)

Now, I know you read that part and might have thought I was getting pretty, what was the word Judge Simonetti once used on me? Granular. Pretty granular, but there was a point. I had the photos of the door, where he had battered in the lower right quadrant panel and then must have reached up to unlock the dead bolt. Like I said, I had the next door neighbor who saw him use a battering ram they keep in squad cars for these situations.

Why he didn't want to admit to this obvious stuff was provocative to me, because the lady who lived there is the one who made the IA complaint about the theft of her money from the master bedroom. And having a guy pinned on lying about why he's in the house and having all these witnesses, I thought I was finally going to expose the systematic theft of money from folks in these narcotics investigations.

We have seen hundreds of cases over the years where the cops take the cash and don't report ninety percent of what they take, but it's always their word against some drug addict, and the courts never want to hear it. You have to catch the guys beating the shit out of Rodney King on videotape to charge them with official misconduct, and even those guys were acquitted by a Los Angeles jury. It wasn't until the feds stepped in and took them to another district to get tried that anyone saw the inside of a prison cell. What I'm trying to say is, we spend careers trying to pin these guys just once for doing this shit, and here was my chance, or so I thought. Let me highlight something in the rest of this cross.

> THE COURT: Mr. Carmody?
>
> MR. CARMODY: Thank you, Your Honor.
>
> (Resumed cross examination of Edward Nestor by Mr. Carmody)
>
> Q. Mr. Nestor, when we broke, I was asking you how long your entire time was inside the house, and you estimated half an hour, did I get that right?
>
> A. Front to back, yes. I might have been outside the home for a portion of that time.

Q. But to be clear, the charges you filed in this case related to a weapon recovered from a grill in the backyard, right?

A. Yes, that and the defendant's failure to obey the command to halt from my partner.

Q. We'll get to that with your partner, but to explain it for the Court's edification, your partner claims he ordered defendant or a suspect to halt, the guy kept running, so your partner signed a complaint for resisting arrest, is that about it?

A. Well, it's a little more involved than that.

Q. Is that the bottom line? Guy didn't stop on command?

A. Bottom line? Yes.

Q. Okay, let's go back to the grill. Where was the grill relative to the back door?

A. There were a couple of steps to the back yard, and the grill was off to the right side of those steps as you looked outside the house.

Q. When you first went out back, was the barbecue grill open or closed?

A. Closed.

Q. Do you know if your partner had been into the back yard prior to your walking out from the kitchen?

A. I don't believe he had.

Q. So to the best of your knowledge, he had not opened or closed the grill before you got there.

A. I don't think he touched the grill at all.

Q. Ever?

A. Well not in my presence. I opened the grill, observed the gun, closed the lid and waited for a photographer to show up and take a picture of the gun exactly as I saw it lying on the grill.

Q. Okay, and when you opened the grill, exactly what did you observe?

A. The gun.

Q. All right, sir, let me try this a different way. May I see the photograph of the gun on the grill plate? Thank you. Your Honor, may I have this photo marked as Exhibit D-1 for identification?

THE COURT: D-1 for identification.

Q. Mr. Nestor, showing you what's been marked D-1 for identification, do you recognize what's depicted in this photograph?

A. The gun.

Q. Anything else?

A. The grill plate.

Q. Anything else?

A. No.

Q. Were you present when this photo was taken?

A. I was.

Q. Did Sergeant Fusco take the picture?

A. He did.

Q. To the best of your knowledge, was the gun pointed in the same direction in the photograph as when you first observed it as you lifted the lid on the barbecue?

A. As far as I know, yes.

Q. And after he took the picture, did you secure the weapon?

A. I did.

Q. And how did you do that?

A. I picked it up, cleared the slide, made sure there was no projectile in the chamber, removed the clip, put the clip in my waistband and the weapon in a paper bag.

Q. Were you wearing gloves for any part of this operation?

MR. MCCLOUD: Your Honor, what's the relevance of any of this? This isn't the trial. I'm sure Mr. Carmody is going to talk about the absence of fingerprints at some point before a jury, but this hearing is limited to the propriety of the search.

THE COURT: Mr. Carmody?

MR. CARMODY: Your Honor, the conduct complained of is the search *and seizure.* Right now, I'm examining the circumstances of the seizure. If police failed to adhere to basic evidence gathering standards, it is one of the facts this court can consider in evaluating the good faith of their conduct in this matter generally. If they had time to request a photographer on scene, query why they didn't have time to request a telephonic warrant to search the premises, including the curtilage. In evaluating the credibility of their response to that question, the court might look to the manner in which they gathered evidence: they took short cuts, including short cutting the constitution, as evidenced by this witness's response to the last few questions. Again, if they had time for a photographer, why not an evidence technician to retrieve the weapon and preserve any fingerprints on the lid of the barbecue and the gun itself?

THE COURT: I'll permit some more latitude on this line of inquiry. Proceed.

Q. Mr. Nestor?

A. Yes?

Q. Wearing gloves?

A. No.

Q. Look, let me address counsel's point right here: your suspect fled the scene, correct?

A. Yes.

Q. And there was no one in the house, correct?

A. As far as I know, correct.

Q. So before you start rifling through drawers and opening barbecues, why not simply apply for a warrant? What was the rush?

A. Who said I was rifling through drawers?

Q. Well, since you asked, the tenant. You did go through drawers when you were upstairs, didn't you?

A. I don't recall that.

Q. You don't recall?

A. I don't recall.

Q. Detective, it was a couple of weeks ago. You ran a protective sweep to secure the bedrooms in a few moments, yet you were in the house for roughly half an hour by your own estimate. It's fair to assume you were looking for identification paperwork, am I right? To identify your suspect?

A. I might have.

Q. You might have? Is that a yes?

A. I might have.

Q. I take it you are aware of the Internal Affairs complaint in which the tenant claims you stole her money from her dresser drawer.

MR. MCCLOUD: Objection, Your Honor.

A. I am.

THE COURT: Hold it, hold it. What's the objection?

MR. MCCLOUD: How is an Internal Affairs complaint, assuming there is one, possibly relevant to this proceeding?

MR CARMODY: Let's start with this, judge. The Rules of Evidence actually don't apply to Rule 104 hearings, except for a valid claim of privilege. That's why paragraph d. talks about a defendant's right not to answer collateral issue questions; it's part of his privilege against self-incrimination. So relevance isn't actually a valid objection. Second, it's absolutely relevant, because again, this goes to the heart of the suppression issue: there was no exigent circumstance. They had all the time in the world and they ransacked this woman's house, stealing her money in the process....

MR. MCCLOUD: Your Honor...

THE COURT: Mr. Carmody, I'm going to have to ask you to confine your remarks to what you can prove, not what you speculate.

MR. CARMODY: Your Honor, the defense plans to call Ms. Brenda Norris to testify both to the condition of her home, including the manner in which her door was kicked in, as well as the theft of her funds, which she indeed reported to Trenton IA. I had hoped to avoid proffering all of this in front of the witness, because now some local cops are going to go to her house and tell her it would be a really great idea if she did not show up here to testify on our next hearing date. But you've asked me for a proffer, and I've given you one.

THE COURT: If you have a point to make here, let's make it and move on.

MR. CARMODY: Yes, Your Honor.

Q. Did you take the money?

A. What?

Q. You heard me: did you take the woman's money from her dresser?

A. I did not.

Q. Fact is, you went through every drawer in every bedroom, starting with the obvious master bedroom, isn't that so?

A. That is not so.

Q. Want to reconsider your answer after I show you pictures of the drawers in that furniture that were left in many cases either pulled out or actually on the floor?

A. How do I know she didn't pull those drawers out to stage a picture?

Q. I don't know, but I could ask you the same question: How do I know you didn't plant the weapon and stage that shot?

A. Because I wouldn't do such a thing.

Q. But this civilian would?

A. People do a lot of strange...

MR. MCCLOUD: Your Honor.

THE COURT: Mr. Carmody, move on.

Q. How about this one: how many gun possession arrests did you make in the last twelve months?

A. Several.

Q. Several? Like three?

A. Like way more than that.

Q. More than twenty?

A. I would say so.

Q. More than fifty?

A. One per week? Maybe.

Q. And you wrote reports for every one of those arrests, right?

A. Of course.

Q. So if we go through every one of your weapons arrests, we will find the weapon itself was turned into the evidence vault, tagged, and a property report was submitted, is that your testimony?

A. Well, that's the way it should happen.

Q. I know how it should happen; is that the way it happened for you?

MR. MCCLOUD: Your Honor, we are way, way off the track from a suppression issue. This isn't a trial.

THE COURT: Please move on, Mr. Carmody. Please try to stick to the issue before this court.

MR. CARMODY: Sorry, Your Honor.

Q. Did you write reports in this case, Mr. Nestor?

A. I did not.

Q. I take it your partner got stuck with that assignment?

THE COURT: Mr. Carmody, please.

MR. CARMODY: Sorry, Your Honor.

Q. Your partner wrote all of the reports in this investigation?

A. He did.

Q. Was that because he was junior to you, he was assigned, how did that come to pass?

A. I think it was his turn, but yes, I was senior to him.

Q. So if I have any questions about any report in this investigation, I'll have to ask Mr. Amico?

A. I would say so.

Q. You're positive you wrote no reports of any kind in this case?

A. I wrote no reports.

Q. And therefore I can assume you handled none of the property retrieved as evidence?

A. That's correct.

Q. Including any money seized from the home?

MR. MCCLOUD: Your Honor.

THE COURT: Overruled.

Q. Including any money seized from the home?

A. I'm not aware of any money seized from the home, but if it had been, yes, it would have been his responsibility to record that fact.

Q. Just to be clear, Detective Nestor, your testimony is that you entered the house, did not run to the back door in pursuit of the suspect, chose instead to secure the house by searching it systematically for possible suspects other than the one who had run out the back door, and only later observed the gun inside the barbecue grill in the backyard in the company of your partner: is that about it?

A. I don't know if I'd put it that way.

Q. Is there another way you'd like to put it?

A. Well.

Q. Is that about it?

A. That's about it.

MR. CARMODY: No further questions, Your Honor.

CHAPTER TWENTY-ONE

Trenton-Ewing border, General Sullivan Way, northbound.

Off Route 29 north at Sanhican Drive is a hairpin right onto County Route 579, known for a couple of blocks as Sullivan Way, becoming Grand Avenue across Lower Ferry Road, then Bear Tavern once you pass Upper Ferry on your way to the county airport, once called Mercer, lately called Trenton (FAA code TTN), located in Ewing. A person could get lost following driving directions here without ever leaving this one road.

Along the Sullivan Way stand majestic trees and institutions with dark histories all. Northbound to your left are the remains of what might have been slave housing, followed by the Trenton Country Club, docile enough now, but once an exclusive domain for white men, non-Jewish (hey, Jews had Greenacres in Lawrenceville.) On your right still stand the vestiges of the original Trenton Psychiatric Hospital and further up, the Marie Katzenbach School for the Deaf.

Trenton Psychiatric remains today, mostly unoccupied, but still a state run mental health clinic of sorts. It has been chopped up, a fitting end to a place where fiendish experiments were once performed on the mentally ill, all in the name of advancing science. It began as the New Jersey State Lunatic Asylum, until even that nomenclature became unfashionable in certain circles. Dorothea Dix opened the place on May 15, 1848. At the time, it was the first public mental hospital in New Jersey, and also the first designed on the principle of the Kirkbride Plan. The concept called for staggering wings of the buildings so everyone had a window view, but if all you're seeing is a suburban streetscape, one might question the wisdom of the conceit.

In 1907, the institution's overseers hired Dr. Henry Cotton medical director. He apparently believed infections brought on mental illness. His fix had a whiff of Josef Mengele: he routinely had his staff remove patients' teeth and occasionally tonsils and other body parts that might become infected. Dr. Cotton stuck around over twenty years killing and maiming mentally ill patients. Fatalities ran to the hundreds, mutilations to the thousands. He made some kind of impression on the remainder of the hospital staff, as reportedly removal of patients' teeth continued to around 1960.

The property runs from brick to limestone to downright gothic. This is a breathing version of Shelter Island, all in plain sight of the folks driving past daily. It's a ghoulish affair on its best day. The hospital was cannibalized by the State for various projects over the past few decades. First there was the Forensic Unit. Criminally insane defendants (those acquitted under the old terminology "NGRI-not guilty by reason of insanity") were committed to the Forensic Unit until declared ready for discharge, a formula guaranteed to eclipse the Hotel California for visitor retention. Those who had worn out their welcome by spitting on, fighting with or mauling corrections officers at the highest security prisons got sent to the adjacent wing, a special place called the "Readjustment Unit" (self-explanatory), all contained within what is commonly known as the "Vroom Building," a grim legacy for New Jersey's ninth governor. There they occupied cells with the amenities afforded Hannibal Lecter on a day he had no appetite.

Later, these two facilities were closed and converted to the Central Reception and Assignment Facility ("CRAF"), the place all county convicts come to receive classification to the State's prison system.

Elsewhere on the grounds is a spanking new hospital entitled the Ann Klein Forensic Center, where the old Forensic Unit population are joined by some pathetic psychotics. They all come for medication and occasional abuse at the hands of a few intolerant Medical Security Officers who lack insight into the peccadilloes of mentally challenged folk. Most of the MSO's and social workers are doing their best, overmatched and underfunded. But as with any institution, the outliers define your reputation. In a state numbering nearly nine million people, this 200-bed facility represents the best taxpayers can do to provide services for the severely mentally ill.

"What's your name?"

"Whah?"

"Your name."

"Who…who 'er you?"

"Doesn't matter if you don't know who you are."

"Juh. Uh, Juh. J"

"Jay?"

"Jay-er."

"Jay R.?"

"Jer."

"J.R. what?"

"Buh-eh…"

"Buh-what?"

"Juh…muh."

"You're talking gibberish."

"Jer-uh Buh-juh-muh Smmm."

"J.R. Bojangles. Got it."

"Jer-me."

"I just need you to turn over for me. I have to give you an injection."

"Smm-uhth."

"That's a nice young man. You'll feel a slight pinch….There. Turn over again. You'll sleep now. I'll check in on you in an hour."

"Jer-uh-me Smmmth."

CHAPTER TWENTY-TWO

Session 8, continued. Carmody, William

...I know what you're thinking: this was way too granular to make any sense to you. Who cares how hard he hit the door, or what side of the road they approached the guy from? Trust me on this: there's a method to this madness. Wait; that's a figure of speech, I swear.

When cops lie, they do it very professionally. They are practiced. They have testified before, and they know how to tailor their testimony to their reports. For years I figured these TAC guys deliberately delayed reports until they saw what they needed to offer in testimony, but now I'm thinking this had something to do with the disappearing money train.

Look: perjury's this way. It's not Perry Mason-style where the lie is confessed and the contradiction completely obvious. And it ain't Bill Clinton stepping on his dick about getting blowed. In the real world, perjury is like a counterfeit hundred dollar bill. It looks like the real thing. Amateurs can't tell, yet you see cashiers at Target holding fifties up to the light, staring at the paper, which is about like your average defense lawyer who starts a question, "Isn't it a fact...," and the witness says, "Nope." If it's professionally done, only an expert can see the bogus bill, and then only under ultraviolet light, or with a really good magnifying glass to see the microprinting.

What I was doing in that Nestor cross was prying loose some arcane details that put the lie to the party line of pursuit of a fleeing felon and a brief protective sweep of the house. Instead, it was chasing a local black kid through his friend's house, then using that event as an excuse to break a door down, search the entire house, and on a good day steal some money.

And before you tell me how paranoid I am, let me tell you, we've been asked to represent cops charged with crimes in the past. I've had cops who had sex with arrestees, cops who've sold drugs, and cops who've stolen money. In each case, the guy told me he was guilty when we first met, then later completely denied the events, confirming that denial on the stand.

I'm stuck in that scenario. On the one hand, the Rules of Professional Conduct prohibit me from allowing perjured testimony to be presented to the court on my watch. On the other, my only source of describing it as perjured is the same guy who's now saying it ain't. I have to breach attorney-client privilege to reveal the problem, then eat my own words when my client renounces the story he told me up front. He'll deny he ever told me such a thing, or insist I misunderstood. Then I'm toast, because I'm forever known as the guy who sold out his client.

So you let them take the stand and tell whatever bullshit they feel like, knowing it's their funeral, but more likely acquittal, because jurors look for all kinds of ways to let these guys off. Hell, in New York, four cops walked for shooting some immigrant kid in a hallway like 41 times for no reason whatsoever, remember? Amadou Diallo? Mean anything? Springsteen? 41 Shots? Nothing? And that other bunch beat the shit out of Rodney King on videotape and walked in state court. You really have to run a plunger up a poor sap's rectum to get yourself indicted and convicted and then only in a federal court.

But back to the motion, the reason for the break in the transcript is that these cases don't play out in order. The judge took a break to take a couple of pleas, and we got bumped to the afternoon session. I had time to return some calls, check on some other cases, and try to figure out how to get paid on the new clients from that week. That's when I caught my first break in my gun case from Wisconsin that got me in all this trouble.

I was actually on the phone with Andrew in my office, so if you had a report on the conversation, please understand that I was talking to my associate even as I was talking to Amy Delaney, who happened to walk by.

"Andrew, listen, this O'Leary guy sent us some pdf's of his wire transfers to his brother. He really did front the guy over three hundred large. Not sure what his brother needed with that kind of cash, and I'm having trouble with one brother shaking another down at his son's expense, just for shits and giggles. So here's what I want you to do: hunt his brother down like a dog. Call Ace...yeah, Ace Bail Bonds, and ask him to get us the full Monty credit and background. I want to know where he's doing business and who he owes money to, and...hang on. Amy, hey Amy! Got a sec? ...Can I ask a favor?... Not you, Amy.... Remember that gun kid from a couple of weeks ago? The one from Wisconsin with the guns in boxes on his back seat? I'm trying to get some pre-indictment discovery or something so I can talk to Delores about him.... I don't even know if it's in grand jury yet, but I thought you might have the file. I'm not looking for anything special, just the invest and the property reports. Hell, I'd take the affidavit of probable cause, but I want the property report to show the guns were brand new in boxes unloaded. Kid's got no record at all and I'm being paid by a nice Midwestern family, you know? They make pies in their bakery, for chrissake. ... Did I mention how good you look? Seriously, I don't know what gym you're going to these days, but I feel like I have to get in better shape just to talk to you. ... Not you, knucklehead....No, I'm waiting on Andrew and he keeps butting in, don't worry about it. Seriously, can I buy you a drink later? I'm so tired of drinking alone, with nobody else... Okay, but next time I will be serious, seriously. Anything you can do....Andrew, I gotta go. Get on O'Leary's brother like a cheap suit and let me know....Amy! Wait up."

I had five more minutes before we had to be back in Judge Winters' courtroom, and I took advantage of all five.

I said, "By the way, Amy, did you look at that file before the bail hearing?"

She said, "I think so, because I had the intern doing the bails, remember?"

That's when I got in my own way again, because I said, "I remember that kid making some shit up in response to the judge's questions about ammunition and stuff."

She said, "Yeah, well, he was nervous."

Why couldn't I let it go? I said, "So when you're nervous you get a pass for lying to a judge?"

And she goes, "C'mon, he wasn't lying. He froze up when he got asked a question he didn't know the answer to, and he didn't know how to say, 'I don't know, judge.'"

And so I said, "So that's the standard for screwing up?"

And she goes, "Can you cut anyone a break these days?"

And I said, "Sorry. You're right. I gotta stop taking drugs or something."

She said, "I'd settle for you switching to decaf." That's when I let it go. Right there.

I said, "Did you look at the file?"

And she said, "I didn't. Or if I did, I don't remember, but tell you what: I'll go get the file right now and bring it to you and we can look at it together, how's that?"

And I said, "That would be great."

So she said, "On one condition."

I said, "What's that?"

She said, "You have to calm down and take a breath. You're beating yourself up over, uh, well, you're being too hard on yourself these days, and I need you to take a step back. For all of us."

I said, "Not sure I know what you're talking about."

She said, "I think you do, but I'm trying to be a friend."

I said, "Right now, I need all the friends I can get."

She said, "Yeah, well, telling the presiding judge he needs to get over himself and his power trip might not have been the smartest thing you could have said. Most accurate maybe, but definitely not the smartest."

I said, "I know, but I've had it up to here with Marty."

She said, "You mean Judge Cooper? I get it, and we all have, but last time I checked, he was wearing a robe and none if us is, including you. I'll bring you the file. You going to be with Winters the rest of the day?"

I said, "At least another hour, maybe the afternoon."

Then she said, "If it goes all afternoon, I'll walk you to Slimey's for the drink you keep threatening to buy me."

So I said, "Deal."

Couple of things. First, I want you to know that flirting is part of the game in getting information out of these people. It doesn't mean you're violating any Rule of Professional Conduct. You're trying to grease the skids without stepping over a line, and I swear it's done every day. Getting her to bring me that file was huge, I'm telling you. But I had to go listen to some more horseshit from the other cop in Wright' case first.

I heard the buzzer and the voice of a deputy sheriff calling "Remain seated," as Judge Winters resumed the bench.

THE COURT: Mr. Prosecutor, do you have a witness?

MR. MCCLOUD: Call Sam Amico, Your Honor.

THE COURT: Mr. Amico? Step up here, please. Place your left hand on the bible, raise your right.

(Witness sworn)

THE CLERK: State your name for the record, and spell your last.

THE WITNESS: Sam Amico. A-M-I-C-O.

THE COURT: Mr. McCloud?

MR. MCCLOUD: Thank you, Your Honor.

(Direct examination by Mr. McCloud)

Q. Mr. Amico, by whom are you employed?

A. Currently?

Q. Currently.

A. All State Security Services in New Brunswick.

Q. When did you start there?

A. Monday.

Q. How's the work?

A. So far, so good.

Q. Directing your attention to October of this year, where were you employed?

A. Mercer County Sheriff's Department.

Q. Is there a reason you no longer work for the sheriff's department?

A. I was laid off.

Q. Fair to say you were an unclassified employee when the budget cuts hit the department?

A. I was.

Q. In any event, you were a junior officer at the time, is that correct?

MR. CARMODY: Could we not lead, Your Honor?

THE COURT: It's preliminary. I'll permit it.

Q. Mr. Amico?

A. Well, I had less than two years on the job.

Q. Directing your attention specifically to October 19, 2012, were you working on that date?

A. I was.

Q. Were you working alone or with a partner?

A. I was paired with Edward Nestor.

Q. And do you remember what shift you were working?

A. Days. 8-4.

Q. And do you recall your assignment that day?

A. We were working fugitive detail, which is basically where you ride around town with a clip board of certain fugitives with warrants outstanding and if you see someone who might be one of the fugitives you're looking for, you stop to check that person out.

Q. Now, did there come a time in the afternoon where you found yourself on Kirkbride near MLK Boulevard?

A. Yes.

Q. What can you tell me about that incident?

MR. CARMODY: Objection to form, Your Honor. Could we have something a little less open ended than "tell me whatever you want about your attempt to arrest somebody in Trenton.'

THE COURT: Sustained.

Q. What if anything unusual happened when you found yourself on Kirkbride?

A. Well, we were looking for a fugitive from Passaic County if I recall correctly, and the description was black male, 5' 10," dreads, slim build, and when we turned onto Kirkbride, there's this guy standing there who matches the description.

Q. Then what happened?

A. Nestor turns the car towards him and we yell at him to stop where he is as we pull up on the street.

Q. Did he stop in response to your command?

MR. CARMODY: Objection, Your Honor. No evidence he heard the command. Assumes a fact not in evidence.

THE COURT: Rephrase your question.

Q. Did you yell at him to stop?

A. We did.

Q. How far away were you when you yelled at him?

A. Twenty feet?

Q. Did he appear to be aware of your presence?

A. Well, he looked right at us.

Q. And what did he do after you yelled to stop?

A. He pulled what looked like a gun out of his waistband, shifted it to his back, and took off for the front door of 18 Kirkbride.

Q. What do you do?

A. Hopped out of the car.

Q. Was it still moving?

A. Well it all happened in a matter of seconds, but Detective Nestor stopped the car, got out his side and headed to the front door. I got out of my side and headed to the far side of the row homes and tried to get to the back yard that way.

Q. Did you see Detective Nestor enter the house?

A. I did not. I ran to a driveway, I think that was number 12 Kirkbride, and there was a driveway along side. I ran up that driveway.

Q. And what did you see?

A. Uh, there was a chain link fence alongside the back yard of number 12, and it had a string of barbed wire on the top of the chain link. And I had a clear view of the back yards of the various row homes from that block.

Q. And what did you see?

A. I saw the defendant exit the back door of the house he had ran into, then he opened a barbecue grill next to the back steps, and he put what turned out to be a gun on the grill.

Q. Then what happened?

A. Well, I ordered him to stop and show me his hands, but he just took off for the back of that yard.

Q. Did you attempt to intercept him?

A. I did, but it was obvious I wouldn't be able to do that or whatever.

Q. What do you mean?

A. There was a fence, as I mentioned, and that fence went all the way to…it ran the length of the back yard of number 12, and it ran all the way to a garage at the back of the property, so there was no way for me to get over to where the defendant was running behind number 18.

Q. So what did you do?

A. Well, I heard the banging that turned out to be Detective Nestor trying to force open the front door, so I figured I should go with him to secure the house and the evidence I had seen in the grill.

Q. I want to be sure I understand you. Where was the suspect when you heard the banging?

A. Not sure I understand your question.

Q. Where did the defendant go?

A. I saw him light out the yard towards West Paul. I kept yelling at him to stop, but he just kept going.

Q. Did you hear the banging before or after you yelled at the suspect to stop?

A. Honestly, I can't recall.

Q. Did you go back to the front of the house?

A. Not right away. I radioed Nestor that the suspect was heading to West Paul and asked for help from other units in the area.

Q. Did other units respond?

A. Eventually, yes. I gave out a description of the guy running with the dreads and the baseball cap and the direction he took off in, and several Trenton PD units showed up, along with some sheriff's officers.

Q. Then what happened?

A. I went back to the front of the house and entered through the front door.

Q. Did you see Detective Nestor?

A. Yeah, he was in the process of securing the premises against possible suspects and what not, so I assisted in that aspect.

Q. Then what happened?

A. Once the residence was secure, I told him about the barbecue grill and we went out back to look at it.

Q. And what did you find?

A. When he opened the grill, there was a .9 millimeter Glock sitting on the top of the tray thing. You know, the grill itself.

Q. Did you take the gun in your custody at that point?

A. No, I waited for the ID officer to show up with his camera and take pictures of how the gun was lying when we found it. Once he did that, I took possession of the gun, secured it, and turned it in as evidence.

Q. Let me show you what has previously been marked as S-1 in evidence and ask if you recognize what this is?

A. Yeah, that's the gun we took and logged into evidence.

Q. How do you know?

A. Green grip, Glock .9 millimeter. Evidence tag on the bag has my signature.

Q. And lastly Mr. Amico, do you see the person who you saw running through the back yard that day in court today?

MR. CARMODY: Objection, Your Honor. What's the relevance of an identification in the context of a suppression hearing?

THE COURT: Mr. McCloud?

MR. MCCLOUD: Is this objection from the same lawyer who said relevance is not a basis for objection in a Rule 104 hearing? I'll withdraw the question, Your Honor. No further questions.

THE COURT: Cross examine?

MR. CARMODY: Thank you, Your Honor.

Q. Mr. Amico, good morning. No, wait, good afternoon.

A. Good afternoon.

Q. Can we start with your layoff due to the budget cuts in the department?

MR. MCCLOUD: Your Honor, is this relevant?

THE COURT: You brought it up on direct, didn't you?

Q. Can we start with your layoff, as you described it?

A. Yes.

Q. You said you were laid off.

A. I was.

Q. And you were an unclassified employee at the time.

A. I was.

Q. Is there a reason you did not disclose the pending disciplinary action to fire you for misconduct after you discharged your weapon in the basement of the courthouse?

MR. MCCLOUD: Objection, Your Honor.

THE COURT: I'll permit it.

Q. Mr. Amico?

A. Yes.

Q. Why did you limit your answer to the budget cuts as the reason for your layoff?

A. Mr. McCloud asked me why I left my job and I said I was laid off, which is true.

Q. And my question is, weren't you in effect told to resign or be prosecuted?

A. I don't think that's true at all.

Q. Well, were you given the option of accepting a layoff the result of which was the dismissal of the pending disciplinary charges, since the result was the same: you were out of a job. Isn't that fair?

A. The result was the same, but I denied the allegation in the PNDA, and I continue to deny it.

Q. You deny you discharged your service weapon in the basement of this building?

A. I do not deny that.

Q. You deny that you did so in a manner that constituted misconduct on your part?

A. I do deny that.

Q. The point here, Mr. Amico, is that you've sworn to tell the whole truth, not the partial truth, was that the oath you took?

A. It was.

Q. So can I count on you to tell the whole story when I ask you a question, not just a nuanced version?

A. I don't understand.

Q. Nuanced? I don't want a shaded version of the truth, okay?

A. Okay.

Q. You turn onto Kirkbride and see a young black man with dreads standing on the sidewalk, is that about it?

A. We did see such a man.

Q. And you immediately decided he was the guy you were looking for on your fugitive sheet, is that also the case?

A. Well, we thought we had a basis to investigate.

Q. Was he doing anything unusual standing on the sidewalk?

A. Not particularly.

Q. Not particularly? You mean nothing at all, except standing there, correct?

A. Correct.

Q. And because he was a black man with dreads, that was a sufficient description to make you want to ask him for ID, correct?

A. We wanted to investigate further.

Q. Investigate what? His choice of hairstyle?

MR. MCCLOUD: Objection.

MR. CARMODY: Your Honor…

THE COURT: The witness may answer the question.

THE WITNESS: What was the question?

Q. Other than his choice of hairstyle, what was the man doing that warranted your attention?

A. I'm not…

Q. Does that mean, nothing?

A. If you put it that way.

Q. What way would you put it?

A. He matched the description we had, so we decided to investigate.

Q. Kind of a snap decision, wouldn't you say, such that you turned onto the street and immediately you're driving a car right at this guy?

A. He drew a gun.

Q. Ah, yes. A car turns on the block, and the man's first instinct is to pull a gun from his waist and then return it to his back, was that what happened?

A. That's what it looked like.

Q. And you're sure it was a gun you saw.

A. Well, I'm not positive, but it had the appearance of a gun.

Q. The appearance of a gun? Never mind. You jumped out of your car, correct?

A. As it stopped, yes.

Q. And you ran at him, is that also true?

A. Yes.

Q. But he was faster, got to the door of 18 Kirkbride and inside, locking the door before you could get to him, right?

A. Right.

Q. What was the weather like?

A. Excuse me?

Q. The weather?

A. Clear.

Q. Was it a hot day?

A. I don't think so.

Q. So, was the front door of the home closed as he approached it?

A. I believe so.

Q. Was there a screen door.

A. I don't think so.

Q. Did the main door open in or out?

A. I believe it opened in.

Q. I take it the running man didn't need a key to enter?

A. As far as I could tell, he opened the door, went in, and locked it behind him.

Q. And he did all that with you a few feet behind him?

A. Yes.

Q. And then he immediately ran out the back of the house and across some back yards to the other street?

A. As far as I know, yes.

Q. Well, you saw him running through those yards, yes?

A. Yes.

Q. But in order to do that, you had to stop your pursuit to the front door, move to your right around two adjacent homes, up a driveway, and stop at a point where you could observe him through a neighbor's fence, right?

A. I did go around the side of the other home, yes.

Q. I'm just trying to figure out why he waited for you to do that before he went running out the back.

A. Excuse me?

Q. Well, it couldn't have been more than a few feet from the front door to the back of that row home, and he was obviously in a hurry. And respectfully, you're not going to be confused with Carl Lewis. Can you explain how or why he would have waited for you to assume a surveillance position at the far side of the back of number 22 Kirkbride before he walked out of the back of number 18, opened a grill lid, placed a gun on the grill plate, closed the lid, then ran to West Paul Avenue?

A. Who's Carl Lewis?

Q. The gold medal track star? Before your time? He's from the neighborhood.

A. He didn't close the lid.

Q. Who didn't close the lid?

A. The defendant. When he placed the gun on the barbecue, he left the grill partially open.

Q. Really? Like half way open?

A. Right.

Q. Do you have a barbecue grill?

A. No.

Q. You do know they have two settings for the lids: open and closed?

A. No.

Q. Or if there's no hinge, it's on or off.

A. I don't own a grill.

Q. How long did it take you to get from the front door of the house to the side of the other house and into the back of the driveway?

A. Seconds.

Q. And when you got there, you actually saw a man coming out of the back door of number 18 into that back yard.

A. Right.

Q. Put the gun in the grill, leaving the lid partially open?

A. Correct.

Q. And you shouted at him to halt?

A. Yes.

Q. Did he look at you when you did this?

A. Not that I recall.

Q. You are familiar with the idea that a shouted command will typically get a person to look in the direction of the voice, aren't you?

A. No.

Q. But whatever that idea might mean, in this case, the person completely ignored your command and went out the back.

A. Yes.

Q. Are you certain he heard you?

A. Would have been hard not to.

Q. You mean anyone in the area would have heard you?

A. I would assume so.

Q. So, if I call the other witnesses who were in the area at the time, and not a single one recalls hearing any shouted command of any kind, it's going to turn out they're all hard of hearing?

MR. MCCLOUD: Objection, Your Honor.

THE COURT: Sustained.

Q. In any case, you're certain of what you saw from the driveway of number 22?

A. Yes.

Q. Was there anything in the yards of any of these houses that would have obstructed your view?

A. Other than the fences themselves? No.

Q. You're sure about that.

A. Well, there might have been stuff in the yards, but
I could see the grill clearly.

Q. You're sure about that.

A. Sure.

Q. It's only a couple of weeks ago, Mr. Amico, I don't want there to be any hesitation on your part. I want you to assume this is critical to the court's understanding of your testimony, that this is a material part of what you have to report. You're under oath and I am asking you once more if there is any possibility that your view was obstructed looking from the driveway alongside number 22 into the back yard of number 18.

A. Not that I can recall.

Q. Well, 'not that I can recall' and 'no' are two different answers. Which is it?

A. No.

Okay, I have to stop you right there if that's where you were reading. Couple of things I want you to understand in terms of how my mind was maybe working a little too hard at that point. I admit I was getting pissed off, because I had been to the scene. I had interviewed the neighbors, and I knew this was another example of these guys just making shit up. Funny thing was, this was going well for me.

See, these judges refuse to call the cops liars unless basically another middle class white man gets on the stand and has documentary proof of the cops' bullshit. Even the cases where the videotape is taken by the bystander get all controversial, 'Was he really an innocent bystander or was he part of some setup?' Who the fuck cares if he was Spike fucking Lee? You still beat the shit out of some guy for talking to you in what you considered a disrespectful way. Private citizen clocks another dude? Fine. Beat the shit out of him. Maybe he will charge you with assault. Maybe he will fight back. Maybe he'll get a gun and hunt you down, especially if you're both at the same school.

But if you're a cop in uniform? You're not allowed to take your aggression out on anyone, including a guy who just called you a pig to your face. You're not supposed to use lethal force except to defend yourself or others against lethal force, but somehow these kids keep getting shot to death for carrying a cell phone that looked like a gun to you.

Why judges put up with this shit remains a mystery to me. They're not elected in New Jersey. But you'd think the governor himself was questioning their commitment to law and order, and they were one file memo away from losing their job and their pension.

Okay, wait, that's actually something they should worry about, but we don't have time to go down that road. Maybe another time. I just wanted you to understand what I was thinking before I lost my shit.

> Q. Mr. Amico, could we just cut the crap for two seconds?
>
> THE COURT: Mr. Carmody.
>
> MR. CARMODY: Sorry, Your Honor, but some days I just can't take it anymore.
>
> THE COURT: Excuse me?

MR. CARMODY: This unadulterated bullshit from this witness.

THE COURT: Mr. Carmody....

MR. CARMODY: Don't take my word for it. Go to the scene. I'll drive you and Mr. McCloud right now. There's a courtesy fence of green vinyl that makes it virtually impossible for this guy to have seen what he claims. I mean he might have peeked through a crack or something, but he's denying there was anything at all, and it just wears you down, you know? You know he's lying, McCloud knows he's lying. He knows he's lying, and I sure as shit know he's lying, a...

THE COURT: Mr. Carmody, please. Sit down!

MR. CARMODY: ...it just wears you down, knowing that you might find a way for me to prevail on this motion without ever getting to the meat of the matter, which is how much more bullshit do I have to listen to from these guys under oath? I mean, what the hell are we doing here, except giving these guys a platform to spin some happy horseshit, and it just makes me sick, and...

THE COURT: We are going to take a ten minute recess and I will see counsel in chambers. Now.

(Whereupon the proceedings were concluded.)

CHAPTER TWENTY-THREE

Law offices of Heinz Beckenbauer, 124 Nassau Street, Princeton, New Jersey.

Traveling to Princeton from Trenton represents a kind of social evolution of capitalism in motion. Starting from a decaying corpse of urbanity, where the mayor is perpetually under federal indictment and cops are scavenger hunting slow moving targets, where junkies and skanks rule certain corners, while junior Bloods and independent dealers rule others, one can head northeast up Route 206 for the scenic tour. It runs right past the Washington Monument. Not that one; a different one. This one commemorates the victory over the Hessians on Christmas night. Once clear of some public housing projects, a creek, some low rent row homes in North Trenton the road lumbers up Brunswick Avenue in pursuit of lower Lawrence Township and the Brunswick Circle.

Once upon a time the Trenton Giants played baseball in a ballyard next to that circle, and Willie Mays roamed a stone littered outfield with his smiling brand of grace. The stands were torn down for an Acme Market, which in turn went bankrupt, the building being bought by the State of New Jersey and rehabbed into the Lottery Commission Headquarters. Right, the Lottery Commission. The official tax for poor people bad at math.

Keep driving north on 206, past Notre Dame High School, which marks the beginning of the stately homes of southern Lawrence lining the once proud boulevard now pockmarked with drug stores, yet another Dunkin' Donuts, pizza shops, and the occasional residential property converted to offices for low rent lawyers and psychics, at times one and the same.

Cross over Interstate 95, politically and culturally the township's Mason Dixon Line, and enter neighborhoods of southern Princeton prestige. On the right is The Lawrenceville School, a premier preparatory institution over 200 years old and offering better facilities than most colleges. On the left is the quaint village of Lawrenceville, now populated with upscale restaurants and a few shops.

Further on the broader mansions start to appear and stare down at cars as they pass, drivers wondering who lives there, what their real estate taxes are, and how they handle the lack of central air in these musty 19th century homes. The road curves and winds in and out of farmland and glens, over well worn paths that once carried another company of British Regulars to Trenton to reinforce the Hessian garrison, too late for anything except the Battle of Princeton, when Washington's troops surprised them from the Princeton Pike, and General Mercer was bayoneted to death by angry survivors of the battle to the south days before.

Beyond that creek and battle site hulks the current governor's mansion, Drumthwacket, which apparently no governor wants to actually inhabit, having lain vacant for most of its existence as the official residence. The lone exception was Jim McGreevey, he of the forced resignation as America's first "gay American" governor, struggling to fend off a blackmail scheme by his boyfriend's lawyer, never mind his boyfriend, an Israeli national, was serving as some kind of Homeland Security advisor. Please don't ask.

A little further on sits the longer standing governor's mansion, Morven, which housed many a governor, perhaps most famously

Governor and later Chief Justice Hughes, an almost mythic figure of 20th century New Jersey politics. Now it's a museum. No one goes.

By Elm Road one can feel the lush greenery and understated opulence that is Princeton proper. Making the 25-minute trip from the Statehouse in Trenton to the Governor's Mansion in Princeton drivers travel through the ugliest underbelly of underfed sons and daughters of slaves and sharecroppers, displaced in search of manufacturing jobs that disappeared half a century ago, leaving behind flotsam, jetsam, and grime, until they emerge in the blinding light of affluence, neither showy nor condescending, just heavy, redolent with the musk of old money.

The borough itself mashes academics with investment bankers' wives, pairing professors with prospective donors in coffee shops, offering sidelong views of the University. Over here is Albert Einstein's house, there Grover Cleveland's, and on Library Place is the leaded glass tomb of that guy who shot himself as his creditors closed in. Surely the new owners cleaned the stained hardwood floors before they moved.

Nassau Street represents the commercial center of this closed universe. Heinz Beckenbauer was the Prussian Prince of Palmer Square.

"Now, Mr. Squitieri, you understand the nature of the transaction as a real estate investment trust?"

"I think so."

"Well, the reason I ask is you do have the right to secure your own attorney to advise you in this matter, and my allegiance is to the trust, not to you, understood?"

"You wouldn't try to screw me, would you?"

"No, of course not. But my responsibility is to represent the interests of the trust, not those of any one investor, and before you sign on to invest, you should be aware of your right to seek counsel from your own lawyer. I'm obligated to tell you this."

"Do I have anything to worry about?"

"I hope not, but I don't know all of your concerns. Obviously, I can answer any questions you might have, but there might be some you don't think to ask, or there might be issues that have different consequences for you than for anyone else."

"You don't look like a guy who would try to screw me."

"I assure you I am not such a person, Mr. Squitieri. I'm simply trying to point out..."

"I wouldn't react well to being screwed in this situation, or any situation for that matter."

"I'm certain that's true, sir."

"I admire your office."

"Well, thank you."

"Nice building, too."

"It is."

"You wouldn't try to screw me, would you Heinz?"

"I would not, sir."

"Then we have an understanding."

"All right then. I'll just need you to sign some papers I've prepared, and of course I'll need your capital contribution of $350,000, which I understand you've brought with you?"

"You'll take a check, right?"

"Of course."

"Where do I sign?"

"Just a moment…May I ask who or what 'Dapper Dan's LLC' is?"

"That's my bank."

"Your bank?"

"My bank."

"Interesting name for a bank. Federally chartered?"

"The check's good. Certified."

"Yes, but…"

"I really like your office, Heinz. Do we have an understanding?"

"Yes. Yes, of course."

CHAPTER TWENTY-FOUR

Session 9. Carmody, William.

You asked me to write down how I got here. Gotta be honest, I worried you'd take notes or ask for my writing and it would wind up in a report. So, this might be a tad literal. You'll let me know?

"I have lost my way. Maybe I've lost my mind, but I haven't lost my nose for right and wrong. I've broken lots of rules, but the one I held firm on was right and wrong. It's one of only two that count.

"For some reason I get totally hacked at other folks who do what I do, not because they are breaking rules, but because they seem oblivious to the fact that they are. It's one thing to break bad, another to break good, but cutting in line while pretending you're parting the Red Sea is annoying. Entitlement infuriates me, especially because I'm petrified it defines me.

"My sense of entitlement led to my betrayal, and my betrayal led to my wife's death, but that's not how I got to this place. I got here because I called some people out in a crowded room where they write stuff down before you can take it back.

"And that leads me to you, where I think about how I'd handle the only other rule: would I do unto others as they surely will do unto me?

"I know they would love to shut me up. I'm a bad apple in a basket of not terribly good apples. I'm not a threat, just an uncomfortable reminder of what they won't see in their own mirrors when they dress for work in the morning."

...I just wanted you to have some sense of how I feel when I'm driving to Princeton. I bust my ass to keep these poor kids from falling into the abyss on the off chance one of them might learn how to avoid spending his young adult life as a guest of the Department of Corrections, while you occupy a solitary recliner, waiting to see if I've slipped a neurological disc so you can report to my masters that I'm unfit for duty.

I used to try harder, I really did. But then the thing with my wife happened and it all started to unravel for me, you know? I hadn't even thought about it. I think I took her for granted and allowed myself to get carried away with my own version of bullet proof. I'd like to tell you I got over her leaving me, but I'd be lying. It still breaks me up every night, when I find myself roaming around our house alone, imagining her sitting in her chair or listening to me read to her.

She used to love that, you know? She loved me reading to her and I loved to do it. I never felt so close to her as when she nestled herself in my shoulder while I rolled Hemingway off my tongue, or grunted Raymond Chandler in a kind of Humphrey Bogart drawl.

And all this was going through my head while I was cross examining this lying cop and I just couldn't take it any more. I wasn't thinking about my responsibilities to the court or to the process. I just lost track of where I was, who I was with, why I was there, and I blew up in my mind. Did I dissociate? I have no idea.

Did my wife jump? Or was she pushed, is that what you're asking? How the hell should I know? She wasn't driving. Do we have to talk about this now? I gotta stick to my story if you want the front and the back of it, or we'll never get done. I'll come back to my wife, promise. Just not now.

So, on the afternoon of that day I lost my shit before Judge Winters, I asked Andrew to draw up a grand jury subpoena. Understand, there are only two kinds of subpoenas in criminal: grand jury and trial. There's no such thing as an office subpoena. You can't just write up a subpoena for documents and serve it on someone to bring stuff to your office. See, a prosecutor has a grand jury sitting somewhere all the time. He wants your phone records. His investigator drafts a subpoena *duces tecum. Duces tecum*; means bring documents with you. It's the other kind from "*ad testificandum*," to testify only. The guy drives to the phone company and hands them the subpoena while showing his badge and identification. Folks want to cooperate with cops, so they say, 'wait, we'll get those for you right now. If we certify them as true records, can we get out of coming to grand jury to say they are true copies? Yes? Well, then, here you are.'

If my investigator shows up, he has to have some kind of trial subpoena and he gets asked for five types of identification and they'll say, 'our lawyer will be in touch.' But I want records preserved and I don't want to wait two years for a trial date to make sure those records are still in existence. And once I get records in the hands of prosecutors, I can demand copies.

What I do in an extreme case is write up a grand jury subpoena, sign it on behalf of the Clerk of the County (lawyers are allowed to do that), and serve it on the custodian of records. That guy doesn't have to contact me, but he can if he wants. I serve a cover letter explaining he can send me copies of the certified records and I'll get them to the grand jury, but the subpoena requires him to get the records to the grand jury sitting in, say, Mercer County on a date I select. Since I know the grand jury sits every Tuesday and Friday, I just pick a Friday a few weeks out.

I don't do it in every case, but the few times I have done it, it's worked in strange ways. Once a prosecutor called and asked what the hell I was doing and I told him, "Your job." Told him to check the rules. There's no prohibition limiting grand jury subpoena power to prosecutors. John Wherry, god rest his soul, once addressed a letter to the foreman of a grand jury investigating his client's role in the death of her boyfriend (okay, she clubbed him senseless and he died, which I suppose is playing a role in his death), letting him know there was a wealth of evidence about her being a battered woman who acted out after years of abuse and inviting the foreman to request reports and testimony from defense experts. The Appellate Division did not disapprove of the approach, although the court also did not chastise the prosecutor for intercepting the letter and refusing to permit the foreman to see it.

With this strange deal in Princeton where my client O'Leary was asking after his $350K, I thought I better get the financial docs as soon as possible into the hands of the prosecutor, who would no doubt shit himself once he realized his victim's father was squeezing my guy for cash in the twelve-plus months before he reported the crime to police. My guy told me his brother had him wire funds to First Bank of Princeton, which has all of two branches. I went to both with the same subpoena, in case the account was at branch two and branch one decided to get cute.

First branch officer took the subpoena, said thank you, and that was that. Second branch manager started grilling me, which was funny, because if you're going to start talking to me, I'm going to let you run your mouth while I pick up information. He was like, "May I ask what this is in reference to?"

"Yes, you can ask."

"Well?"

"I said you could ask."

"We are not accustomed to receiving subpoenas here. I'm just looking for some guidance."

"Have I come to the correct branch for Mr. O'Leary's account information?"

"Mr. O'Leary is a valued client, and we will of course comply with, with whatever this is about. Did you say you were from the Attorney General?"

"I didn't say."

"I suppose I should have asked for some identification."

"It's not necessary. The document is authentic, and there's a number you can call for further instructions. My information is on the cover letter, and you should feel free to turn this over to your lawyers. I think the bank is represented by Bob Risoldi's firm."

"Are you a lawyer?"

"I am."

"Is Mr. O'Leary in any kind of trouble?"

"Look, if you know something and you want to tell me, I'll listen, but the grand jury is a confidential proceeding and I'm sure you'll understand why I cannot discuss my role in that process."

"Of course, of course. Only reason I ask is that you're not the first law enforcement person to be asking about his deposits and balances."

“Oh? Was another lawyer here?”

“No, no. A police officer. Detective. Italian name. Big fellow. Asking if Mr. O’Leary could cover a large check.”

“How large?”

“I don’t recall. Three to four hundred thousand, I think. Strange conversation. I thought you were from the same agency.”

“Sorry to disappoint. No worries. What did you tell him?”

“I couldn’t release confidential customer account information, but I did check Mr. O’Leary’s balance while the detective was here, and I assured him there would not be a problem handling a large check.”

“Think you could identify the detective again if you saw him?”

“I’m fairly certain. I’m sure I would recognize his partner, who had this strange haircut, like a Mohawk, I think they call it. Hair sticking straight up down the center of his head.”

“Like a lizard’s mane?”

“Yes, precisely.”

“Well, thank you for your time.”

“Glad to be of service, Mr?”

“Carmody.”

CHAPTER TWENTY-FIVE

Dapper Dan's, Route 12, Wisconsin Dells, Wisconsin.

Tim was in no mood. "Who told you to bring guns along for the ride?"

Tim's snarl got Aaron's German-Irish up. "No one told me not to."

"Oh, a wise guy, eh? Remind me who sent you to me."

"My boss?"

"Right. You work for Joe McGarrity. At the golf course. What did you do there? Mow grass?"

"Maintenance."

"And who was your friend and why was he along for the ride?" They sat stiffly across Tim's desk, Tim leaning hard against the back of his Naugahyde executive chair, Aaron hunched, one elbow on the edge of the blonde teak.

"Jeremy? He's just a kid I went to high school with. He didn't know anything."

"Did he know about the guns?"

"Uh, yeah, we bought those together."

"Oh, great, a gun shop appearance."

"Hey, I bought them, didn't show my ID, place was a hole in the wall and I didn't see any cameras."

"And when do you have to be back in court?"

"Lawyer says a couple of weeks at least."

"Who's your lawyer again?"

"Some old dude my parents found. He's like friends with some lawyer from Middleton my folks know."

"Did you tell him anything about what was going on?"

"Nope. Just the guns. Kind of hard to deny that part. They found them on the back seat."

"What the hell were you doing leaving guns on the back seat of your car?"

"I didn't. Cops said that's where they found them, but they were packed in the trunk when we left the train station."

"Have you spoken to your buddy's family?"

"Not yet. They're out of town for a few days, and he doesn't talk to them much anyway. I ain't worried about that part."

"Oh you're not worried. That's helpful." Tim stared at the ceiling, fingers steepled.

"Did you call his girlfriend?"

"Did I call his girlfriend?" Still staring, talking to the fluorescent lighting in his drop ceiling.

"Seriously..."

Tim lowered his gaze and his voice. Both penetrated. "Seriously, you need to shut the fuck up and listen. I gotta send you back there to find your buddy and get him the hell out of there. Then you gotta go to court and resolve your stupid gun case. Then you gotta leave New Jersey and never go back. Then I never want to see you. Ever. You need to disappear."

Aaron crossed what might prove to be his last bridge. "Am I still going to get paid?"

"You really like to push your luck, don't you."

"I'm out like a grand on the two guns. My folks had to send my lawyer $7,500. My bail was another $2,500 up front. I need help, man."

"Get your friend out of New Jersey. Get back to Madison. I'll take care of your travel expenses."

"I don't know where to look for him."

"Jesus, you really are an idiot. I will tell you where to find him. You get him, come back here, then the two of you disappear."

"What do you mean by disappear exactly?"

"Get out of my sight."

"You mean don't bother you?"

"I mean: get out of my sight.

CHAPTER TWENTY-SIX

Session 10. Carmody, William.

Here's the thing: sometimes timing is everything. Right place, wrong time? You're early or late. Wrong place, right time? You're lost. Right place, right time? This is what I'm talking about.

I knew once I lost my shit in court on Friday, I'd have to get some stuff done quickly, because I had to face the very real possibility of getting suspended immediately. But this was not the first time I had acted out in front of this judge. If you spread bad acting around, you might get away with it, but this might have been once too often at the same well. Maybe wrong place, wrong time would be more accurate.

About six weeks earlier I had been on trial before the same judge against a Deputy Attorney General on an official misconduct case. The guy was insufferable, and coming from me that's saying something. He was badgering witnesses, marking up my exhibits, just acting like a total jackass. He said something to a witness after the judge had told him to knock it off, and I turned to my client and whispered, "What an asshole."

I guess he heard me, because he stopped in mid-question, turned to the court, and said, "Did you hear that?"

The judge must have heard that, because he looked right at me, chin down, eyebrows up, and said, "I'll see counsel at sidebar. Off the record." Sidebar meant outside the hearing of the jury, and off-the-record was telling the court reporter to stay where she was. This was going to be a private dressing down.

What you didn't read was the sidebar exchange, which went something like this:

> MR. CAFONE: Your Honor, did you hear what he called me? I've never been called that before.
>
> MR. CARMODY: I find that very hard to believe.
>
> THE COURT: Mr. Carmody, you can't be calling counsel disparaging names on the record.
>
> MR. CARMODY: I was speaking privately to my client, Your Honor. I didn't realize counsel had such acute hearing.
>
> THE COURT: His hearing isn't that special. I heard you, and judging by the smirks on some of the jurors' faces, you made the front row there too.
>
> MR. CARMODY: I'm sorry, Your Honor, and permit me to apologize to Mr. Cafone. Just because he's an asshole doesn't mean I have to comment even semi-publicly on it. My bad.

Funny thing was, we had a new court reporter, who took down everything she heard, and she must have heard this, because I think you have a transcript of what I said in front of the jury.

Now for the second time in recent memory, I went into chambers and apologized profusely, this time for calling out the detective for being a bald-faced liar. Unfortunately, that's when I told the judge I didn't know where I was. I just meant I was kind of out of it, and he reported it as a dissociative event.

I knew all about dissociative events. I once had a guy who dissociated himself from: going to work to calling out sick, to buying a ski mask and grabbing a kitchen knife so he could go to his wife's hairdresser and stab her in her chair. Then he ran away, dumped his coat and mask and knife, and when they caught him five minutes later, he said he couldn't remember a thing. He was a good kid whose wife literally drove him crazy. With a stick. And a dog.

My shrinks believed him. So did the jury, up to a point. Attempted murder got written down to simple assault. If only he hadn't robbed those other ladies in the salon, I'd have gotten him off altogether. Anyway, the jury got confused, the judge got confused, and the robbery convictions got tossed on appeal. My guy got cut loose in two years. That's about 18 less than he would have done without the hypnotist and the forensic psychiatrists. But I digress.

The problem with dissociative events like sleep walking or accidentally driving to Ohio on your way to the grocery store is that judges don't know if you're capable of representing your clients. They have to make a quick judgment on whether you're up to the job while they investigate whether to sit you down for six months. That's where you come in.

I knew I was okay in the bank account, and I was confident my partner could carry the load if need be while I was on the shelf. But if you ever stop and think about it, you've got a hundred things to do to bring your files to current shape for someone else to understand, and I had to put these new files in some kind of working order in case Alan had to step in and figure out what to do. Plus, there was something nagging me about Bellow's gun case and TAC's involvement.

That weekend I had some work to do. I had to figure out what happened to those kids in the gun case; I had to interview those folks in Wright's cousin's house; and I had to figure out how to pin the extortion scheme on O'Leary's brother, which was looking like a problem now that I knew Squid and Klingon were interested in him. What was the connection there, you know? And if I followed that through, and I did, I'd have my answers to a bunch of questions at one time if I got lucky.

Anyhow, it's Friday night, which means a weekend is coming, and I gotta go back to my house alone. And I don't want to do that, so I plan to get drunk, conk out, and get an early start. And that's where my next problem came up, but please understand it was just bad luck or bad timing.

I was no more than three beers onto my porch in the early evening when my cell rings and it's Patty Voorhees. She's an LCSW case manager at Ann Klein who I've worked with for years. Few years back I had a kid there with schizophrenia, diagnosed after he raped his stepmother, she called me when the MSO's beat him up. Apparently, he called some Gold Gloves boxing champ a chump, and a worthless Puerto Rican grease ball, and god knows what else. But paranoids will get under your skin if you let them, because they are always spoiling for a fight.

Tell you something else about me and Patty. When the AG started loading guys about to be released from ADTC (another acronym, Adult Diagnostic and Treatment Center, you know, the sex offenders prison) into her facility on involuntary civil commitment orders, Patty called me to ask for help in getting those guys lawyers to get them out of her hair. They weren't truly mentally ill, just a bad social experiment in declaring guys with paraphilia diagnoses to be permanent members of a latter day Soviet-style psychiatric ward.

I use "Soviet-style" as shorthand for, 'you must be crazy to think you don't need our help after you finish serving your sentence; you don't want our help; you're crazy; that's reason to civilly commit you.' In the Soviet Union, they used to hold guys in the psych ward who were political prisoners. The rationale was, 'you know we're going to lock you up if you protest against the government; you protested; only a self-destructive nut would do that; we'd better hold you until you change your tune.'

Don't get me started on that whole 'sexually violent predator' issue, but Patty asked for guidance. I got 25 out of the first 26 released within 30 days of commitment because the retired judges who held those hearings knew the politics didn't justify keeping those guys locked in. That's changed now, and New Jersey has about 500 guys hidden in a gulag on the chance they might commit some new sex crime, but that's another story for another day.

The point is that Patty and I had worked together in the past. The unit was less than a mile from my office, and she was not shy about asking me for legal advice the AG would never give. I guess I should mention that every state agency has a Deputy Attorney General or five assigned to that department, whose job it is to give them ongoing advice on any legal matter that might come up. Anyway, those DAG's can't get themselves arrested most times when funky issues come up, like, what do you do with an MSO who's beating up your patients?

So Patty gets me on the phone, and I might be a little tight from the three beers, because truth is I'm not much of a drinker. And the conversation goes something like this.

"Hullo."

"Hello, Bill? Is that you?"

"Who's this?"

"Patty."

"Patty Powers? Patty Tribuani? Paddy Chayefsky?"

"Jesus, Bill, how many Patty's do you know?"

"A lot, if you include the Irish bugs."

"It's Patty Voorhees, from Ann Klein?"

"Patty. How the heck are you? What time is it?"

"Did I catch you at a bad time?"

"Dunno, 'cause I don't know what time it is."

"It's a little after six."

"At night?"

"Is it dark out where you are?"

"It's dark everywhere."

She said, "Okay, that's enough. I've got a problem. I couldn't call from the hospital; had to wait 'til I got home. Can you talk for a second?"

I said, "Of course. How can I help?"

She said, "Remember that time I called you about the guy who was here from out of state, and it turned out DOC was exchanging prisoners with other states for change of scenery purposes?"

I said, "Yeah, yeah. And he turned out to be a sicko that DOC hadn't bargained for."

She said, "That's the one. So, I thought I was having déjà vu all over again today. I'm looking at a kid's chart and it's making no sense. He came in on a police hold, but there's no paperwork explaining what he's being held on. Kid asked to see a social worker, and of course it's a problem so you know it fell into my lap."

I said, "Who are you kidding? You grabbed the kid's chart as soon as you smelled a rat."

She said, "Okay, that's possible, but I was the duty social worker when the request came in, so..."

I said, "So once more into the breach."

She said, "Shakespeare? You have been drinking. Here's the kid's story. He has no idea how he got to Ann Klein. He remembers being taken into custody by police, not sure where or what department, as he is not from New Jersey, but he does recall being taken from where he was arrested to some remote area, then passing out, then waking up in his bed here, then passing out again, now he's awake and disoriented. Wants to know where he is and why he's being held. I go to check out paperwork and I can't find anything. No complaint, no warrant, no retainer,"

"Detainer."

"Whatever; no what-do-you-call-it, extradition thing either. And I called someone over in Mercer to run a Promis/Gavel check. Empty. He doesn't recognize his own name, but he doesn't show signs of amnesia. Just seems perplexed about why we keep calling him 'J.R.'"

"Okay, that's weird."

She said, "Doesn't know how long he's been out of it, thinks it's several days. I'm just having a hard time figuring this one out, and when I thought about who I could call to look into it for me, your name kept popping into my head."

I said, "I'm flattered."

She said, "Is that what they're calling it these days?"

I said, "You want me to talk to the kid?"

"I think he needs a lawyer and he wouldn't have the first clue how to go about hiring one, and it doesn't sound like anyone knows where he is. He's got to have family, but I have no idea how to get in touch with someone when I'm not sure I know their kid's real name."

"Does he say where he's from?"

"Wisconsin."

"Wisconsin? Does he have any ID whatsoever?"

"Zip. Zero. Nada. That's part of the weirdness."

"Did he have any other helpful information when you talked to him?"

"He said he was a passenger in a car stopped by the cops, and his friend, Aaron something, apparently got taken into custody separately."

"Say again?"

"What?"

"His friend, who? Whom?"

"Oh, I have it in my notes in my desk. I think it was Aaron, can't remember last name."

"I'll be right there. Where am I going?"

"You're picking me up?"

"How else am I getting onto a state-run psych ward without someone like you to navigate?"

"Good point. Meet me in the Klein parking lot in an hour."

"Okay."

"And Bill?"

"What? I'm fine, I swear."

I drove to the Psychiatric Hospital without a problem. My head was clearing, so I don't want you reporting I was driving drunk on top of everything else. Three beers, what, point oh-six? Tops. The parking lot was empty except for the night shift cars, and no one was manning the booth out front.

I pulled up next to Patty's car, which I wouldn't have recognized, except she was standing next to it smoking a cigarette in jeans and sneaks, looking very Pink Lady in what for her I suspect was not retro wardrobe.

I said, "Hey."

She said, "Hi, Bill."

I said, "Do I need ID to get in?"

And she said, "Just bring your driver's license. They don't have to know you're a lawyer."

I said, "Hang on."

Then she said, "C'mere."

"What?"

"Come over here."

"Patty, what? You're not going to smell my breath, are you?"

"Just don't want to have a problem getting inside. You're fine. Let's go."

We walked right through the front doors like we owned the place. She nodded to the MSO in the bubble, said something about needing to interview someone for something, then gave my ID and her badge to the guy through the tray under the plexiglass. We got buzzed through immediately like it happened every day this way, which kind of amazed me. Within three minutes I'm walking down this all white corridor headed for a day room with tables and chairs and some books on the shelves.

She left me there for a few minutes, then came back with this kid who couldn't've been 20 years old. Turned out later he was like 25. I stood up and shook his hand, but he's all shaky and shit. Don't know if he was out of it, going through withdrawal, or maybe a little paranoid at that point. Hell, who wouldn't be? I introduced myself and got to it.

"So I understand you're not sure what you're doing here, is that right?"

"I have no idea. And who exactly are you?"

"I'm a lawyer. Your social worker called me to talk to you right away, because she couldn't figure out why you were here either. I figured you could give me some information about yourself, and on Monday I can ask a judge to order your release."

"I don't think I can pay you."

"Don't worry about that. If someone locked you up here for the wrong reasons, we might be able to sue somebody, get my fees paid and maybe even get you a few bucks to buy a ticket home. Which is where, by the way?"

"Wisconsin. "

"Whereabouts. It's a big state."

"Madison. Middleton actually, which is sort of part of Madison."

"And how did you get to New Jersey?"

"Buddy of mine and I drove."

"Where's your buddy now?"

"No idea. We got separated after the cops picked us up."

I said, "Where did that happen?"

He said, "When?"

I said, "Where. I think I know when."

He said, "Dunno. We were on some dark street near the Trenton Train Station. Lights went on, they took us out of the car, my friend went in one car, and I went in another."

I said, "Did they take you to the police station?"

He said, "I don't know. I remember going to some place with a bunch of tall grass and weeds, not a lot else going on wherever it was."

I said, "Who took you there?"

He said, "Two guys. They had guns."

I said, "Black polo shirts?"

He said, "Yeah, how did you know?

I said, "Took a guess. What did they look like?"

He said, "One big guy with red hair and like brown spots all over his face."

I said, "How about the other one?"

He said, "Not as big. White guy. Shorter, crew cut."

"What happened?"

"They were talking and one guy walked away from the car while the other guy stood along side where I was sitting. After that, I'm not sure, because I passed out. At least that's what I think happened. I don't remember anything after being handcuffed in the back of that car."

"Any idea why cops stopped you?"

"Nope."

"None whatsoever?"

"Unh-uh."

"Okay, and who's your buddy?"

"Really don't think I want to get him in any trouble."

"Oh, he might already be there."

"Why do you say that?"

"Well, if he weren't in trouble, wouldn't he be here helping you out? Sounds like you were both arrested. And you have no idea why?"

"Told you I didn't."

"All right. Would you like to get out of here?"

"Sure."

"Okay. Here's what we're going to do: you're going to stay here for the weekend. Don't say anything to anybody about anything, understood? Your social worker is going to talk to the nurse about making sure you don't get any more medication until I get back. I'll see the judge first thing Monday morning and ask for an order authorizing your immediate release, and I will personally pick you up and get you on a plane back to Wisconsin. How's that?"

"Cool."

CHAPTER TWENTY-SEVEN

Route 1 and Quakerbridge Road, Lawrenceville, New Jersey. East conference room, Sherman Susskind Bloomberg Cohen and Fineman

Barry Sherman, politician-short, brought a mouth-only smile to every transaction table. "Hello Heinz."

"Barry, how are you?" Heinz shook his hand, bracing for the *faux pas.*

"I'm well, thanks. How's Sarah?" Heinz's sister, Sylvia, suffered from advanced Parkinson's. With some help, he had cared for her in his home for nearly six years.

"She's good. You know she had that back surgery, but she's recovering nicely."

"Oh, right. Please give her my best..."

But chitchat grates on the impatient, fingernails on blackboard. "Excuse me, can we cut to the chase here?"

Barry took charge. "I'm sorry; you are Mr.?"

"I'm Mr. Would Like To Get The Fuck Out Of Here To-night."

"All right then, Mr. Night. Let's get started. Have you reviewed all the paperwork with your counsel?"

"We signed earlier."

"I don't believe that was my question."

"Maybe not, but that's my answer."

"Their check cleared my trust account, Barry. We have our other participant's funds as well, and we have wire instructions."

"Thanks, Heinz. Did everyone execute signature pages for the wrap around notes and mortgage?"

"They did. Signature pages have been pdf'd to the bank's lawyers and hard copies are in the red manila folder in front of you."

"All right, and what about your third participant, who I understand is out of town."

"He has also signed, and we have POA's for the remaining corporate resolutions."

"Then we have nothing left to discuss. Could you authorize your bank to release the funds?"

"I'm doing that right now." Heinz emailed an authorization.

"Can we leave?"

"Don't you want to know how this will work going forward?"

"Nope. Can we leave?"

"You aren't under arrest, sir. Of course you can leave."

“Interesting choice of words. It’s been real.”

Two men in casual clothes, one with beefy biceps, one patting his hair spiked with gel, abruptly stood and left the conference room, no handshakes.

“Charming fellow, Heinz. Where did you find him?”

“My client had a nasty case of the shorts and needed an infusion of cash. These two were his fifty percent partners. No idea who’s behind them, but their check cleared.”

CHAPTER TWENTY-EIGHT

Session 10, continued. Carmody, William.

Patty told me to take off while she got this kid back to his room and probably tampered with his chart, so I headed out the security corridor and signed out. When I was walking towards my car, I noticed a Human Services cop was now standing in the guard booth. I think you know the booth is at the east entrance to the TPH complex, right next to Ann Klein. You can head out to the west if you just take a left instead of a right leaving the parking lot. I had signed out with a facsimile of a signature that vaguely resembled the name "Don Mattingly," and I doubted the MSO would check my signature against the D/L I showed him on the way in.

I thought I saw the guy in the guard booth holding a radio, but that could have been my paranoia. Okay, bad choice of words, but you get what I'm saying. Reason I mention it is, I turned left and started winding around the old stone buildings that get just a little creepy in the dark. I'm pretty sure I saw headlights behind me, and I knew I had those three beers, so I kicked it a little over the speed bumps to get to Sullivan Way on the other side of the grounds. Then I burned a right and a quick left into the Trenton Country Club driveway.

I had been a member there until about ten years ago, when they told me every member would have to undergo a Megan's Law background check, which I thought was beyond insulting to my dignity.

Plus my wife wasn't much for country clubs, so it got to be a cash drain.

Point was I knew what the deal would be there on a Friday night. Front door would be valet parking and lot of folks coming for dinner upstairs. But I could bypass valet, park behind the pro shop, walk around the side of the main building and let myself into the men's locker room without a key or anyone likely to see me. Plus, very few current members knew who all the old members were, and I could run that bluff with anyone.

I'm only telling you this part of the story, because after I parked behind the pro shop, I saw another pair of headlights driving up the driveway, and I couldn't be sure it wasn't the Human Services police. They patrol the Psych Hospital grounds, but they can arrest anywhere in the state.

I snuck around the side of the clubhouse, went into the men's room outside the locker room, and waited a minute. I thought about grabbing a vacant locker and taking my clothes off to take a steam, but that would have really been tempting fate, so I just washed up and walked back out the way I came like a man who just finished dinner. I'm guessing someone saw me, because now they want to know if my trespassing at the country club is another sign of my illness. I wanted you to know it was nothing more than me avoiding a DUI stop on a Friday night in Trenton.

I made it home otherwise without a problem. But now I'm starting to freak out. I was 90% sure this kid was with Aaron Bellow when they got stopped by TAC for the bogus gun search. I went out of my way not to spook him with the idea I knew who he was and what he was doing in town. Hell, he probably would have broken out of the hospital had he suspected me. Not sure he didn't anyway. Shouldn't have asked him five times if he knew why he was there.

Here's a hint about cross examination: if you want the witness to know you know when he's lying, ask him the same question a few times, marking it with, "Are you sure? Positive?" Because he will know you have something in your file that says he's full of shit, and you're trying to figure out if now is when you're playing the card.

Give you an example. I had to cross examine a cop a couple of weeks ago on another gun search. TAC is full of them. Gun searches. It's like they know ahead of time who has a gun. Or maybe they have extras. I haven't decided yet. Anyway, cop stops some guys in a parking lot for public drinking. Cop swears he gave all three guys in this target Range Rover tickets for open consumption of alcohol. Claims he saw them drinking from Solo cups when he and his partner rolled up on them, and I'm sure they were. Only problem was the car's engine was off. They were sitting in a parking lot on private property. Couldn't see the violation from where I sat, which would have been the issue for probable cause to start searching the car, but we didn't get that far. I asked him,

> Q. Now you testified you gave all three of these men summonses for open container?
>
> A. I did.
>
> Q. You're sure about that?
>
> A. Positive.
>
> Q. So you would have written them out of a summons book you keep for that purpose?
>
> A. Correct.
>
> Q. And that book contains tickets with four color-coded parts, right?

A. I believe that is correct.

Q. Well, the white one goes to the court, right?

A. Right.

Q. Defendant gets the blue one?

A. Right.

Q. Pink goes to records?

A. Right.

Q. And there's a yellow copy that stays in your book, right?

A. Right.

Q. So if you gave these three young men summonses, each should have a copy?

A. If they didn't lose them.

Q. And the court clerk should have a copy, right?

A. Same answer.

Q. And police records should have a copy?

A. Should.

Q. And your book should have a copy?

A. For the time being it would.

Q. For the time being?

A. Do you have any idea how many ticket books I go through?

Q. I'm sure I don't.

A. Thousands. I throw them out when they're done, because I have no need to hold onto them.

Q. Is that right?

A. Yeah.

Q. You have no need of them because the clerk of the court and records both have copies, right?

A. Supposed to.

Q. Detective, I want you to assume this is a critical fact in this case, a "material fact," if you will. I want you to assume your career depends on the truthfulness of your answer. If you don't recall the answer, feel free to simply say, 'I don't recall.' The question is, do you have a specific recollection of giving these three young men tickets for open container?

A. Absolutely.

Q. Let me represent to you, sir, that once you are through testifying, I will be calling representatives of both the municipal court and the records bureau to advise they have no copies of these tickets and no records, digital or otherwise, that these tickets were ever issued. Further, all three young men are prepared to testify they never got any tickets for open container, and one of the men actually gave you a fake name, begging the question of how you wrote a ticket to someone whose identity you never accurately established. One last chance, detective, did you write those tickets? Or did you intend to write them and just not get around to it during your tour of duty?

A. I'm telling you, I issued all three summonses.

And it went on like that. I called the folks from records and the court, as well as all three guys from the car. No tickets. It could not have been clearer. But here's the thing: this cop lied his ass off under oath in front of a judge and prosecutor. The prosecutor should have opened an internal on this guy immediately, and the judge should have formally referred the matter to the prosecutor for a perjury investigation. Didn't happen. You need to understand my mindset. Even when I get the cop cold on the stand, and the judge threw us the motion by the way, on completely different grounds. My client is happy, because his gun case gets tossed. So once again I have a lying cop in my cross hairs and... nothing.

You have to understand, I represent cops. My partner handles their cases through their PBA. I've taken more cop cases to trial than anyone, except maybe my partner. Cops charged with stealing money and champagne from drug dealers; cops charged with having sex with female prisoners in the cell block; cops pulling their guns in off duty traffic stops, while drunk of course. You name it, we've handled it. I once told Phil Donahue I represent sex offenders, drug dealers and cops, and on a good day I get all three rolled into one. You know what? He didn't find it funny. Come to think of it, it wasn't.

I'm telling you, these guys are immune. That's why they steal the cash and jewelry from the kids in the street, because they can, and no one's going to challenge them. Even on the rare occasion when they do get busted, they almost always beat the rap, to the point where the average cop thinks there's no way he can go down for misconduct for some little shit he did that everyone else's doing. Serpico was a sap.

CHAPTER TWENTY-NINE

Electric Earth Café, West Washington Avenue, Madison, Wisconsin

"Got a piece of paper?" Tim had no patience for Madison, hipster coffee shops, and less for Aaron Bellow.

"Hang on....Okay."

"Here's your contact information. Write it down."

"Why can't I just take this?" For Aaron, another lesson in listening not learned.

"Write it down."

"Okay."

"You have to drive back to New Jersey and be there by 7AM Monday. Leave tonight. Don't be late. Be there by six."

"Okay. But what if...?"

"There ain't no what ifs. Be there by six."

"Got it."

"You make your pick up and drive straight back here, but do not use a toll road."

"But that will take forever."

"Did you hear what I said?"

"Got it. No toll roads. What's my alternate route?"

"You're a college kid. Figure it out. And turn off your cell phone for the duration."

"But that's…"

"That's another way you can be tracked. Tower hits."

"Can I at least get gas money?"

"Take this. It's enough for you to find a U.S. highway without an interstate number and keep going for a while. Buy gas with cash, no tolls, no speeding or traffic stops."

"What about motels?"

"Who said anything about motels?"

"Can we stop to sleep anywhere?"

"Only if they rent rooms by the hour, cash only, no ID. If they ask for ID, you got a problem. Sign a book with your own name and we will have a problem. I got enough problems."

"One last thing?"

"Jesus, Mary and Joseph, now what?"

"What if he doesn't want to come with me?"

"He will be very happy to see you, trust me."

CHAPTER THIRTY

Session 11. Carmody, William.

...So if you're following me, that last weekend was already going to be a problem. I was a tad hung over from three lousy beers. Telling you, I don't drink; three beers and I wake up with a crashing headache. I had to get to Wright's cousin's house on Kirkbride before they went out for the day. I grabbed my camera, headed out, and called Wright from the road asking him to meet me there.

When I got down to the street, I saw Joe leaning against a car talking with his videographer. Not kidding. He had a guy with a digital camera to record every significant event involving him and the cops. I wasn't making that up. The young man was playing for keeps. Or else he was melodramatic. He nodded towards me as I walked up to Brenda, who turned out not to be his cousin. Seems she was raised next door to him by her grandfather as though they were related. I didn't have to knock on the door; she waited on the stoop.

"You Mr. Carmody?"

"Are you Brenda?"

"Yeah."

"Here's my card, but I think Joe can vouch for me. And I have photo ID if you'd like to see it."

"No, I believe you."

"That's a good sign."

"You want to come inside?"

I said, "I do, but before we do, can I ask what happened here?"

She said, "This is where they broke the panel of my front door in. We just patched it and it's been like that. We have to get our landlord to fix it."

I said, "Do you mind if I take another picture?"

She said, "No, no. I thought you had pictures."

I said, "I do, but these will be time stamped, and you will be able to verify when I took them, because you are standing right here." Someone cracked open the adjacent door an eye's width, then whipped it open. I said, "Hello, how are you? Long time no see."

She said, "That's Mr. Wilson from next door."

I said, "I hope he's from next door, or else has a good reason why he's standing inside that apartment in his pajamas. Just pulling your leg, Mr. Wilson. Everything okay?"

Mr. Wilson said, "Fine, fine. You looking at that door again?"

I said, "I am."

He said, "I told you how they broke it down, didn't I?"

I said, "You said they had a small battering tool they got from their car."

He said, "It was like a long metal pipe. They was just banging, banging, you know? Like this: Bang! Bang! Till it just broke in."

I said, "Yeah, you told me that last week. You still going to come to court and tell the judge?"

He said, "Sure I will. When is it?"

I said, "Well, it was going to be Monday, but now I'm not so sure. We might need to get a new date. Can I get back to you?"

He said, "Of course, of course."

"Brenda and I are going inside, but I'll stop by on my way out, okay?"

"Of course, of course."

That's the thing about independent witnesses. They want to tell you their story sometimes over and over. They are showing solidarity with a friend or neighbor. But when court rolls around, they go completely blank, and even then only on the days where they actually show up. You have to massage these guys like crazy to keep them interested, and then hope they don't have some petty bench warrant for unpaid parking tickets or some shit that cops use to scare them out of coming to testify. No one wants to get locked up, ever.

I had come alone. I was taking a calculated risk here, but that doesn't make me crazy. It just makes me foolish if the witness blows up in my face, because a lawyer can't testify in his own case. If I don't have an investigator present when I interview these folks, I'm stuck with whatever they give me in open court. In a Rule 104 hearing...sorry, you know, a pretrial hearing, like a motion to suppress or *Miranda* hearing or whatever, well, okay, maybe not a *Miranda* hearing, but anywhere hearsay is admissible, I can ordinarily call an investigator to testify to an interview if the witness either doesn't show up or backs off an earlier statement of what he saw with his own eyes.

Look, here's the reality of what we do: Wright couldn't afford an investigator, and I wanted to be sure I understood what everyone was saying before they came to court to say it. When a guy has limited funds, sometimes you do double duty as lawyer and investigator, even photographer. In a lot of cases, that's what separates the good lawyers from the careless or the lazy.

If you haven't been to the scene of the event, or the scene of the crime, you can't really ask questions with that authority of personal knowledge. You don't know where the street lamps are, where the curb is cracked, where the stoop meets the door jamb, in this case where the courtesy fence would have made it impossible for the officer to see what he claims he saw. And if you haven't talked to the witnesses at least once, preferably twice, you are going to be surprised at what they say under oath, because what they do say in court is rarely what they saw or heard.

Here's something that might surprise you, but did not surprise me: when I walked into Brenda's home, I found it immaculate. Every inch of floor was spotless. Books and papers were in their places, toys were in crates, and there were no stray cans or plates or evidence of two kids in a living room. She had known I was coming, but this was not the one time effort of a housekeeping slacker. This was the tiger mom of clean, and my prejudice is that I doubted the father was the enforcer on this front.

"I had my husband take the kids out for breakfast so you could look around."

"That wasn't necessary."

“Maybe not for you, but they had a tough enough time when we came home and the house was turned upside down. Took us a couple of days to put all their stuff back in the right place.”

“Cops gave it a thorough look?”

“I’ve heard of worse, but they must have been mad at Joe for running. Clothes was everywhere, boxes turned upside down.”

“How do you know it was Joe who ran?”

“Must have been. Who else would go through my house?”

“Did he have a key?”

“No. I had been to a funeral that afternoon and left the door open because he was next door with my uncle.”

“Did your family go to the funeral with you?”

“Yes. My aunt’s cousin passed. She was very close to my kids.”

“So, is this about how the house looked inside when you left?”

“Except for the door over there.”

“How about the money?”

“I kept the money we were saving to get a new car in my dresser upstairs. I counted it last time I put some towards it. I had close to $3,500 in my jar.”

“Is the jar still there?”

"Jar's gone. Money's gone. I went to Internal Affairs."

"In Trenton? On North Clinton?"

"Yeah."

"But these guys were county sheriff's officers. You should have gone to the county."

"For real? 'Cause when I came home, there was Trenton Police on the cars outside my house."

"Well, did the man at IA tell you? Did you talk to somebody?"

"Yeah, he gave me his card. He said they would do an investigation. He was very nice."

"Have you heard anything since that day?"

"No. It's only been like a couple of months or so. I don't know how long it takes."

"Fair enough. Would you be willing to tell this story to a judge in court?"

"Will I get in any trouble?"

"Why would you think that?"

"Telling on cops is supposed to be dangerous."

"What did you think you were doing when you went to Internal Affairs?"

"I was just, like, filing a complaint. Court is serious."

"It's all part of the same thing, and I promise you, you will not be in any trouble. The judge will protect you. I will protect you. Promise."

"Well, when is it, because I have to let my job know."

"I will find out from the judge on Monday and call you. How's that? We will work around your schedule."

"Okay, but when do they give me my money back?"

"I can't promise anything about the money, but I will make sure these guys pay up, one way or another. Best I can do for now."

"Okay, 'cause we really need that car. And now I gotta pay to fix this door."

CHAPTER THIRTY-ONE

Between Sullivan Way and Stuyvesant Avenue. Residents' Wing; Ann Klein Forensic Center.

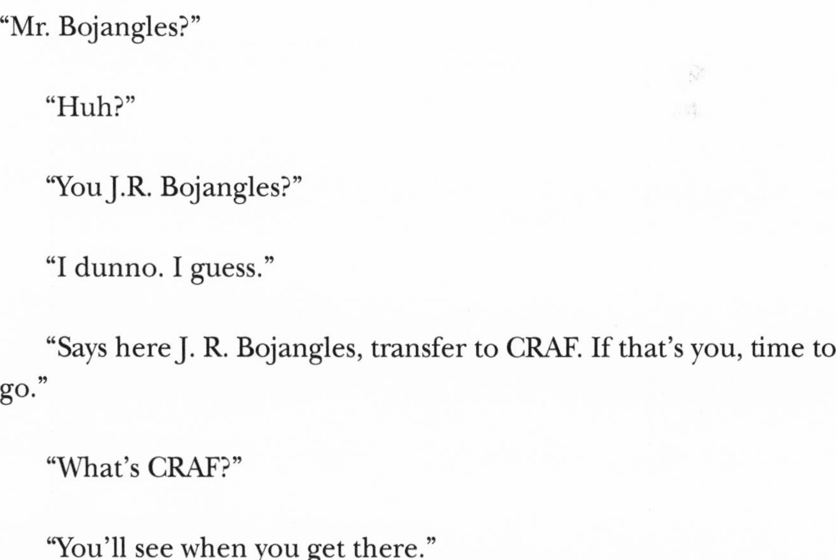

"Mr. Bojangles?"

"Huh?"

"You J.R. Bojangles?"

"I dunno. I guess."

"Says here J. R. Bojangles, transfer to CRAF. If that's you, time to go."

"What's CRAF?"

"You'll see when you get there."

"Can I get dressed?"

"Give you two minutes. They ain't gonna let you keep your clothes anyway, so just throw something on."

"Who's they?"

"CRAF, man. Orange jumpsuit for you."

"Can I make a call?"

"You can put your hands out?"

"What for?"

"I have to put these on."

"Am I under arrest?"

"You're officially in the custody of the Department of Corrections, and that means bracelets. Let me know if these are too tight."

"Too tight."

"Too bad."

CHAPTER THIRTY-TWO

Session 12. Carmody, William.

Here's a side of the practice that can drive a man to drink, and they probably didn't tell you about. Sunday night, early Monday morning actually, I finally dozed off after a couple of Advil, some Nyquil, and two Coronas, when my cell phone starts buzzing like it's been possessed. We have this program that shoots wav files from our server to our cell phones, but only if it's an emergency call.

For years I used an answering service, even after automated calling was acceptable, because I wanted a live operator to make a judgment before I got a middle of the night call. But too many guys would bullshit their way into a sleep interruption by making some outrageous claim.

One guy who was the boyfriend of my client called a couple of times during a week, and I didn't call him back. A) She was behind on payments, so the extra care involved in calming a boyfriend was not on my list of things to do, and B) I wasn't allowed to discuss the details of her case with the man anyway.

So he calls one Friday night around 11PM, says it's an emergency, and the service calls me. Knowing who the client is, and she was a hopeless junkie-shoplifter—and if you know any female junkies, you know junkie shoplifter is probably redundant-- who occasionally abused her own kids (no, she was white, why did you think otherwise?), I figured she's been arrested boosting from the local Burlington Coat Factory or some stupid shit. So I took the call.

"Hello."

"Mr. Carmody?"

"Reginald? How can I help?"

"It's about Stacey."

"I figured. What's happened?"

"Nothing. I just wanted to know what was going on with her cases?"

"You mean there's no emergency?"

"Well, you didn't return my calls this week, so I figured this was the only way to get you on the phone."

"Really? That's what you figured?"

"Yeah, and it worked. So, what's going on with her cases?"

"Well, I can report one development, very recent."

"What's that?"

"Her lawyer just quit her case. She needs to find a new one ASAP."

"I don't understand."

"Of course you don't. Here it is in another language: I resign as her lawyer. Please tell her to expect my letter in the mail. She needs to start looking for another one immediately."

I hung up the phone, but you get the idea. People are always stealing my time, and the more they owe me, the more willing they are to commit the act of theft. It's exhausting.

Anyway, my phone buzzed off the night table at close to 2AM and I struggled to play back the message. A young woman was near hysterical, but I think she said, "Mr. Cromartie, my husband, actually we're not married but we've been together a long-long time and anyway he's been taken by the police after he shot a man who attacked us in our bedroom when I woke up and saw him struggling with Michael I hit him with a screw gun but I didn't shoot the screw in him he was wearing a mask and had a gun and I thought he was going to shoot Michael and he was yelling about the fucking money give him the fucking money and ohmygod ohmygod I just whacked him with the screw gun and Michael had his own gun at the bedside table and he grabbed it and shot the guy who took off and the cops came and he hid the gun and said he didn't know what happened other than my hitting the guy with the screw gun and they said ok and left but they came back and took Michael away and they're searching the house right now and I don't know what to do but Michael said to call you 'cause his boss is someone you helped out a few years back in the taxi service and I don't know what to do and please please please call me at this number, um, ohmygod ohmygod I forgot my number but call me anyway I gotta go please please please..."

Our system recorded the incoming number so that's what I called. I figured the taxi service must have been a reference to a company that got jammed up a few years back for running a prostitution ring using their cars as mobile brothels, actually more like twenty years ago, but I remembered the guy who ran the company as a good man with an entrepreneurial streak that might have exceeded the limits of our vice regulatory scheme. I recall thinking the racketeering indictment was a tad strong, but we beat that down.

Anyway, she answered the phone before the first ring echoed.

"Hello? Mr. Cromartie? Is that you?"

"It's Carmody, and yes, it's me. How can I help?"

"Thank you so much for calling. They took Michael away and now they're searching our basement and backyard and I can't see where else, all because Michael hid the gun."

"What gun?"

"The one he shot the man with."

"The man who tried to rob you?"

"Yes, yes. The masked man came in and tried to rob us and woke us up screaming 'Where's the fucking money? Where's the fucking money?' and I was so scared and Michael started tussling with him and I thought he was going to be shot, so I grabbed the screw gun on the floor next to our bed…"

"Why did you have a screw gun next to your bed?"

"We were doing work fixing up our bedroom before we get married and I had put it down before I went to sleep, so I knew it was there and they were tussling and I got scared, so I hit the man with the screw gun, and he fell back and turned towards me and that's when Michael grabbed his gun from the nightstand and shot the guy in the leg or thigh or something because he screamed and grabbed his leg and ran out the door and next thing I know the cops are banging on our front door."

"Okay, couple of quick questions, if you don't mind. First, what's your name?"

"Denise."

"Good. We're making progress. What's your last name, Denise?"

"Loffredo."

"And Michael? What's his last name?"

"Francesca."

"Like the radio guy?"

"Exactly."

"Okay, and where are you right now?"

"I'm in my kitchen watching the cops dig up my back yard."

"Where is your house?"

"On Liberty Street."

"Well, that's a long street, couple of miles at least. Can you give me a street number?"

"Sorry, 734."

"What's it near?"

"Across the street from the EMS?"

"On the Hamilton side, couple blocks up from Broad?"

"Yeah."

"Which cops are there now?"

"The ones in uniforms?"

"Yeah, Trenton or Hamilton?"

"Both, I think."

"And did they tell you who took Michael?"

"No, I just saw them put handcuffs on him and walk him outside into a car."

"Hamilton or Trenton, any idea?"

"Sorry, sorry, no."

"Don't worry, just trying to figure out where he is. I will be there in 30 minutes. If Michael calls you before I get there, ask him where he is, as in Hamilton or Trenton, okay? I'll try to track him down from here, but it would be helpful if you found out from him first. If he does call, I need you to tell him one thing for me, can you do that?"

"What is it?"

"Tell him not to talk to anyone without me being there, can you remember that? No talking without his lawyer."

"I can do that."

"Good. See you in half an hour."

And from there it was a race, grabbing the least dirty jeans from my laundry basket and a sweatshirt to get to my car, to head south on Route 1 to 129 to Broad, figuring it would be faster than waiting for one of those long 129 lights on Lalor or wherever. I made it in about twenty-eight minutes, which probably challenged some laws of physics in addition to the other kind.

In the meantime I called Hamilton PD and was told they didn't have anyone in custody on the Liberty Street shooting, which was odd, because I was pretty sure it fell into their jurisdiction, Liberty being the municipal border between Hamilton and Trenton. Then I called Trenton and got jerked around until I got voicemail at CIB, where at least I could leave a taped message stating the time and date by which Michael Francesca had invoked his right to counsel.

When I got to the Francesca household, cops were standing outside and seemed to be winding down. I brought attorney ID and asked to see Denise. They brought her outside and we had a chance to get acquainted.

I said, "Feel up to talking?"

She stood five-four, five-five. Hard to tell with her shoulders hunched over. Straight brown hair, a little matted, fair skin, smoking. She said, "I guess. [Exhale.] It's just weird, you know?"

I said, "Not really. Never hit a guy with a screw gun, much less got robbed at gunpoint. You handled yourself pretty well. Ever been in a jam like that before?"

She said, "Nope. Had my purse snatched once. I reacted is all."

I said, "If that's how you handle pressure, I admire you. I have to track down Michael. Anything from him?"

She said, "Nothing. And these guys aren't the most helpful."

I said, "Any idea what they're looking for?"

She said, "They're probably looking for the gun, but they might be looking for pot."

I said, "Is that what the robber was looking for?"

She said, "I guess. [Exhale.] Maybe the money too."

I said, "Well, that's usually interesting to lots of folks. Any idea how much?"

She said, "You'll have to ask Michael. More than twenty for sure."

"Thousand?"

"Yeah."

"Any idea how much pot they might find if they get lucky?"

"Don't know. Ten? Fifteen?"

"Pounds?"

"Uh-huh."

"Have the cops interviewed you yet?"

"Nope."

"Well, let's keep it that way. I'm going to find Michael and arrange his bail. You staying here or do you have someplace to go?"

"I can't stay here. Too scary now. I called my mother. Think I'll go there."

"Need a ride?"

"She's on her way, but thanks."

I finally found her boyfriend in Trenton lockup after driving to Hamilton police headquarters and being told they had no one by the name of Francesca in their custody. Yeah, that's right: I didn't take their word for it. Trenton PD is an island on North Clinton, bad sixties brick and concrete jutting out into the muddy waters of the crack and heroin dealers' version of an urban enterprise zone. You can't park near the building, remember? There's that free lot about a block away, but it's a different game at that hour. By day, not getting run over by high speed traffic on North Clinton defines success for the slow footed. At night, it's not getting shot, right? Nah, not really. Trenton isn't nearly as tough as newspapers and cops make it out to be.

Entering the pillbox, you head right to the sergeant's window and ask for your client. If you're lucky, you'll get a "stand by" from the handbook of terse responses. Five minutes later I got "he's on the third floor." This meant he was in the act of being interrogated in a windowless room with soundproof peg board walls in the middle of CIB.

"I'd like him brought to the second floor for attorney interview please." It wasn't really a request. Still, constitutional rights, like the right to counsel and the right to remain silent, are funny things. You can assert them all you want, but if the guys with guns show no interest in honoring your assertions, you have little to do but plot how you will bring this constitutional contempt to the attention of the court. It's on the order of "Badges? We don't need no stinkin' badges."

About 20 minutes later I'm in a small space, three feet wide, maybe four feet deep, metal chair, plexiglass window and a phone set. The interview room is across the hall from the records window I had been to get the Bellow arrest report. Mike Francesca shambles in, maybe five-ten by 265, barely able to shove himself onto his plastic furniture, picks up the phone and says,

"You my lawyer?"

"Bill Carmody. Fine, thanks, yourself?"

"What?"

"On the order of, nice to meet you. How are they treating you?"

"I got some crackers and a Coke a little while ago."

"Did they stop talking to you to let me see you?"

"Uh, we were about done when the one guy stepped out. Came back in and said you were here."

"Did you give them a statement?"

"What?"

"Did you talk to them?"

"Well, yeah. I mean, I was attacked."

"I understand. Did you sign anything?"

"Not yet."

"*Miranda* form? Anything?"

"I haven't signed a thing."

"That's about right. I'm going to talk to them. You are not allowed to talk to them any more, understood?"

"Can I go home?"

"I'm going to have that conversation with them now, but I understand they found a bunch of pot in your house. They might hold you on that, along with the gun."

"I did have some pot in my house."

"Any idea how much?"

"Honestly?"

"Or you could lie to me. Might not be helpful."

"A little over twenty pounds."

"Twenty pounds? Good work if you can get it. Any cash in the house? Guns?"

"About $40,000. Just the one gun I buried in the back yard and my uncle's shotgun I use for hunting."

"Did you tell them about the cash or the pot?"

"No, they told me they would find whatever I had in the house. I said there's no use in me talking about what's there then, right?"

"Good man. Let me talk to them about your bail and then get hold of your girlfriend to see what she can do to get together with a bondsman."

"Where am I going now?"

"Probably to a cell on this floor. I will see you in court on the first floor in a couple of hours."

We wound up that little chat; I went to the third floor to talk to the detective running the shooting, but not yet murder, investigation. Seems the guy who tried to rob Francesca got himself shot in the thigh during the struggle, and when he ran to his friends' car downstairs, they drove him to a hospital and dropped him in the ER. Kid bled out from a severed femoral artery and died on the cart. That meant the prosecutor's homicide unit would become involved, but cops hadn't made the connection between the shooting and the ER drop off by the time this investigation was taking place. Detective agreed to stop interrogations (pretty sure he had what he wanted by that point, but still) and put this kid in a cell until morning.

I texted Ace, who I swear sits up nights waiting for money calls.

"BC: u up?"

"AA: Yo."

"BC: nu guy."

"AA: Yo."

"BC: Pot, gun, body. Local kid."

"AA: Yo."

"BC: Bail in morning; TMC. Will text info."

AA: Yo."

"BC: Michael Francesca. G/F is Denise Loffredo."

"AA: Yo."

"BC: Plenty of scratch. Family. House."

"AA: Yo."

"BC: Do this for me?"

"AA: Yo."

"BC: OKIOU1."

It was pushing 4:30 when I got out of there, so I didn't have a lot of time before the bail hearing. Drove home to shower and shave and put a suit on, back to Dunkin' Donuts where the coffee cups had my name scrawled on the lids, and then on to Trenton Municipal Court. The courtrooms are one floor down from the detention block, very convenient for moving prisoners to their bail hearing. They started those a little after eight, and indictables went first. I listened patiently to a municipal prosecutor recite the crimes against Francesca: possession, possession with intent, possession with intent in or near school property. No mention of a weapons charge or a homicide or aggravated assault. Then the judge asked about the weight of the pot.

"Third degree, Your Honor. About four pounds. Police also seized about $16,000 in cash."

Bail was set at $75,000 cash or bond. Bail source hearing required. I had to go, texting Ace as I walked to my car.

"BC: 75k. Source hearing. u got this?"

"AA: Yo."

CHAPTER THIRTY-THREE

Sullivan Way: Trenton Psychiatric Hospital; Ann Klein Forensic Center; Central Reception and Assignment Facility.

On the grounds of the Trenton Psychiatric Hospital, two units once stood side by side: the Forensic Unit, long term temporary residence of the criminally insane, and the Readjustment Unit, a Department of Corrections site for inmates too antisocial for even Trenton State Prison, which is saying something for a population two-thirds of whom are convicted murderers and one-third are even more hard-core. FU and RU have been transformed into CRAF, the Central Reception and Adjustment Facility. The word "adjustment" figures prominently in correctional philosophy. Corrections folk want to know what kind of adjustment you will make to life in prison. Recall the scene in *Shawshank Redemption*, where hardened inmates take bets on which of the new blood coming into their institution will break down first and proclaim that he does not belong there. In native parlance, the question is, do you jail well?

On the long frog march from Klein to CRAF, sandwiched between two security guards, a skinny young white man learning the language of institutional life could be excused for developing intestinal distress. And if offered an opportunity to depart the premises by simply walking to a waiting sedan driven by a familiar face, his decision to accept that offer uncritically might be reminiscent of another prison life classic, Midnight Express. Faced with the prospect of indeterminate detention, who amongst us would not pursue an obvious avenue of escape?

"Aaron?"

"Shut the fuck up and get in."

"I need help."

"Give me your hands."

"What?"

"Put your hands out."

"What's that?"

"Cuff key. Now how do we get to Route 29?"

CHAPTER THIRTY-FOUR

Session 12, continued. Carmody, William.

This is where I started to really lose it, because I had my big break and he disappeared. I drove straight from Trenton Municipal back to Dunkin' Donuts, funkin' for the Dunkin,' now pushing 8:45. My West Trenton Dunks was half a mile north of Trenton Psychiatric, so I grabbed a medium with 'Mr. Bill' scrawled on the plastic and headed down Grand Avenue.

When I pulled into the Stuyvesant Avenue parking lot, I saw Patty Voorhees' car already there. When I pushed through the double security doors, she was waiting for me in the lobby.

She said, "He's not here."

I said, "What do you mean, he's not here?"

She said, "He's not here."

I said, "Where is he?"

She said, "According to his chart, he was sent to CRAF."

I said, "I give up: how do you go to CRAF without a judgment of conviction?"

She said, "No idea. Doesn't matter."

I said, "How so?"

She said, "Because I called CRAF. They have no record of him there, and they've had no admissions in the last 24 hours in any case."

I said, "Hey, this is great. We can't even keep a guy in a forensic hospital for the weekend without losing him? This should make the neighbors feel safe."

She said, "I'm still trying to figure out what happened. We interviewed the MSO's on his wing. They didn't see him leave or have any idea where he might have gone."

I said, "How well do you know those MSO's?"

She said, "I don't think they're smart enough to pull this one off, if that's what you mean."

I said, "That's what I mean."

She said, "You should go. If I find anything out, I'll call you."

"Hey, Patty. I recognize this is not your fault, and I appreciate your trying to help. Keep me posted, and let me know if there's anything I can do."

"Okay."

And that was it. Back in my car, back to my office, drank my cup of coffee. Hard to think on short sleep, so I checked my calendar, spoke to Andrew, told him to cover whatever I had that morning, and went home for a nap. Coffee wasn't going to make a difference. I needed to consider my options.

I took off my suit, pulled back the covers, and slumped into bed debating whether to take more Advil. Lying on my back, thinking about my future and my past, I had started to drift off when my phone started vibrating on my night table.

"Hello?"

"Hey, Bill."

"Andrew?"

"Yeah. I just got a call from Judge Black's chambers. Did you know you were scheduled to pick a jury at 1:30 in Beanie Johnson's case?"

"You're shitting me, and if you're not shitting me, I'm shitting myself. I thought we got that adjourned."

"Well, snatch some toilet paper, because you're confirmed for 1:30. I grabbed the file and started copying discovery. I'll have binders ready in an hour. Any idea what you need me to do before this afternoon?"

"How about call the client and make sure he's dressed for jury selection. Long sleeves, tie if he has it. Collared shirt at a minimum. Can you bring the file directly to the court so I can meet you there?"

"Sure."

"Get any empty briefcase from my office with a pad and pen in it."

"Anything else?"

"My evidence book."

"Anything else?"

"That should do it."

"Sounds good. See you there at 1:15." This was my day, and it was not yet noon.

There's a lot that goes into trial preparation as it's depicted in movies and TV, but once you get the hang of it, routine cases can get rung up much more quickly with some spit and sandpaper. Beanie Johnson was a small time drug dealer from Hightstown who found himself framed for the burglary and boosting of the local police chief's 40-inch flat screen. I took the case on a light retainer months ago, because I never thought it would go to trial. None of the proofs made sense, unless you knew, as I did, that the chief's 33-year-old son was a heroin addict. This fact was concealed from much of the public, but the street level cognoscenti were well aware.

We had gone to half a dozen status conferences, each time getting better plea offers from the prosecutor. What started out as a flat 10, which is an extended term for a guy with nine (count 'em, nine) third-degree possession priors, wound its way down to a seven, then a five, then a three, and finally a probation/364. That's where you get placed on probation, but as a condition of your probation, you have to go "smell the cell" for about nine months, in the memorable phrase of one state trooper I interviewed after an off-duty bar fight few years back.

When we rejected the 364 (named because it is one day less than an actual calendar year, the threshold for a state prison sentence), we figured they'd offer a Disorderly Persons offense, fine the kid a hundred bucks, and call it a day. Beanie swore he wouldn't take the DP for something he didn't do, but I knew he was a realist who would not take a chance on a 10-year bid just to prove a point.

You have to understand, I've probably tried, I don't know, 250-300 cases to verdict before a jury. Most of these kids today are lucky to get two to three jury trials in five years. Nobody goes to trial anymore, and those who do tend to be the heavy hitters with nothing left to lose. When the offer for stealing a couple billion dollars from investors is life in prison, going to trial is an obvious choice. If they're offering you the gas chamber, you don't ask for a room with a view. You might as well run for it. Make them shoot you in the back.

So I knew before I got to court what the day would look like. I knew I could handle this aspect without heavy lifting. The judge would call the case, and I would note a couple of preliminary concerns I had about how evidence would be handled. Then we'd have some review of questions for jury selection. Jurors would be brought in and called up at random. All of this would kill the afternoon and maybe run into the following day. I had time to hone my preparation.

By one o'clock I was setting up at counsel table in Judge Black's courtroom, going through the loose-leaf notebooks Andrew had prepared for the judge and me. We had copies of the indictment and other pleadings. We had the State's discovery with numbers on the lower right hand corner of each page. We had a grand jury transcript. We had some pictures I had taken of the front and side of the chief's house. Couple of yellow legal pads. Exhibit stickers, pens, markers for the chart pack in case I had to ask a witness to draw a diagram, the basic stuff for a show and tell exhibition.

Because that's all a trial is: we go in front of twelve strangers and say, 'here's what happened, do you think my guy did it?' Did they give you this transcript?

BAILIFF: All rise!

THE COURT: Be seated ladies and gentlemen. All right, I'm calling for trial the matter of State v. Beanie Johnson, Indictment Number 11-09-1342. Appearances of counsel.

MR. STEPHENS: Good afternoon, Your Honor, Assistant Prosecutor Jim Stephens for the State.

MR. CARMODY: Good afternoon. Bill Carmody, Carmody and Scott, on behalf of defendant, who is seated to my left.

THE COURT: Good afternoon, counsel. I have in front of me a copy of the indictment, which appears to charge burglary in the third degree. Any motions or requests with respect to the form of the indictment?

MR. STEPHENS: No, Your Honor.

MR. CARMODY: Not for the defense, Your Honor.

THE COURT: Preliminary matters. Any motions unresolved?

MR. CARMODY: Your Honor, my client has a few priors, and ordinarily I would want them sanitized. But in this case, he has no convictions for burglary, and if he elects to testify, I would prefer the jury know he's a small time drug dealer and not a burglar.

THE COURT: Understood. Is there a *Sands* argument?

MR. CARMODY: I would ask the court to consider that defendant is 42 years old, and although he has two convictions in the last ten years, he also has a couple of convictions that date to his teens. They're over twenty years old and I would argue they should not be permitted to bear on his credibility should he elect to testify.

THE COURT: Mr. Stephens?

MR. STEPHENS: Your Honor, Mr. Johnson actually has nine convictions for indictable charges, and that does not cover the many arrests and dispositions he has in municipal court. The whole point of admitting evidence of prior convictions is to let the jury know that a witness may have demonstrated some level of contempt for the rules of society in the past when they are weighing his ability to tell the truth under oath. I think they should all come in if only to demonstrate a consistent disregard of those rules and how that might impact on his testimony.

MR. CARMODY: Your Honor, I object to the use of impact as a verb.

THE COURT: Mr. Carmody, are we to be graced with your celebrated wit today, or do you think you might spare me, just for the sake of brevity?

MR. CARMODY: Sorry, Your Honor. Permit me to observe that counsel's argument bolsters my application under Sands. He fully intends to argue that because my client has a bunch of convictions, he must be guilty of this offense, because he's a logical person to convict. I should tell Your Honor that part of our defense in this case is that police lacked a credible suspect, and because they knew Mr. Johnson was in the area at the time of the burglary, he was a good candidate to pin this charge on. I'd like to give him an opportunity to deny the allegations without being tarred and feathered by his prior record that simply reflects a long history of drug abuse and small sales to support his habit. There's a reason he has nine priors and only a little more than eight years of total time in prison. The cases were all small potatoes and he only got one state prison bid out of the lot of them.

THE COURT: All right, counsel. Thank you. Under *State v. Sands and Sheldrick*, 76 N.J. 127 (1978), the test for admissibility of prior convictions of a defendant rests in the sound discretion of the court. On the one hand, there is a presumption of admissibility consistent with N.J.S. 2A:81-12. On the other hand, I am entitled to undertake an analysis under Evidence Rule 403 as to whether the prejudice to the defendant substantially outweighs the probative value of the evidence to be introduced, namely defendant's prior convictions.

I should note the federal evidence standard is that any conviction older than ten years is presumed to be inadmissible, and understandably so, because it is hard to judge a man by something he did more than a decade in his past. That presumption can be overcome if the prior conviction goes to the heart of what is at stake, namely the credibility of a defendant who is testifying under oath. If the conviction is for, say, perjury, that certainly would have an impact—okay Mr. Carmody?—on how a jury might see his credibility.

But here, where the convictions are all for possession of CDS, and I see one theft in the fourth degree and receiving stolen property, again, consistent with a drug dealer and user in terms of what might be revealed by a more searching analysis of defendant's record. Under the circumstances, I am going to grant the relief in part and deny it in part. I will permit reference to the theft and receiving convictions despite their age, as they go to a defendant's honesty, not as a basis for conviction, but rather as a basis for evaluating his testimony for truthfulness should he elect to testify.

I will also admit the possession convictions for the past decade. I will not allow reference to those convictions for drug offenses that are more than 10 years old, which I believe will permit the prosecutor to hold up at least five separate judgments of conviction for emphasis. If I were to permit wholesale use of defendant's priors, I fear a jury would be unable to fairly weigh his testimony, perhaps convicting him merely for having a lengthy record. And that's not the point here, is it gentlemen?

All right, what's next? Jury selection. Peremptory challenges 10 and 10?

MR. STEPHENS: I believe so, Your Honor.

MR. CARMODY: Actually, Your Honor, burglary is one of the enumerated common law crimes. 20 and 12.

THE COURT: What's the rule?

MR. CARMODY: 1:8-3, Your Honor.

THE COURT: Give me a second. I stand corrected. Peremptory challenges shall be 20 for the defense and 12 for the State. Agree, Mr. Stephens?

MR. STEPHENS: Yes, Your Honor.

THE COURT: Two alternates sufficient for this length of trial?

MR. STEPHENS: Yes, Your Honor.

THE COURT: Any stipulations?

MR. STEPHENS: I haven't discussed any with counsel, Your Honor, but if I could get a stipulation with respect to chain of custody, I could take one or two witnesses off my list.

THE COURT: How about that, Mr. Carmody?

MR. CARMODY: Sorry, Your Honor, no can do. Cops claim they found my client with a flat screen TV, which he denies. They'll have to bring someone in.

THE COURT: There's your answer, Mr. Stephens. How long is your witness list.

MR. STEPHENS: Well, if I have to lug a TV in here, it'll be four or five, Your Honor.

THE COURT: Mr. Carmody?

MR. CARMODY: I have mostly the same names on my list, Judge. Add the defendant and the guy he was arrested with and I think I have eight names total.

THE COURT: The guy he was arrested with? I only have one name on my indictment. Did a co-defendant plead?

MR. CARMODY: No, Your Honor, long story, but one guy got let go and one guy got charged. Mr. Johnson was on the second list.

THE COURT: Any statements by defendant? *Miranda* hearing?

MR. STEPHENS: No, Your Honor. He denied the offense.

MR. CARMODY: While we're on that subject Your Honor, I'd like a representation from the State as to any oral statements made by defendant not otherwise recorded in any report.

THE COURT: What's the nature of that request again?

MR. CARMODY: Under 3:13-3, discovery shall include any oral statements or admissions against penal interest known to the prosecution but otherwise unrecorded. So, when they interview witnesses in preparation for trial, cops will sometimes tell them, 'By the way, he told me he did it when I was booking him,' or some such, and we hear that for the first time in open court, because it's not in any report. I'm entitled to that information now if it's in the prosecutor's possession or knowledge.

THE COURT: Mr. Stephens?

MR. STEPHENS: I don't have any admissions, Your Honor.

MR. CARMODY: Any statements at all, admission or otherwise?

MR. STEPHENS: None, Your Honor.

THE COURT: Witness lists?

MR. STEPHENS: May I approach, Your Honor?

THE COURT: You may. Mr. Carmody, why don't you hand yours up as well. Let's see. Hightstown police. Custodian of records. Defendant. Who's Cleon Green?

MR. CARMODY: The man who got away, Your Honor.

THE COURT: Oh, okay. I see. Shall we go over the jury questionnaire?

And it went on like that for another 20 minutes until we broke to let the jury panel file in. Everyone was fine, but something started bothering me. See, I don't process information at the same rate as smarter people. I mean, I'm quick with some stuff, but other stuff, it takes a while to roll around in my head and rattle a few synapses. Hits me later.

When we were done with jury selection for the day, still no final 14, I sat with Andrew to go over some evidence issues I thought he might have to research over night. The courtroom was virtually empty, doors open, client gone, a deputy clerk cleaning up some paperwork. Then I saw McCloud coming through the back door.

"Billy, gotta talk."

"What's up Sean?"

"Hey Andrew."

"Hey Sean."

McCloud said, "Are you representing that Francesca kid?"

I said, "Is that yours?"

"No, it's on Lew's watch." That wasn't good. Lew Stein was head of homicide. Had to be careful here.

I said, "I talked to the kid. Having trouble figuring out how I'm going to get paid."

McCloud said, "That's what I said to Lew. Far as I'm concerned, they should pin a medal on your guy. Kid he shot was a scumbag."

I said, "Hard to have sympathy for armed intruders."

McCloud said, "Yeah, with three open files and four priors. Your kid saved us a lot of time and effort."

"Is that where we are? Summary execution to assist case management?"

"C'mon. Kidding. Lighten up, man. I'm trying to do you a favor."

"Sorry, Sean. I get on a horse sometimes."

"No problem. Anyway, your kid had some cash in the house."

"So I heard."

"I was going to offer to split it with you so you could have a retainer."

"I can appreciate generosity in almost any form. What's the catch?"

"No catch. Just curious is all."

"About what?"

"How much cash does your guy claim he had in the house?"

"Do you really want to know? They always have more than the cops report, and it's never bothered you."

"Yeah, well this one's bothering me. What's your guy say?"

I said, "Ready? Forty grand. No reason to lie about it. I understand cops are coming in at a much lower number."

Sean said, "Yeah, sixteen grand, right?"

I said, "That's the number my kid heard."

Sean said, "'Cause that's the number they put in their report. Funny thing happened on the way to the evidence room. They had to make out property reports for the different places they found the cash: the big stash in the basement, the jar next to the bed, the cookie tin in the kitchen, wherever. Each got its own report, right?"

"Okay."

"Turns out there were five reports filed. Guess how much money the five reports totaled?"

"I'm guessing less than forty grand."

"No surprise there. But less than sixteen grand? Try a little under twelve five."

"Hold it. So they didn't bother to square their evidence receipts with the invest?"

"You got it."

"What do you do now?"

"I come see you and ask if your guy will talk to me. Which is what I'm doing here."

CHAPTER THIRTY-FIVE

Pennsylvania Routes 32, 611, and 33, northbound.

"A fuck nigga, that's that shit I don't like
A snitch nigga, that's that shit I don't like
A bitch nigga, that's that shit I don't like
Sneak disser, that's that shit I don't like
Don't like, like, don't like, like
A snitch nigga, that's that shit I don't like."

-Chief Keef and friends.

Interstate highways received their route designations largely consistent with the existing grid. Odd numbers run north and south, even east and west. Interstate Five runs the length of the west coast; I-95 the east. In between, you'll encounter I-15; I-25, the balance of the two-digit fives, and the occasional wedge route installed at the insistence of local business folk who pressure their congressman to pressure the House Transportation Committee to fund highway construction that will bolster local economies. The further east you go, the more Congressional pressure you'll see in terms of roads running through areas that might not have justified Interstate Route designation.

The strangest designation was I-195 as an offshoot of I-95 in central New Jersey. The road is nothing more than a commuter strip from Trenton to the Jersey Shore, funded at the insistence of Congressman Jim Howard, long time chairman of the House Surface

Transportation Subcommittee. There's a sign on the highway in his memory. For irony, consider there used to be a commuter rail line that ran from Trenton to Manasquan in Monmouth County, where the line hooked up with the Jersey Shore rail line. That roadbed was removed thirty years ago, around the time they funded the interstate extension. Smart stuff that.

Of the east-west routes, I-90 was supposed to run the furthest north, I-10 the southern tier. I-10 is practically in the Gulf of Mexico, so it remains the bottom of the grid. I-94 now courses further north than I-90, through such heavily trafficked areas as Eau Claire, Wisconsin and Bismarck, North Dakota. If you pay close attention to route information, you can find ones lacking tolls for portions of their length, but as states become more cash starved, these roads, legislatively enacted to be toll free, become toll magnets, latching on to spare change in transient pockets to help pay for services governors want desperately to cut.

Four score and seven years ago this nation adopted a route designation system featuring federal shields for even numbered routes running east to west, with the lowest numbers in the east, starting with the fabled Route 1, from Fort Kent, Maine to Key West, Florida.

A hundred years ago some ambitious guys got the government to dedicate the "Lincoln Highway," first of several federal highways to run the width of the continent. A young man told to go west, but by all means stay off the grid, might ask himself, is there a search query for such a route? That's the ticket, or at least the way without one.

To avoid paying tolls from New Jersey to Pennsylvania, avoid toll bridges. This translates into avoiding major highways, including most Interstates and state-named turnpikes. Finding less traveled routes means nothing more than understanding America's highway system from its earliest design. To get across Route 1 from Trenton to Pennsylvania, pay a toll. From Ewing to Pennsylvania, five miles north of Route 1, take I-95. No toll. Go figure.

"Where are we going?"

"Home."

"How?"

"Slowest route possible. We gotta plan and think and make sure we live to tell."

"I thought they were gonna kill me."

"Who?"

"Cops. Crazies. Zombies. Nurses with needles. You name it."

"Well, you made it out."

"Were you ever gonna tell me what this was all about? This is way deeper than dropping off some pot or whatever was in that gym bag."

"Hey, let's get across PA and talk on the other side, okay? Right now, I need you to find a way to get to I-80 until just before the bridge to Youngstown."

CHAPTER THIRTY-SIX

Session 13. Carmody, William

I recognize some stupid trial on burglary of a TV set wouldn't seem to figure on my, um, behavior issues, given the allegations. But you have to understand how it fits into the larger picture. For me, it was a fulcrum, a window, a tumbler rolling into place with some clicks and clacks. Did they give you the transcript? If not, I have an extra copy.

We finished jury selection the next morning and launched into openings, and I started to get the germ of an idea.

> THE COURT: Ladies and gentlemen, the trial you are about to hear consists of five essential parts. First, the lawyers will give their opening statements. The prosecutor will go first, outlining what he expects to prove in support of the indictment I read to you earlier. Then, and only if he chooses, defense counsel may give an opening statement. He doesn't have to, because he is under no obligation to prove anything.
>
> After opening statements, the State will call witnesses from the list I read to you. At the conclusion of the State's case, the defense may call witnesses, but the defendant is presumed innocent, so he is under no

legal obligation to call any witnesses, or indeed produce any evidence whatsoever.

After all the evidence is received, the lawyers will give their closing arguments. In this case, the order of presentation is reversed, and the defendant's lawyer will go first. During closings, the lawyers will argue the merits of their respective positions and presentations in an effort to persuade you to find what they will argue is the proper verdict.

When the lawyers finish, I will give you the legal principles upon which to base your findings of fact. This legal charge will help you to understand the law and how it fits together with the facts as you find them.

The final part is the most important, because it is exclusively yours. The deliberations of a jury are central to the proper operation of our system of justice. You have taken an oath to well and truly try this case, and we expect you will do so. Upon conclusion of those deliberations, it is our sincere hope you will have arrived at a unanimous verdict as to the guilt or innocence of the defendant on trial.

I will now turn to Mr. Stephens to delver the opening statement for the State.

MR. STEPHENS: Thank you, Your Honor. May it please the Court, counsel, ladies and gentlemen of the jury: good morning. My name is Jim Stephens, and I'm an assistant prosecutor with the Mercer County Prosecutor's Office. With me at counsel table is Michele Barone, our lead investigator. She handles marshaling of evidence and presentation of witnesses, so I wanted to give you a heads up if you see her walking in and out of the courtroom. It's not because she's rude, but she is getting the next witness lined up to keep the trains moving on time.

Beanie Johnson is a burglar and a thief. I'm not calling him names, just stating a fact. On March 17th, 2010, which of course was St. Patrick's Day, he broke into Robert Armstrong's home in Hightstown, stole several personal items, and even found time to unbolt a 40-inch flat screen TV from the wall of Mr. Armstrong's den and haul it off. I'd say that was his first mistake, but arguably his first mistake was deciding to break into a man's house in broad daylight. Or to break into any man's house for that matter.

In any case, police were called to the scene several hours later, when Mr. Armstrong returned to find his house in disarray. A patrolman studied the outside of the house for signs of forced entry and found pry marks on a window alongside the...on a side yard that faces a garage, basically out of sight to anyone not looking directly into that narrow area.

A detective going over the inside of the house found some dirty footprints under the window, and although they weren't specific enough to get an impression, they were able to be measured and appeared to fit someone with feet at least size 10, perhaps as long as men's size 12. No usable fingerprints were found, although the surfaces around the window were dusted, as were the areas near where the TV was removed and certain items were taken from the bedroom.

Police interviewed neighbors across the street and on either side to see if anyone had noticed a suspicious person in the area on the 17th. You'll hear from one such person, a Mrs. Coffee, who remembers two black men riding bikes in the area sometime in the late afternoon of the 17th. None of the other neighbors had anything unusual to report.

So, police had very little to go on, but they kept their ears open. They went to their informants in the street and asked if anyone had any information about the possible burglars. Couple days later, they caught a break when one informant...

MR. CARMODY: Objection, Your Honor.

THE COURT: What's the objection?

MR. STEPHENS: It's okay judge, I understand Mr. Carmody's concern. I was not going to relate hearsay from an informant. I was simply going to say the officer received information from an informant, and as a result of that conversation, he went to defendant's apartment.

MR. CARMODY: Well, the damage is done, Your Honor. Mr. Stephens has now introduced hearsay from an informant who I will never have an opportunity to cross-examine, and indeed, I haven't even heard from the officer yet.

THE COURT: Ladies and gentlemen, the argument counsel are having stems from an evidence issue not yet upon us. I should remind you that what the lawyers say during their openings, and indeed their closings, is not evidence of any type. The evidence will come from the witness stand. Mr. Carmody is expressing concern about how evidence might be received during the trial, and Mr. Stephens is trying to anticipate that objection in the way he has couched his recitation. I can't tell if this will be a problem or not at this point, so I will merely caution you that what the lawyers say is not evidence. Please proceed, Mr. Stephens.

MR. STEPHENS: Thank you, Your Honor. As I was saying, police obtained some information from an informant, and without going into what was said, one thing led to another, and police went to Mr. Johnson's apartment. They knocked on the door, which he opened, and let them in. Inside, they saw a bike against the hallway wall, some muddy Timberland work boots, which turned out to be size 11, and in the room beyond, they saw a flat screen TV. It wasn't hooked up, just leaning against a couch in the living area. It was a Sony, and yes, it was a 40-inch LED. There was another man in the apartment, but he has not been charged in this case. We will present the testimony of the victim, the police officers' investigation, and show you the Sony television taken from the defendant's apartment. Mr. Armstrong will identify that TV as his, and then we will ask you to find Mr. Johnson guilty as charged. Thanks for your time.

THE COURT: Thank you, Mr. Stephens. Mr. Carmody, do you choose to open?

MR. CARMODY: I do, Your Honor, thank you. And good morning, ladies and gentlemen. Thanks for being so patient. I recognize I'm going to have to fight for your attention after listening to preliminary instructions followed by the prosecutor's opening, and now asking you to listen for a few more minutes. But I will try to keep it short. I'm mindful of the words of my dentist, who when he leans me back in his chair just before he jams with me a needle full of Novocain, posts a hand written sign so that when I look at the ceiling I read, "It could be worse. You could be on jury duty."

Okay, bad joke, sorry. Here's another one: Beanie Johnson is on trial for burglary. And while Mr. Stephens wove a very smooth tapestry for you these last few minutes, I can assure you he came no closer than setting up an argument for circumstantial evidence that Beanie cannot be excluded from the universe of people who might have taken Chief Armstrong's TV set.

Oh, right, I called him Chief Armstrong. I listened carefully to Mr. Stephens's opening, and I don't recall him mentioning that salient fact: the "victim" of this burglary is the recently retired chief of Hightstown police. I'm not saying he got special attention, but I think I'm safe in saying that this is the only burglary in the history of Mercer County law enforcement that rated an evidence technician looking for fingerprints around various less-than-porous spots in the chief's living room.

Nowadays you're lucky you can get a cop to respond to a burglary the same day, manpower is so short. They had detectives hitting the streets for informants and intelligence on what happened. This was Priority One for these guys from the minute it got called in, whereas I suspect you and I would get a neat report to send to our insurance company, and that would be that.

So, who would have the nerve to break into the chief's house in broad daylight on St. Patrick's Day to steal some stuff, including his Sony flat screen? And didn't leave any fingerprints?

I wonder if it might have been someone who knew the chief would be out all day. If it was someone who knew what the chief had in the way of valuables. If it was someone who knew how to take the TV off the wall without damaging the wall, at least not according to the photo I saw. Someone who was familiar to neighbors and would not have stood out as not belonging in the neighborhood.

His son, perhaps? Bobby Armstrong, aged 36, heroin addict, shoplifter, stealer of folks' money to pay for his habit. What about him? Did we check his alibi? I don't like to give this much away in my opening in a typical case, but this time, I want you thinking about him from the first witness the State calls to the last word the court utters before the judge tells you to commence your deliberations, because this guy's fingerprints are all over the house, literally, and they weren't included in any report. I intend to call young Mr. Armstrong to the stand and ask him where he spent St. Patrick's Day, and I will let you be the judges of the credibility of his answer.

I'm not going to bore you with a lot of talk about the presumption of innocence, because my client doesn't have to prove anything. And let's face it: nowadays

> defendants are presumed guilty. I mean, the grand jury indicted him, he must have done something wrong, right? I'm not going to tell you the grand jury will indict anyone the prosecutor asks them to, including a ham sandwich, if the proofs look ordinary and there's no reason not to. We're not going to talk about that, because it's not necessary in this case. Beanie didn't do it. He was just one of the usual suspects.
>
> Remember where that phrase first got used? Last scene of Casablanca. Rick shoots the Nazi colonel as his former girlfriend and her husband 'get on that plane.' Rick, played masterfully by Humphrey Bogart, then turns to Claude Rains, superbly cast as the French police captain, and gives him the chance to arrest him for shooting the colonel. The captain looks at Rick, then at his arriving men, pauses, and says: "The colonel has been shot. Round up the usual suspects."
>
> And now you know how Beanie got fitted up for this case. I'll tell you more when we are done here. Until then, stay tuned. This should be entertaining. Thanks for taking a couple of days out of your lives.
>
> THE COURT: Thank you, Mr. Carmody. I think we should take our morning recess at this time.

And off we went. It wasn't all cut and dried, but there were a few exchanges that would probably interest you, and I'll try to explain what was going through my mind. As I'm sitting there reviewing police reports in anticipation of these cops getting called in, I'm thinking about the money in young Mr. Francesca's case. It was one thing for the cops to give these kids a haircut by reporting half of what they actually confiscated. But it was quite another to put one figure in your report, then have the receipts for evidence fall short of that number by several thousand dollars. Was it possible one cop lied to another about what he counted? Were they getting greedy and not telling each other what the final split was? Didn't they think someone would check the money in evidence?

And that might have been my lightening bolt moment. It occurred to me that in terms of evidence retention, no one was minding the store. Look, I get that you're a shrink, so this is inside baseball, but I have to make you understand how this stuff works, or at least used to work. Otherwise, you'll write me off as another paranoid with delusions or some crap. Please. I'm begging you to listen to me. Remind me to explain chain of custody and stipulations.

But first, Stephens calls the patrolman who responded to the burglary call to start his presentation, and I figured I had caught a break. He wouldn't have prepped the guy for a cross that went to the heart of my theory. He'd be all about assessing the crime scene. Signs of forced entry. Preserving the integrity of the evidence and all that happy horse manure. Did you read that? Because that was way before I lost my shit.

THE COURT: Mr. Stephens, call your first witness.

MR. STEPHENS: State calls Patrolman Harry Headley, Your Honor.

(Witness sworn.)

DIRECT EXAMINATION BY MR. STEPHENS:

Q. Sir, by whom are you employed?

A. Hightstown Police Department.

Q. In what capacity?

A. Police officer.

Q. And for how long have you worked there?

A. It'll be six years in March.

Q. And what are your duties currently?

A. I was recently assigned to the detective bureau.

Q. And before that?

A. I was a patrolman.

Q. Directing your attention to March 17, 2010, were you working on that date?

A. I was. Day shift.

Q. 8-4?

A. That would have been our normal assignment, but it was St. Patrick's Day, so there's an understanding we will be working at least two hours of overtime because of the parade and all.

Q. And by 'all' you mean the goings on associated with a kind of holiday where people might have something to drink along the way?

A. Exactly.

Q. Were you assigned to respond to the scene of a burglary in the late afternoon hours on that date?

MR. CARMODY: Objection Your Honor, assumes a fact not in evidence.

THE COURT: What fact would that be?

MR. CARMODY: A burglary. This was an inside job and calling it a burglary is like calling employee theft shoplifting.

THE COURT: I'll sustain the objection. Mr. Stephens can we re-phrase the question?

MR. STEPHENS: Yes, Your Honor.

Q. Mr. Headley, were you assigned to respond to the scene of an *alleged* burglary that afternoon?

A. Yes.

Q. Where did you go?

A. 108 Park Way in the Borough.

Q. Where is that?

A. It's about half a block off Stockton Street, which is County Route 571, the main road through town.

Q. And who lives at that address?

A. Robert Armstrong.

Q. Did you speak with Mr. Armstrong upon your arrival?

A. Yeah, the chief was standing outside waiting for us, so we talked to him right away.

Q. And what did you discuss?

MR. CARMODY: Objection, hearsay.

THE COURT: Sustained.

MR. STEPHENS: Sorry, Your Honor. Did you talk to Mr. Armstrong?

A. Yes.

Q. As a result of that conversation, what if anything did you do?

A. Well, first we walked around the house to see if we could locate a point of forced entry. Then we went inside and stepped through the areas where things had apparently been taken to see if there was any obvious evidence inside as well.

Q. Let's start with the outside: did you find any evidence suggesting forced entry on the exterior of the house?

A. There were what looked like pry marks on the bottom of a window sill along side the house, on the side that faces a hedge, as opposed to the garage side.

Q. Did you take any pictures of those marks?

A. I did not, personally, no. We had an evidence technician respond to the scene and directed him to take some pictures of certain areas, including the window on the side of the house.

MR. STEPHENS: Your Honor, I'd like some photos marked for identification.

THE COURT: How many, counsel?

MR. STEPHENS: Well, let's see, looks like eight in total, Your Honor.

THE COURT: Okay, we will mark these S-1 through S-8. Please show them to counsel.

MR. STEPHENS: Yes, Your Honor.

THE COURT: Mr. Carmody? Any objection?

MR. CARMODY: May I *voir dire*, Your Honor?

THE COURT: Certainly.

Okay, look, I'm not showing off. I just want you to understand this inside baseball stuff, because it tells you something about how our minds work. I mean all trial lawyers. We are always looking for an edge in court, and it doesn't matter if we are scoring points, as long as we think we are, or at least getting information before we are supposed to or rattling the cage of the other side. *Voir dire* is old French, meaning to speak the truth. There are variations of the phrase throughout criminal practice. "Verdict" is the same thing, only it's two Latin words strung together. *Veritas dicto*—to speak the truth.

In modern parlance it's about asking a juror or a witness to spill in an effort to uncover some stuff. So, *voir dire* just means getting to ask some preliminary questions to satisfy yourself before passing on a particular procedure. In this case, it's admission of evidence. You can ask a few questions as to the reliability or foundation of the exhibit and then say you object or do not object. It's a kind of early shot at cross-examination, because once the evidence is in, you can't back it out. The same phrase is used in jury selection: once you say the juror is acceptable, you can't challenge for cause. You either waste a peremptory challenge or you live with that juror. That's why they let you ask a few questions before you have to pass, one way or the other.

What I'm doing here in this dinky trial is get some stuff out about how the pictures were taken and why they were taken without giving the witness a chance to consult with the photographer. Prosecutors usually fail to anticipate where we are going with most of our cross. They tend to concentrate on the big stuff, like identification or recovery of evidence. Here's how you do it.

> *Voir dire* examination by Mr. Carmody:
>
> Q. Now Detective Headley, I just want to be sure I understand the sequence of events relative to these pictures, okay?
>
> A. If you say so.
>
> Q. You scoped out the exterior of the house first, is that right?
>
> A. Correct.
>
> Q. Then you went inside, also true?
>
> A. Correct.

Q. Okay, when did the photographer arrive?

A. I would say about twenty minutes after we did.

Q. Was the procedure that you walked to various spots and asked the photographer to take pictures of those areas you considered important?

A. That's fair.

Q. But you did not take the pictures?

A. I did not.

Q. And this was done digitally, I assume? No film? No negatives?

A. I'm not sure what you mean.

Q. God, I'm old. Did you ever review the photos that were taken by your technician to see if they matched up what you personally observed at the scene?

A. At some point I did. I don't recall when that was.

Q. Well, did you look at the pictures on the view finder at the back of his camera while you were at the house?

A. I don't think so.

Q. And at some point he downloaded his images to a computer with a program, fair enough?

A. I suppose. I'm not a photographer.

Q. So, as a non-photographer, you would have no idea whether he edited these photos in any way, using any of the many editing programs available for that purpose?

A. No way of knowing that.

MR. CARMODY: That's all I have, Your Honor. I would ask that the photos Mr. Stephens has offered and any others he plans to introduce not be admitted until the photographer has verified their authenticity and absence of editing.

THE COURT: Mr. Stephens?

MR. STEPHENS: That's fine, Your Honor. I just don't want to have to recall this witness after the technician testifies, so if he can identify them now, that would save a step.

MR. CARMODY: I have no objection to that, Your Honor.

The point of this exercise is that once upon a time, proof beyond a reasonable doubt meant you had to jump through every hoop as a prosecutor. You couldn't just ask someone who didn't actually take the pictures to identify them and then admit them into evidence. And until they're in evidence, you can't show them to the jury. So if they are a big part of your show-and-tell, bring the technician into court and we will move on.

The other approach is to ask your adversary for a stipulation. That's lawyer-talk for an agreement that the evidence is an accurate depiction of what was recorded at the scene. Some things you can stipulate to; a lot of others you can't. You can agree that New Year's

Day, 2012, fell on a Sunday. Stipulating that a lab report claiming your client's DNA was found at the scene of the crime, probably not a good idea. You can't make it easy on these bastards, because your client is already presumed guilty. But you also don't want to make the trial look like an imposition visited on jurors by the defendant.

I knew Jim Stephens was going to ask for some stipulations to move this trial along, but something was bothering me about the flat screen, and it wasn't' necessarily bothering me in this trial. My brain isn't that quick all the time. I mean, I get distracted, and I might have some stuff on my mind that we ought to get to, and I hope we will have time to, but this was the backdrop I wanted you to appreciate when the other thing happened the next day.

As it turned out, Judge Black was the emergent duty judge on this particular court day, which made absolutely no sense at all. This meant that any time a cop needed a search warrant signed, or someone got brought in on an unscheduled arrest in the building, or maybe even a photographer for a local paper wanted permission to shoot court room scenes that day, this was the judge you had to see. Why a judge sitting on a trial caught that duty, I couldn't tell you, but we got the afternoon off, which was lucky for me. I still had to take my best shot at Chief Armstrong, and the delay gave me some prep time. After all of our sparring and circling, the chief came up later on the second day of trial.

CHAPTER THIRTY-SEVEN

U.S. Route 41, north, Winnetka and Wisconsin

About four miles east of the Ohio border in western Pennsylvania, Interstate 80 offers a well worn exit onto I-376 south. About one mile south on 376 comes the exit for West Middlesex, in Mercer County, no relation, except the likelihood it too was named after the Revolutionary War general who died in the Battle of Princeton. Travel west on East Main, cruise through a calm country town of former iron workers and their kin, until Route 318 passes below the Oak Tree Country Club and above the West Middlesex Airport, and straight across the state line into Ohio. No toll, no camera, no notice, no reason for any.

Picking up U.S. 6 west of Cleveland gives a driver the opportunity to appreciate the scenic beauty of Lake Erie, without sentiment or surveillance, until the road bends south after Sandusky, right through the border into Indiana. From Indiana the roads get easier to navigate, except looping around Chicago, where it seems every ward heeler has a toll bridge to boost local revenue. Still, with an abundance of personal caution, a driver can easily make his way into Illinois without an analyst figuring out his whereabouts in under ten minutes. U.S. 41 marks a good northbound route if one is careful not to get trapped on the Interstate ramps for I-94 until after entering Wisconsin. In Wisconsin, toll roads do not exist.

"How long 'til we get to Madison?"

"Couple of hours. But we're not going to Madison."

"Where we going?"

"Gotta go to Dapper Dan's first."

"How long 'til we get there?"

"Couple hours."

"What are we doing when we get there?"

"I gotta settle up for our trip. Way I figure, he owes us some coin."

"What way do you figure?"

"His boys took our guns. I had to post bail, buy a lawyer, and still have to go back there. I'm actually looking at jail time for having a perfectly legal gun in New Jersey."

"How much time?"

"Like ten years."

"Huh."

"And you had to take a vacation in that hospital."

"Yep. Think you could drop me in Madison on your way to the Dells?"

"I suppose. You don't want to come along?"

"Had enough vacation time, to be honest. Could use some sleep and a shower."

"Okay. Understood. I'm sure it'll be fine."

"Why wouldn't it be fine?"

"He asked me to bring you along."

"Tell him I said thanks for the offer."

"I'll tell him you got out of the car."

CHAPTER THIRTY-EIGHT

Session 13, continued. Carmody, William.

MR. STEPHENS: Your Honor, we'd like to call a witness out of turn. Sergeant Schultz has a commitment this afternoon and he shouldn't be long.

THE COURT: Very well. Any objection?

MR. CARMODY: No, Your Honor.

THE COURT: Bring in the jury please.

(WILLIAM SCHULTZ sworn)

Direct examination by Mr. Stephens:

Q. Sir, by whom are you employed?

A. Hightstown Police Department.

Q. And how long have you been so employed?

A. This March will mark my eighteenth year.

Q. And what is your current assignment in the department?

A. I run the evidence room. I'm also the armorer and the firearms field training officer.

Q. Now, directing your attention to March 17th, 2010, were you on duty that day?

A. If I recall, that was a weekday, in which case the answer would be yes.

Q. If I represented to you that March 17th, 2010 was a Wednesday, would that jibe with your recollection?

A. As I said, if it was a weekday, I was working Monday through Friday, 8AM to 4:30PM throughout the year.

Q. And during the day, what were your duties?

A. Mostly desk work. Firearms applications, training reports. Scheduling officers for semi-annual instruction. And of course, receipt and retention of evidence.

Q. Where is the evidence room in Hightstown?

A. We have a locker near the chief's office. There's a log book maintained in a desk under lock and key adjacent to the locker.

Q. How about oversized items? What do you do in those instances?

A. Well, with cars, we typically put them in the police parking lot until we are through dusting them for prints or taking inventory or what not. We make a decision as to whether they will be subject to forfeiture and if the car needs to be retained for evidence purposes. If not, we might move the car to the county lot, which is secure.

Q. How about items other than cars too big for the locker?

A. Like a TV?

Q. Like a TV.

A. We don't get a lot of televisions, so this one was unusual in that respect. I put it in a separate closet in what used to be the traffic captain's office. That also has a lock on it, and the key is kept in the chief's secretary's desk.

MR. STEPHENS: Okay, if you'll bear with me here, I'm having a flat screen TV rolled up here on a dolly for your inspection. Your Honor, I recognize this is being shown to the jury before being moved into evidence, but I will represent to the court I will link it up through the succeeding witnesses. Could we mark it S-9 for identification?

MR. CARMODY: No objection, Your Honor.

THE COURT: S-9.

Q. Sergeant Schultz, you can come off the witness stand if you need to, but my question is going to be whether you've seen this television before.

A. I have.

Q. When was the last time you saw it?

A. Well, I brought it with me this morning.

Q. How?

A. I unlocked the closet, used this dolly to wheel it to a police van, drove here from Hightstown, pulled up out back, unloaded it and the dolly and brought it up the back elevator to this courtroom.

Q. How do you know this is the same television?

A. Well, it has my evidence tag taped to the base right here, this red piece of reinforced paper.

Q. And what does that say?

A. It bears my initials and the date 3/19/10, along with the case number and Detective Headley's name as the person received from.

Q. And is this television in substantially the same condition now as it was when you received it a little less than three years ago?

A. It is.

MR. STEPHENS: Your Honor, subject to its being identified by Mr. Armstrong and Detective Headley, I move S-9 into evidence.

THE COURT: Mr. Carmody?

MR. CARMODY: May I *voir dire*, Your Honor?

THE COURT: You may.

(*Voir dire* examination by Mr. Carmody):

Q. Sergeant Schultz, good morning.

A. Good morning.

Q. I want to make sure I understand your testimony correctly about the identification of the set. I noticed you made no reference to the serial number on the TV, is that right?

A. I did not record the serial number.

Q. Why not?

A. Well, first of all, that's the job of the officer who makes out the property report, in this case I believe it was Detective Headley. Second, not every item of evidence carries a serial number, so we try…well, let me put it this way: you've got to have a consistent protocol in these things. The tag is my personal, I guess you'd call it certification, that this is the item delivered to me by Detective Headley on that date. It has his case number, a unique number on the evidence tag, and my initials and date.

Q. So if I understand you correctly, you can't even tell me if this is the TV that was taken from Chief Armstrong's home?

A. I can't tell you if this is the TV taken from the defendant. I can only tell you this is the TV entrusted to me by Detective Headley. He can tell you if it's the TV taken from defendant's home, and Chief Armstrong can tell you if it's the same TV that used to hang on his wall.

MR. CARMODY: Nothing further, Your Honor. May I reserve on my objection to this item going into evidence until we hear from Chief Armstrong? I have no objection to it being displayed to the jury in the meantime.

THE COURT: Very well. Subject to the linking of this television to the item described in the indictment by its owner, S-9 shall be admitted into evidence. Anything further, Mr. Stephens?

MR. STEPHENS: That's all I have, Your Honor.

THE COURT: Mr. Carmody? Cross examine?

MR. CARMODY: Thank you, Your Honor.

Q. Sergeant Schulz, can I just follow up on what you told me about serial numbers?

A. Of course.

Q. By the way, do you have any idea how many millions of flat screen TV's were shipped to the United States last year, or any year, for that matter?

A. None whatsoever, but I have friends who are... well, I bet it's a lot.

Q. Fair enough. And to the best of your knowledge, television sets come with serial numbers, do they not?

A. I think that's right.

Q. I think you said previously that a lot of evidence you handle does not contain serial numbers, right?

A. Sure, think kitchen knives, shotguns manufactured before a certain date, tire irons, burglary tools, whatever.

Q. Whereas handguns of recent vintage, cars, and TV's do have numbers unique to each one?

A. Cars and guns for sure.

Q. So, I understand why you can't record serial numbers in cases where the evidence does not have a number, but why not when it does?

A. Well, for one thing, you have a lot of different numbers rolling around. We start with a police case number, and that's what we want to keep consistent within our department. Drugs don't carry serial numbers, but we tag them with our case number. When we send those drugs to the State Police lab for testing, that evidence bag, those drugs, get assigned an entirely different and unique number from the lab's own log book. The idea is for each agency that handles evidence to have its own numbering system to keep track of what it has or has handled and returned.

Q. Don't you record serial numbers for guns, virtually every time?

A. We do, but for different reasons than evidence retention. We are under orders from the Attorney

General and I think ATF to request trace reports on every gun we seize to see if it was used in an earlier crime, reported stolen, what have you. Plus, a defaced serial number is a separate crime.

Q. For the benefit of the rest of us, ATF, or BATF, is a federal agency, no?

A. Right, Bureau of Alcohol, Tobacco, and Firearms.

Q. Named when booze and smokes were considered as dangerous as guns?

A. If you say so.

Q. Don't you record VIN numbers for cars as well?

A. Again, there are external agencies that want our VIN, Vehicle Identification Numbers, to make sure the car is not reported stolen or uninsured, et cetera.

Q. So, other than electronic devices, are there any other types of evidence where you don't record the serial number?

A. I can think of one common one off the top of my head.

Q. What's that?

A. Money. We take cash into custody all the time and I don't sit there recording the serial numbers on bills. Sometimes the officers will make a photocopy of the bills confiscated, but I don't encourage that. Just count it, record the denominations, and put it in the safe.

Q. Hold on. May I have a moment, Your Honor?

THE COURT: Certainly. Are we going to be much longer?

MR. CARMODY: Almost finished, judge.

THE COURT: Take your time. The jurors' morning drinks have arrived and we will take a break when you're done.

(Continued cross-examination by Mr. Carmody):

Q. Sergeant, when you take money in, do you verify the amounts and denominations before you sign your evidence log book?

A. I do.

Q. Does the officer turning in the money show you his property report at that time?

A. Not as a rule. I think evidence gets turned in generally before reports are written.

Q. And once you put the money in the safe, does it come out for any reason until the case is disposed of or taken to trial?

A. No, not that I'm aware of.

Q. Well, what if the money is not part of the proofs in the case, or there's a stipulation that money was seized or whatever, and the prosecutor moves to forfeit the funds? Do you turn the money over to the County in those situations?

A. We do not release funds without a court order or other document authorizing transfer. Typically the money is considered contraband, like proceeds of a drug transaction, so we keep it unless ordered to give it to another agency, or bring it to court.

MR. STEPHENS: Your Honor, how is this relevant?

MR. CARMODY: It's probably not relevant here, Your Honor. It was more for my edification. I have nothing further.

THE COURT: Re-direct, Mr. Stephens?

MR. STEPHENS: No further questions, Your Honor.

THE COURT: The witness may step down. We'll take a fifteen minute recess.

Can you appreciate how distracted I was when I heard that stuff about the serial numbers and the cash? It simply hadn't dawned on me until that moment how easy it would be for cops to cover their tracks even if someone did set them up or believed even one of the drug dealers who claimed to have been ripped off. All this time I had thought it was nothing more than hubris: 'Who you gonna believe? Me, a ten-year veteran police officer or some scum bag drug dealer?'

Now I realized there was no check on what they put into the evidence vault in the first instance. And if no one showed up to claim the cash later, who's to even suspect a problem? No wonder Francesca's money didn't line up between the property reports and the investigation reports.

The civil forfeiture cases get resolved between the prosecutor and the defense attorney with no actual cash changing hands. The county cuts a check for your end after a consent order is filed with the court. So no one asks to see the cash. Ever. It would be genius if that were indeed the plan.

And on the off chance someone demanded to see the actual cash in evidence at a trial, what would happen then? Nine times out of ten, hell, ninety nine times out of a hundred, the lawyers stipulate to the amount of cash seized and the money is never brought into court. It's not because defense counsel are sitting on their hands. It's because the book play is to stipulate to the amount to avoid having a police officer place four or five grand in wadded twenties on a table in front of the jury and basically ask, does this look like a guy who just visited an ATM? Did we mention he reported he was unemployed on his arrest form?

But this led me to another idea that I needed to figure out how to test. I was still sitting in my chair in the courtroom after everyone else had left when my cell phone started vibrating on the table.

"Andrew, what's up?"

"Hey, I thought you'd want to know the bank just dropped off the records for Mr. O'Leary."

"Did you look at them?"

"Didn't you want me to?"

"Of course I wanted you to."

"Wanted to make sure. Yeah, real interesting. He took all the money from his brother and wired it in a single transaction to a trust account for a lawyer in Princeton named Heinz Beckenbauer. Know him?"

"Sort of. I went to high school with him forty years ago and we shared study hall and stuff and see each other at reunions, but other than that, nah."

"Too bad. I think he might be helpful."

"I was kidding. Of course I know him. I'll call him as soon as I get out of here."

"Okay. Sounds good."

"And Andrew?"

"Yeah."

"Draw up another subpoena *duces tecum* for Mr. Beckenbauer's trust account. Make it returnable in five days before Judge Black."

"Got it."

CHAPTER THIRTY-NINE

South of Wisconsin Dells, maybe a mile off I-90/94.

Death speaks:

There was a merchant in Baghdad who sent his servant to market to buy provisions and in a little while the servant came back, white and trembling, and said, Master, just now when I was in the market-place I was jostled by a woman in the crowd and when I turned I saw it was Death that jostled me. She looked at me and made a threatening gesture; now, lend me your horse, and I will ride away from this city and avoid my fate. I will go to Samarra and there death will not find me. The merchant lent him his horse, and the servant mounted it, and he dug his spurs in its flanks and as fast as the horse could gallop he went.

Then the merchant went down to the marketplace and he saw me standing in the crowd and he came to me and said, "Why did you make a threatening gesture to my servant when you saw him this morning?" " That was not a threatening gesture," I said, "it was only a start of surprise. I was astonished to see him in Bagdad, for I had an appointment with him tonight in Samarra."

"Welcome to Dapper Dan's. I'll need to see your ID and take your twenty bucks."

"Yeah, I'm not here to see the show. Just need to see the manager."

"Still need to see your ID."

"Yeah, okay. Is the back door open?"

"See the sign? Twenty bucks cover to get in, man."

"Not here for the entertainment, man. Just here to report to Tim."

"Dude, nobody gets in without paying the cover and showing ID. Take it or leave it."

"Do me a huge favor. Tell Tim, Aaron is here. If he doesn't want to see me, I'm happy to turn around. Don't want to deliver the message? Up to you. Not sure I'd be taking that chance in your shoes. But whatever."

"Aaron who?"

"He'll know."

"Is he expecting you?"

"Since, like, two days ago."

"Wait."

"What?"

"I said, wait."

"I got nothing but time."

Five minutes later: "Okay, I'm supposed to tell you to head to the VIP room. Know where that is?"

"Yeah. Been there, done that."

Aaron had it worked out in his head: $7500 for the bond; $5000 for the lawyer; $2500 for the two guns; $5000 for all the aggravation. $20,000 to settle accounts. His cell phone started buzzing in his pocket as he walked down the puce carpeted stairs. "Yeah, this is Aaron."

"Aaron, Bill Carmody."

"Who?"

"Your lawyer."

"Oh, right, right. Sorry Mr. Carmody. What's going on?"

"Not much. Quick question. Two actually. First, did you ever look into the gym bag you had in the trunk to see its contents? Second, did you or your passenger have any cash taken off you at the time of your arrest?"

"Thought I told you I never looked in the bag."

"How about pick it up? Was it heavy? Any sense of what kind of stuff was inside?"

"Can't help you, man."

"How about the other issue? Did the cops take any money from you at the time of your arrest?"

"I'm sure they did, but it wasn't a lot. I probably had $200 in travel money in my pocket. No idea where that went."

"How about Jeremy? He have any cash?"

"You know, he might have. I'll have to ask him."

"So he was with you at the time of your arrest?"

"Wait, what?"

"Reports have you alone when arrested, and you told me the same thing back when you were scared shitless. Now that you're clear of this wreck, you want to come clean about Jeremy being with you? Because the cops were trying to hide him out at a psych hospital, and now he's gone missing. Any ideas?"

"None whatsoever."

"Think hard about that one. Your life might depend on it."

"Serious?"

"Dead serious."

"Let me call you back. I gotta talk to some dude."

"Please tell me you're not anywhere near a place called…hang on…uh, Dapper Dan's."

"I really gotta go."

CHAPTER FORTY

Session 13, continued. Carmody, William.

I asked Andrew to tell me more.

"So I already looked through the stuff the bank dropped off." Andrew had the inexhaustible energy of youth mixed with ambition and an interesting caseload. He knew what to search for more by instinct than experience, and gave meaning to the hackneyed 'fresh eyes' reboot.

"And?"

"He's having a cash flow crisis, but you wouldn't know unless you realized that every major deposit for the last year plus has been from our client. Mostly in $20-25,000 transfers, but one $15,000 and a bump recently for $40,000. We are now over $350,000."

"You mean he's paid since we started representing him?"

"He wired the $40,000 two weeks ago."

"So when he told me about the payments and I asked him, 'Are you fucking crazy?' he took it as a purely rhetorical question?"

"Looks like it."

"Let me call Heinz."

And I did. Heinz Beckenbauer and I did indeed attend high school together. I was boarding at this prep school, while he was a so-called day student. He had to partner up with a boarder to stash his stuff (they don't believe in lockers at The Lawrenceville School, and that capital "T" is no accident), and I was his boarding buddy or whatever we called it. We stayed in touch, and now he was our class historian, which meant he'd post to the alumni magazine whenever one of us crossed his path. I hated the school experience, and desperately avoided mention in his demi-blog, but I suspected this call would not make the quarterly report.

I have to tell you, though, Heinz was always a straight shooter. His father ran his own tool and dye shop just north of Trenton near the Brunswick Circle. Heinz was not to the manor born. But he got solid grades at Lawrenceville, matriculated at Princeton, and graduated with honors from NYU Law. There are worse pedigrees out there, but he stuck to his roots, transplanting them slightly north of the family homestead. He practiced retail law as a solo on Nassau Street here in Princeton, representing local schools and charities in addition to his small business and real estate work. As long as you caught him before he bellied up to his first martini at the Alchemist and Barrister off Witherspoon Street, you were going to get what you asked for.

"Bill Carmody? Is this a business call? It can't be school, because you missed the reunion dinner eight months ago. How the hell are you my friend?"

"You know, for once I can answer 'fine thanks, yourself?' and it's not a *non sequitur.*"

"Using a Latin phrase in your opening sentence. Mr. Coomber would be proud."

"Okay, enough *pas de deux.* What can you tell me about Pat O'Leary without violating privilege?"

"How the hell do you know I represent Pat O'Leary?"

"I've got his brother Thomas, who appears to be the source of all those funds you've received."

"This does not sound like it's going to be a good day for me."

"I wouldn't go that far."

"Yeah, but you're used to having clients with, um, checkered pasts."

"Heinz, we all have checkered pasts. Some of us are better at checkers."

"Where did I go wrong?"

"I don't think you did anything wrong. Did Pat buy something you own?"

"Good lord, no. I did a real estate investment for him. He bought Barry Lenk's office building next to Quakerbridge Mall."

I said, "Really. That ugly white thing? What's that, three stories, I'm guessing 60,000 square feet?"

Heinz said, "Actually 74,000, and it's bigger than that. They wasted a lot of space on that atrium, and yes it will win no awards for architecture, I agree."

I said, "I'm guessing he paid, what, $160 per square foot? $12,000,000 or thereabouts?"

Heinz said, "I'll say you're in the neighborhood. More like $150 and $11,000,000, little less. Place throws off about one point five in annual rent, so it's a no brainer if you have the cash. Did he have the cash?"

I said, "Well, he sent you about $350,000 he borrowed from my client."

"Am I about to hear a margin call?"

"You should be so lucky."

"Please tell me these are not drug proceeds or that your client is a Colombian cocaine cowboy."

"Cocaine cowboys? I think you're watching too many Miami Vice reruns, Heinz. What does it take to get bank financing for a three story office building?"

"In some cases you can get by with fifteen percent down, even ten, if your buyer is J. T. Moneybags, because the rent is so stable the bank doesn't mind holding first position."

I said, "How about in this case?"

Heinz said, "Ah, you know, no one named Moneybags showed up at closing."

I said, "More like Moneypenny?"

Heinz said, "More like Son of Sam."

"Huh?"

"O'Leary must have had a case of the shorts, and this phone call confirms that, I guess. He brought in some outside investors to carry his load. Bank insisted on twenty percent down. O'Leary cut it up into $350,000 lots. He could only manage one of the six. That still left him like a hundred grand short, but they made that up at closing."

"I don't get the Son of Sam."

"This guy who is his partner. I thought he was mobbed up or something. Felt like The Sopranos. I think the guy was threatening me, but I'm not savvy enough to know when I'm being threatened."

"What made you think you were being threatened?"

"Kept telling me how nice my office was and how he hoped nothing bad ever happened to it. Not sure what that means."

I said, "Means you were being threatened. Who was the guy?"

Heinz said, "Some bullet head named Manny something. Italian name. His name wasn't on the check or the LLC paperwork, because they were using this other LLC to secure the interest of Manny, another guy he brought with him, and the other three units."

I said, "What was the LLC?"

Heinz said, "I think I can tell you that without checking on privilege, right? Strange name: Dapper Dan's, LLC. Address in Wisconsin."

I said, "You said the guy who liked your office was named Manny?"

Heinz said, "Yeah."

"Last name Squitieri by any chance?"

"That's it. How the hell did you know that one?"

"He was our classmate at Lawrenceville."

"Really? I don't remember him."

"I made that up. He's not a mobster, at least not that I know of."

"What does he do?"

"He's a Trenton cop."

CHAPTER FORTY-ONE

Brittingham Bay, a few hundred yards east of West Shore Drive

In winter, the lakes freeze up around Madison. Not so much the big ones, although if the cold lasts long enough, even Monona and Mendota will turn to solid ice. But Lake Winagra and Monona Bay surely do, and local ice fisherman pitch their elaborate tents and ice fishing gear in proprietary fashion, dotting the white with REI-studded bungalows featuring breath-taking amenities so guys can drill a hole in the shelf and drop a line to catch walleyes in the frosty mornings.

The fish put up pretty good fight because they don't know the lake is frozen or that this is the time of year when sturdy Midwestern men will stay with a line for an eternity, hell having already frozen over by the time the fish takes the hook in his mouth. The fight can catch some folks unawares, and a 20-pound walleye can fight like a sonofabitch.

Sometimes the lagan and derelict fishermen hook up isn't as obviously inanimate as the routine sneaker or small appliance one might encounter. A fisherman will reel in, pull the line; reel in some more; pull the line; reel in again, trying to show the fish who's the boss. But once an ice fisherman has a load on his line, he'll see it to the end. No sense giving up until you see what you've got.

"Any ideas, Chin?"

"White male, roughly 20-25 years of age, well nourished, evidence of what looks like blunt force trauma to the base of the skull. Impossible to tell time of death because of the hypothermia, but I think we can say with some degree of confidence he was unconscious before he hit the water."

"What degree of confidence is some?"

"Like 95%, plus or minus."

"Did he drown?"

"Wait for Paul to get him on a table. He's the doctor. This guy's a stiff. Between his lungs and his stomach Paul should be able to tell you within a couple of hours and whether he drowned or froze to death. Doubt he knew the difference."

"Who went through his pockets?"

"No one; waitin' for you, LT."

"Okay, good to know.'

"Hard part for Paul might be the trauma to back of cranium."

"Why's that?"

"Because he was pulled up through this hole by a fisherman using his gaff. Head would have bounced off the bottom of the ice sheet more than once on this trip. Just shouldn't be any evidence of active bleeding when those bruises were inflicted. Paul will be able to tell. I'll just take pictures."

"Anyone talk to the guy?"

"The fisherman? Nah, like I said, waiting for you, lieutenant.... Sure you wanna go through his pockets out here? What do you got there?"

"Piece of paper. Looks like a pawn slip or something. Have to get the lab guys to look at it."

"Any ideas?"

"Some kind of receipt or ticket for a piece of something....Wait. I don't have my glasses. Can you read that?"

"Well, it's wet."

"Who knew?"

"Letters are running together. Looks like, uh, hang on. I don't know, might be Grampa's something something. Can't read the last two words."

"Gun shop?"

"Could be. And there's some smudged ink. Can't read the first word. Second word looks like, I don't know, 'Whou'?"

"What?"

"I don't think so. Maybe it's 'Blou.' Definite 'O.' Not sure about the second letter. Might not be an 'E.' Might be an 'A-L.' 'Balo'? 'Billo'? Something like that."

"Thanks, Chin."

"That's it?"

"I gotta go."

CHAPTER FORTY-TWO

Session 14. Carmody, William.

I think I've told you I'm not the sharpest tool in the shed, but if you give me enough time to chew on something, I'll figure it out. Problem for me here was I was losing my mind as I was finding out stuff. I don't think it was any one thing that set me off. But there were days when I missed her so much I couldn't concentrate. She had a way about her. It's hard to describe, but she filled a room when she walked in, and that's in sync with how she filled my life.

I spend a lot of time on these little cases, maybe too much time. Okay, definitely too much time. Kid gets tagged with a gun or some weed, another one gets into a beef and winds up cutting the other guy. Sometimes kids get killed and the shooter can't tell you how it happened, let alone why. Not sure why I try so hard to stick up for these kids, but it's what I do. The pay's not bad, and it's indoor work, no heavy lifting. I shouldn't have any complaints, and for the most part that's the deal. You get paid, you do the work best you can, and hope for a decent outcome. But I'm too invested in the outcome, and that's probably where I went sideways.

I could never separate my days and nights. I brought work home, talked about it over dinner, took rides on weekends to take pictures of dirty alleyways or broken down row houses with crack heads wasting on the porch. I lived this shit. I don't think I took a vacation for the first ten years of my marriage. Hell, I haven't taken a vacation in the last ten years either, and I wasn't married twenty years. She was right to lose interest. I'm so slow I didn't get that she was unhappy until the night she, uh, you know....

But here I was with more information than I could sort out. I knew these guys had been stealing money from local dealers for years, and I had seen them fill out forms and deny taking proceeds over the same time span. But now I had some facts that fit together.

On the front end, I knew they were jacking the cash, but I could never figure out how to prove that. Then I'm listening to the Hightstown evidence custodian tell me how they record stuff in his log book and the light bulb goes off for me about the serial numbers and the tagging of the property. There's no way to track what's submitted beyond that book, and every department has one, that says, 'ten thousand in U.S. currency' or something on a ledger. I don't know if the money is actually in the safe. I don't know if the money was actually turned in. If the evidence custodian is in on the deal, he could be verifying the receipt of cash that isn't even making the vault. Who's going to challenge him on it?

Here's a little known fact: for years, New Jersey State Police refused to videotape DUI arrests. They wouldn't put cameras in their cars, which is kind of new, but they wouldn't tape the station house sobriety testing either. Know why? They didn't want to establish a protocol for taping what they do in that house. Because as often as not, they are doing some crazy shit, like maybe roughing up the suspect who gets lippy with them. They definitely don't like that, and they don't care what color you are.

Couple years ago they got tagged for racial profiling on road stops. Driving while black, whatever.

Anyway, an inspector general gets appointed, and long story short, now all troop cars carry dash-mounted, audio-included cameras to record what happens on field stops. Problem is, trooper has authority to turn off the camera, or just sound, any time he wants. I understand why, but it does kind of defeat the purpose of having the camera in the first place.

I tell you this, because it would be the simplest thing in the world to have a contemporaneous recording of the surrender of evidence to the evidence vault. If we could see that video every time, we probably would stipulate to the evidence coming in over our potential chain-of-custody objections. But even that would only record money going *into* the vault.

I realized it is even more important that the money almost never comes *out of* the vault, or at least not for many, many months after it goes in. Evidence sits there forever these days, because we have almost no rules for speedy trials. Guys are sitting in county jails for months, hell, more often years, waiting for a trial or at least a bail reduction. There aren't enough judges, prosecutors, or public defenders to keep the system moving at pace with the arrest and detention of tons of these kids.

I don't know if they're stealing the money before they put it on a property report, or splitting the cash with the custodian, or using some other ruse to get the book to reflect a deposit of ten thousand bucks when in fact they handed over four. What I do know is they must have got it out somehow, because they had no trouble forking over $350,000 to buy a major piece of an office building, and I don't think any of them is doing that on a police officer's salary.

And I was racking my brain on this Dapper Dan's. Who the hell were these guys? Whatever or whoever they were, it was not going to be good for my poor schmuck Aaron Bellow, if he was connected to them at all. I had no idea where Dapper Dan's was relative to Bellow's home, but it was all Wisconsin and seemed way, way too coincidental to me. Turned out later I was taking a flyer, because the club's a good hour north of where this kid's family lived. But still, hard to believe Wisconsin people had any interest in Trenton, New Jersey, one of our nation's reigning armpits of urban attitude and decades-long decay.

Turned out I was right on that score, but I didn't know it at the time.

CHAPTER FORTY-THREE

East Williamson Street, near the Yahara River.

If Wisconsin's pristine capital has a dodgy area, East Madison would qualify for the title. Long after the 2008 collapse, real estate remains at a premium, so even low rent districts now run high, and mom and pop stores close daily. So it will go with GramPa's Guns. The squat yellow pillbox sat on a lonely corner of East Williamson Street, hard by the Yahara River. Well, "river" is a relative term in those parts. More like an urban lagoon cutting through the leafy streets from Mendota to Monona around Tenney Park.

Now bikers and alt-hipster postgrads litter the landscape, having been displaced from Bedford and Bassett and points west, all that student housing demolished and remade with high-end lofts to accommodate the retirees and undergrads supported by helicopter parents of means.

The front door of GramPa's had a tinkle bell, thrown back from dustier pasts, when technopop did not blast from the Aeropostales and Urban Outfitters in plastic malls dependent on plastic cards from plastic moms and their elastic kids.

"Hello."

"Hello."

"Looking for something specific?"

"I am actually. You're GramPa, if memory serves?"

"I've been called worse."

"Lieutenant Ray Severson, Madison PD. How are ya'?"

"Do you look familiar to me?"

"I might. You sold me a Kimber Montana you had gotten your hands on couple years ago."

"That's right. Deer hunter, worried about the kick of those light .308's."

"That's me."

"How'd it work out?"

"Once you get used to the jolt, you're fine. Accurate as hell."

"You in the market for another?"

"'Fraid not. This is official business."

"How can I help?"

"Someone literally fished a kid out of Monona Bay with some kind of receipt in his pocket. We had it examined by a forensic technician who identified the script as your store. Man's name appears to be something like Ballou. I'd like to see your recent sales receipts, unless you have them indexed by name."

"Indexed by name? Like on a computer? That's a good one. Hang on a second." GramPa went to a rolltop desk in the corner of the room. He opened a lower cabinet door and pulled out a small cardboard box. "This is every gun sale for the last month."

"How's business?"

"Ah, you know. This and that. Probably have to close up one of these days, but I ain't getting any younger."

"Can I look through these while I'm here?"

"You're the lieutenant, lieutenant. Sit at my desk. Shouldn't take that long."

"Suppose not." Not ten minutes later, he placed an invoice on the transom. "Remember this guy? Robert Bellow?"

"Let me take a look. Oh, yeah. Two guys actually. Ruger Lites, right? Paid cash. Couple boxes ammo. Nothing special."

"Remember what he looked like?"

"Both kids were white, probably 20-25 years old. I thought they went to the University."

"Why did you think that?"

"Used a couple of fifty-cent words. Clean cut. Thought I was an easy mark."

"Why do you say that?"

"I wasn't sure about his ID. Thought it might not be him. So, just to be safe, I wrote down the plate."

"Of what?"

"His car. Parked across the street."

"Recall the number?"

"Right there on the back of what you're looking at. Wisconsin plate. Little SUV."

"GramPa, you're a good man."

"Helpful?"

"You have no idea."

CHAPTER FORTY-FOUR

Session 14, continued. Carmody, William.

I still had to cross-examine Chief Armstrong. And that's the thing about trial lawyers. We don't have time to get sentimental. I didn't have the luxury of an artist, to put the brush down and ponder my palette. I couldn't call in sick. By this point I was stressed to the max. I was starting to get paranoid, thinking cops were following me. Even worse, I'm pretty sure they actually were following me, which probably promoted me from the rank of paranoid to hypervigilant. I doubt that's an improvement.

But this young man, Beanie, closing on middle age, was depending on me. He was clearly innocent. I suspect even the prosecutor knew by now, and unlike a lot of his peers, this would bother a conscience-driven man like Jim Stephens. Still, he would be committing professional *hari kari* is he were to stand up and announce he was dismissing the indictment, even though that's what prosecutors are sworn to do: seek justice. I know. I did it once when I had been an AP for all of two years on a case where a high school girl accused a midshipman from Navy of rape. She recanted, and I dismissed, no permission from my supervisor sought or obtained. I got suspended for three days by the head honcho. I offered my resignation. She refused to accept it. I took a long weekend without pay.

THE COURT: Mr. Stephens, call your next witness.

MR. STEPHENS: State calls Robert Armstrong, Your Honor.

THE COURT: Mr. Armstrong, please come forward and be sworn.

(Witness sworn.)

Direct examination by Mr. Stephens:

Q. Mr. Armstrong, where do you live?

A. 108 Park Way, Hightstown, New Jersey.

Q. And how long have you lived there?

A. Thirty-seven years.

Q. Do you live alone?

A. I do now, yessir.

Q. Okay, directing your attention to March 17th, 2010, were you living at this address?

A. Yessir.

Q. Do you recall your schedule that day?

A. Well, it's almost three years ago, but I do remember what happened, because it was St. Patrick's Day, and my house was broken into.

Q. Do you recall what time you left the house that day?

A. I had to be at the head of the parade in town, so we met in front of the floats around 11AM. Parade kicked off at noon.

Q. What were you doing in the parade?

A. I was the grand marshal.

Q. Oh, congratulations. And how long did the parade last?

A. Well, the parade itself was about three hours to go the mile and a half from the prep school to downtown, then up Main to the Presbyterian Church. I was actually there about five hours, figure an hour before hand and an hour after.

Q. So you got out of there sometime after four?

A. Yessir.

Q. And what did you do when you left the parade grounds?

A. Well, what I did was caught a ride from the church back to the Peddie School parking lot, where I had parked my car.

Q. And did you leave from there?

A. Yessir.

Q. Do you remember where you went?

A. I went home to change, put my sash away and what not.

Q. And what if anything unusual did you observe when you got home.

A. House had been broken into.

Q. How did you know that?

A. TV was missing, some other stuff moved around. It was pretty obvious.

Q. What did you do?

A. Called the station.

Q. The police station?

A. Yessir, just filed an initial report of burglary, asked them to send a car out.

Q. And did they do that?

A. Yessir. Dispatcher sent a patrol unit to inspect the house and take my statement.

Q. Did you have occasion to inventory what was missing?

A. Well, sort of. Obviously the TV was gone, and my wife had some antique silverware in the cabinet in the dining room. That was gone. Also, I kept a jar with a couple hundred bucks worth of change on my dresser. Gone. And I had a bible next to my bed where I always kept a hundred bucks in case of emergency. You know, "The Lord will provide?" Took that too.

Q. Is that all?

A. That's all I could say for sure. Other stuff had been moved around, but I honestly could not say what else might have been taken.

MR. STEPHENS: May I approach the witness, Your Honor?

THE COURT: You may.

Q. Mr. Armstrong, I want to show you State's Exhibit S-10 for identification and ask if you recognize what is depicted in this photograph?

A. That's my TV.

Q. How do you know?

A. Well, it's a Sony Bravia model flat screen, 40 inches, black. If it ain't mine, it looks just like it.

Q. And now may I ask you to step down from the witness stand and take a look at S-9, standing over here. Do you recognize this?

A. My TV.

Q. Sure?

A. Course I'm sure. Think I wouldn't know my own TV?

Q. Just making certain.

A. It's mine.

MR. STEPHENS: Your Honor, The State moves S-9 and S-10 into evidence.

THE COURT: Mr. Carmody?

MR. CARMODY: Your Honor, I'm not sure why counsel is trying to admit both the TV and the picture of the TV, but may I reserve *voir dire* for cross-examination? I think Mr. Stephens is getting close to the end of direct and I don't want to hold him up.

MR. STEPHENS: Actually, Your Honor, subject to admission of S-9 and S-10, I have no further questions of this witness.

THE COURT: I sensed that was coming. Please proceed, Mr. Carmody.

(Cross examination by Mr. Carmody):

Q. Morning, Chief, how are you?

A. Could be better.

Q. Just so we are clear, you retired as chief of police when exactly?

A. My last day on the books was December 31st, 2010.

Q. So you were still serving as chief of police when you called this alleged burglary in?

A. Oh, it was a burglary, no alleged about it.

Q. Understood. You were chief at the time?

A. Yes and no. I was not actually working by that time. I was suffering from a chronic condition, using sick time, and I had put my retirement papers in, effective end of that year. So my captain was acting chief in my absence.

Q. All right, and from the time of your call to the stationhouse, do you recall how long it took for a car to get there?

MR. STEPHENS: Objection, Your Honor, how would this witness know that?

THE COURT: Mr. Carmody?

MR. CARMODY: I'm asking how much time elapsed from call to response, Your Honor.

THE COURT: I'll allow it.

Q. Did you understand my question?

A. Can't say that I did.

Q. Neither did I. Let me try a different one. How long from the time you called in the alleged burglary until a marked car showed up at your door?

A. I don't recall. It was a burglary.

Q. So you keep saying. Was today the first time you looked at this photo, marked S-10?

A. I don't believe so. Mr. Stephens showed it to me when we met to prepare my testimony.

Q. You're sure he showed you this photo, and not some other copy that looked very similar?

A. I'm fairly certain.

Q. Well, I appreciate "fairly certain" must mean pretty sure, but what I'm getting at is whether you see any identifying marks on this photo, like your initials or a case number, or some other indicia of uniqueness?

A. Did I sign the back? No. Do I see any case number or like that on the back? No. It appears to be the same as the picture Mr. Stephens showed me last week.

Q. By the way, where were you when he showed you the photograph?

A. At home.

Q. So, the prosecutor and I'm guessing at least one investigator actually drove to your home to prepare your testimony and show you this picture?

A. That's right.

Q. Do you always get special treatment, Chief?

MR. STEPHENS: Objection, Your Honor.

Mr. CARMODY: I'll move on, Your Honor.

Q. Do you have any children, Chief?

A. I have a son.

Q. How old is he?

A. 44.

Q. When was the last time you saw him?

MR. STEPHENS: Your Honor, how is this relevant?

THE COURT: I know how it's relevant, Mr. Stephens. Mr. Carmody told us in his opening his theory of the case. My question is: Is this proper grounds for cross-examination?

MR. CARMODY: Your Honor, we can go to sidebar if you like, but there is a wealth of case law on third party suspects and a good faith basis for examining on the issue. Surely I should have some latitude in this situation where the primary item stolen is the subject of a challenge to its authenticity.

THE COURT: Mr. Carmody, I'm going to give you some latitude, emphasis on the word, "some." Get to your point quickly.

MR. CARMODY: Yes, Your Honor.

Q. Chief?

A. Yessir.

Q. Last time you saw your son?

A. Couple months ago.

Q. But he lives in Hightstown, no?

A. Yessir.

Q. And he's your only child, yes?

A. Yessir.

Q. I hope you can appreciate I'm not trying to embarrass you, but can I assume you might be estranged from him as a result of his chronic substance abuse?

MR. STEPHENS: Objection.

THE COURT: Sustained.

Q. Has your son ever stolen from you?

MR. STEPHENS: Objection.

THE COURT: Overruled.

Q. Well?

A. Not sure what you mean.

Q. Look, chief, I'm not trying to make this difficult. Your son has a substance abuse problem, and he has been known to support his habit by stealing, true or false?

MR. STEPHENS: Objection, Your Honor, calls for speculation.

MR. CARMODY: I'm asking for a lay opinion on a subject he should be familiar with, Your Honor.

THE COURT: I think the witness can answer this question, if he knows.

Q. Chief?

A. What.

Q. Your son is a heroin addict who boosts, as they say in the trade, right?

A. My son struggles with addiction and I struggle with him. Sometimes he borrows money from me and doesn't pay it back. You want to call that stealing? Be my guest.

Q. Well, how about this: was your house ransacked when you came home on the afternoon of the 17th?

A. Ransacked?

Q. Yeah, bed sheets pulled down, drawers pulled out, sofa cushions thrown on the floor, that sort of thing?

A. I wouldn't say ransacked.

Q. Well, the burglar, as you would describe him, entered your home presumably in search of valuables, right?

A. That's why they're called burglars.

Q. And he didn't ransack the place?

A. Not as you are using that term.

Q. Yet he knew enough about your personal habits to head for the bedroom and remove currency from your bible, did I get that right?

A. He took money from inside my bible, yes.

Q. All right, let's turn our attention back to this photograph. Can we agree there is no serial number on this photo that would mark it as uniquely yours or even the same one you looked at last week, true?

A. True.

Q. And the same with the TV, S-9, we simply don't know if that is yours or one of the several million other Sony Bravia's that might be making the rounds of the neighborhood. Agreed?

A. I don't know about millions.

Q. You are aware that Sony has sold millions of LED Bravia flat screens, fair enough?

A. If you say so.

Q. And may I correctly assume you don't know the serial number of the TV taken from your home?

A. Nosir.

Q. Any idea where you bought the TV?

A. H&H Appliances in East Windsor.

Q. And when was that?

A. I believe it was 2009, but I would have to see the receipt.

Q. Do you have the receipt?

A. I don't believe so, but it's possible.

Q. How is that?

A. Well, I'm not in charge of keeping receipts and things like that. I had always given those kinds of chores to my wife.

Q. Could she tell us where the receipt is, or where the warranty is, or where any document is that might yield the serial number?

A. No, sir, she could not.

Q. Oh, why not?

A. Because she died last year. Dumbass.

Q. Excuse me?

A. You heard me. You knew damn well she was dead, but you had to bring it up anyway.

Q. Chief, I honestly had no idea.

MR. STEPHENS: Your Honor,

THE WITNESS: You did. You read it in the paper or your client told you, but you knew damn well she was dead. At least my wife didn't step out of a moving car with me driving it.

THE COURT: Mr. Armstrong. Mr. Armstrong.

MR. CARMODY: What did you say? What did you say? Goddamn it, Chief, tell me what you just said.

THE COURT: Mr. Carmody, counsel. Ladies and gentlemen of the jury, we will take a recess. Counsel!

MR. CARMODY: Who do you think you are, you piece of shit? You think you're too old to get knocked out? I'll knock you out right here.

THE COURT: Mr. Carmody!

MR. STEPHENS: Your Honor, may I remove the witness?

THE WITNESS: If you think you can take me,

THE COURT: Off the record.

(Whereupon the proceedings were concluded.)

CHAPTER FORTY-FIVE

Hubbard Avenue, Middleton, Wisconsin

Middleton, Wisconsin was named the best place to live in America in 2007, a distinction Madison had held many years earlier. As Madison pushes out in all directions, it bumps heads with Middleton to the northwest, where competition for titles like New Urbanism ranks high in the minds of eco-minded parents scouting for near perfect school systems and a residential lifestyle for raising progressive, sensitive children, or at least progeny who avoid the alt-alt moniker, "budding young sociopath." These folks prefer to self-identify their kids on a non-existent end of the autism spectrum, the realm of the merely moody, or disagreeable, or perhaps terminally bored. These are the ones who occasionally smoke pot, steal a car, or on rare occasions, drive contraband across country for cash.

"Mrs. Bellow, I'm Lieutenant Severson from Madison Police. This is Detective McGinley from Middleton PD. He's here at my request."

"Is this about Aaron?"

"Why would you think that?"

"Because he's the one who's in trouble?"

"I'm sorry, I don't understand."

"Let me call my husband. He's at the diner."

Mrs. Bellow left the expansive front porch without inviting the officers inside. They turned to examine the garden, but perhaps more importantly, the cars parked in the driveway, one of which was not a green Ford Taurus.

Not five minutes later another Ford pulled into the driveway, a man wearing a black t-shirt reading "Hubbard Avenue Pie House" got out slowly.

"Mr. Bellow, how are you? Didn't mean for you to leave work on our account."

"On whose account would you like me to leave?"

"Excuse me?"

"This is about my son, ain't it?"

"I'm afraid it might be."

"Aaron's a good boy. He's never been in trouble."

"Aaron? Do you have a son named Robert?"

"Robert? He's at the diner right now. You need to talk to him?"

"Maybe not. When the last time you saw Aaron?"

"Spoke to him a couple days ago. Told me he had to go out of town, but I expect he'll be back any day now."

"Does he drive a green Ford Taurus?'

"It's my car. He's driven it the last three years."

""How about Robert? What does he drive?"

"He's got his own car." Mrs. Bellow had assumed a position by the front door, listening. Detective McGinley had nothing to offer, present as a courtesy to a detective from a neighboring jurisdiction.

"May I ask if you have a picture of Aaron you could show me?"

"Honey?"

"I'll be right back." Mrs. Bellow retreated from the door for a moment, then stepped out with what appeared to be a high school graduation eight by ten glossy. Severson looked at it, tightened his mouth, then stared at Larry Bellow.

"Mr. Bellow, I think you'll need to accompany me to Madison."

"Can you please tell us what this is about?"

"About seven o'clock this morning, an ice fisherman on Monona Bay hooked what turned out to be a young man's body under the ice. The body had no identification, but we found a scrap of paper that led us to a gun shop in Madison, where the owner sold a gun to two young men recently. He wrote down the license plate of the car they were driving. The plate matched your Ford Taurus. We think the body we recovered might be your son. I can't say for certain, but I personally viewed the young man before he was removed from the scene. He strongly resembles the person in this picture. I'm terribly sorry, but I have to ask for your help."

"Oh my God." Mrs. Bellow fainted on the porch, but McGinley saw it coming and caught her before she hit the deck.

CHAPTER FORTY-SIX

"Ace?"

"Yo."

"Alan Scott."

"Yo."

"I need a favor."

"Yo?"

"It's Bill."

"Yo."

"Bill Carmody?"

"Yo."

"He needs to get bailed out."

"Yo. Wait, what?"

"Threatened a witness. In open court."

"Where is he?"

"Mercer County Courthouse, probably in the holding area of the sheriff's office. $25,000 bond for third degree terroristic threats. Can you do it?"

"Have him back to you before the day is out."

"Thanks, man. You're more eloquent than I appreciated."

"Yo."

Session 15. Carmody, William.

You know what a mistrial is? That's where the judge stops a case cold for some typically unforeseen reason, like hospitalization of one of the lawyers, or a blurt-out of inadmissible evidence by a witness, at least if it's over-the-top prejudicial. Or, say a cop telling a jury the defendant flunked a polygraph test for no particular reason. The grounds for a mistrial are as wide as the mind's eye, and it's up to the judge whether to grant one. Usually it's a do-over. Jeopardy does not attach to a mistrial. You just do the whole thing over.

There are a couple of rare exceptions, but this was not likely to be one of them. Let's face it: if a defendant could get off with no new trial after his lawyer went psycho, lawyers would be offering to do just that for a healthy fee every time. I'm not sure where the line lies in the sand for granting a mistrial, but crime victim and defense counsel challenging each other to a fight in the presence of a jury is probably over it. The hell of it was I was going to have to be the one asking for it. This would likely be why I got sent here.

Judge Black wanted to see me in chambers, but I sent word through his clerk that I was in no condition to talk to anyone rationally. I asked for the rest of the day off and a night to clear my head.

Not sure if the court was used to lawyers blowing him off like that, but he got back to me: go home, see you in the morning. Maybe 30 years of showing up on time was worth something after all.

I never made it to the front door. Sheriff's officers told me I had to go with them, and next thing I knew I was in their basement across the street getting printed and ID'd. Tell you the truth I was half expecting to get tagged, just didn't realize they would take Armstrong's citizen's complaint as a basis for a warrant.

The bail amount was fixed by a deputy clerk and somehow the information leaked back to my office, because Ace had me on the street before I took a wagon to the Workhouse. I think McCloud okayed on the bond application, but I'm not a hundred percent sure of that. I took my personal property from a brown envelope and found my car still on the street.

Dunkin' Donuts might not have been my best choice for next stop, because caffeine has an effect on me. My partner must've been in the office, because he got word of what happened. He met me in front of the cash register as I was ordering. Let me tell you about Alan Scott.

We met in a courtroom shortly after he became a lawyer, maybe seven years behind me. Our paths crossed a couple of times, in a deposition, on a trial call, and I had always appreciated his calm. He didn't fluster, and that's a trait trial lawyers need in spades. We played in the over-35 basketball league at the Y, at least until I got thrown out for too many technical fouls in consecutive games. Finally, when I watched him cross examine a witness in that multi-defendant prison case one day, I decided this was my future law partner.

In my line of work, you need foxhole guys. Alan was a foxhole guy. Better still, he had an ineffable quality in the neighborhood of fearlessness. He stood forever rail thin, but in school he played power forward and shortstop. Steel limbs say something about a man. At 6' 3", I used to consider myself an imposing figure. At 6' 4", he wasn't imposed. I made him an offer, and twenty years later, we've operated on the same handshake. We make good money, not great money. We work hard. We don't rattle. Still, his face read worry even washed out against the orange décor that marks every franchise from here to Boston.

"I guess the good news is you didn't ask him to step outside, like that time you challenged Randy Barnes to a fight in front of Judge Maloney."

"Yeah, but there was no jury present for that one, and Barnes did accuse me of sandbagging the alibi notice."

"What the hell's the difference?"

"Barnes called me a liar."

"What did Armstrong call you?"

"A liar."

"I'm missing the distinction."

"Chief couldn't believe I knew nothing about his wife's death. Swear I didn't know. Like I read the Hightstown Herald or some shit."

"Did you remember I represented his kid on that DUI a few years back?"

"You know, I forgot until you just mentioned it, but yeah."

"I'm thinking he figures you know all about this, and you knew about his kid's drug habit from us representing him, know what I mean?"

"Hadn't thought about that."

"Hey, it's done, and there's nothing we could do. And that's that." Alan was forever quoting *Goodfellas* dialogue.

I said, "Any suggestions?" Must've been the look on my face. For once the question wasn't rhetorical. I needed help. Not the kind of thing I admit.

He said, "I think you should take a few months off, for one."

I said, "I'm thinking about tomorrow morning?"

He said, "Let me handle Judge Black."

I said, "How you gonna do that?"

He said, "I'll ask for a mistrial. Tell him you're in no condition to continue. Jury's probably in shock anyway, although they loved the show from what I heard."

I'm looking at him, like 'who did you talk to this time?' because he knows everybody in the building. "Now how did you hear that?"

He said, "C'mon, man. J.P. had to walk the jury to the transport bus. He already called me with the skinny. Jury loved your whole shtick, didn't believe your guy was guilty, and figured they're on their way home as of 10AM tomorrow."

I said, "Maybe I should ask to close up the case."

He said, "Can't. If your guy does go down, he'll say it was because his lawyer blew up on his dime."

I said, "Hate it when you're right. Tired of this case anyway. Tired of the grind this month. Just tired."

He said, "Who wouldn't be, Bill? You lost your wife. It wasn't your fault. You gotta stop."

I said, "Stop what? Working?"

He said, "Beating yourself up."

I said, "Easy for you to say."

He said, "What's going on with your other guys. Anyone who can't wait for a few weeks?"

I said, "I got three clients with issues that need immediate attention, then I can go take a nap. Everyone else can wait. I got Joe Wright and the gun on the barbecue. I think Judge Winters is going to grant that motion to suppress, but we have outstanding testimony, and Internal Affairs is still waiting to see if we are going to let the civilians cooperate on that theft of money allegation. It's connected to another case somehow, but I can't get my arms around it."

He said, "That doesn't sound too difficult to resolve. What else has to move now?"

I said, "My hedge fund bachelor from the Twin Cities. He got shaken down for three-fifty large by his own brother to keep quiet about molesting his nephew. Gallegos is apoplectic about how to resolve the case. He's got my guy's confession, but now he has a victim's father shaking down the defendant, and the confession was taken by

Minneapolis police, and they didn't Mirandize until after the statement was completed. Dr. Witt says it's a one-off fluke; no evidence of pathology, just needs to deal with being gay. I think Gallegos will cave."

He said, "What's a cave look like?"

I said, "I need a non-custodial, but I also need no PSL, because the guy lives and works in the Twin Cities. He can get a probation transfer, but Parole ain't letting him relocate if he's on Parole Supervision for Life."

He said, "How you gettin' that?"

I said, "I need a fourth degree criminal sexual contact, or maybe a child abuse violation under Title Nine. Both are fourth degree, even the Title Nine stuff. Difference is the sexual contact will require registration under Megan's Law. I doubt prosecutor's are going to let this guy go without a registration requirement coming out of the end result."

He said, "Agreed, but where did the money go?"

I said, "That's what's weird. Looks like it went to Heinz Beckenbeuer's trust account to help pay for purchase of an office building. Turns out Squid and Klingon are in on the real estate deal. Can you believe that shit? They also ponied up $350,000 for a one-third share somehow, but I'm still piecing that together."

He said, "Okay, that's crazy shit you're talking now. You got proof of that?"

I said, "From Heinz himself."

He said, "I stand corrected. What else?"

I said, "This kid from Wisconsin with the guns in the back of the car. Another Klingon case. Passenger in the car disappeared after being detained in Trenton Psych. My client is back in Wisconsin. Have to be back on court for PIC in about three weeks, but my guy says he didn't do anything and he wants a complete pass."

He said, "Tall order."

I said, "Tell me about it."

He said, "That's easy for now. Turn down the PIC offer and wait three months for them to indict it. They like to run traces through ATF on all these gun cases. He might not have to show for an arraignment before summer. Good stop?"

I said, "Crappy stop. Driving on North Clinton with Wisconsin plates in a Ford Taurus. After dark. Classic driving while white."

He said, "You funny Joe. You gonna answer your phone?"

I said, "Guess I should....Hello....Hey Frank, what's up?... Yeah....Yeah....Who?....Got it. Sure. Give him my number. What happened?....Frank, I'm in no mood....You're kidding....Jesus Christ. Okay, thanks. Yup. See ya.'"

He said, "Everything okay?"

I said, "Frank Sabatino. His office just got called. My gun stop on North Clinton? They just fished the kid's body out of some lake in Wisconsin. My number's like the last call on his cell phone."

He said, "Jesus Christ."

I said, "Yeah, he wasn't there."

CHAPTER FORTY-SEVEN

West Washington Avenue, Madison, Wisconsin.

Coffee frequently defines a community. Starbucks started a trend that has metastasized in middle America. Seattle represents Patient Zero were we to trace the origins of brown plague. Perhaps we should treat the disease, where millions of Americans queue up to order mocha java lattes, scones, and buckets of refills at cross purposes with productivity. Or we could adjust to a new normal, where caffeine controls our rhythm in ways nicotine can only dream.

Dunkin' Donuts may have displaced Starbucks by simply recognizing bitter is not better, or that two bucks at speed trumps four bucks in an interminable line. But the success of both spawned small scale successors, market systems signaling entry in microeconomic terms. So it was for the proprietors of the Electric Earth Café, 546 West Washington Avenue, Madison, Wisconsin, at four years a model of stability in a pop-up/pop-down world.

Jeremy Benjamin Smith nursed a latte at a table in the back room near a window overlooking West Wash. Not a news reader by habit, Jeremy had become a State Journal junkie in the past 48 hours. When he read Aaron's name in the second story describing a suspected student's body pulled from the ice, he knew police would come looking. Matter of time, and no time to be going home.

“Jeremy Smith?”

“How’d you find me?”

“Wasn’t that hard, but you could have made my life easier.”

“Is this real?”

“My badge? Of course. Here’s my ID. Raymond Severson. Not what I usually get, but I think I understand. Can I sit?”

“Are you going to kill me?”

“Good God, no. Man, you have been spooked, haven’t you?”

“I don’t want to go to a hospital either.”

“Are you injured?”

“You know what I mean.”

“Honestly, I don’t.”

“You gonna arrest me?”

“Do you want me to arrest you?”

“No.”

“How about this: May I sit down?”

“May I leave?”

“I wouldn’t recommend it.”

"You gonna ask me a bunch of stuff?"

"Would you rather do this at the police department?"

"I'd rather not do this at all."

"Jeremy, I get it. You've got a lot on your plate here and I'm trying to make this easy. Best I can tell, you're a material witness in a homicide investigation. Might be connected to your recent trip to Trenton, might not. I don't know all the details, but I spoke to Aaron's lawyer in New Jersey, and he told me to find you. Wouldn't tell me a whole lot, which I guess is par for the course back east, but he did tell me that if I so much as mentioned the Trenton Police Department around you, you'd probably run for the hills. Not sure what that's about, but I have a job to do. Think you can cut me some slack?"

"Where do you want to start?"

"How about you tell me. When's the last time you saw Aaron?"

"He dropped me off right here four days ago, on his way to Dapper Dan's in the Dells."

"The strip joint?"

"You been there?"

"Uh, um…"

CHAPTER FORTY-EIGHT

Session 16. Carmody, William.

I'm not sure I believe luck is the residue of design. I have my doubts about karma. I've seen the higher power of money. I've known way too many guys who were born on third base and thought they hit a triple. Truly catching a break might be completely random. You tell me, doctor.

I caught a break, or maybe I forced a fumble. The same day Judge Black declared a mistrial, Joe Wright called me. Seems his cousin, who owns the house Joe never ran through, got a call from one Detective Edward Nestor, offering to meet her and provide her with something she might want. Anyway, she agreed to the meeting, and he gave her an envelope with four thousand bucks inside. She took it, and Wright called me to ask what she should do with the cake. I told him to bring it to my office. We were going to deposit it in my trust account and wait for further instructions. Just like a kidnapping.

I filled out the deposit slip and handed the four grand to a teller. Nestor wanted her to waive off her IA complaint, and he reasonably assumed if she got her money back, she wouldn't pursue the claim. I figured I'd wait for Nestor to make his move, but turns out, I didn't have to: the proverbial check bounced. Or in this case, the bank called. The money was no good. Secret Service Agents were my next order of business. They would want to know: "Where'd you get the cash?"

Then they would no doubt try to explain to me: "You know, attorney-client privilege doesn't apply in this scenario."

I would ask, "Where did you say you went to law school again?"

Which of course would bring a snarled version of, "Don't act like a smart ass, we could charge you with a federal crime." In fact that's about how it went.

I told them, "I'll have to do some research on the source of funds, try to figure out if I have an obligation to protect a privilege." I doubted they would know the distinction between a business account and a trust account for lawyer purposes, because otherwise they might get the bank records and notice I had very little trust account activity. Still, there was a federal subpoena in my future, and I needed to get ahead of that curve as well.

So, I was now facing disciplinary action for two or three separate incidents in court with a grand jury subpoena *duces tecum* chaser. That I was my own worst enemy was not helping, and maybe you could help me with that.

But why had he given her counterfeit money? Did he know the bills were bogus? Did someone else pass the envelope to him? Whoever had the paper, where did it come from?

That's when it struck me, and this is the idea I haven't been able to shake. I knew cash was coming in all over town. I had heard the stories, seen the paperwork, and lately I had a strong suspicion a couple of TAC supervisors were laundering their take through a real estate investment.

But there was still the business about evidence retention. What was in the evidence locker? It occurred to me the evidence was almost never produced in court. I kept seeing Schulz barking at me: the serial numbers were never written down. Transfers were all about bookkeeping entries.

What if they were putting phony paper into evidence? Anyone looks in the vault, there's paper there. Bring it to court to show a jury? Not a problem. The charge isn't counterfeiting. It's drug dealing. Nobody's going to challenge the authenticity of currency in a drug case. Prejudice? Relevance? Yes. Authenticity—is it real money?—not a chance.

When they seize the drugs, the stuff gets tagged and sealed. It gets a case number. When it gets checked out of the evidence room in TPD, the courier signs the book dating the removal. When it gets to the State Police lab, it gets assigned another number, and the courier and the receiver both sign the New Jersey State Police lab receipt. When the lab tech handles the specimen, he or she signs it out of the NJSP locker, then signs it back in. When the evidence gets retrieved for court, the courier signs the State Police lab book, then transmits it either to the prosecutor or his or her investigator. None of that happens with cash.

I had spoken to this Detective Severson in Madison, and he actually seemed like a straight shooter. Didn't matter. Point was, he was in Wisconsin, and he had no allegiance to Trenton PD beyond the law enforcement fraternity thing. He had Midwestern values. He had a murder on his hands. I couldn't tell him what I knew, but I could ask questions. I called him back.

"Did you find Jeremy?"

"Wasn't all that hard. His girlfriend told me the coffee shop he never leaves."

"Did he put you on to Dapper Dan's?"

"Boy, you like to hold cards close, huh."

I said, "Not following."

He said, "Oh, I think you're following just fine. Any reason you wouldn't have told me about that place last time we spoke?"

I said, "Lieutenant, I have professional obligations that don't die with my client. I'm not trying to play games, but if I can help, I will. Have you subpoenaed Dapper Dan's bank records?"

He said, "Why should I?"

I said, "Have you asked yourself who would have had a motive to burn this kid, and was it a big enough deal to kill for?"

He said, "You don't think this was a random beef?"

I said, "You mean someone punched him and he fell in the water where it wasn't frozen over? Or he tripped and fell through the ice?"

He said, "It's a titty bar. Kids go off all the time and get roughed up by a bouncer. Maybe they were covering up a problem. Sometimes these cases are just involuntary manslaughter and abuse of corpse."

I said, "All the way to Madison? Have you seen his tox report?"

He said, "Couldn't discuss it with you if I had."

I said, "I guess I'd have to ask myself if this kid came to Trenton for any reason on earth that involved moving some kind of contraband by car. And if he did, did something happen that might have exposed a pretty sophisticated conspiracy? And if Jeremy Smith was there, is he in danger right now?"

He said, "C'mon, Carmody. If you know something, can you just spell it out for a slow thinker like me?"

I said, "I'm only asking in the interest of protecting my client."

He said, "Your client's dead. How does he need protecting?"

I said, "If dead men tell no tales, even through their lawyer, it generally goes better for their family and friends, and their lawyer, for that matter."

He said, "You're wearing me out."

I said, "I'm asking if you checked all the bank records for Dapper Dan's because I'd like to know if there's evidence of a substantial transfer of funds to a real estate development in Lawrence Township, New Jersey. Office building. Trust account for a Heinz Beckenbeuer, Esquire of Princeton. If I were a betting man, and I am, I'd bet there is."

He said, "And what if I find that kind of information?"

I said, "Wouldn't you want to know if the owner of Dapper Dan's had any contact with my client couple days before he was arrested in Trenton? And did he have any contact with him in the last week? Wouldn't you be on the track for motive and opportunity?"

He said, "You left out method."

I said, "That's your end, right?"

He said, "Mind if I call you again sometime?"

I said, "I'd be disappointed if you didn't."

CHAPTER FORTY-NINE

West Doty Street, Madison, Wisconsin.

An autopsy bears little resemblance to those seen on television. They are quiet, sometimes messy affairs, where first timers have been known to faint or vomit while taking autopsy photos. The cadaver is indeed placed face up on an examination table, a Y-incision is part of the process, and most important organs are removed and weighed, coupled with tissue sampling. Pictures play an important role, as do diagrams, clothing, indeed anything of interest recovered along with the body that might inform a forensic pathologist about the circumstances of an otherwise unexplained death.

Without giving away the secret, it bears noting that pathologists can tell if a defenestration was voluntary or induced. Put another way, when someone goes out a twentieth story window, these docs can tell you if she jumped or was pushed. The way a noose breaks a neck can often reveal whether a hanging was suicide or lynching.

These are the kinds of questions that can shape a medical examiner's judgment: she must determine the cause and manner of death. In the matter of Aaron Bellow, the cause of death might be drowning, blunt force trauma, or something else consistent with a drunk falling through the ice (jumped). Or he could have been fed into the water after being rendered unconscious (pushed). Once the cause of death has been established, the medical examiner must determine the manner of death: natural, accidental, homicidal (unlawful killing of another human), suicidal, or undetermined.

"Hey, Paul."

"Hello, Raymond. This young man yours?"

"He is. Did we thaw him out?"

"We had to, but we took body temps along the way. I can say within some degree of medical certainty he died around 10PM on February 2nd, plus or minus about three hours."

"Water in his lungs?"

"Are you asking me if he drowned?"

"Yeah, I guess I am."

"It's a little hard to say about his condition when he hit the water, because there was some water in the lungs. If I had to guess, I'd say he might have been unconscious and dying when he went under, and some shallow breathing got some small quantity in his lungs."

"How about the trauma to the head? Ice bumps?"

"Most likely. There was a pretty good sized piece of wood that came up with him. The hook was sturdy, in his cheek, then the line wrapped around his body, trapping the wood against his hip. Probably bumped his head against the ice multiple times. There's not a lot of swelling or bleeding around these wounds, suggesting he was ice cold when they happened."

"You telling me it might go in the books as undetermined manner of death? Ain't going to help my murder case if my pathologist says he can't rule out a drunk falling into the water where the ice was shallow."

"Well, I'll have to wait for the tox report on his BAC, but I'm prepared to enter a finding of homicide."

"Was there a trauma to the head you can say for sure preceded the time under the ice?"

"Oh, sure."

"How can you tell? What makes one blow to the head more obviously antemortem than the others?"

"See, that's the thing about bullet holes: unless someone was waiting underwater with a firearm, I have to assume that single shot behind the right ear was inflicted prior to him going in."

"What?"

"I'm sorry. I thought you knew. Small caliber bullet to the brain. Professional job. Probably went into the water within minutes of the fatal wound."

"Ah."

CHAPTER FIFTY

Session 16, continued. Carmody, William.

So, turns out there are a couple of ways you can get to Madison from Trenton. You can fly Philadelphia to O'Hare and rent a car, fly to Milwaukee and change planes, or fly direct from Newark to Madison. I drove to Newark. The flight from Newark to Madison ran late but had no stops, which was good, because I had this nagging feeling that this tiny aluminum tube they run to regional airports had no business being aloft.

Lieutenant Severson met me at the Madison airport, which was smallish, but still big enough to look empty mid-afternoon with only two gates active. We walked down an escalator and into an icy wind that I admit hit me square in the jaw before it undressed me in my cotton sweater. My pea jacket didn't quite do the trick.

His not-really-undercover cop car stood in a loading zone. I was relieved he didn't ask me to sit in the back of a marked unit, complete with handcuffs at the ready and no handles on the inside of the car doors.

"They feed you on the plane?

"Kidding, right?"

He said, "I don't get out much."

I said, "You got a better shot at getting a bagel in the back of a cab."

He said, "I don't get it."

I said, "Not important. Bad East Coast joke. Where we going?"

He said, "Didn't know if you wanted to eat first."

I said, "Probably better if I see the kid before I eat."

"Understood." The airport was at the near eastern edge of town, couple of blocks from Lake Mendota. We were in the Dane County complex just off the capital square within minutes, where parking for cops came even easier than it had been at the airport.

The medical examiner's offices were clean, modern, tan, stony, stainless. I wanted to get through the morgue experience as quickly as I could. To his credit, Severson had understood the importance of having me identify the body. Aaron Bellow's name had not appeared on the purchase receipt for the guns at GramPa's. His father identified Aaron. Now Severson wanted me to confirm the same guy who I bailed out was on the table.

If you've never seen a dead person other than the embalmed, it can be jarring. Depending on the progress of decomposition, you might not recognize a family member. Years ago an assistant prosecutor was murdered in a gay pickup scene gone horribly wrong. If I remember correctly, he was strangled, maybe as part of the sex. Two prosecutors who worked with him looked at the body and denied it was him. That might have been emotional. It's much easier if the body was frozen at the time of death, then kept close to on ice afterwards.

I can tell you it was surreal. There was a lot of bruising around the face. I had only met the kid the one time at the Workhouse, plus seen him on video during the bail hearing. He hadn't made an appointment or come to my office after he was released, which is standard procedure for local clients. I nodded and they slid the steel gurney away.

Ray Severson knew what he was about. I figured as much when he suggested we get a cup of coffee. We drove a couple of blocks west down this broad boulevard away from the top of the hill where the capitol building sits. One of those granola-serving indie latte-machined blue-pastel-painted former head shops where the impulse buy items at the counter include rolling papers and tiny mints instead of batteries and bubble gum. The newspaper stand carried free copies of the Isthmus and The Onion (headline: "Pregnant Jessica Simpson Pulls out Fetus for Photo Op").

I tried to fit in, ordering a medium latte, but I tripped when asked if I wanted that with soy milk. I think I mumbled something about gluten free, but in the end I just said, "Whatever." This was not helpful.

We sat at a larger table in a mostly empty room, a vestibule and some distance from the counter workers.

He said, "First time in a morgue?"

I said, "Wish I could say it was."

He said, "Huh. Here I thought defense attorneys only saw the pictures without having to smell the chemicals and decay."

I said, "Yeah, that's about right. I had to identify my wife last year."

He said, "Oh my god, sorry. I didn't mean to..."

I said, "No, I know. It's okay. That was the last time, and I was hoping it would have been the last time, but that's the way it goes."

He said, "You all right?"

I said, "Nah, not really. Just can't let anyone in New Jersey know that. Once you get marked as a casualty, your clients dry up. Crime's a growth industry for lawyers, but there are enough of us that we don't seem to mind eating each other alive. You take one bad step and your friends are telling potential clients they're running a risk if they give you money. "

He said, "Didn't know your fraternity was so vicious."

I said, "Well, they're not cops."

He said, "Hey now."

I said, "Oh, I don't mean anything harsh. Just seems like cops have no conscience about eating their own. Not just IA types. I mean one cop does something out of line off duty, makes a mistake or a bad judgment call, and he's either snagged on an internal or turned in by one of his own guys. Unless his own guys are part of the problem. In which case the rules don't apply."

He said, "You've been trying to tell me something from the day I first called you."

"Can't tell you anything."

"You keep saying that."

"It's like this: the Rules of Professional Conduct bar me from revealing anything I have learned from a client or in a privileged context absent his permission. Aaron Bellow can't give me a waiver from the grave."

"What if I get a court order?"

"Until a judge in the state where I'm admitted orders me to answer a question, think of me as a locked box."

"We already got a peek at Bellow's cell phone records, waiting for the full printout and tower hits. Looks like you spoke to him the night he bought it."

"Can't even confirm that. Figure out where the Dapper Dan's guys do their banking?"

"We're working on it. Started with the county search and found his mortgage holder. Guy owns about six acres with about twelve thousand square feet of building if I include the basement, couple hundred parking spaces, and he owns the RV resort and bar across the street for another twenty acres and another mortgage. Guess how much he owes on the two properties?"

"Two million bucks? I have no idea."

"Yeah, commercial real estate's a lot cheaper in the Dells than Princeton, but that's not a bad guess."

"So what's the guy owe?"

"He's got a $65,000 mortgage on the club property and $40,000 on the RV resort. Looks like he put about 85% down on both purchases in cash."

"Cash cash?"

"Can't tell that. Fifteen years ago, before a lot of the rules changed. Any ideas?"

"Lots. Probably can't discuss."

"You know, I thought you might say that. Know this kid?" As we were talking the front door opens and Jeremy Smith walks in with another guy who had to be a detective. Bad hair, cheap shirt and tie, heavy coat about two sizes too big.

"Hey Jeremy."

"Hey Mr. Carmody."

I said, "Long time no see."

He said, "Right?"

I said, "You under arrest?"

He said, "I don't think so."

I said, "Did this guy drive you here?"

He said, "Uh, yeah."

I said, "Did you ride in the front seat or the back?"

He said, "Front."

"Okay. You're not under arrest. Want some coffee?"

"Sure." He said 'sherr,' the way all these Wisconsin folks talked. I turned to Severson. "In answer to your question, no. I'm not going to have a conversation with Jeremy in your presence."

"Won't be necessary. You already answered my biggest question, which was whether you ever met him or just knew of him from Bellow. Now I just gotta figure out where you spoke to him and if anyone else was there. Care to share?"

"Wish I could."

CHAPTER FIFTY-ONE

Hubbard Avenue, Middleton, Wisconsin.

To some, the Hubbard Avenue Pie House marks the center of the American universe. Folks can be found cupping coffee, wolfing waffles, choking on cheeseburgers starting around seven every morning. The building squats fifties-style near the heart of Middleton. Middleton makes Madison seem dark and dirty. Streets have been paved and repaved to accent retro sandstone facades in the modest downtown. Boulevards are, by definition, broad, leafy, lined with predominantly craftsman bungalow homes. It's hard to envision tradition in a town planned to replace farmers with retailers roughly four hours before one arrives.

Still, there's no hurry in the gaits of pedestrians, perhaps owing to a sense of tranquility, perhaps straining from the leash of self-induced girth, a product of bratwurst and beer, along with cheese Wisconsin's leading exports.

At nine in the evening, the last customers take pies to go and ease out of the diner. Staff keeps cleaning until ten thirty. Typically Harry Bellow reviews the day's receipts from a large booth near the rest rooms in the east corner of the building.

Harry rarely missed the dinner rush, let alone the closing count. For a couple of nights in February, he missed both: one for a viewing; one to meet his son's lawyer. This night he is absent.

"Mr. Bellow, thanks for seeing me at your home. I'm very sorry about Aaron."

"Mr. Carmody, you came highly recommended from our friend Chris. We wish we met in some other way. But your coming here tonight tells us something about the character he assured us you had."

"I hope that's all he said."

"Well, he said you're from New Jersey, and we'd have to deal with that."

"I hope you don't mind my coming with Lieutenant Severson."

Severson said, "Hello again, Mr. Bellow."

Mr. Bellow said, "Hello."

I said, "He was kind enough to pick me up at the airport today and to help me with the business I had here on Aaron's behalf."

Mr. Bellow said, "What kind of business?"

I said, "Well for one thing, I'd like to clear his name, especially because of all this."

Mr. Bellow said, "Is his name needing to be cleared?"

I said, "Depends on who you ask. He's been charged with a couple of counts of gun possession in New Jersey; that's why you hired me. Turns out he drove there to make some sort of delivery, and the cops are going to look pretty closely at what he was doing."

Mr. Bellow said, "Why do they care? My son's dead."

I said, "I think they want to know why he's dead. And if they know that, then they might be able to figure out who killed him."

Mr. Bellow said, "Okay, but please understand: my wife is not doing well. Not well at all."

I said, "I understand completely."

Mr. Bellow said, "Do you? Do you know what it's like to have your heart ripped out? What it's like to lose someone whose life is more important to you than your own? Do you have any idea what that's like?"

I said, "I know exactly what that's like."

He said, "Oh. I'm sorry. Your child?"

I said, "My wife."

He said, "Should I ask how she died?"

I said, "I'm not exactly sure, but I think I killed her."

CHAPTER FIFTY-TWO

Session 16, continued. Carmody, William.

I have to tell you, the rest of my evening with Lieutenant Severson was a tad strained. I'm sure the local cops or prosecutors told him something about me before I ever got out there to ID the body, and I think we got along okay, but there's something about a guy hearing that you killed your wife that puts a little bit of a chill in the air. Little bit. I sensed from that moment on, it was a thaw in reverse, which was fine, but it's one of those things that's never going to get easier, is all I'm saying.

I had persuaded Mr. and Mrs. Bellow to permit Severson and me to look through Aaron's room, where he stayed most nights. Something about this generation, I'm telling you, they still live at home well into their twenties and thirties. I think I'd rather be homeless, except I've met homeless people and I realize I don't mean that.

There wasn't much to look at, probably because kids today don't have shit. They have tech. Everything of importance to Aaron Bellow was in or on a cloud somewhere, and that made it much more difficult to count him down. Hard to get a sense of someone without seeing his music collection, or posters on the wall, but if I had access to his search history, I'd be in pretty good shape. No computer in his bedroom.

But there was one item, and in retrospect, I think showing it to Lieutenant Severson might have been a mistake. Guess I could've been charged with tampering if I had shoved the envelope in my pocket, but, um, hmm, not sure. It was in what I guess we would call his desk, a little table with a couple of drawers underneath the top, which I think qualifies as a desk.

Don't know why I went through his mail, but this envelope caught my eye. Might have been the scribbling on the back, and I couldn't make it out. When I opened it, twenty-five one-hundred-dollar bills spilled out. You could say I got a rush. More like a hard on.

Kids today don't carry that kind of cash. The boyz who hustle on street corners trade in cash, but almost exclusively fives, tens and twenties. You just don't see twenty-five C-notes on a kid today. Not many adults either, for that matter. And the bills were crisp, like right out of the bank drawer.

Severson took possession of them and put them in a piece of printer paper he found on Aaron's desk. He folded the paper in thirds, grabbed a rubber band, and stashed the bundle in his pocket. He kept the envelope as well. Then he offered me a ride to the airport, which I accepted. I'm pretty sure he thought I was getting on the late plane back to Newark, and I did not disabuse him of that notion. We were out of there by 7 and I still had time to catch the 7:45 flight. But I didn't.

As soon as he dropped me off I walked to the Hertz counter and picked up the car I had rented for the next 24 hours. I had ordered a GPS to go with my map, but I-94 isn't that hard to find and follow from the airport. I made the trip to Dapper Dan's in an hour.

The exit was non-descript, and the county road took me to the entrance on the right side inside a mile. There was an R/V resort and bar across the street that Severson had told me were owned by the same guy who owned this club. The parking lot was mostly empty when I pulled in after eight-thirty. I noticed CCTV cameras all around the faux log cabin building as I approached the front door from the side parking lot.

You had to buy a rubber band for your wrist. Twenty bucks, and I didn't need an ID.

"Welcome to Dapper Dan's, mister. By yourself?"

"Do I need a date?"

"No, no. Just trying to find out if you're with the bachelor party we have coming in tonight."

"Is it that obvious?"

"Let's just say you're a little older than our average guy stopping by for a couple of beers."

"Well, I'm afraid I don't even know the groom. I'm a guest of a guest. Am I early?"

"You're fine. You staying across the street with the group?"

"No. They're a hard drinking crowd and a little young for me. You know how it is. Thanks for looking out for me." I pressed a twenty into his hand and shook it.

"Got it. Well, main event is on this floor. VIP room for specials is through the back, downstairs. You want to head down there, find me and I'll take care of you."

"Appreciate it." I walked to the lonely rail and grabbed a stool. Maybe five guys nursing drinks, some staring at the mangy, too-inked girl with no meat on her bones doing a so-so job with the pole. Not that I would know what she should have been doing.

I noticed another black globe in the ceiling to my right, another camera that might or might not be monitored in real time, might or might not tape its feed, might or might not have been purged of recordings from a few nights back. The crowd was thin enough to warrant few personnel beyond the two guys tending bar, one of whom was chatting with what I assumed was the next dancer. The sign to the rest rooms pointed in the direction of the VIP access area, and I took the opportunity to relieve myself after a long ride. Well, long for a guy in his fifties.

In the back I found still another black globe, this one with obvious sight lines to the office door down the steps and across the hall, and what appeared to be a fire escape or panic-barred, metal reinforced door around the far side of the building. I could see a light creeping under the office-designated, wood paneled door on the lower level, so on my way back from the loo I walked down and knocked quietly.

"Yeah?"

"Got a minute, boss?"

"Yeah." I turned the knob and counted my breathing. This was ballsy, even for me.

I found myself looking at an unreconstructed biker from the 80's, long straggly hair, either greased back or very unwashed, bad t-shirt over post-steroid paunch, leather jacket, Fu Manchu moustache. He looked up, frowned, said, "Who are you?"

"Bill Carmody. Lawyer. From New Jersey. Heard of me?"

"Shittin' me, right?"

"I shit you not." I think he pushed a button on his desk as he spoke, leading me to reconsider my last comment as premature. "I lost a client a couple of nights ago. Aaron Bellow. Know him?"

"Seriously?"

"Dead serious."

"Well, Mr. Cromartie…"

"Carmody."

"…Cromartie, I don't know who you are or what you're doing in my office or my establishment for that matter, but I think I'll have to ask you to get the fuck out before I call the cops. Serious enough for you?" And at that moment, my friend the bouncer walked in and stood behind me with a distant look on his face, unsure if he should say something like, 'Hey, don't I know you?'

"I'm hearing you loud and clear. Guess I'll take my counterfeit money with me and leave." I got maybe two feet towards the threshold when he must have nodded to my friend, who didn't so much as move as stand still, arms akimbo.

"Whoa, whoa, whoa. Who said anything about counterfeit money?"

"I did, just now."

"What makes you think I give a shit about phony bills?"

"I'm sure you don't, which is why I'll be going."

"Maybe you'd like to tell me what's on your mind before I decide to hold you for police investigation."

"What's the charge? Trespassing through an unlocked door?"

"Maybe you'd like to tell me what's on your mind for your own good."

"I think we're getting warmer."

"What the fuck is that supposed to mean?"

"You can't threaten me. I'm not a fucking kid. Wanna call the cops? Be my guest. They know I'm in town. Give you their business card if you like. What are you going to do? Kill me? At my age you'd me doing me a favor. But you couldn't if you wanted to. Guys like me don't disappear off the map like Aaron."

"Fuck you."

"Nothing if not straight forward. Here's the part you need to understand. I'm not the cops. I was Aaron's lawyer. I'm obligated to keep my mouth shut, which is more than some of these pukes can say." My friend was not smiling.

"So?"

"So I don't care about a Wisconsin murder investigation. They have no idea about Aaron and this place. They got a body on ice in Madison and I had to ID it to confirm the same guy was in New Jersey before New Jersey would consider dropping its case against him."

"I'm not seeing your angle."

"I got an office building in my town paid for with bogus money. I got dirty cops stealing everything not nailed down in some of my clients' homes and cars. All I need is confirmation that these cops are getting it done with counterfeit bills and I'm good to get a dozen cases tossed over the next month. I can get paid by clients for figuring this out and forcing my prosecutor to eat crow."

"Is there an end in sight to this stupid shit?"

"Yeah. Ready? Don't tell me I'm on the right track with these cops and the counterfeit bills. Just give me some of the money. A round number, like ten thousand. My plan is to use the paper to flush their spending and compare it to their income. When it turns out they came up with three-fifty large or even spend a few, say, twenty thousand more each year than they make, heads will roll and I will go to my grave a happy man."

Then I said something like, "If any of it comes back to you, you can always point to a lawyer from New Jersey, who just happens to have ten thousand and a letter signed by both of us on my letterhead. You retained me in case the New Jersey investigation came back to haunt you. You were shocked the money might be counterfeit, because it was actual proceeds from your club. How do they know I didn't substitute Monopoly money for what you gave me? I have a retainer letter right here, and you have a witness to retaining me standing right there. I'll be stuck on attorney-client privilege. You know I'm good for it, because if I were here to burn you, the cops would already be at your door."

Finally, I dropped the closer. "It's really that simple: if Squid and his crew are dirty, isn't it a matter of time before one of them rolls on you? I'm telling you, if you do it my way, no one will ever know it came from you, and they'll tie off the New Jersey cases without ever looking your way. And as a special added bonus, I'm giving you an airtight defense."

There was a long pause. The man looked at his book, his hands, the guy behind me, his TV. Finally he looked at me.

"You know what?"

"What?"

"You make me sick. I'm sending you off the premises. We'll return your cover charge."

CHAPTER FIFTY-THREE

Liberty International Airport, Newark, New Jersey.

If you've never been to Liberty Airport, formerly known as Newark and still identified on radar as EWR, there's really no reason to break your streak. Like nearly every other monument to modern transport, Newark represents an architectural tradition born under a bad sign. Or a rock. Congealed sand. Concrete to be precise.

Americans know no scenic, comfortable airports. Most are constructed of stone and steel, stuck in a minimalist paean to pragmatism, nothing of beauty left to capture, let alone thrill the imagination. A noted architect, noted because he was quoted in the New York Times, suggested concrete is the modern era's marble. One conjures Herodotus and Thucydides asking Socrates to pass the hemlock upon hearing the news. Airports reinforce everything, including the notion that history retreats.

They tried hard renovating Newark/Liberty. Both Amtrak and New Jersey Transit trains stop awkwardly at a small station connected to the airport tram. Those trains run in and out of New York Pennsylvania Station (NYPenn to those born after 1960; NYP to those born after 1980; #WTFisupwithAmtrak? for the rest). The tram runs a lumbering course along the terminals to some of the outlying parking, neither efficiently nor clearly. Likewise traffic funnels through and around a circuit that would challenge Rubik for decryption.

Parking and signage match wits with the dimwitted, meaning most of the civilized world.

"Ladies and gentlemen, welcome to Newark, New Jersey, where the local time is 10:45. Please feel free to resume use of electronic devices. However, the captain has asked that you remain seated until we are parked at the gate. Thank you for your cooperation. On behalf of everyone in the flight crew, I want to thank you for choosing United Airlines."

New text messages:

Andrew: "Madison PD wants to know where u r."

Alan Scott: "Where are you?"

Amy Delaney: "Call me about Bellow file."

Amy Delaney: "ASAP."

CHAPTER FIFTY-FOUR

Session 16, continued. Carmody, William.

By the time I caught the plane back to Newark the night after my trip to the Dells, I couldn't remember if I had my car keys. I had left my car in the short term lot outside Terminal C, but it was entirely possible my keys were sticking up in the center of the console. It was entirely possible my car might be there still. I've been doing this a lot lately, and I suppose you could assure me this is a product of stress and not early onset of dementia.

Lots of times I forget things like keys and wallets and passports, and phones, which at least you can ask people to call, although that doesn't help if your ringer is silenced, only to figure out after much gnashing of teeth and high wire anxiety, including lengthy, wandering conversations with myself ("Are you really this stupid? Are you an even bigger idiot than I thought you were, which is next to impossible?" "Yes, actually, I am that big an idiot. Don't try to stop me.") that my keys/wallet/passport/phone are precisely where I put them in my briefcase.

Leaving airports is way faster than getting in. Follow any sign reading "exit" or "salida," and you are bound to find yourself ramping onto a high speed limited access highway, regardless of direction or designation. But before you can cut and run, you have to navigate the parking garage, beginning with a riff on the once-campy cinematic question, "Dude, where's my car?"

I knew I had beached my ride near the back of one level, but which one? Surely not ground level, but I couldn't remember up or down a flight from bridge crossing to departing flight ticket counters. Best to start up and work down, checking an elevator to discover I only had three levels above grade.

Good thing, too, because when I got to the end of the top tier, I looked down to see if I could spot my beat up black Beemer below. I couldn't see squat, but I did see Squid standing in a corner talking to Klingon, long enough for the thought to register, "What the hell are they doing here?" Followed by, "They're here to harsh me."

I called Alan immediately. No answer; left him a detailed message. Andrew next, and he took down the stuff I handed him with no lame questions. Then I checked my phone's recording function, "Test, test."

I walked down a flight of steps and onto Level Two. I headed vaguely towards where by all rights my 3-series should have been. It was and I popped the trunk to throw my bag down, leaving my briefcase over my shoulder. I expected to turn around and see these two characters facing me. They didn't disappoint. Here's a rough transcript from my tape, but I didn't turn this over to the committee.

UI.1-Unidentifed male 1
UI.2-Unidentified male 2
BC-Bill Carmody

UI1: Been on a trip, big shot? (No response.) Looks like you've been on a trip. (No response.) What, you ain't talking? Bill Carmody with nothing to say?

BC: Fine thanks, yourself?

UI2: What's that supposed to mean?

BC: It means, I'm fine, thank you for asking, and how are you doing?

UI1: Know why we're here?

BC: Taking a trip? Helping me find my car? I give up.

UI1: Let's just say we have an issue.

BC: What's the issue?

UI1: I think you know what I'm talking about.

UI2: You're the issue.

BC: Have you guys ever done this before?

UI1: (unintelligible)…this one time.

BC: Oh, I doubt that.

UI1: Why's that?

BC: I don't think you have the stones.

UI1: This ain't a courtroom, fuckface, so you can cut the shit right now.

BC: No, seriously, no shit. Right now's good.

UI2: What the fuck are you (unintelligible) dickhead.

BC: That's it? That's your best shot? Dickhead? Ever heard that profanity is the last refuge of the (unintelligible)...

UI1: Hey, hey, both of you. Knock it off. Just listen Carmody. Listen. This ain't a courtroom, you don't get to talk, and we ain't answering your fucking questions right now, okay? Just listen.

UI2: (unintelligible)

UI1: Whatever you think you know, you don't know. You don't know. That's all. It's absolutely in your interest to forget whatever it is you think you know, (unintelligible) you don't. fucking. know. Can I make that any clearer?

BC: You wanna know what I know?

UI2: Tell you what I (unintelligible)...

UI1: Don't go there, man. Not if you know what's good for you.

BC: Tell you what. I won't tell you what I know. But I will tell you this. I know enough. Enough to put you both away and break up your stupid assed party. Trust me. But here's the thing. I don't need to forget. I can't tell what I know. I got a dead client who never authorized me to reveal anything, so I'm kind of stuck with what I know. Wanna know what's worse?

UI1: What.

BC: I wouldn't tell anyway.

UI1: Why not?

BC: Did you ever know Dave Rhoads?

UI2: He died.

BC: That's the one. He broke me in as a prosecutor 30 years ago, and then broke me in as a defense guy five years after that. He's the one who told me never to rat anyone, and make money off of your bullshit. He used to say we didn't get that many chances to look good by making cops look bad, and we should never look to clean up your mess. We ain't in the position to tell you how to act. Just do our jobs on behalf of our clients, one at a time. So I probably could have gotten this kid off, but he got killed. Next client....

UI1: I should trust you why.

BC: Don't care if you do or you don't. But when you do get jammed, and you will, you can call me, because I will defend anybody, even you.

UI1: That's it?

BC: Yeah, but one more thing.

UI1: What's that?

BC: When I ask for a retainer, don't even think about paying me with your fucked up counterfeit bills.

UI2: Sarge, we (unintelligible)

UI1: What's that?

(remainder of tape unintelligible.)

Okay, I have to ask for the transcript back. I can't stop you from referring to it in your report, but I would prefer that you not. Just wanted you to know how I see my ethical obligations. And since you're asking, that was the point where the airport security showed up yelling and screaming for everyone to freeze and show our hands and stuff. Took us an hour plus to get things straightened out, but when it was done, those guys were going to an office to file reports and I was headed for la salida.

CHAPTER FIFTY-FIVE

Witherspoon Street, Princeton, New Jersey.

In the realm of cognitive cultural dissonance, perhaps no demarcation divides more than Trenton from Princeton. Both occupy Mercer County, sitting at opposite ends of Route 1, America's first highway. Roughly 12 miles separates one of the poorest cities in the nation from one of the richest. Jay Gatsby might have tried to navigate the distance, but likely he would have been turned away at the gates of the University that educated F. Scott Fitzgerald: too loud.

Princeton. The best academics, the best thinkers, the best therapists all flock to this near utopian idyll, orange and black, but mostly white, beleaguered only by bad parking and perhaps a nagging sense that one cannot belong here. A condescending order of rank and privilege permeates nearly every nook and cranny of a faux borough and its gothic university environs.

Palmer Square. Poor people expect to rub police the wrong way, simply by being there. Even the affluent are on edge. But restaurateurs try and some succeed, along with independent coffee houses, national name retailers, and the Nassau Inn, if only because pride of place stands for something.

Nassau Street. There are several mainstays, businesses that have survived multiple generations of boom and bust, changes of scenery and taste, the American impulse for creative destruction. P.J.'s

Pancake House; the Garden Theatre; The Annex, some of these have changed hands, but never names or locations.

The Alchemist and Barrister has occupied a pre-War (of 1812) space between Witherspoon Street and Palmer Square East for decades. The back bar used to feature bucolic outdoor seating with a floral view, until Nassau Square became such valuable real estate that a multistory retail/residential megaplex just had to be imposed on the landscape. It's all about maximizing value. The A&B has a stable of regulars, most of whom can be found tethered to the mahogany bar wedged into the back room of what used to be a garden behind the main building.

"Heinz Beckenbeuer?"

"And you are?"

"Jim Stephens. And this is Michelle Russell."

"Hi."

"Hello, Michelle. Would you care for a drink?"

"We're from the Mercer County Prosecutor's Office. We were wondering if we could talk to you for a minute."

"I think that's a 'no' to the drink."

"Could we sit at a table?"

"Would you rather talk in my office?"

"If you prefer. We had some concern your office might be under surveillance, which is why we came here. Seems to be some view that this is where you can be found most late weekday afternoons."

"Under surveillance? Why do I think Bill Carmody's name might creep into this conversation?"

"It could. Why do you ask?"

CHAPTER FIFTY-SIX

Session 17. Carmody, William.

So what I did was schedule a meeting with Delores Santucci. She's one of the two "deputy first assistant prosecutors" in the office. Used to be a prosecutor and some assistants. Then they designated a "first assistant prosecutor" in order to have someone in charge who knew how to try a case. Seems the top job became increasingly political, which meant it went to guys (and two women in the history of Mercer County) with little or no trial experience but loads of political yank.

The county needs about two chiefs and 20 native Americans. The current numbers are something like 20 and 16, with roughly ten lawyers doing nearly all the important work. That's how Sean McCloud got his job. He does shit.

If there's one higher up who gets things done by making the call it's Delores (same with judges: up or down, make the call. Make the call, for crissake! Every judge I know these days is like frigging Hamlet, scared to make a decision that might haunt him at a tenure hearing. Was Solomon the last judge who knew how to make the call? Okay, okay, back on topic.)

What was I saying? Delores. She reads the files, has a solid head for practicality on her shoulders, and knows instinctively both what a case is worth and how it can resolve to everyone's satisfaction. I didn't say happy. Satisfied is as good as it gets in most cases. Add to that the 98% rule...sorry, 98% of all cases get taken out of the stream with a plea, diversion or dismissal, all lumped as plea bargaining... and you get a sense of the importance of having a prosecutor willing to do the right thing or the practical thing, in most cases those being the same thing.

As a rule, prosecutors never travel. Defense attorneys are supposed to go to the prosecutor's office, on the order of 'If the *mountain* won't come to *Muhammad* then...' you get the picture. Prosecutor's Office alumni used to wander in, knock on an office door, and say, "Gotta minute?" Now, you check in at a desk, sign your name, and wait for your hostess to escort you in.

"Hey, Bill, c'mon back."

"Thanks. How's your summer?"

"Hasn't started yet. Don't we have to get to June?"

"Just wanted to beat the rush."

"Sounds like we have a problem."

"Why do you say that?"

"Whenever you start with your stock lines, I know you've been rehearsing."

"Ouch."

"Too close?"

"Too true."

She said, "Your call was a little cryptic. Do I need Mike Gallegos?"

I said, "Nah, I'll give him fair grades. Plus, this one wandered off in a direction I didn't actually see coming."

She said, "You didn't see something coming? I find that hard to believe."

I said, "Well, it's not every day I see the father of a child sex crime victim blackmail the perpetrator for $350,000."

She said, "Excuse me?"

I said, "So Mike and I have this case. Kind of run of the mill. My guy is the loving uncle who got a little too close to his nephew. Somehow the kid's penis wound up in his uncle's mouth. It happens."

She said, "So I've heard."

I said, "Kid complains to dad."

She said, "How old?"

I said, "Nine. Anyway, it doesn't get reported right away."

She said, "How long?"

I said, "Like fourteen months."

She said, "Fourteen months? How long from when it happened to when the kid told his father?"

I said, "Oh, same day as far as I can tell."

She said, "Did they take him to the ER or a therapist or something?"

I said, "No, I don't think so. Check with Mike, but it looks like they had a family pow wow and decided to report nothing so long as my guy went back to Minneapolis and got himself into therapy."

She said, "Interesting."

I said, "Hey, black people are not the only ones suspicious of the system. These folks might have figured out that my guy was toast for 20-do-17 with a lifetime of supervision when he got out, assuming he lived to be 70."

She said, "Still."

I said, "No, I hear you. You'd think they'd have known what the right thing to do was just by watching *Law and Order, Special Victims Unit* or some other happy horseshit."

She said, "How about watching Mr. Rogers' Neighborhood?"

I said, "Or that. Whatever, that's not what they did."

She said, "What did they do?"

I said, "Talked to the kid. Told him Uncle Tommy- his real name is Thomas Francis Xavier O'Leary, known only in his family as Uncle Tommy- wasn't right in the head. Not his fault, nothing to worry about, he wasn't in trouble. I mean, right out of the playbook, you know?"

She said, "Is anyone in the family a licensed professional?"

I said, "Fair question. Fair answer? No. Unless you're talking about a real estate license."

She said, "Um, not helpful."

I said, "Right, until you get to chapter two."

She said, "Which is?"

I said, "Uncle Tommy goes back to Minnesota and gets into therapy with some New Age guy who talks to him about sex for twenty minutes before focusing on more important stuff, like why he left the priesthood."

She said, "Why did he leave the priesthood?"

I said, "If I say because he had a conscience, do I get in trouble with the pope?"

She said, "Probably. Aren't you in enough already?"

I said, "I'm about to go under, which is why I'm here. I have to wrap this and a couple of other things up before they punch my ticket."

She said, "Really? More than a reprimand and a fine from the bench for contempt?"

I said, "Dee, I'm on my last nerve. I'm running on fumes and they have me talking to a therapist who's going to write a report that says I'm a member of the lunatic fringe."

She said, "Please don't tell me you made the mistake of being honest with her."

I said, "Worse. I told her what actually happened."

She said, "In your mind or what you can prove?"

I said, "Both."

She said, "Wait, are we talking about your wife or that Bellow case?"

"Yes."

"Let's get back to Tommy Boy."

I said, "Right. So Uncle Tommy is sitting in my office and asks me if his loan is ever going to get repaid. And I ask him what loan, and he says, 'the three-fifty large I handed over to my brother.'"

She said, "You're kidding."

I said, "I kid you not. We subpoenaed the guy's records once we got copies of our guy's wire transfer reports showing twenty-five to thirty-five thousand a month for over ten months. Couple times larger hits, came to about three-fifty when you tote it up."

She said, "How'd you get the subpoena?"

I said, "*Ex parte* application to the court for the return date of the arraignment. Judge Winters was curious, to say the least."

She said, "So what's in the records?"

I said, "Looks like a real estate deal run by Heinz Beckenbauer in Princeton. Know him?"

She said, "Should I?"

I said, "Not unless you're doing REIT's in Princeton."

She said, "I'm not. What's a reet?"

I said, "Real Estate Investment Trust. R-E-I-T." You put a group of guys together with units to sell like stock. Bunch of tax benefits."

She said, "Legitimate deal?"

I said, "From what I've seen, but I haven't seen everything. One problem. Some of the investors might not be the best citizens."

She said, "Anyone I know?"

I said, "Can't tell you what I know, but if he were alive to tell, I bet Aaron Bellow would be worth interviewing."

She said, "You can't breach privilege after a guy dies?"

I said, "Not unless you get a court order. 'Cause from where I stand, the privilege is absolute, and death does not do us part."

She said, "Where does this leave Tommy Boy?"

I said, "Looking for a lesser included that doesn't send him to jail. He doesn't want to go to jail, directly or otherwise, but he's not looking to pass Go or collect two hundred dollars either."

She said, "What does he want?"

I said, "Fourth degree criminal sexual contact of a minor. That gets you registration and probation. It avoids Parole Supervision for Life, which would make him a permanent resident of New Jersey."

She said, "How's the family going to take this?"

I said, "They'll be fine. Mike had already offered me non-custodial on a second degree endangering, apparently after the family told him they didn't want Uncle Tommy to go to prison. Once we found out about the cash, mom got a little pissed at dad, who she thinks was pimping out her son after the fact."

She said, "I wonder why she thought that."

I said, "Exactly." We heard two quick knocks on her door.

She said, "Hang on. Come in."

I said, "Hey Mike."

Mike said, "Hey Bill. Delores. Did I miss anything?"

I said, "The three-hundred-fifty-thousand dollar question."

Delores said, "How do you feel about fourth degree sexual contact no jail and probation? No contact and comply with Interstate Agreement on probation transfer. Bill says it will fly with the family."

Mike said, "Yeah, I talked to mom. She's not happy with dad, but she sees the handwriting on the wall. This could get ugly in a heartbeat, and I think she wants to avoid that as much as anyone."

Delores said, "Bill, do we need to know anything about the real estate deal that would blow up in the middle of this plea?"

I said, "Up to you. I'm not saying a word. You can look at it as much or as little as you want. I think you'd find it interesting, but my focus is on Tommy Boy. If I throw him clear of the wreck, my work is done here."

Delores said, "Okay, Mike. Write it up and I'll sign off on the memo. Do you guys need to run this by Judge Winters in chambers before you put it through?"

I said, "I'm doing what you tell me. If Mike wants to meet the judge, I'm in."

Delores said, "Let's make sure we get his team leader on board. Who's that?"

Mike said, "Ethel? She won't know what day it is, let alone the deal. We should be fine."

Delores said, "When do you want to do this?"

I said, "I'll probably be suspended by the end of next week, so sooner the better."

Mike said, "You say it like it's a foregone conclusion."

I said, "Well, I called a DAG an asshole, basically cussed out a judge, then threatened to fight a witness, who happened to be a retired police chief, while he was on the stand. Now I got an indictable citizen's complaint for terroristic threats hanging over my head. What could my chances be?"

Mike said, "Is calling a DAG an asshole a violation? Me and about two hundred other guys have done that."

Delores said, "Bill, I'm so sorry. Is there anything I can do?"

I said, "Like what?"

Delores said, "Well, you've been under an awful lot of stress. It just seems like…"

I said, "Please don't. Beating myself up is the least I can do to deal with my guilt, you know?"

Delores said, "That's encouraging. At least you know what this is about."

I said, "For all the good it will do me. It won't bring her back."

Mike said, "Would you let Alan do the sentencing?"

I said, "Of course. My life is in his hands. Tommy should have the same treatment."

CHAPTER FIFTY-SEVEN

Mount Lucas Road, Princeton, New Jersey.

Many professionals maintain offices in their homes, because they do not fear their clientele might know where to find them after business hours. By contrast, every law office, every bank, every retailer, every state office in Trenton empties at precisely 4:30pm daily, and by six, there's that bowling ball on West State.

The home office of Nancy Fortescue, PhD, squatted below an elegant two story bungalow off Lucas Road, an artery connecting what was once Princeton Township to Princeton Borough, the two governments having merged the previous year. Parking was cramped and quiet.

"He's coming in for his final appointment in about half an hour."

"Can you share your opinion at this point?"

"At which would point would I be now?"

"The point at which I'd know whether I can or should seek his indefinite suspension."

"Well, I'm not prepared to take a position other than the one you'll find in my evaluation, but he's not crazy, if that's what you're asking."

"You got this referral almost three months ago. You're not finished?"

"I'm not at liberty to discuss how I conduct evaluations, other than to say this one took considerably more time than most. No two are alike."

"Is he in control of his faculties?"

"Is he what? Do you even know what you're asking?"

"Maybe you could help me."

"Maybe you could wait for my evaluation. This is not proper procedure in these matters, and I'm of half a mind to alert the court."

"But I'm sure you understand…"

"Yes, but I suspect you don't, and there's the rub. Good day, Mr. Marquand."

CHAPTER FIFTY-EIGHT

Session 18. Carmody, William.

"…So, after all these sessions, I'm still not sure what you want to know at this point."

"What do you think I should know?"

"Well, I've been babbling for a couple of weeks now, and maybe I should tell you how some of this stuff worked out in ways that I felt were within my ethical constraints."

"What are your ethical constraints?"

"I guess there are two. First, I swore to uphold the Constitution and laws of this state and nation when I was admitted to practice. The RPC's are part of that oath…"

"RPC's?"

"Oh, uh, Rules of Professional Conduct. Our little ethics handbook."

"I see."

"Anyway, I've always felt there was a competing ethical narrative for the defense lawyer. These days, we're more like priests, without the fixation on kids. People want to tell us stuff, because they need to know what to do, and because they think we can give them advice without calling the cops."

"Aren't there other professionals trained to offer that service?"

"If you mean priests, no. Too many of those guys are all into judgment. They say they're not, but judging is what they do. Not all. I know some who actually subscribe to the New Testament and say things like, 'judge not, lest ye be judged.' But they are in the minority, by which I mean, I don't know, eight in the entire country?

"Most of my clients want to stop what they're doing, get a clean break, not go to jail, basic stuff. Priests can't help with most of it, and they make these guys feel like shit along the way. Confession may be good for the soul, but it's a bitch on the psyche. Guys stress all day long on how prayer is going to get them out of prison."

"There are other options."

"Therapists? You folks are even worse. You blab to anyone. Guy mentions he was thinking about porking his niece in her cheerleading outfit, and you call Family Services before the guy is back in his car."

"Is that opinion based on fact or just your view of therapists?"

"Doctor, I have files all over my office with sex offenders who were outted by their therapists, who felt a child's safety was at risk and contacted some agency or another. I don't blame the therapist. It's the law. We are all responsible for notifying an agency if a kid is getting molested. But if the molester knows that, he's never going to step forward, and way, way too often that's how this stuff stops. Not because the kid reports, but because the guy comes clean somewhere, because he wants to get caught, or stop, or get help."

"Well, if he wants to get caught, aren't you accommodating him if you report him?"

"Seriously? They don't come in with the conscious design of turning themselves in. They want to be stopped by someone else, right? But going to prison as part of the stopping isn't something they can face. Then I have to tell them about the Megan's Law angles that make any plea a life sentence, and they freak out."

"But what about the child?"

"What child? If a guy tells me he's having sex with his kid and planning on doing it again that night, that's one thing. I have to tell the guy, 'I can't let you do that, even if it means I come take your kid away tonight.' But I've never had a guy tell me that in twenty-five years of listening to this shit. The guy who is actively molesting someone isn't seeking me out for advice. Maybe he is, but I ain't seen it."

"What have you seen?"

"One, guys who have been threatened or sort of caught, or who are so paranoid they think they're about to be caught. Two, guys who can't take the stress and want to stop."

"This is our last hour together, and once again, we are talking about everything but you."

"You saying I'm avoidant?"

"Are you admitting you're avoidant?"

"Well, at least I heard you use a declarative sentence for once. I was going to ask you if you dream in interrogatory."

"This isn't about me now, is it?"

"I suppose not."

"Would you like to take a stab at why we are here?"

"My wife."

"What about your wife?"

"I killed her."

"How did you do that?"

"I set her in motion until she stepped out of my car and died."

"Do you really think that's what happened?"

"Not only do I think that. It's actually what happened."

"Why don't you tell me what happened?"

"Confess? Wouldn't I be better off telling my priest?"

"Do you see a priest?"

"No, but I have talked to one."

"Really?"

"My wife's brother. He's a priest. He talks to me by phone. Prays for me."

"How do you know that?"

"Because he tells me that. He is the purest soul I know, and unlike the others, I honestly don't think he judges."

"The other priests?"

"The other family members. And other priests, I suppose. Look, when this happened, I had to call her family. I called her sister. Big mistake. She started screaming at me, calling me names. I was already a mess. That made it a thousand times worse."

"What kind of names?"

"Murderer. That was enough."

"How did that make you feel?"

"How do you think it made me feel? I felt like shit before I picked up the phone. I dreaded making the call. My wife was still warm in the gurney they wheeled her off in. They wouldn't let me see her. And there I am crying like a baby, staring at my phone, pushing Kathleen's number, and when I heard her answer, I couldn't control myself. I just blurted it out to get it over with."

"What did you say?"

"I said, 'She's dead, Kat. I killed her and she's dead.' And she starts losing it on the phone, 'What do you mean you killed her?' And I'm like, 'She stepped out of my car when I was pulling to the side of the road. She hit her head, and that's it.' And she's getting more agitated, saying, 'Why was she trying to get out of a moving car? How did you let this happen?' And I said, 'I was trying to pull over. She wanted out. She wouldn't wait.' That's when she started screaming, 'How could you let this happen? You killed her. You killed her! She told me there was something going on. What was it? Why did you kill her? You're a…you're a murderer!' I couldn't take it. I hung up. I think I said I was sorry, but I had to hang up. I just couldn't take it."

"Is that what happened? Did she step out of your car while it was moving?"

"We had gone to dinner in Philadelphia. She really is not a drinker, but she had a couple of glasses of wine. Big mistake."

"For her to drink?"

"For me to let her."

"Are you in charge of how much she drinks?"

"Just the opposite. She's in charge of my entire life. She was. Now I don't know what to do. She picked my clothes, my food, our trips, you name it. She liked being in charge of me. And I let it happen."

"Why?"

"You know, I don't know. It was something that slipped under my radar. Maybe I liked not being in control for once in my life. You know what I do for a living? Stage manager. I have to know everything that goes on in a courtroom, what everyone is going to say, and when to object if someone goes off script. It gets old, and so am I."

"What happened at dinner?"

"She knew something was wrong, and I'm not as good at hiding my stress as I used to be. We bumped through the meal, and that's probably why she ordered a glass of wine. And a refill. And that's way more than she can handle. Could handle."

“What did you tell her?”

“I said I couldn’t live like this anymore. She figured I meant I wanted a divorce, but that’s not what I meant. She started crying. I should have said something, but I sat there like a blob and stared. I got the check and we got out of there.”

“Were you asking for a divorce?”

“I wanted a different life. One that didn’t revolve around her and her family 24/7. As rough as it was before I met her, I wanted my own life back. All we ever did was hang out with her family. When we went on vacations, when we took a weekend drive, didn’t matter. Someone from her crew was along for the ride, flight, pick your poison.”

“Couldn’t you have talked about it?”

“You have no idea how strong her personality is. Was. It runs in her family. They’re bulldogs, survivors. That’s the irony: she didn’t survive.”

“But you don’t think you killed her, do you? Honestly?”

“At a practical level, I controlled the car. We’re driving up 95 and we cross the bridge into New Jersey, and she was talking about carving up the property and I said she could stay in the house, I would leave. And she starts all over again, ‘I don’t want to stay in your suburban shithole, commuting three hours every day,’ and, ‘You have no idea the sacrifices I’ve made for you. I know you’re seeing someone else, I just didn’t say anything.’

“And that’s when I went off the deep end, because I said, ‘Yeah, and so have you, and I know all about him.’ And she acted shocked, like I didn’t know what I was talking about, bluffing, whatever. But you can't play a playa, and I told her that. That I knew the guy was running a practice group in her firm. That she risked pissing off everyone who didn't like the guy, which was everyone in his practice group. Then I told her the managing partner knew all about it. That sent her into orbit. And I pulled off the first exit and got on 29 North, and it's dark and there's not much of a shoulder, so when she started screaming to pull over so she could get out of the car, I should have hit the brakes and stopped even without a shoulder. But I was looking for a bit of room, and she opened the door.

"I hit the brakes and she went out while the car was still moving. I heard her hit the pavement and I knew it was bad. I jumped out of my side and went around, and her head was all bloody in the back. And I'm trying to call 911 and they're asking me where is my emergency, and I'm trying to tell them I'm either in Ewing or Hopewell, but I need an ambulance, and they're asking me questions and I couldn't answer. I was crying and holding her and she was moaning and gurgling and barely breathing and all I kept saying was 'Please don't die, please don't die,' but she wouldn't listen to me. She never listened to me."

"I'm so sorry."

"Yeah. Me too. More than she will ever know. Thing of it was, I didn't have to play that card, or any of those cards. I should have worked on our marriage. I should have asked her to go to counseling. Something. Anything. Instead, I acted like an asshole, and in the process drove her to another guy."

"And was she right about you and another woman?"

"Narcissist trial lawyer bedding a piece of strange? That never happens. Of course she was right. It wasn't serious, but it was betrayal 101. Like I said, I killed her."

"Do you want me to let that go, or would you like to consider your answer more closely?"

"Which part, 'wasn't that serious?' Serious enough for her to be devastated?"

"Was that the extent of it?"

"Okay, it might have been more serious, even if the sex wasn't."

"What does that mean?"

"We went to a charity function sponsored by her firm. We got seated at the head table. I met the managing partner and his wife. They also had their daughter at the table. The daughter was randy as all get out, and like an idiot, I chose to accommodate her."

"Right there?"

"Not at the table, no. The event was at a hotel. She had a room. I slipped out for a few minutes."

"Really?"

"Still would have been okay, but then she started calling me and texting and wanting to get together, blah blah blah. So I accommodated her a few more times, but then I tried to cut it off, and she was not so amenable. And this is the boss's daughter, so, I don't know, do the math."

"And did you?"

"Yeah, and I suspect my wife did too. We were completely stuck, all because I couldn't keep my dick in my pants. It was pathetic. I'm not a young man, fer crissake."

"Do you understand that your choices, however reckless and irresponsible, did not lead her to step out of a moving car?"

"I don't understand that at all. I see a straight line from an open and loving woman whose only crime was to love me too much to the point of wanting to control me like a kewpie doll. All I had to do was dial her back. Stick up for myself. I'm a goddamn man, not a potted plant."

"Let me change topics for a moment and deal with my inquiry. How has this crisis affected your professional responsibilities?"

"You mean can I practice law feeling like this? I suppose. I'm under a lot of stress, and these folks keep coming in. I'm not sure if work is good therapy, but it beats sitting at home, staring at pictures of us on vacation."

"When was the accident?"

"September 27th."

"How long did you take off?"

"I didn't, except for the funeral. Her family wouldn't talk to me, except Father Bob. He was kind, and I think he was the designated driver."

"I don't understand."

"Someone had to move the proceedings forward after the funeral. He separated from the pack and drove me home. We prayed together, and for that briefest of moments, I actually felt the power of prayer. Because I was on the edge. Guess I still am."

"How about the last couple of weeks?"

"You know, I should have gone into therapy, but I didn't believe in it. Now, I'm not so sure. And the proof was in these last two months. I've been telling you these case histories so you could understand my frustration and how I finally lost it, in open court of all places."

"Do you understand now how your stress leaked out? How it forced itself into the courtroom with you?"

"I can't hide anymore, and I don't want to. I need help. I can't keep praying for forgiveness. Prayer alone isn't enough. I need help. Can you help me?"

CHAPTER FIFTY-NINE

Richard J. Hughes Justic Complex, Market Street, Trenton, New Jersey.

As the city of Trenton progressively decayed after the civil rights riots of the late 1960's, white flight accelerated with a vengeance. This once proud manufacturing center, still sporting a sign for every incoming train passenger to see, claims to this day that "Trenton Makes, The World Takes." Whether it was the Brooklyn Bridge, the tires you rode on, or the commode you sat on, there was once truth to the slogan. No more.

Italians fled for Hamilton. Irish left for Lawrenceville. African-Americans went to Willingboro if they could, Hiltonia if they could not. Latinos filled the old row homes in Chambersburg, "Burger Bits" (Guido slang for themselves) having sold out for cash and the chance to abandon ship. The Polish remained in North Trenton. Some had moved to Ewing, later moving back, having missed their friends on the stoops around St. Hedwig's.

Today, the lower Trenton skyline reflects the sky from the tarnished, overpriced aluminum skin of the Hughes Justice Complex, housing the New Jersey Supreme Court, the Attorney General, and the Public Defender. Even this awkward edifice, with its soaring multi-story atrium, severe surface angles, and chronically dirty glass overstates an overall design that on a cloudy day pays surreal homage to the homeostasis of the 1980's. Dickens' Miss Havisham had a kind of equilibrium: this building too had not evolved in thirty years, its sleek aluminum skin decaying in the elements, another testament to the law of unintended architectural consequences.

Tuesday, May 14, 2013. Final day of oral arguments for the Supreme Court of New Jersey's 2012-2013 term.

> SERGEANT-AT-ARMS: All rise! Oyez, oyez, oyez, all persons having business before this honorable Court, give your attention and you shall be heard. Mr. Chief Justice Stuart Rabner, presiding.
>
> CHIEF JUSTICE RABNER: Please be seated everyone, and good morning. First matter this morning comes from the disciplinary docket, Matter of William H. Carmody, admitted to practice in New Jersey, December 6, 1982. Appearances of counsel please.
>
> MR. MARQUAND: Good morning, Your Honor. John Marquand, on behalf of the Office of Attorney Ethics.
>
> MR. SCOTT: Alan Scott, Carmody and Scott, Your Honor, on behalf of Mr. Carmody.
>
> CHIEF JUSTICE RABNER: Good morning, gentlemen. Your burden, Mr. Marquand.
>
> MR. MARQUAND: Thank you, may it please the Court, Mr. Chief Justice, Associate Justices of the Court, counsel: this matter comes before the Court by way of a complaint filed *sua sponte* by two separate judges in the same courthouse. Respondent was admitted…

JUSTICE ALBIN: We know when he was admitted. December 6, 1982. Why are we here?

MR. MARQUAND: Thank you, Your Honor. On diverse dates within the last two months, respondent acted inappropriately before two different judges, using profanity after repeated warnings from the trial court, and challenging a witness, a retired police chief and senior citizen, to a fight. He also disparaged a Deputy Attorney General with profanity, although that appears to have been a private comment overheard by the court reporter.

JUSTICE HOENS: And the court.

MR. MARQUAND: And the court.

JUSTICE ALBIN: Perhaps you didn't understand my question: why are we here? What's the rush?

MR. MARQUAND: Your Honor we are seeking an immediate suspension of Mr. Carmody's license to practice until we can complete a psychological evaluation to determine his fitness to provide competent representation.

JUSTICE HOENS: You're not suggesting he has failed to provide competent representation on this record, are you?

MR. MARQUAND: Well, in one case, his conduct led directly to the declaration of a mistrial.

JUSTICE HOENS: I understand that. The trial court acted out of an abundance of caution. But

Respondent had positively put the prosecution case to rout, would you not agree? If anything, the mistrial will now give the State an opportunity to reevaluate its proofs against Respondent's client, no? I'd be surprised if this indictment ever comes up for retrial, wouldn't you? The client even wanted the jury to decide the case, but he was overruled by the trial court.

MR. MARQUAND: Yes, Your Honor, but...

JUSTICE ALBIN: Look, we understand that Respondent has behaved inappropriately, and he may well have to suffer sanction. But what I'm having trouble with is, why now? Why this instant? This is a deliberative body.

MR. MARQUAND: We have reason to believe Respondent is under enormous stress, has begun to exhibit paranoid tendencies, and may be in the throes of a nervous breakdown, for lack of a better term. He practices criminal defense law, and every case he handles is a potential PCR for ineffective assistance. Given the volume of his practice, this could be procedural nightmare for the Criminal Part.

CHIEF JUSTICE RABNER: Those are strong accusations, Mr. Marquand. Can you support them in this record?

MR. MARQUAND: On this record? Perhaps not. The psychological functioning piece is very circumstantial. But the conduct is not disputed, and we have had Mr. Carmody evaluated by a neutral forensic psychologist who should be rendering a report within a matter of days.

CHIEF JUSTICE RABNER: Are you suggesting we suspend respondent prior to receipt of that report?

MR. MARQUAND: Out of an abundance of caution, Your Honor.

CHIEF JUSTICE RABNER: And if the expert does not find him incompetent, what then?

MR. MARQUAND: Then he can resume practice under court supervision pending a final disciplinary hearing.

JUSTICE ALBIN: Why is court supervision necessary? Do you know something about the contents of this upcoming report that we do not?

MR. MARQUAND: I'm not suggesting…

JUSTICE ALBIN: Would you care to share your insight from that preliminary review?

MR. MARQUAND: I have had no preliminary review, Your Honor.

CHIEF JUSTICE RABNER: Perhaps this would be a good time to hear from Respondent. Mr. Scott?

MR. SCOTT: Thank you, Your Honor. Respondent has enjoyed an unparalleled and more importantly, unblemished reputation, first as a prosecutor, then as an ardent defender of those accused of infamous crimes, for over thirty years. He lost his wife in a tragic accident, and it threw him off his game. He has struggled to cope with his loss, and in the process, has slipped up in court on a couple of occasions. It happens. What is not at all clear to me is why the Office of Attorney Ethics thinks this is an ethics issue at all. While respondent may well suffer sanction for failing to control his emotions under very difficult circumstances, I'm not understanding how this translates into an Order to Show Cause.

JUSTICE BLACK: How do you respond to petitioner's claim that your client is endangering the rights of criminal defendants. Obviously, he has behaved recklessly at a minimum. Don't we have a duty to protect those defendants from risk of loss of a competent defense, or perhaps more accurately, a competent defense attorney?

MR. SCOTT: If that were truly a concern, Your Honor, I would suspect we would have seen several things that are missing from this record. First, Mr. Carmody has made multiple appearances before multiple tribunals over the last eight-plus months, and I am aware of no other complaints of unprofessional or reckless behavior from any quarter: not judges, not prosecutors, not clients. Second, the judges who made these referrals were, I think I can honestly say, circumspect in their characterization of the offensive behavior. I think Judge Black called the episode "unfortunate," as opposed to reckless or willful.

JUSTICE BLACK: You know, I know Judge Black. He's a good man. He's a better man than I, as our mother repeatedly told me growing up. But seriously, he would not unnecessarily tarnish another man's reputation. I wouldn't draw too many inferences from what is not in his referral.

MR. SCOTT: I understand, Your Honor.

JUSTICE SAPP-PETERSON: Counsel, I respect your spirited defense of your partner. I also recognize the record at this point is sparse. But you cannot challenge the transcripts, can you? What are we to conclude when a lawyer knowingly uses profanity in the courtroom, or continues to do so after admonishment by the trial court? Or how do we respond to a lawyer who challenges a witness to a fight, regardless of the provocation? Certainly there must be witnesses who would have liked to challenge Mr. Carmody to something over the years after sitting through his cross-examinations. There are a lot of very qualified defense attorneys in this State. Couldn't we all breathe a little easier if we asked one of them to step in for your partner while he takes a breather? It is obvious he has been under, and continues to be under, by his own description, an enormous amount of stress.

MR. SCOTT: Well, he hasn't been indicted…

JUSTICE ALBIN: Not yet.

MR. SCOTT: Yes, Your Honor.

CHIEF JUSTICE RABNER: By the way, do we know who is handling the aggravated assault complaint filed by the one witness, Chief Armstrong? I'm assuming the Mercer County Prosecutor would recuse herself in this situation, no?

MR. SCOTT: That's correct, Your Honor. He has been charged with a crime in that citizen's complaint, and the file was sent to the Division of Criminal Justice for review and presentation if appropriate. But he has not been subjected to any kind of ethics complaint by a client. The only charges he currently faces, although criminal in nature, do not reflect on his fitness to practice. There has been no showing whatsoever of unethical conduct, and I fail to see why this Court should take action as drastic as an immediate suspension pending the results of a forensic evaluation.

JUSTICE SAPP-PETERSON: How do we know none of his clients has complained? Because they have not perfected a document with the Office of Attorney Ethics? Have you considered they might not know his situation? Or might not have seen it?

JUSTICE ALBIN: Candidly, that's my concern as well. It's not just about use of profanity, which I'll admit probably happens more frequently than has been reported on the transcripts.

JUSTICE HOENS: Well, if the clients didn't know about his situation until now, they'll certainly know about it tomorrow morning. If I had to guess, it will be those cases where he was unable to get a desired result where PCR's will start popping up. Are we pushing a self-fulfilling prophecy?

JUSTICE SAPP-PETERSON: Isn't that the problem, counsel? Your partner has a lot of clients, has had and represented many more. Each of them is going to learn of this hearing, which is after all a public event. Can't we expect a torrent of PCR's in the coming months, if not years as a result? Don't we have some duty to stem the tide until we are satisfied there is either a basis or no basis for those complaints?

MR. SCOTT: I suspected someone on this Court would pose that question, Your Honor, and in anticipation of it, I spoke to as many of his current clients as I could reach, and our staff called many more. You might be wondering what the intense public interest is in this case that would lead to this courtroom being filled beyond capacity.

If you look behind me, you'll see this is a standing-room only crowd. We are not debating a health care law, or public education, or even gay marriage. This is a preliminary hearing regarding the fitness of a single lawyer with a narrow practice area, and yet we are filled to the rafters. Permit me to tell you why: these are his present and former clients, who've shown up in force, as a mark of support, a mark of solidarity, and an unmistakable mark of respect. Bill Carmody's personal life may be in total disarray, but his professional life is defined by these people, every one of whom took time out of his or her life to attend. I know I can't expand the record during oral argument, but I will ask every one who is or has been a client of Bill's to stand up and shoulder to shoulder with Bill, who has stood up for them for so long.

CHIEF JUSTICE RABNER: Mr. Carmody, do you need a moment to compose yourself? No? Continue, counsel.

MR. SCOTT: And let me speak for myself, if I might, because as you have pointed out, I am Bill's partner, and I have been for 20 years. We've survived and thrived on a handshake, because Bill's word is good. I hope mine is too, so when I tell you I would not vouch for the man unless I was absolutely convinced of his fitness to practice, I ask you to take me at my word. I offer it to you as an officer of this Court.

Bill certainly needs help. But then we all do. A prophet once said, "Go and learn what this means. I desire mercy, not sacrifice. The healthy have no need of a physician." Bill's been helping people find justice or mercy, hopefully sometimes both, for over thirty years. In the process, he's sacrificed himself. Maybe we could throw a little help his way, and maybe we would all feel a little better about ourselves if we did.

CHIEF JUSTICE RABNER: Thank you, counsel. We will take the matter under advisement.

(Whereupon the proceedings were concluded.)

CHAPTER SIXTY

West Washington Avenue, Madison, Wisconsin.

When Madison's face turns towards the spring sun, one can appreciate why Edward called April the cruelest month. Lilacs shoot up from the dead land, mixing memory and desire with dull roots and soft rain. May is a tease. June haunts....

Jeremy Benjamin Smith kissed his sleeping girlfriend before hoisting his ten-speed to the stairs and the front door. Within twenty minutes he was sipping stiff coffee at the New World, reading The Onion, chuckling at a headline ("Jessica Simpson goes on tour to promote novel she read.") He had another ten before he had to be at the law library on Bascom Hill. He was considered on loan from the Memorial Library on Lake Avenue, but with luck, he hoped to make the move permanent. He heard the shop's front door open, not looking up until the voice wafted in his direction.

"Hey, Jer, long time no see."

"Hey, Brian."

"Whatcha' been up to?"

"Absolutely nothing."

"You still at the library?"

"You still at the PDQ?"

"Yup."

"Yup. Except I'm on loan to the law library at UW."

"Really? How's that going?"

"Good. Thanks, man."

"Hey, did you hear about Aaron Bellow?"

"What?"

"Aaron? Your buddy?"

"What about him?"

"He got shot or something. Found his body in a ditch. I heard he pissed somebody off in a poker game or borrowed some money and didn't pay it back or something like that."

"Huh."

"Yeah. Cops arrested some dude from the Dells. Biker. Hells Angels or some shit."

"Nope, didn't hear a thing."

"Probably ran his mouth once too often, know what I mean? He could do that."

"No. I mean, I guess."

"You mean that's not what happened?"

"I meant, no, I don't know what you mean. Don't know a thing about it."

"Dude should have figured out you have to keep your mouth shut in this world if you want to stay alive."

"Sounds like good advice."

"I'm tellin' ya.' Hey, see you around. Say hi to Amanda."

"Okay."

Jeremy Benjamin Smith rode his bike quietly to work. Parked and locked. Opened the contemporary law building door, rode the elevator to the fifth floor. On his way to the reference desk, he stopped to open a well worn copy of the United States Constitution. "No person… shall be compelled in any criminal case to be a witness against himself, nor be deprived of life, liberty, or property, without due process of law."

CHAPTER SIXTY-ONE

Law Offices of Carmody and Scott, West Trenton, New Jersey.

I looked at the envelope. I looked at Alan Scott. I looked at the window over his shoulder. I looked at the envelope.

"Did you see this?"

"What is it?"

"Might be my death sentence. Can you read it to me?"

"I don't even read to my kids."

"That's 'cause they're in college."

"Relax, big shot. I'll give you the highlights:

Psychological Report (Redacted Version)

Name: William Carmody
Age: 57
Dates of Examination: April 1,4, 8, 11, 12, 15, 18, 22, 26; May 2, 6, 8, 9, 13, 16, 17, 23, 29.

Examiner: Nancy H. Fortescue, PhD., NJ Lic. No. 1325

Reason for Referral: Mr. Carmody is a practicing lawyer who has been accused of misconduct by court officials. The Office of Attorney Ethics obtained Mr. Carmody's consent to undergo an evaluation to determine his fitness to practice law pending further investigation.

Sources of Information:

(1) Interviews of Mr. Carmody;
(2) Transcripts of trial proceedings supplied by the OAE;
(3) Investigation, toxicology and accident reports, motor vehicle accident of September 27, 2012;
(4) Psychological assessment instruments, including:

-MMPI-2-RF. The MMPI-2-RF contains 338 items, comprising 9 validity and 42 homogeneous substantive scales, and allows for a straightforward interpretation strategy. The MMPI-2-RF was constructed using a similar rationale used to create the Restructured Clinical (RC) Scales. The rest of the measure was developed utilizing statistical analysis techniques that produced the RC Scales as well as a hierarchical set of scales similar to contemporary models of psychopathology to inform the overall measure reorganization. The MMPI has been considered the gold standard in personality testing ever since its inception as an adult measure of psychopathology and personality structure in 1939.

-Personality Assessment Inventory. The PAI is a 344 item objective personality test designed to assess 4 validity indicators, 11 clinical scales, 5 treatment consideration scales, and 2 interpersonal style scales, as well as a number of more specific subscales.

Background:

On September 27, 2012, William Carmody was driving northbound on Route 29 in Ewing Township, New Jersey, when his wife removed her seatbelt and exited the vehicle. Although the car was nearly stopped, Ms. Carmody did not maintain her balance as she stepped out and fell, fracturing her skull in the process. The wound was fatal. Ewing Township Police and Mercer County Prosecutor's Office investigators conducted a rigorous review of the facts and circumstances and concluded no basis for preferring criminal charges. Mr. Carmody's Blood Alcohol Concentration ("BAC") was .03%, below the legal limit for driving while intoxicated. His blood was also negative for other medications or controlled substances. Mr. Carmody was cited for careless driving and failure to ensure a passenger was wearing a seatbelt during operation.

Thereafter, on diverse dates, Mr. Carmody acted inappropriately in a courtroom during trial or motion hearings, including cursing at another attorney, cursing at a witness, and challenging another witness to a fistfight. The behaviors exhibited led two separate judges to file reports with the Office of Attorney Ethics, suggesting Mr. Carmody may be emotionally unfit to appear in court.

Interview of Mr. Carmody:

Mr. Carmody presents as a tall, athletically built but perhaps undernourished white male who appears older than his stated age of 57 years. He was at all times oriented as to time, place, and person. His thought processes, as assessed through multiple interviews, were relevant and coherent. There were no signs of hallucinations or delusional thinking. There were no overt signs of suicidal thoughts or intent. However, some self-destructive commentary was noted, particularly with reference to the recent accidental death of his wife. This may have been the product of careless choice of metaphors or vocabulary. Likewise, some opinions he expressed in response to certain outside influences suggested the possibility of paranoid thinking. However, none of these responses would rise to the level of a thought disorder. In summary, Mr. Carmody gave generally valid responses and appeared intact.

Mr. Carmody was fully informed as to the nature of the evaluation, including the lack of confidentiality, in that this writer's report was to be turned over to the Office of Attorney Ethics and the Supreme Court. Mr. Carmody indicated his understanding of the process, and he was cooperative throughout the several interviews.

William Carmody is the middle of three children born to Robert and Miranda Carmody. He was raised in Monmouth County, attending the Lawrenceville School and later Christian Brothers Academy, where he played baseball. His academic performance was by his description unremarkable, but he gained admission to Seton Hall University, where he studied English as an undergraduate and law in graduate school.

Mr. Carmody was admitted to the bar in 1982, following his education at Seton Hall. He spent several years as an assistant prosecutor before leaving to join a small defense firm. In 1993 he left to establish his own firm with Alan Scott, a long time friend and colleague. This firm has operated for 20 years without controversy, and apparently rather successfully.

In 1996 at the age of 40, Mr. Carmody married Mary Margaret McSorley. There were no children born to the marriage. Mr. Carmody described a whimsical romance and courtship resulting in a "fairy tale wedding...we eloped and got married overlooking the caldera of the biggest volcano in Hawaii."

In the early years of their marriage, the Carmody's traveled, socialized, and worked in tandem, both being lawyers. However, Mrs. Carmody's commercial practice with a large Philadelphia firm began taking her further away from their household, straining an already tightly scheduled existence that may have worn both spouses down. Although not delved in detail, there appear to have been multiple signs of marital alienation suitable for therapeutic inquiry going forward.

In 2012, Mrs. Carmody died in an automobile accident, which Mr. Carmody described as "totally my fault...I killed her." When asked to explain the foundation for those statements, Mr. Carmody described an unpleasant personal conversation with his wife immediately before she opened the car door to escape a moving vehicle. He believes his harsh words drove her to attempt a spontaneous exit, notwithstanding the immense physical risk. Efforts to probe his rationale were unavailing and should be the subject of future therapeutic treatment.

By his own description, Mr. Carmody suffered through the traumatic loss without professional intervention. He continued to practice law in a high stress environment, failed to properly grieve his wife's death, and withdrew from friends and colleagues instead of seeking out their support. The internal pressures began to "leak" (his term), manifesting themselves in dealings with clients, attorneys, witnesses and ultimately judges. Mr. Carmody is aware of the wrongfulness of his actions in open court, expressed genuine remorse, as well as a willingness to seek professional guidance going forward.

At the time of the incidents detailed in the judges' referrals, Mr. Carmody was in the midst of an extraordinary criminal investigation, one that apparently implicates several police officers and conceivably some attorneys as well. While the details of that investigation remain privileged, suffice it to say the thoughts expressed by Mr. Carmody as the investigation progressed were either extremely insightful or the subject of a paranoid delusion. Given his validity scales on his MMPI, the former seems plausible, but this examiner cannot rule out the latter.

As to the actual episodes of improper conduct, Mr. Carmody describes an "infuriating" exchange with prosecution counsel in the first incident, and his uttering of the profanity ("What an asshole") was not meant for public consumption. He was speaking to a client at counsel table a little too distinctly, and (he reports) "a new court reporter" assigned to the courtroom simply transcribed what she heard, although not intended for the record. According to Mr. Carmody, the prosecuting attorney heard the comment, reported it to the court, and told the judge, "I've never been called that before," to which Mr. Carmody allegedly replied, "I find that hard to believe." None of this was reported initially by the trial judge, who apparently admonished counsel informally.

In the second instance, Mr. Carmody felt he had been lied to once too often by a particular witness, whom Carmody claims lies with impunity and the indulgence of both prosecutors and criminal part judges, all of whom know the witness is lying and none of whom is prepared to take any action as a result. Here again, Mr. Carmody expresses his opinion with considerable agitation, but not without some clarity. While his thought process in reporting this incident was intact, I cannot rule out another paranoid fantasy.

The third instance was described by Mr. Carmody as "the one where the wheels finally fell off," as his wife's death became the subject of an exchange between Carmody and a witness he had long known as an antagonist in the local criminal justice system. Mr. Carmody claims he had been unaware of this retired police chief's wife's death, and based on his own keen sense of loss, he felt doubly ashamed to have engaged in a verbal duel with another widower, when both were still grieving the loss of their respective spouses.

Mr. Carmody advised this examiner of his intention to step back from his practice and take a leave to undergo therapy, reflection, and rehabilitation "for as long as it takes." This appears to be a positive and constructive approach to an otherwise intractable emotional dilemma.

Psychological test results:

Examination of the validity scale pattern on Mr. Carmody's PAI indicates that he presented himself in a negative manner on this test, focusing on faults, flaws, and problems. I do not see evidence that his negative self description was an intentional effort to malinger, or fake psychopathology, given that his history does indeed indicate some psychological disturbance. Rather, I see his negative self description as reflective of his generally distressed emotional state. Interpreted conservatively, his clinical scale elevations indicate a significant amount of anxiety, emotional instability, and impulsivity. He also reports some suicidal ideation, although as noted during the interview, he reported no actual suicidal intent or plan. On scales assessing interpersonal style, he presented as alternately passive and aggressive, unassertive and dominating, emotionally distant yet craving intimacy, but who most likely has significant difficulty establishing and maintaining close, intimate relationships. On the scale assessing attitudes toward treatment, he presented as well motivated. He acknowledges personal problems and recognizes the need for professional assistance with these issues.

In the alternative, the scales do not properly reflect the subject's insight into issues an objective test cannot fathom. Mr. Carmody's personality inventory also revealed a moderately defensive, insecure adult struggling with issues of guilt and abandonment, probably dating to childhood. Here again, the test results were within normal limits and revealed no evidence of active psychosis or self-destructive tendencies.

Integration of findings

Based upon a combination of test results and multiple interviews, this reporter can state to a level of reasonable psychological probability that Mr. Carmody does not present a danger to self, others, or property. Additionally, there is no evidence to support the proposition he cannot manage his professional responsibilities, provided he seeks treatment for his persistent issues, if only to avoid a recurrence of the behaviors that brought him to this evaluation.

Axis I: Disthymic depression; r/o paranoid delusions
Axis II: r/o Paranoid Personality Disorder; r/o Narcissistic Personality Disorder
Axis III: Hypertension
Axis IV: Preoccupation with legal system
Axis V: GAF 85

Recommendation

Mr. Carmody is probably fit to continue in the practice of law. There are no overt signs of psychological dysfunction that would interfere with his ability to discharge his professional responsibilities. However, to address his long term needs, Mr. Carmody should commence an intensive therapeutic regimen, to include modules in anger management, grief counseling, and perhaps group therapy for survivors. He should be evaluated for possible administration of antidepressant medication.

While there are legal issues beyond my purview, from a forensic psychological standpoint, I can report to a degree of high probability that William Carmody presents no significant risk to the community. While there might be support for assigning an interim monitor to oversee his professional practice, such a decision should not be taken solely on account of this report.

June 18, 2013 Nancy Fortescue, PhD.

"Is that it?"

"Isn't that enough?"

"Does that mean I'm crazy?"

"It means for once in your life you were wrong: you're not an idiot after all."

"Jury's still out."

CHAPTER SIXTY-TWO

Hughes Justice Complex, Market Street, Trenton, New Jersey.

SUPREME COURT OF NEW JERSEY

In the Matter of William Carmody, DOCKET NO M-136-12

Respondent.

THIS MATTER, having been opened to the Court on the application of the Office of Attorney Ethics for an Order to Show Cause why the respondent, WILLIAM LEE CARMODY of West Trenton, a member of the Bar since 1982, should not be immediately suspended from the practice of law pending further disciplinary proceedings, Charles Marquand, Special Counsel, appearing on behalf of the Office of Attorney Ethics; Alan Scott, Esquire, Carmody and Scott, appearing on behalf of the respondent, and the Court having considered the arguments of counsel and the exhibits submitted on behalf of the respective parties, and for good cause shown,

Now it is on this 8th day of August, 2013, ORDERED, that the respondent shall cooperate with the Office of Attorney Ethics as follows:

1. Within 10 days hereof, the OAE shall submit the names of three monitors to oversee respondent's practice, respondent having three days to object to any one name thereafter;

2. Upon receipt of these names and any objection thereto, this Court shall appoint a monitor to oversee respondent's professional activities, including the authority to review case files, business practices, courtroom conduct, and any treatment plan crafted by respondent consistent with the June 18, 2013 report of Dr. Nancy Fortescue, PhD.;
3. Within 180 days of appointment, the monitor shall report to this Court as to the therapeutic progress respondent has made in that time frame, the issues if any regarding the conduct of respondent's professional practice, and the mental status of the respondent; and,
4. Respondent's request for a 90-day voluntary leave of absence from the practice of law in lieu of suspension be and hereby is GRANTED.

_______/s/___________________________

STUART RABNER, Chief Justice

Filed: August 10, 2013
Stephen Townsend, Clerk

CHAPTER SIXTY-THREE

Mercer County (New) Criminal Courthouse, 400 South Warren Street, Trenton, New Jersey.

If all roads truly lead to Rome, the path from Trenton starts with more than a single step. The road to perdition probably leads elsewhere. The road to hell is allegedly paved with good intentions. If one man takes the high road and another takes the low road, they're both going to Scotland. 'I shall be telling this with a sigh somewhere ages and ages hence: Two roads diverged in a wood, and I, I took the one less traveled by, and that has made all the difference.'

On a cool morning in November, 2013, Bill Carmody spoke to his court-appointed monitor as evenly as his keel would permit. "So, you're going to follow me to court too?"

"I think I should, don't you?" She stood close to six feet in pumps, cradling a shiny leather Montblanc slim case, minimum fifteen hundred bucks. Carmody eyed it suspiciously.

"I don't think you should."

"Well, this is your first appearance since the court lifted your suspension. Aren't you worried someone might try to cause you a problem?"

"You know, sometimes I worry about the future of our profession. I appreciate your concern, but why is your default setting a problem from other lawyers? The trial bar in Trenton is a small fraternity. These are not my enemies. Many are my acquaintances, some are my friends, a few are family. I'm insecure about a lot of stuff, but these folks ain't on the list. They'll take care of me."

"Then you won't mind if I tag along."

CHAPTER SIXTY-FOUR

Provisional discharge session. Carmody, William.

So, one year almost to the day from my bail hearing with Aaron Bellow, I was allowed back in a courtroom under my own power, which apparently included carrying this minder on my back. I'm sure you got some kind of report, but it actually went about like this in the new courthouse where the video was working and they fixed the leaks in their brand new roof.

"Hey, J.P."

"Mr. Bill, what's up?"

"Uh, my suspension?"

"Okay, that's not bad first day back."

"Say hello to my sponsor."

"Could you place your bag on the belt, miss?"

"Why doesn't he have to put his bag on the belt? And I'm not his sponsor. I was appointed by the court."

"If you could make sure to take any metal out of your pockets."

"How's your mom, J.P.?"

"She's good, Bill. Resting quietly. With your wife. Thanks for that. That was a special day."

"Yes it was."

We headed to the second floor for a Monday morning call of Judge Black's list, which included some of my stuff that had been held for a few months. After that, I would meet with some new client who managed to get himself charged with kidnapping without ever leaving his house. Then I had to drive to the Shore to meet a client and some forensic people at his house. Some workmen digging in his basement had unearthed the remains of a human skull. No idea.

Anyway, I slid into a back bench of Judge Black's courtroom just before nine. With my minder. Did they give you the transcript?

November 6, 2013

Sergeant at arms: All rise!

> THE COURT: Please be seated everyone. Good morning. I'm going to call the list in order, but first, I see private counsel on several matters, and I will try to accommodate them in order to get them to other courts promptly. Let's see, Mr. Carmody? Nice to see you. How have you been?
>
> MR. CARMODY: Can't complain, Your Honor. No one would listen if I did.
>
> THE COURT: You're probably right. You have several short matters?

MR. CARMODY: I do, Your Honor, thank you. On page three, State versus Joseph Wright? It's on for a status conference, but I believe that's going to be a dismissal.

THE COURT: Mr. McCloud? Good morning. Good weekend?

MR. MCCLOUD: Peachy, Your Honor, thank you. On Joseph Wright, given Judge Winter's ruling granting the motion to suppress, which he handed down last month, the State has decided not to appeal, leaving us no choice but to move to dismiss the indictment. I have an order to hand up to the Court.

THE COURT: Mr. Carmody?

MR. CARMODY: No objection.

MR. MCCLOUD: For the Court's reference, the older case was resolved as a DP a couple of months ago in municipal court, and I think that file was removed from your list.

THE COURT: It was, thank you counsel. All right. In the matter of State versus Joseph Wright on Indictment Number 12-10-0987, the State's motion is granted; bail is discharged. You're free to go Mr. Wright.

THE DEFENDANT: Thank you, Your Honor.

THE COURT: Anything else, Mr. Carmody?

MR. CARMODY: On page five, Your Honor, I have Mr. O'Leary. That's also apparently from Judge Winters' list. That's going to be a diversion to PTI with the State's consent.

THE COURT: Mr. McCloud?

MR. GALLEGOS: That's actually mine, Your Honor, and we have signed a consent to permit Mr. O'Leary's entry into the Pre-Trial Intervention program on conditions, which are spelled out in the first order of postponement, which should be in Your Honor's file.

THE COURT: Okay, here it is. Mr. O'Leary, raise your right hand and face the clerk.

(Thomas O'Leary, sworn)

THE COURT: Mr. O'Leary have you reviewed the terms and conditions of your diversion with your attorney?

THE DEFENDANT: I have, Your Honor.

THE COURT: And you understand that you must comply with those conditions as part of your participation in this program?

THE DEFENDANT: Yes, Your Honor.

THE COURT: And has your attorney answered all of your questions regarding this program?

THE DEFENDANT: Yes, Your Honor.

THE COURT: You are to return to Minneapolis, remain employed, seek treatment until discharged by your treatment provider, perform 500 hours of community service, have no unsupervised contact with children under the age of 16 and no contact at all with your nephew, A.O., and pay the assessments listed on page one of your order of postponement, understood?

THE DEFENDANT: Yes, Your Honor.

THE COURT: All right, I'm satisfied the defendant understands the terms and conditions of PTI. I'm familiar with the facts of the case and concur with the program coordinator's and prosecutor's recommendation, so I will sign the first order of postponement. Anything further, gentlemen?

MR. CARMODY: Move for reduction of bail to O.R. status, Your Honor?

MR. GALLEGOS: No objection, Your Honor.

THE COURT: So ordered. Mr. O'Leary, you'll have to wait for my clerk to fill out some forms for you to sign. Have a seat in the courtroom until she's ready, okay?

THE DEFENDANT: Yes, Your Honor.

THE COURT: Is that it, Mr. Carmody?

MR. CARMODY: One more, Your Honor, from your trial list? State versus Beanie Johnson, Indictment 11-09-1342.

MR. STEPHENS: That's mine, Your Honor. We've decided to dismiss.

THE COURT: Good choice, Mr. Stephens. Do you have an order?

MR. STEPEHENS: I do, Your Honor, if I may approach.

THE COURT: You may. All right, I have before me an order dismissing Indictment 11-09-1342, which having considered the previous application for a mistrial and my recollection of the facts of that trial, this motion will be granted. You're free to go Mr. Johnson.

THE DEFENDANT: Uh, Your Honor?

THE COURT: Yes, Mr. Johnson.

THE DEFENDANT: I just want to say thank you, you know.

THE COURT: Don't thank me, Mr. Johnson. You might want to direct your comments to your attorney next to you.

THE DEFENDANT: Well, I wanted to say thanks to Mr. Carmody, even though he messed up, but I didn't know if I was allowed.

THE COURT: You're allowed Mr. Johnson. Good day to you, sir. Bail is discharged.

THE COURT: Anything else on my list, Mr. Carmody?

MR. CARMODY: That's it for me, Your Honor. May I be excused to Judge Winters' court?

THE COURT: You may. Moving on to other business.

(Whereupon these proceedings were concluded.)

O'Leary had gotten a huge break, but he still looked dazed and confused. We had to get him out of the building and back to the airport without stopping. Beanie was at the opposite end of the jaundice spectrum. He was two blocks from the courthouse before I turned to leave, and I was pretty sure he owed me money.

I wanted to talk to Joe Wright about his cousin and her money and ask if they had seen the cops since she got the envelope. It's not like the Secret Service reimburses you for the counterfeit bills. I had to figure out how to get her $3,500, or at least a new car. Maybe I could get her on Oprah.

I wanted to ask O'Leary about his brother and the $350,000 and if they had spoken. It was a sex case, which means no contact with your victim or his family, direct, indirect, text, email, carrier pigeon, whatever, so Thomas shouldn't have been talking to his brother at all, but as Judge Politan once said, cash flow is thicker than blood.

I didn't think I could talk to Joe or Thomas with a third party monitor present. She would never have understood why I would be asking about TAC cops under any circumstances, and certainly not these. Wright would know better than to say anything to me in front of her anyhow.

Then my monitor wanted to know what was going on, and I know it sounds paranoid, but I honestly didn't think she'd understand.

"What's in Judge Winters' court?"

"The rest of my morning list."

"Do all of your cases get dismissed or diverted like that?"

"They should. But I'm not that good. I like to think my clients get the results they deserve, but it turns out deserves got nothing to do with it."

"But how do you know when to fight and when to fold?"

"Mostly it's instinct, but knowing your client is a big part."

"What was all that with the sheriff's officer and his mother?"

"She died a while ago and he didn't know what to do with her ashes. I had the same issue with my wife. I got an idea. His family and I took a ride down the shore one day and scattered them on Barnegat Bay. We had a nice dinner and raised a glass to women we had loved."

"Was that hard just now to stand up in court?"

"You know, I'm not sure what they told you. For those of us who do this for a living, that's our living room."

"You didn't answer my question."

"Okay, now you're starting to sound like one of us. It wasn't hard; it was rote. We take on the clients who ask us for help and have some ability to pay for it. Get them a result they may not deserve, but at least they can live with."

"What can they live with?"

"Knowing their lawyer didn't sell them out in the process is a start. I can't speak for the rest of our crowd, but that's my story. Picking them up and putting them down. Kind of a 24/7 arrangement."

"When do you sleep?"

"Guess I'll sleep when I'm dead. Wait, does that sound suicidal? I didn't mean that."

Judge Winters was sitting in the fourth floor courtroom that day, at the west end of the building. Tall, arched windows flooded light on the floor, giving a broad view of the Hughes Justice Complex, the Delaware, the Trenton Makes bridge, and on its near side, Route 29, a few miles south of where my wife bought it.

That's the direct route to the Workhouse, but I had left the highway at Jacob's Creek and driven around that one section every time for the last thirteen months. I hadn't put a cross or bouquet of flowers on the shoulder.

Maybe when I finished with Judge Winters, I could drive straight to the jail without detouring. Some things were in my control, some weren't, but the road wasn't to blame. I had no one to blame but myself.

My cell phone vibrated. I could see my monitor looking at me as I answered.

"Hello?"

"Billy?"

"Who's this?"

"Heinz."

"Beckenbauer?"

"Do you know more than one Heinz?"

“Got me there.”

“Actually, I was wondering if I could get you here.”

“You okay?”

“Depends on how you look at it. I’ve got a room full of Secret Service agents who want to ask me some questions about some counterfeit money and a real estate deal.”

“Don’t be nasty, but don’t talk to them either. Tell them I’ll be there in 30 minutes. Buy them some coffee.” I hadn’t put the phone in my pocket before she turned back towards the elevators.

“Where we headed?”

“Princeton. Do you know anything about REIT’s?”

“I did a law review article about REIT’s.”

“I could have guessed that. C’mon.”

Made in the USA
Charleston, SC
03 September 2014